THE
SILVER
GUN

THE
SILVER
GUN

L.A. CHANDLAR

KENSINGTON BOOKS
www.kensingtonbooks.com

KENSINGTON BOOKS are published by

Kensington Publishing Corp.
119 West 40th Street
New York, NY 10018

All Kensington titles, imprints, and distributed lines are available at special quantity discounts for bulk purchases for sales promotion, premiums, fund-raising, educational, or institutional use.

Special book excerpts or customized printings can also be created to fit specific needs. For details, write or phone the office of the Kensington Sales Manager: Kensington Publishing Corp., 119 West 40th Street, New York, NY 10018. Attn. Sales Department. Phone: 1-800-221-2647.

Kensington and the K logo Reg. U.S. Pat. & TM Off.

eISBN-13: 978-1-4967-1342-1
eISBN-10: 1-4967-1342-7
First Kensington Electronic Edition: September 2017

ISBN-13: 978-1-4967-1341-4
ISBN-10: 1-4967-1341-9
First Kensington Trade Paperback Printing: September 2017

10 9 8 7 6 5 4 3 2 1

Printed in the United States of America

Dedicated to the wonderful performing arts schools of New York City and a special thank you to the Fiorello H. LaGuardia High School of Music & Art and Performing Arts. You have carried the torch that Fiorello LaGuardia lit over eighty years ago. You give the city a soul and a bright future. He would be proud.

AUTHOR'S NOTE

The Thirties in New York City was the age of Art Deco; a modern place of grand architecture, chic fashion, and unfettered ingenuity. It was a time of brokenness, but we don't hear enough about the fact that it was also a time of Depression-defying wit, art, and innovation. It was the era of soup lines, and at the same time, the era of the cocktail. According to art historian David Garrard Lowe, Art Deco inspired an "unabashed advocacy of beauty," and its exhilarating influence was felt in every sphere. Women were assuming new roles and responsibilities in the workforce, skyscrapers were being erected in staggering numbers at a seemingly impossible pace, and people everywhere began to feel the compelling hope that perhaps they weren't the lost generation after all. Perhaps they were the generation that created beauty out of turmoil. They didn't just survive. They *lived*. The Art Deco Mystery Series seeks to bring life to characters and stories that embody that very spirit. The indomitable spirit of 1930s New York City ushered in a whole new era for the world. An era that has left its mark on every decade since.

Paris is self-consciously beautiful;
New York, careless of beauty, is thrilling.

—From *New York: City of Cities,* by Hulbert Footner, 1937

The ashes of the cigarette struck the rocks with sparks and bloodred cinders. The wind beneath the bridge played with the wisps of smoke coming from the tip, making spidery webs in the air. The rising sun splashed a honey-colored glow on the buildings. From the shore, a trumpet, of all things, blew loud and clear like a call. The hooded head turned up abruptly, alert like a hunter on the prowl. Ready. At ease, knowing that it would come full circle. Destiny was working its odd magic. Like he said it would.

Something bright appeared at the edge of the bridge—halting, tipping, and then falling. The eyes beneath the dark hood followed it carefully, one corner of the mouth curving slightly into a gratified grin. The shining bit of destiny hit the shore just out of reach of the water on a small hill of gravel. The figure gracefully slunk across the shore, an arm slowly reaching out like a white snake about to grasp its prey. The coveted reward. The one he'd said was worth waiting for. The hand gripped the handle and tenderly pocketed the prize.

The cigarette was thrown to the ground, discarded. A lingering whistle echoed softly in the breeze as the hooded figure drifted up the shore into Manhattan.

CHAPTER 1

My father was skating up ahead, faster, faster; my mother and I were laughing, joyously racing to catch up. Colors and sensations swirled like a dancer teasing the audience: the cold, gray day, the gentle snowflakes kissed my cheeks and coated my eyelashes, my mother's blue scarf, my father's scratchy red mittens. He was skating along the outside edges of the rink. We almost had him! A loud crack suddenly ripped through the air. A heart pang of panic, and my father's fearful, wide eyes flashed back to us, arms reaching out. Then frigid, terrifying darkness. The intense cold made my bones and muscles ache to the point of cracking; then a slow, heavy, downward pull to blackness . . .

Three familiar images drifted into focus: the ugly grin of the lady in the green hat; the dark brown eyes intently staring, willing me to wake; and finally, the silver gun with the bloodred scroll on the handle.

I opened my eyes. A cool spring breeze ruffled the white drapes with the city's fresh, energetic air. The familiar dark brown dresser with glass drawer knobs poking out and a charming porcelain pitcher and bowl on top looked steadfast and comfortable after the eerie dream. The cotton sheets in my smoky blue and white bed felt soft and reassuring as I rubbed them between my fingers. I stretched like a cat, and the only lingering remnant of the dream was those eyes. Those dark brown eyes.

I'm a big believer in dreams—well, at least some of them. But who's to say which dreams are just dreams and which are an issue your subconscious is working out, or perhaps, in my case, eclipsed memories of the past? A past I was still piecing together.

The piece I'd already figured out was the dark brown eyes. If this were a novel, those intense eyes might bring a sense of fear or unease. Perhaps they'd be a harbinger of my death and open up a vast mystery.

Surprisingly, those eyes were the only part of my dreams that absolutely brought me comfort. Were they the eyes of a long-lost love? No. Were they the sinister yet seductive eyes of a criminal? No. Tall, dark, and handsome stranger? Try squat, rather tubby Italian who never stopped moving and was, most of the time, bellowing. Which was actually occurring downstairs right this second.

I jumped out of bed, threw on my favorite black skirt and white blouse with the long, full sleeves, raced a washcloth around my face, brushed my dark brown hair, tossed on some mascara and bright red lipstick, slipped on my high-heeled red Mary Janes, and ran down the stairs to greet that bellower. Who just happened to be my boss and a friend of the family.

He was also the ninety-ninth mayor of New York City: Fiorello LaGuardia.

"Good morning, Laney Lane, my girl!" boomed a voice loud enough to be worthy of a six-foot-eight giant versus this five-foot-two, rotund man.

"*Grrrrr*," I replied. I only went by Lane. Lane Sanders. And I happened to take a perverse pleasure in never telling him, or anyone, for that matter, whether Lane was my full name or a nickname. Plus, his voice was loud enough to be a giant's but also *very* screechy, especially before breakfast.

"Good morning, Aunt Evelyn," I said as I strode right past him, across the dining room, and gave my aunt a quick kiss on her soft cheek.

My Aunt Evelyn—Evelyn Thorne—was a marvelous mix of classy city lady and bohemian artist.

Her jet black hair was neatly pinned up, and she was sporting a crisp, navy blue pinstriped dress. I smiled to myself at the stark contrast of her attire this morning compared to her red skirt and her long hair trailing down her back while she was painting in her studio last night. Her childhood in France and Italy gave her a worldly and almost exotic air mixed with an earthy authenticity that loved to dare convention.

She smiled up at me from the breakfast table laden with scrumptious-smelling scones, eggs, and sausages. Her eyes crinkled with amusement at the exchange between Fiorello and me.

"Were you dreaming again, dear?" she asked. Her eyes squinted slightly as she expertly analyzed my face.

"I don't have dark circles under my eyes, do I?" I asked as I contemplated running back upstairs for some face powder.

"Oh, no, not at all, Lane, not this morning. I can just tell," she replied. I had no doubt about that. Aunt Evelyn's intuition and attention to detail were uncanny at times.

I turned to the buzzing and humming human being I had swept past. Fiorello was in a consistent state of perpetual motion, but especially if he had not been greeted properly. Having had him suffer sufficiently, I rounded on him with a huge grin and cocked eyebrow. "And *you*, my cantankerous friend. How are you this morning?"

I heard his chuckle as I dove to the table, eating what I could as fast as human digestion and general dignity could handle, for I knew he would give me mere seconds to eat before we had to bolt out the door.

"All right," he began, with eyes still smiling but with an air of getting down to business. "We have a lot to do today. I was just telling Evelyn that I have a meeting with my commissioners this morning." He said this with a great roll of his eyes. Most of the time, his commissioners were the bane of his existence.

He continued, ". . . a meeting with Roger down at the docks to discuss the conditions at the dock houses and . . ." He went on and on about the day's activities as I slurped down a cup of tea and loaded up a scone with homemade strawberry curd and butter.

Mr. Kirkland came in and scooped some scrambled eggs onto my plate. Even though I had lived with them for over thirteen years, John Kirkland was still a bit of a mystery to me. I would have thought that Aunt Evelyn would require a butler and cook who would be refined and stern in a European fashion. He was anything but that; Mr. Kirkland's craggy face was weather-worn but appealing. I liked how his light gray hair was somewhat unfashionably long, touching his collar; how his eyes were tough, blue, and intelligent. He looked more suited to being captain of a sea vessel, barking orders to swarthy sea mates while battling hurricanes and pirates.

He had been with Aunt Evelyn since before I came to live with her when I was ten. He kept to himself and never really talked with me at great length, other than his usual muttering with the colorful language that also reminded one of seafaring life. And much to Aunt Evelyn's chagrin, I couldn't help but pick up a few of his more colorful words here and there.

As I ate my breakfast, last night's dream kept tapping my shoulder like an insistent child trying to get my attention. So I began walking down the lane of the old memories it triggered.

It was the music I remembered most. The early Twenties was ripe with new sounds and new life. Our Victrola played them all: Paul Whiteman, Trixie Smith, Al Jolson. Songs like "Toot, Toot, Tootsie! Goodbye" and "Three O'Clock in the Morning." They were always the backdrop to every memory, every feeling. My parents owned a bookstore on Main Street in Rochester, Michigan, and our brown Tudor-style house had a lovely garden in the back.

My attention snapped back to the present as I heard Fiorello say, as he did every day, "We've got work to do!" He started to bolt out the door, which meant I'd better follow or be left behind.

"Bye, Aunt Evelyn! Bye, Mr. Kirkland!" I yelled as I grabbed my large purse with my two notebooks tucked inside.

One I always carried with me to take notes. The other was my prized possession: a deep red leather notebook with engraved curls and leaves around the edges. It was filled with notes and mementos from my parents and it never left my side. With my bag securely over my shoulder, I ran out the door after Fiorello.

His legs moved rapidly down 80th Street toward Lexington, where we'd pick up the subway at 77th. In my high heels, I was actually much taller than Fio, but his commanding presence more than made up for his height. I never *felt* taller than him. I had to fairly run (not an easy task, but damn, I loved those red shoes) to keep up with his pace. As he walked, he started to rapid-fire tasks for me to do for the day. I brought out my notepad and took down copious details.

We took a variety of routes to work every day, depending on Fio's mood and whom he wanted to see on his way in. Sometimes we took one of the elevated trains down Second or Third Avenue, sometimes the subway down Lexington, or, once in a while, his car and driver would pick us up. When we came to Lexington and started south, we went past Butterfield Market with its heavenly aroma of baking bread wafting out. The many languages of the city rolled around us, making the energy and bustle of the thousands of people heading to work and school that day a physical force so palpable you could almost touch it. Packs of children were being walked to school while packs of dogs were being given their morning exercise. There was Murrey's Jewelry store, which had just opened, with sparkling rings and bracelets in the window; the shoe store with its tantalizing new spring line; the dusty newspaper stands . . . I loved this city. It was challenging, stimulating, vibrant. A place of many layers and depth.

I was writing as fast as I could, fortunately using the shorthand I learned in high school. It looked like Sanskrit, but it was infinitely faster than longhand, especially when trying to keep up with the Little Flower—that's what Fiorello means in Italian. He was only called that by people who loved him, but I never really could tell how he felt about that. His small stature seemed to haunt him. He acted like he was at least six-foot-four, but in actuality he was always looking up at people. He had a bust of Napoleon in his office.

Mr. LaGuardia was loud, abrasive, rude, purposeful, fast, incredibly intelligent, sometimes scary; did I mention loud? And yet he was also kind, generous, intuitive, and something I could never put my finger on. . . . Wary? Insecure? I don't know. He was an enigma at the same time that his feelings were written all over his face.

I loved my job. I interviewed for the job right when Mr. LaGuardia took office two years ago, and after an hour of back-and-forth discussion (rather like a speed game of ping-pong), I was hired. I started in the secretary pool for over a year. Then, at the youthful age of twenty-three, I was recently promoted to Mayor Fiorello La Guardia's personal aide.

We clanked down the two flights of steps at 77th, and Mr. LaGuardia said, "Good morning" and, "How are ya?" to many people, interspersed with things like, "Tell that Fletcher guy I'm watching him!" and, "Hey, Micky, how ya doin'? Tell your pop I hope he's feeling better."

We stopped, finally, at the end of the platform. I pointed and flexed my foot, working out the usual high-heel cramps. I felt someone brush up against me from behind; it was a mother with two young boys pulling on her arms, both prattling on to her at the same time. She looked tired, but she was smiling.

My eyes flicked behind her, and my stomach lurched with a sickening drop. Standing there was one of the scariest men I'd ever seen in my life, which is saying a lot, since I worked in the mayor's office. He was a grungy white man with a grungier brown hat smashed on top of his head, a stained white shirt, a grotesque stomach jutting out over wherever his belt would have been, and a slimy black cigar poking out of his mouth. All that was enough, but it was his face that sent a ripple of fear into me. His eyes were mean and flat but hinted that *something* was lurking back there. His nose encased a dense collection of black, bristly nose hairs poking out. He locked eyes with me for one second. I blinked and looked down as he gurgled a satisfied grunt at my unease. Just then, the train roared into the station.

Fio glared at me. "Lane? You with me? You okay?"

I looked at him and said, "Do you see that guy watching us?" I turned, but he was gone.

"What guy? Watching us?" he asked.

"He's gone." Before I could say more, the train stopped, the doors swung open, and a mass of humanity crushed its way onto the train. The train lurched downtown with all of us packed into place with someone's elbow in my back and a corner of a briefcase poking my thigh. I couldn't get that guy out of my mind.

In an effort to think of something else, I tried humming the new song by Bing Crosby, but all I could remember was the part that had the title of the song in it: "Benny's from heaven . . ." We finally pulled into our station, Brooklyn Bridge–City Hall. We smashed our way back out of the train and up several flights of stairs, and burst out into the refreshing open air at city hall. I straightened my red pillbox hat, which had gotten jostled a bit, and began copying down the onslaught of instructions once more.

Fio went right to his office after greeting everyone by name. I got to my desk and immediately started organizing my schedule. There was already a lineup of petitioners to see the mayor. From the young man whose wife had gone into labor unexpectedly early and the closest hospital was an expensive one that they couldn't afford—Fio was sure to get the fees reduced—to the pushcart peddler who had come in to complain that he couldn't get his license renewed. Fio always listened to each and every person and did something about their problem.

I helped Fio get through the line of people, listening, directing, and taking down information. Stifling a yawn, I felt the need for coffee and walked over to the coffee room. Fiorello didn't believe in coffee breaks, so I had to make it quick.

"Hey, Lane! How ya doin'?" exclaimed Ralph, one of the other aides in the office. Ralph's curly dark hair fell over his brow, and his smile was wide as he talked at breakneck speed. He was a nice guy; however, he never let me finish a sentence.

Ralph always knew what was hot to do in town. I could never fathom how much he crammed into a weekend. "Hey, Ralph, what's up t—" I asked. Before I could finish my greeting, he started in at a pace worthy of a Gilmore Special.

"There's a bunch of us going out to Club Monaco tonight, want to come along? I hear there's a great band, play all the new songs, too, not just the oldies. Hey! Great shoes, Lane. You should wear that red dress you wore last time we went to Wit's End. You looked amazing. Do you think you could bring Annie?"

He looked at me expectantly. Ralph had a hopeless crush on Annie, a secretary downstairs. But then again, he had a hopeless crush on a dozen women a month. He was lucky he was so good-natured.

"Sure, I'll see if she wants to c—" I tried to reply.

"Great! Save me a dance, Lane! Gotta run, Mr. Fitzgerald's extra grouchy today, better get back before he realizes I've been 'Gone too long, Popeye!'" He mimicked his surly boss perfectly and flew out the door, managing to throw his empty coffee cup into the garbage can with a very nice backhand. He really did resemble Popeye from the radio show and on the Wheatena box.

I walked back to my office with my creamy, sugary coffee and looked forward to going to the new Club Monaco. I got to work typing up notes for some points of contention Mr. LaGuardia had on the conditions of the housing organizations, adding up some numbers of the budget for this month, and transcribing my notes from the morning train ride.

The first meeting of the morning was a big one. It was a Boner Award day. Today's winner of the monthly award—a sheep bone decorated with ribbons like a Christmas present—was Fire Commissioner McElligott. He burned himself with a firecracker while giving a presentation about the dangers of Fourth of July fireworks.

The day went along its merry way until after lunch, when stern voices (aka yelling) floated out from Fio's office. I had learned to diagnose how important the yelling was. There were three categories. Category one: normal yelling that occurred on a daily basis, when Fio was only nominally annoyed at something, like at the Boner Award earlier. Category two: louder yelling accompanied by some desk-thumping and perhaps a pen whipped at the door out of frustration. This often led to a swift departure by the one being yelled at, brisk action taken by the mayor (more rapid-fire notes on my part), and a lot of activity all day long as we metaphorically put out fires to undo the damage that caused the yelling.

And then there was category three. Ooh, category three. There was usually one big outburst that contained an ominous tone, only one single, loud thump of an agitated fist hitting his desk, and then an eerie quiet that was like the calm before the storm. I usually walked away from my desk at that point, went to the ladies' room, and basically hid for a few minutes to prepare for battle.

This event turned out to be a category one. I wrote out a quick note on a minuscule piece of paper that said *C1* and went out to the main office toward Val's desk to give her the alert.

The entire office full of secretaries and aides was abundantly aware of the categories of our Little Flower. Valerie was my closest friend, and we navigated the office politics together. There had been a bit of a territory war ever since Fio decided to have me, a woman, be an aide versus a secretary. As I walked out to Valerie, I was already receiving dirty looks from my least favorite people: Lizzie and Roxy.

Val looked over at me with her green eyes flashing. With her light brown hair and thousands of tiny freckles, she looked fantastic as she sported a sage green suit with large buttons and three-quarter-length sleeves.

Lizzie and Roxy were eyeing me with constipated snarls on their faces. I waved in their direction and smiled, tossing the note to Val. She made some cryptic hand signals, like a catcher to the pitcher, to George across the room, and he ran off to another part of the office to inform them that the yelling was a mere category one.

"Hey, Short 'n' Shorter are particularly snarly today. What's going on?" I asked Val as I leaned up against her desk. Lizzie and Roxy were very tiny and they had an adorable aura around them that made me feel like a Clydesdale. I looked over at them, noticing how Roxy's curly white-blond hair hugged her perfectly round face in the latest style. She was very attractive except for the fact that she looked like she was perpetually displeased, or smelled something rotten. Today she had on a gorgeous yellow scarf and matching yellow, curve-hugging sweater that perfectly highlighted her best assets.

"Oh, they just figured out that since you were made an aide, you actually outrank them in the office."

"Just now? But I got that promotion six months ago," I said, with a quizzical, cocked eyebrow.

"Yeah, well, they might type like lightning, but the rest of them isn't so quick," said Val.

I looked over at them as Lizzie whispered something to Roxy like a gossipy schoolgirl. Lizzie's long red hair more than made up for her sort of mousy looks. She had a terrible squint, like she might need glasses, and her shoulders were the tiniest bit hunched (which made me constantly want to scold, *Stand up straight!*), but with her luxurious hair and wonderful figure, I'm pretty sure no one else noticed. Lizzie and Roxy were devious backstabbers. But they did type like lightning.

Since word traveled fast around there and I wanted to get back to my desk in case the C1 turned into something else, I said bye to Val and started to walk back. Just as I was getting to my desk, a lean, muscular man came barging out of Fio's office, and we charged right into each other. He was obviously surprised and said with a soft and rather intoxicating British accent, "Sorry, love." Before I could blink, he gently took my shoulders, set me aside, and in about three strides, was out the door of the office. The man was quick and efficient, yet I had time to glimpse dark eyes that sparked. And since I had literally run my face right into his collarbone, I also knew he smelled wonderful.

Just then Fio came out of his office with a crease furrowed between his brows, tapping his lips with his forefinger in thoughtful consideration.

"Who was that?" I asked.

"*Hmm?*"

"That man that you were yelling—I mean *speaking*—with just ran into me, and I didn't get a chance to meet him," I said, eyes squinting in assessment.

He hesitated, tapped his lips one final time, and replied, "*Hmm.*" Then Fio turned right around and went back into his office, closing the door behind him.

CHAPTER 2

Later that evening, Valerie and I met up with Ralph and his buddies at Club Monaco like we'd planned. His friends were fun and carefree as puppies as we danced all evening. I noticed Val had a particular shine in her eye when she was dancing with a guy named Peter. He was very tall. So it was pleasant, I'm sure, for my tall friend to wear high heels *and* get to look up at a guy for once.

I went to get a drink at the glossy black and silver bar and saw Ralph taking a break from the gals and all the dancing.

"Hi, Ralph," I said. I told the barkeep, "I'll have a Bad Romance."

"The drink?" he asked, waggling his eyebrows.

"I knew you'd say that," I said, with a smirk.

"Comes with the territory."

"Hey, Lane," greeted Ralph, with a casual elbow perched on the bar, while scouring the crowd for cute girls. "Great you could come tonight. Looks like Val's having a good time. Too bad Annie couldn't come, but it's a fun night anyway. Hey, don't forget you said you'd save a dance for me."

"Sure, sounds f—," and he was off and running, having spotted a partnerless gal at the edge of the dance floor. I took a sip of my Bad Romance while I enjoyed the view. In the belly of the cavernous club, dozens of tables surrounded the dance floor, with the band up front. The fifteen-piece band had on white jackets and black pants, and they were playing their hearts out, sweat dropping from their brows. It was hot inside the club with all the people dancing and the many glowing, low candles in the center of each table. My feet were just beginning to ache; I hadn't sat down the entire evening.

The club was a swanky place, so Val and I had dressed to the nines. I had on one of my favorite dresses, which was, in fact, the one Ralph had mentioned. The dark red number, almost off the shoulders, short, ruffled sleeves, and the skirt was close-fitting down to where my knees peeked beneath the hemline ruffle. My feet were decked out in black patent leather high heels. I thought about heading home soon. It was nearing midnight, and prying my feet out of these delightful shoes was sounding attractive. Just then someone came up beside me and rested his arms on the bar right next to mine, brushing up against me.

"How are you, Roarke? I haven't seen you around much lately." I smiled up at him. Roarke was a friend who worked across the street from the mayor's office. He was part of the ever-present press, and his job was to camp out in front of the city offices, waiting for my boss to give him some good headlines. Fio never disappointed.

"Nice dress, Lane. Want to dance?" Roarke was very easy on the eyes, with sandy blond hair and, to his extreme annoyance, blatant dimples that appeared when he smiled.

We walked out onto the dance floor, and he took me around the waist with his right hand. Roarke was wearing his signature black and gray, wide-striped suit. He cut a dashing figure with his white shirt, wide black tie, and black and white wingtip shoes. We danced to my favorite song of the month.

"Benny. Benny's from heaven . . ." I sang softly to the music.

"Uh, Lane? It's pennies. Pennies from heaven," said Roarke, with a smirk.

"Really? Are you sure?"

"Pretty sure," he said, with a nod.

"Huh," I said. For someone with excellent mental recall of events and people, I was terrible with song lyrics. "I like Benny better. Hey, I'm getting hungry. You want to go get something to eat with us?" I asked him.

"Yeah, that sounds good. I've got a lot of work to do, I'd better get something in me," he replied.

"Work? Roarke, it's almost midnight! You got something hot going on?" I asked.

"*Ehhhh*. Nah, nothing like that, just some big deadlines coming up." I didn't believe a word he said. Roarke was always on the prowl for a good story.

"Uh-huh. Right," I said, under my breath. But before I could question him further, he pulled me off the dance floor, yelled to Val to bring Peter along, and shooed us all out of the club. He was like a magnificent border collie herding us effortlessly out the door.

Outside, the air was much cooler, with a pleasant crispness. I filled my lungs with the fresh air, a delightful sensation after the smoky club.

"So . . . Marty's Place?" I questioned. They all barely nodded, as it was our mainstay late-night diner. We started walking, all of us lost in our own thoughts.

Clearly Val and Peter were only thinking of each other, truly enjoying their time together. They weren't holding hands, but they leaned into each other as they walked. Roarke was presumably consumed with the story he was working on.

And me? Well, I just couldn't stop thinking about two things. All day I found the image of the silver gun with the red scroll coming to mind. My recurring dream had a peculiar strength last night. Why did it make me so nervous? Maybe it was just intensified after I saw that disturbing guy on the subway platform. And secondly, more interestingly, I was thinking about that mysterious visitor of Fio's. His looks, his cologne, his accent . . .

Before I could delve into those enticing thoughts any further, a siren broke through my musings as a fire truck raced right by us with an ear-splitting racket. Roarke and I locked eyes and said simultaneously, "Fio!" We started to run down the block after the fire trucks. I yelled back to Val and Peter that we'd see them tomorrow.

Sure enough, as Roarke and I were all-out sprinting down the block, my sore feet forgotten, a black sedan careened around the corner in pursuit of the engines. In a split second I saw that the driver had dark hair and a maniacal smile full of excitement and childlike glee.

Fiorello had an insatiable need to be at all the big fires, traffic accidents, and crime scenes in the city. He kept police radios in his office at work, at home, and, believe it or not, in his car (it filled up most of the front seat). If something of interest came up, he jumped into his car and flew like the wind. Most of the time he had a driver, so he had the backseat of his car outfitted with all sorts of useful tools, including a folding desk to get work done while being driven about the city.

Roarke outstripped me, of course, but when I bounded up to the fire engines, I almost ran into him as I got distracted by the enormous fire shooting out of a town house. The flames looked impossibly tall as they soared into the black sky, almost twice the size of the actual town house. Firemen were running in every direction; they all had their jobs and knew them well. I located Fio and ran over to him. The FDNY had given Fiorello an honorary fireman's coat, which he was currently wearing.

"Anyone in there?" I asked him, out of breath. I pretty much knew the answer already, since he didn't look too solemn. Instead, Fio looked a bit like a seven-year-old watching his heroes go to work, his hands clasped behind his back, bobbing up and down on his toes.

"No. They say that this was an abandoned house, which means it looks like arson. The bigger concerns are the homes on either side, but the people have all been evacuated. In fact, the neighbors came home late and saw the flames, so they started banging on the doors around them after they called in the fire department. Thankfully, it's not a windy night, and they've been soaking the buildings next to them as well as putting out the main fire," he said.

Roarke came over and suggested we go across the street to stay out of the way. His investigative reporter spirit took over as he whipped out his notebook. He was scribbling furiously as we walked across the street. He'd been talking to a few people already, and I'm sure he wanted to take advantage of being on the scene. He spotted a friend of his and murmured a quick, "Be right back."

The flames were slowly dying down. While the heat had been intense even where I stood across the street, it started to feel cooler again. It was dark on this side of the street, the inhabitants not even opening their blinds a crack to peek out. That was odd . . . everyone enjoys a good gawking session. From the shadows behind me, I saw some of the darkness shift. The hairs on my neck and arms pricked. Even though it was warm out, I felt a chill. *Someone is watching me.*

My stomach clenched and my breath quickened, my thoughts going directly to that man from the train station that morning. I suddenly realized I was very alone; everyone's attention was on the fire, and I happened to be in a very dark and shadowy place. In the city, that just was not smart.

My aunt always told me I had an excellent sense of self-preservation: I moved. Fast. Just not fast enough.

Someone caught my arm and twisted it hard. I tried to yell out, but a hand went over my mouth and pulled me farther into the shadows. My shoulder was on fire, roiling with the pain of being slowly wrenched out of the socket. My crazed thoughts raced, but as I struggled to get in control, I realized it was definitely not that slimy man with the nose hairs. This guy was shorter and very slim. I could see jet black hair in my peripheral vision, very slicked back and shiny. And when I looked down, he had on equally shiny black shoes. He jerked my head back against him, and his rough stubble from a five o'clock shadow raked against my face.

A higher voice than I expected whispered in my ear, "You tell LaGuardia we don't appreciate him poking his nose in our business. I've got a message for you to send him. Tell Fio we've got sumthin' good planned for him. Something to shake up the city. And we've got a lot of help. He can't . . . aw, shit."

Just as fast as he caught me, he let me go and backed away, having said "Aw, shit" with the disappointment of getting his carefully prepared message cut in half. Just as he rounded the corner, his suit coat opened, and I saw a glint of silver coming from his shoulder holster.

I spotted Roarke coming back, the obvious impetus of the sleazy guy's departure. The satisfied grin on Roarke's face slowly melted into a frown as he got a better look at me.

"My God, are you okay?" he asked, taking my shoulders between his hands.

I started shaking. *Damn it. Get it together. I'm a New Yorker, for crying out loud.* "Yeah. Yeah, I'm okay. There was a guy in the shadows who came up behind me and just about wrenched my arm out the socket," I said, massaging my shoulder.

"Did he say anything?" he asked as he carefully tucked my hair behind my ear, gently smoothing it back into place.

"He started to mumble something crude, but didn't get far. He saw you coming and let go." I had to get my mind around this before I made a big deal of what the guy had said. Fio, not to mention all mayors of New York City, received threats all the time. This was just the first time I was involved. "Probably just some weirdo. I smelled a lot of alcohol on him." Which wasn't a lie, but he also smelled like cheap men's cologne, and I could feel that he was on the shorter side, taller than me but definitely under six feet.

"Did you see what he looked like? What he had on?" asked Roarke as he delved into figuring out the facts of the story.

"No, and don't go talking about this to your paper," I said sharply. "Or to Fio, for that matter. He's got enough on his plate without worrying about me taking care of myself." I took a deep, steadying breath. "Seriously, it was random, just a crazy guy. Okay? No telling Fio."

"*Hmmm,*" he murmured skeptically.

We started to walk toward Fio, who was talking amiably with some firefighters as they wrapped up everything.

"All right," said Roarke. "I'll let it go. For now. Just be careful. You work for the most important and the most controversial man in the city. He has enemies, which means you have enemies, too," he said, looking down at me.

"Thanks, Roarke. I will." His words rang undeniably true as I considered what the guy had said.

I let Roarke say good night to Fio, who was blissfully unaware of my adventure. I smoothed down my hair some more and tried not to hold my arm, which was still throbbing. Nothing was too wrong with it, maybe a light sprain.

I waved to Fio with my other arm as Roarke and I started the long walk back to Broadway to grab a taxi. Up ahead I saw a very familiar yellow sweater and shining white-gold head of hair, the owner of whom was clinging to some guy's arm. Then, with a quick glance our way, she quickly ducked out of sight. What was Roxy doing over here, far from the clubs, restaurants, and shows?

CHAPTER 3

Huh, no dreams. You'd think that after a night like last night, I'd have all sorts of nightmares. Instead, I awoke with a headache, my hair smelled a lot like a barbecue, and a canary yellow sweater was flitting through my mind. Oh, and when I went to get out of bed, I winced from my painful and stiff arm. *Fantastic.*

I took a shower, slowly washing all the smokiness out of my hair and letting the hot water ease the weariness out of my shoulders and the ache out of my head. I stretched my arm gingerly and loosened it up a bit. I took an aspirin and hoped my cool demeanor would deflect any questions from Aunt Evelyn.

"Good morning, Aunt Evelyn," I said with a sleepy smile as I sat down in the creaking dining room chair.

"Good morning, dear. And what did you do to your arm?" *Of course.*

"Oh, I don't know, must have slept funny on it," I said, in a very convincing tone, I thought.

"Really," she said, with a *don't even think about lying to me, child,* look.

"Oh, for crying out loud," I declared, with a frustrated gust of air to my bangs. I spilled the beans about last night. It had been harder to stop thinking about those terrifying moments than I wanted to admit.

I told Aunt Evelyn how I had left things with Roarke last night.

"Yes, I think that's a good idea for now, Lane," she replied, to my surprise. I took a piece of toast as I sipped my black tea. It was heaven.

"As one of my favorite friends from Egypt is fond of saying, I think we need a council of war," said Aunt Evelyn, with a portentous finger raised. "And perhaps we should start some kind of list. A list of people who could be behind this." Aunt Evelyn had friends all over the earth. I didn't know this one, but I smiled at the serious tone of her statement.

"Okay, what are you thinking as far as suspects?" I asked her.

"Let's see. Fio is forever getting into trouble. It's trouble the city needs; God knows he's worked miracles already just to get voted in. But then to take on Tammany Hall and all its corruption . . . Good heavens."

Nobody had expected Fio to win the election two years ago. Tammany Hall was a corrupt political machine within the Democratic Party. Its bosses had influence on city officials from the police force to the lawyers and the judges. It was a miracle Fio won on the Fusion ticket. Believe me, they gave it their best shot to try to circumvent the system.

On voting day, Tammany had thugs all over the city "assisting" voters . . . With brass knuckles, blackjacks, and lead pipes. Some public figures came out to help. Even Tony Canzoneri, the prizefighter, showed up to back Fio. But Fiorello was galled at the outright chicanery of Tammany. They went against everything he wanted for Gotham. So, in his usual style, Fio was everywhere at once, scurrying around to as many polls as possible to "enforce honesty" as he liked to say.

But Fiorello did it. He became New York City's ninety-ninth mayor.

"Well, who would have it out for him? What do you know of the leftovers from Tammany?" I asked, getting my pen ready.

Aunt Evelyn had friends in all places, high and low. She was in the know about everything and was always connecting with people from all different worlds: art, finance, education, politics. She deliberated about possibilities as she sipped her steaming cup of tea. "I know the Tammany crowd is still very angry and not convinced that Fiorello can make his changes permanent. I think they're hoping that they're only on a hiatus. Jimmy Walker and the old Tammany Tiger crew were disgraced, but power and greed do not relinquish their hold very easily. Plus, New Yorkers love Walker! I never understood the cheers and hoots and hollers for him every time he showed up somewhere—even after he was out of office! He is a charismatic man, I'll give him that. His wisecracks carried him farther than anything he ever did."

I wrote down the names of Fio's biggest opponents as Evelyn started naming them, ticking them off on her long fingers.

"Besides Tammany, there are the gangsters," I said, flipping to a new page. Gangs like Lucky Luciano's and Louie Venetti's were running monopolies on anything they could get their hands on, with unpredictable and brutal scare tactics.

"Yes, it's likely one of them has a grudge and is willing to do something about it. Every time I see Fiorello wielding a sledge-hammer across his shoulders on another anti–slot machine campaign, one moment I want to cheer out loud, and the next moment I want to yell at him to stop making such a show of himself," she exclaimed, with a shake of her head.

I nodded in complete agreement. Once in the mayor's seat, Fiorello began a quest to rid the city of everything that the good people had been tempted to try their luck on in these hard times after the crash. He especially hated the slot machines that filled the delis and grocery stores. He was convinced that people were spending their milk money hoping for a little luck. He started a campaign to get rid of them, loading thousands of them onto barges and then dumping them in the sea. Those machines, which Fio so blatantly and joyfully crushed with his very own sledgehammer, were mostly operated by gang bosses. You can imagine what they thought of Fio as he destroyed a very lucrative part of their businesses.

She held her chin in her hand and tapped her cheek with two fingers. She murmured something about talking to a friend named Ellie.

"Who's Ellie?" I asked. Mr. Kirkland kept coming in to replenish the breakfast items, and I couldn't help but notice that he was taking a deep interest in our conversation. He wasn't his usual mut-

tering self as he kept looking directly at Evelyn like he was trying
to get her attention.

"*Hm?*" she said, as if I had woken her up from her thoughts. "Mr.
Kirkland, did you need something?" She had obviously noticed his
unusual interest as well. Or possibly she was avoiding my question
about Ellie.

Mr. Kirkland's light blue eyes opened wide. He looked like a kid
caught with his hand in the cookie jar. "*Mmmmuuundddertttss,*" he
said, then grabbed the nearest dish and raced off to his lair.

A smile tugged at one side of Aunt Evelyn's mouth as she blithely
continued, "I think that when Robert Moses and Fiorello tore down
Jimmy's casino in Central Park, it was the coup de grâce. It was a
move that made both Tammany *and* the gangsters upset. I think we
are at a pivotal moment. Jimmy's supporters will either die out, or
they will become vengeful and take things into their own hands."

Fio had denounced Walker's casino as a whoopee joint. He had
it razed and replaced it with park space. Personally, I wished he'd
kept it; I'd have loved to dance in the gorgeous black glass ballroom
with those dazzling chandeliers. But Fio was trying to root out the
rampant corruption. Walker was "charmingly corrupt," as many reporters loved to say, but corrupt nonetheless.

"With that, I regret I must leave you to ruminate, Lane. I have
plans with Lucille later today. Would you like to come? We're going
to go to the Whitney."

"No thank you, Aunt Evelyn. I have some things to think about,
plus it's beautiful outside. I want to take a walk along the river,
maybe read more Agatha Christie," I said, with a smile as I felt a
ripple of delight at the thought of having a day to myself.

She looked at me a little skeptically, assessing my arm, my curiosity, and whether or not the trouble of last night would follow me
today. She smiled back, releasing her pursed lips, and ended with,
"Just watch your arm, Lane. And don't get yourself into a lonely
spot again. Until we know what last night was all about, we need to
be more careful. When it gets dark out, make sure you're not walking around alone, all right?"

"Definitely. Thanks." I watched as Aunt Evelyn swept around

the room collecting her hat and her capacious purse. She passed by the pair of a man's riding gloves on the little desk and a beautiful sketch of Evelyn with a young man in a chic Paris café with their heads close together. She opened a drawer and retrieved a small lavender book that I had never noticed before, then quickly left the house, softly closing the door behind her.

I collected my notepad and pen as I strolled through the empty kitchen and poured myself a lemonade from the icebox. It was new, and Mr. Kirkland told us it was officially called a *refrigerator*. "It even uses the new cooling agent, Freon-12, to keep things cool!" he had happily explained. It was the most excitement I'd ever seen Mr. Kirkland show.

I leisurely strolled farther back and swung open the door to my favorite part of the house, the patio. We lived in a four-story brownstone and had an outdoor space in the back where Mr. Kirkland showed a surprising and charming talent.

He had landscaped a beautiful green space full of climbing plants like ivy, morning glory, and moonflowers that opened their enormous white petals in the summer evenings and let off a spectacular scent. In large clay pots set in strategic places were tall grasses, annual flowers of bright colors, and more ivy. A long table hosted many dinner guests on warm evenings. And above that table was an old, sprawling maple tree. Ingeniously, Mr. Kirkland kept the branches pruned over the years to form a canopy over the table and part of the small yard. He and Aunt Evelyn strung lanterns and even some small crystal chandeliers that they filled with tiny lights in the evenings. It was a magical place. A place that stirred thoughts of Peter Pan, where fairies flew and danced and created their own magic.

I let out a contented sigh and found my favorite spot, a chaise longue in the corner. There was a small teakwood end table next to it, where I set my things down. I stretched as I sat back on the soft cushions, flexing and pointing my feet, enjoying the cool air running through my toes.

I started to make some notes. There was a lot going on in the city. This summer the new Triborough Bridge was to be opened, as well as the huge Randall's Island complex. And we had already broken ground for the World's Fair that would be coming in 1939.

Lying beneath all these names and ideas and lists, puzzling and teasing my mind, was that quick glimpse of silver in my assailant's jacket. Could it be the silver gun in my dreams?

Just as I was massaging my cramped right hand, the doorbell rang. I set my notes down and ran to the front door.

"Roarke. What are you doing here?" His presence was completely unexpected. We usually only saw each other during the week at work or dancing on the weekends. "Is everything okay?"

"Oh. Yeah. Everything is fine," he said, rather unhelpfully. We stood there looking at each other for a few long seconds before I decided to be the forthcoming one and ask him in. I took him to the patio; it was too nice to stay inside.

"Lemonade?" I asked as we went through the kitchen.

"Sure, sounds good." I poured another glass and got some potato chips for us to share.

"Wow! This is a great space!" exclaimed Roarke, with his head swiveling all around, taking in the trees, the lightly tinkling chandeliers, and the colorful comfort of the patio. He had on a white polo shirt open at the collar, and a pair of light blue slacks with loafers. He looked pretty darn great with his sandy blond hair as he took off his boater hat.

"Yeah, I love it here. Have a seat," I said as I gestured to the outdoor couch and chair striped in a worn green and white fabric. I curled my legs up on the couch and sipped some lemonade.

"You look surprised to see me," said Roarke, with the kind of know-it-all smirk on his face that drives women to criminal fantasies.

"*Euuhhh*, Roarke," I said, with exasperation. "Do you have something to share?"

"*Mmm hmm!*"

"Well?"

"I'm just enjoying the anticipation of your reaction."

"This can't be good," I muttered.

"All right, I'll put you out of your misery."

"Really? Leaving so soon?" I said, with the same smirk he had been giving me.

"Ha. Funny. I heard through the grapevine that Fio has found out about your little misadventure last night."

"Well, that's not that big of a deal. He'll be mad that I didn't go to him right away, but . . ."

"*And* that a little gal who loves yellow sweaters was . . . the . . . tattletale," he finished, with a flourish.

"What?" I yelled. He jumped, making lemonade splash onto his sleeve. "That little, conniving . . . Wait a minute. How did she know about that? When we saw Roxy, she was far up ahead of us. The fire was in a residential area away from the restaurants and shows."

"She says she saw the whole thing from across the street. She'd been walking home just like we had, heard the sirens, and went to see what was going on. Saw what happened to you, but after I had arrived and the guy had fled, she figured that you were all right and just went home."

"And I suppose out of the goodness of her heart, she called Fio to 'check on Lane' and gleefully pass on the information," I surmised.

"*Yyyyup,*" said Roarke as he crunched another chip.

Something still wasn't right about it. "That was pretty far away to see all that, and we were in the shadows. Is it possible that she knows more about it than she should?" I asked.

Roarke gave me a sidelong glance, his eyebrow lifted skeptically. "Lane, I know you and Valerie don't get along with her and Lizzie, but . . ."

"No, Roarke, listen. I didn't tell you everything about last night."

"I figured," he said smugly.

So I filled him in on what the guy had actually said to me in the shadows.

"Well, it was clearly just a message," said Roarke. "He could have hurt you if he'd wanted to, but he didn't."

"True. So what about Roxy? She knows I would eventually tell Fio everything, probably Monday morning. Why make sure he gets the news now? You know, interrupting his weekend, making sure he got the message *now*." Roarke looked at me as he gave it some thought, then another realization struck me a terrifying blow. "Oh, my God," I said, with the blood draining out of my face. "Fio's going to come here!"

"What's wrong with that?" said Roarke, unbelievably naïve.

"Are you kidding? He'll give you and me the third degree . . . *for hours*." He still looked at me a little blankly. I spelled it out. "No. More. Weekend."

"Oh, my God."

"We gotta get outta here!"

We swept out of that house as fast as humanly possible. As I closed and locked the door behind me, the phone started ringing. Close one.

We decided to go for a stroll along the East River walkway. Later, we caught up with Val. The three of us decided to spend the evening down in Little Italy. Moneta's had the best food in town, but was way out of our price range. Copioli's was a close second and fit our budget. I especially loved their crumb-coated, fried green olives. I could eat about fifty of them.

As we were drinking our red wine and soaking up the last of the sauce on our plates with the fresh bread, a small band of diminutive Italian gentlemen came up to play some music.

The music was making people move; the whole crowd felt the vitality of the place, plus, the wine helped. We got up, helping to move tables out of the way, and Valerie was scooped up by an admirer. It was dark, smoky, and sparkling from the candle flames dancing off the glasses.

Just as I was helping the people next to me move their table, someone came up, put his arm around my waist, and pulled me toward the middle of the floor. He pulled his arm in toward himself and me along with it, pressing me in close.

"Hi, love."

My eyes opened wide in surprise as I smiled. The music had a fast tempo, but was very smoldering. My right hand clasped his left as sparks and tingles flowed through his fingertips. The whole place moved to the rhythm, everyone caught up in their own world. He'd left his hat at the door. My mystery man from the office had on a black form-fitting suit with a bright white shirt, open at the collar. We turned and swayed to the music.

Hey mambo, mambo Italiano . . .

His looks were full of opposites. His eyes were dark gray, or maybe green, and had that intangible quality that makes eyes sparkle. His slight five o'clock shadow darkened a strong jawline. He looked like he could take a punch and give one back, yet there wasn't an ounce of arrogance. His arms were hard and strong, yet he moved with grace. He was intense, yet there was a hint of a smile dancing around the corners of his eyes and mouth.

Hey mambo, mambo Italiano . . .

Years later Rosemary Clooney would sing a similar song, but I would be forever convinced this one was even better. Maybe it was the wine. We turned one last time, and as I breathed in, deeply savoring the moment, the song ended. We stopped dancing. The next song started up, but we were motionless, still very, very close, our eyes and arms locked tight. My right hand clasped his hand a little more tightly, and my left pressed up against his chest, feeling the warmth underneath. His face was intent and serious, and something in me wanted to make him smile.

Concern suddenly etched a crease on his brow, and he bent to whisper in my ear, "I . . . I'm sorry." And he left. I let out a breath. He made his way easily through the crowd, gathering his hat and heading toward the door. He placed his fedora on his head at a slight angle and looked back at me. A smile pulled up one side of his mouth, making me smile back like we shared a good secret.

I got back to the table, sank into my seat, and took a long swig of my wine. Roarke finished his dance with a blonde on the other side of the room just as Val came back and sat down.

"This place . . . it's the best!" exclaimed Roarke. Val was grinning ear to ear.

Val took a closer look at me and said, "Hey, Roarke, I think Lane and I are going to go freshen up, right, Lane?"

"What?"

"Let's go, girly," she said, and she took my hand, leading me down the rickety stairs to the basement.

When we got to the ladies' room, Val turned to me. "So *who* was *that*?" she said, with her hands on her hips.

"You saw him, too? I was just beginning to think he was a figment of my imagination," I said, a little breathlessly.

"I thought you knew each other. You sure *looked* like you knew each other, *danced* like you knew each other," she said, with a smile mixed with a furrowed brow. Val liked to keep tabs on me, but a lot had happened the last two days.

"Well . . . I saw him, actually ran into him, coming out of Fio's office yesterday. He smelled so good. . . . Did I say that part out loud?" I said, with a smirk.

"So . . . did he smell good tonight?" Val the inquisition officer was replaced with the giddy best friend who wanted to get the scoop.

"Oh, yes. Really . . . really, really good. I couldn't even talk, it was . . . ho, boy," I said as I plopped down onto the tiny pink couch in the lounge.

"Wow, you're not usually so lost for words."

"I know. Shocking, isn't it?"

"So, what's his name?"

"I have no idea. We didn't get to names."

"Maybe you can ask Fio. Did he say anything? Did you make any plans to see each other again?"

"No. We really didn't say anything. Just danced. And then he left. Just like that," I said as I snapped my fingers. I wanted that dance again. It was like a hunger, and I wanted to replay it over and over again.

"Well, if he found you tonight, he'll find you again," said Val.

"What makes you say that? It was just one dance."

"Oh, no," she said, with conviction. "It was more than just a dance." Back upstairs we found Roarke talking to the guys next to our table and enjoying a cannoli.

"So, are you going to ask her to dance again?" one of the guys asked Roarke.

"Yeah, I think I will," said Roarke as he took one last sip of his dark espresso and then walked over to the blonde's table.

"Hey, he didn't even finish his cannoli," I mumbled as I finished his cannoli.

After our fill of dancing and dessert, we headed home. I went up the steep steps and discovered music floating down from Aunt Evelyn's studio upstairs. I climbed all those stairs to the attic, singing softly to my new favorite song. During the day, the attic skylights gave the perfect light for an artist, but at night, Aunt Evelyn painted by lamplight. She liked to see how her pieces looked in shadow and the warmer lighting. The room was golden, accompanied by the soft sounds of Rachmaninoff.

"How was your night, dear? Did you have a good time?" she asked while dabbing her pinky lightly on some soft, white patches of clouds she'd been painting. She wasn't upset, but I could tell something was up by the look on her face.

"It was a great day, a great evening. I'll tell you all about it, but what's going on? I can tell you're waiting to tell me something. Everything all right?"

"Oh, yes, Lane, just fine," she said wearily. "But Fio has been ringing the phone off the hook! Literally! It rang so hard once, the receiver fell off the hook in the hallway. What am I going to do with that man?"

All of the day's earlier events came flooding back to me at once. I had forgotten about Roxy's little tattle; it seemed a world away. It turned out that Fio was out of the city for the weekend, and instead of running over to our house, he had opted for calling every few minutes to talk to me—at me. Aunt Evelyn had talked with him and told him the details, but apparently, that wasn't good enough.

"Did you tell him what that man said?" I asked.

"Yes, I decided it was better to tell him, and also, you wouldn't have to face the full wrath on your own. Don't worry. You know Fio, darling, all the fire dies out after a while, and then a different fire comes along to consume him. I hope you feel that telling him was the right thing to do."

"Of course. Thanks. And did you hear about how he found out?" I told her about Roxy, and she clucked her disapproval.

"What is it with her and that Lizzie girl? And how did she even know about that incident? I believe you said that man pulled you into the shadows," said Aunt Evelyn, with her usual acumen.

"I said the same thing to Roarke. He's not convinced anything is amiss; she's just silly and immature, in his mind."

"Maybe," mused Aunt Evelyn. "But something makes me think there is more beneath her demeanor than she lets on."

"What do you mean? You've only met Roxy and Lizzie a couple of times."

"Just a feeling; there's a look in her eye that says she is not weak-minded. I'd keep my eye on both of them, if I were you."

"I think I'll be keeping my eye on a lot of people. . . ."

"*Hmm*, yes, I think that would be prudent. Good night, dear. I'll see you in the morning." She turned to her canvas like it was speaking to her and she was excited to listen.

I went to bed, a cool breeze floating into my third-floor window. I heard Aunt Evelyn's occasional step or two above me and the soft sounds of traffic, the hum of the city. It had been a humid day even though it hadn't been very hot. But the night air had blown all the heaviness away, leaving the city cool and comfortable. There was a lot to think about, but my mind was, of course, dancing again. That thrill that ran up my spine as he pulled me close; breathing in the scent of his cologne; that enticing jawline, neck, and collarbone; moving to the spellbinding rhythm of the music. Was he thinking of me right now? And, most importantly, who was he, and what would make him say, "I'm sorry?"

CHAPTER 4

Monday morning came with a bang. Literally. Fio had thrown open the door with his usual gusto.

We were eating breakfast at the dining room table, and between us, we had worked out our plan on how to handle Fiorello. "Come in, Fio, darling, come in!" said Aunt Evelyn, with a gracious sweep of her arm as she stood up and bustled Fio over to the table, handing him a steaming cup of coffee and a freshly baked muffin with crumbles on top and blueberries peeking out. She "helped" him sit down with a ladylike shove as I broke into a commanding lecture about the events of Friday night. Between Fio's favorite food by Mr. Kirkland, hot coffee, and Aunt Evelyn and myself, the poor guy didn't have a chance. All his outrage just melted off as easily as he took off his bowler hat.

After finishing her part of the thorough recount, Evelyn stopped and daintily sipped her tea. Fio took a deep, steadying breath, narrowed his eyes, and looked from one of us to the other without moving his head.

"All right. Seems like you two have covered all the pertinent details. But next time, and I'm sure there will be a next time, *Lane* . . ." he said, with a meaningful, piercing look, "I want you to come directly to me. TO ME." He emphasized the important words with a fist on the table, rattling the cups.

"Deal, Chief. I know it sounds like backpedaling, but I was going to discuss it with you today, after I got my head around it. I don't know what it means, what that guy meant . . . exactly."

"*Hmmm*, yes. *Exactly* is the key word. I've irritated many, many people." That was putting it catastrophically mildly. "But I've also made some powerful friends. It probably doesn't mean anything; maybe someone trying to get our attention, maybe just a weirdo getting high off threatening people. Anyway! We've got work to do!" With an effortless flick of a switch, Fio moved on to more pressing issues, suddenly bawling out his workday mantra.

I promptly said good-bye to Aunt Evelyn and Mr. Kirkland. We hopped into the awaiting car out front, and as the driver picked his way through the neighborhood, Fio recited the long list of things to do for the day. Anytime we drove to work or the LaGuardias went home from an event, the driver would take a unique route. Former mayors and political leaders had had well-known and not-so-well-known assassination attempts. Most mayors had two detectives along for protection. To save the city money, so he said, Fio got rid of the detectives and had two pistol compartments added to his car: one for the driver and one for him. Both he and his driver had gun permits. *Good Lord.*

We arrived at work, and his first meeting of the day was with Mr. Thomas Dewey, special prosecutor for New York City. With these two, I was going to have to add whole new chapters to my list of people who had a gripe against Fio.

The city, the whole country, actually, was going through an era of the gangster. Everyone was obsessed. Gangsters filled books, movies, theater, and real life. But let me tell you, for someone actually living in New York and not vicariously through the romantic movies, it wasn't glamorous. It was terrifying and excruciatingly frustrating. And those damn machine guns that were all the rage—they took out just as many innocent bystanders as gangsters.

Organized crime syndicates had a hold on just about every market you can imagine. Fio made it his business to try to take down every stronghold. Last year, he'd made a lethal strike against the Artichoke King, Ciro Terranova. Yes, there was a stranglehold even on artichokes. Fio rustled up the mayoral car and good-sized police escort to add to the spectacle and paraded up to the Bronx Terminal Market, the Artichoke King's command central. Happily surrounded by a grinning audience of policemen, Fiorello regally declared, from an ancient law he had discovered, that in an emergency, the mayor could ban the distribution of food. With trumpets blaring (he really did bring in two trumpets), he actually unrolled a kingly scroll and pronounced that the Artichoke King was shut down. While the lawyers were scrambling to find a judge to overrule this proclamation, Fio had West Coast dealers flood the market with artichokes. Reporters wrote that prices dropped thirty percent within just a few days. This was absolutely a publicity stunt, but damn, did it have pizzazz.

"Good morning, Mr. Dewey," I said, greeting the slender, thirty-four-year-old special prosecutor.

"Good morning, Miss Sanders. Fiorello? I have a thought about that Parker guy and his crew. . . ." His voice faded off as the crime-fighting duo started to make their plans.

I typed up my morning notes for the day and decided to go get a cup of coffee. I waved at Valerie as I passed by. I poured a cup and started to add the sugar, when I heard a quiet, "Ahem." I turned around expecting Val, but saw Lizzie. Dark circles rimmed her eyes, and she looked like she might be coming down with a cold.

"You okay, Lizzie?" I asked.

"Oh, ah, I just didn't sleep well last night, that's all. Um, I have a favor to ask," she said while taking a quick glance out the door of the break room. "Ah . . . could we go get a cup of coffee or take a walk later or something?" She'd never been this nice.

"Well . . . sure. Do you want to do lunch?"

"Oh, I can't do lunch, I'm having lunch with Roxy." She took another look out the door.

"All right, when? After work?" I asked, looking out the door myself to see what she was looking at. Nothing there.

"Great, let's walk to the station together. Thanks. See you then." And she ran out the door. I mentally shrugged my shoulders and went about my day.

I tried to pin down Fio several times to find out more about my dance partner from Saturday night, but it never worked out. The workday finally came to a close, and I met Lizzie by the café out-side in the nearby park. We each bought a Coca-Cola and walked around the path.

"So, what's up, Lizzie? You don't usually like to go for walks with me," I said, deciding to cut to the chase.

"Oh, yeah. Sorry about that. I know this is really out of the or-dinary." She took a thick strand of her glorious red hair by her ear and started to twirl it with her fingers. The gesture made her look self-conscious and unsure. It was like a veneer had been lifted.

"It's okay, Lizzie. No big deal. What did you want to talk about?"

"Well . . . it's kind of hard to say. I mean . . . Well, I know you and Roxy don't get along. Well, for that matter, I know we're not ex-actly friends, either, but . . ." She tripped over her words, trying to find the right thing to say. "Well, anyway, I'm getting worried about Roxy. I *am* worried about her. She's just not herself lately." Lizzie started to talk fast, unloading her thoughts as quickly as she could. "I mean, she's not talking to me as much, I find her just staring at you and Val. She says she's going to do one thing over the weekend, but then I find out she's been doing other things. . . ."

"Whoa, whoa. Wait a minute. Go back. She's *staring* at me and Val?" Of course that was the main thing I zeroed in on.

"Well, she's never liked you guys. I don't know, maybe she's just envious of your job. I mean, I'm not that crazy about the fact that you get to be Mr. LaGuardia's aide, either, but . . . it's just normal fun office stuff, you know?"

"I guess," I said hesitantly, not sure how to respond to her sense of what *just normal fun* meant.

"But I mean, she's been quiet and so aloof lately. I don't know. Maybe I'm worried over nothing. I feel a little silly for bringing it up."

"Oh, I'm sure it's nothing. Maybe she's got some big work dead-line or something with her family that's just occupying her mind. But why talk to me about it? Do you want me to do something?"

"I don't think so, I just wanted to say something to you or Val. I don't want you to think that there's something more than just office banter going on. You know, I wanted to clear the air."

"Sure, any time. And don't worry, this city takes a toll on every-one at some point. Maybe Roxy just needs some time off."

"Maybe so," she replied, with a small smile and a shrug. "Thanks, Lane. I'll see you tomorrow," she said as she walked away, sipping her Coke. I had to find Val and tell her about this bizarre conversation. Roxy was indeed behaving strangely, and maybe there was something big behind it. But then again, Lizzie was acting even stranger.

Later on, Val and I met up on my side of town. We decided to go to my place and get something to eat. I got us a couple of sandwiches and two bottles of root beer, and we sat down at the small, scrubbed pine table in the kitchen. It was cozy in its small alcove, which jutted out into the patio area—the perfect place for a tête-à-tête. I recounted my entire conversation with Lizzie.

"That's really hard to believe, Lane."

"I know. I'm not sure what to do about Roxy. If I should talk to her, follow her . . ."

"No, no! I mean Lizzie! Whenever we've even tried to talk with her in the past, it always looked like she found it difficult to even be in the same room with us, let alone have a heart-to-heart with you."

"I know what you mean," I said, taking a sip of my frothy root beer. "I kept thinking that she'd end up making a joke of it or something. But you should have seen her! She was hesitant, and even . . . sweet. I'm not sure I liked it," I said, with a curl to my lip.

Val let out a laugh and said, with her chin in her hand, "Well, I think we should just keep watching the situation. We still don't know what's going on here, what your incident with the threat to Fio really means. Things with Roxy are tough to put a finger on, but it can't hurt to be careful. Do we know much about her background?" Val asked as she finished off her sandwich and crumpled up her napkin, then thoughtfully put her elbows on the table.

"I don't know anything about Roxy or Lizzie. Maybe I can ask Fio about them," I said.

"Well, the main guy who hired them was Ralph, let's ask him."

"*Ralph?* He worked with management to hire the secretary pool?"

"Yep. His boss was supposed to handle it, but he let Ralph take over. Much to Ralph's surprise and pleasure."

"Okay, then. I'll chat with him tomorrow."

* * *

The next morning, I headed to work on my own, since Fio was going in early to start working out the plans for the new housing being developed on the Lower East Side. I took the train down to Grand Central to drop something off for Fio at the main post office. I made a point of walking through Grand Central Station whenever I could; it was my favorite building. The enormous main hall was captivating with its giant curved windows at the top and the sea green ceiling painted with constellations and pinpoints of glittering, starry lights—made me wish I could fly. The energy was palpable, with thousands of people going to work or going on some vacation or other, and hundreds of tourists standing around with their jaws hanging open.

After the post office, I walked back into Grand Central and ran down several flights of stairs to the passages that led to my downtown subway line. There was a rollicking band playing a lively number with fiddles, banjos, and a washboard for percussion.

I walked down the final flight of stairs to my platform, watching my plum-colored dress flare just below the knees as I skipped down the steps in my spectator pumps. The train had probably just departed, as the platform was pretty empty. I walked a little farther and stopped. The area began to fill up fast, this being one of the most popular stops. I adjusted my purse, took out my pad of paper, and perused some of my notes for the day.

A gust of wind came down the tunnel, signaling a train coming shortly. I looked up at the people across the platform; an uptown train was about to pull in there as well. A man right across from me flicked his wrist, and a large pile of ashes from his cigarette fell to the ground with a red gleam.

The uptown train pulled into the station with a rush of air blowing the hair about my face, a couple of strands sticking in my eyelashes. Our train was getting closer, the white light at the front appearing as I peered down the tunnel. A group of loud tourists came up behind and around me, chattering about their plans.

Suddenly, something shoved into me, forcing me right to the edge. I lost my balance as I felt one more push and fell down onto the tracks. A lady screamed as I fell, then I heard several more screams as people saw the oncoming train. My palms hit the black ground hard, jarring my head as my knee slammed against the metal track. I whipped around to see what the hell had happened.

Right where I'd been standing, I spotted slick black hair, and a leering face looking right at me. In a sardonic gesture, he brought the barrel of a gun up to his lips, hushing me with an evil smile. *Oh my God. It* is *the silver gun.*

All my fear instantly slipped away and was replaced by seething anger. It was the same man who had grabbed me at the fire and he had that silver gun of my nightmares. Damn it, I was *not* going to be one of those ridiculous damsels in adventure novels who fall and are completely witless and helpless.

The horn of the oncoming train blared relentlessly over and over again above the screams of people who looked infinitely far away on the tall platform that I had been standing on just a second before. I was between the first and second tracks. I looked at the third, taller track, which carried the electricity that powered the train, and then over to the farther side of the tracks, where the uptown train was pulled into the station, blocking an escape.

I dashed over the top of the deadly third track to the middle, where the uptown and downtown trains would pass each other within just a couple of feet, which seemed like inches, bracing myself against two pillars just as the train careened by with a wild surge of wind and power.

I was sandwiched between the two trains, but not dead. And that was a damn good feeling. There was a ruckus of yelling as people tried to figure out exactly what happened. Panicked faces started peering down from the windows of both trains. I was able to give a thumbs-up and saw plenty of relieved smiles and enigmatic gestures that were surely telling me to hold tight. That I could do.

Apparently, this situation rarely happened, and it took quite a while to figure out what to do, but finally people motioned through the windows that the uptown train would pull out. I gave another thumbs-up, my heart still trying to thump its way right out of my chest.

The train pulled out slowly, and I stood completely still, not wanting an inch of me to extend past those columns on either side

of me. The last car went by, and I exhaled a big breath. I probably hadn't fully breathed in about fifteen minutes, but it felt more
like fifteen hours. I wobbled over to the other side, again carefully
stepping high up over that electrified track, to where several kind
people held out their arms to haul me up onto the platform. The
police were already there, and that was about when the adrenaline
started to ebb. Curse it, my hands started to shake.

An arm wrapped around my waist just in time, and kept me
firmly upright. The man's head bent down, and his cheek touched
the top of my head. "I've got you, love."

I let out a short, rather indignant gasp, saying, "What? Hey!" Just
then, he firmly pushed me down onto a bench. About five other
people quickly clustered around me, trying to assess if I had any
injuries . . . and he was gone.

A medic came over and started looking at my banged-up knee. I
had torn a hole in my ivory stockings, and my knee was swelling up
underneath the blood that trickled down my shin. My shoulder was
throbbing, but I could move that as well. He handed me a hanky
and said, "It's all right, do you want something for the pain? Or are
you crying from the scare?"

"I'm not sad! Or scared. I'm mad! I'm crying because I'm really,
really mad!" He blinked. "I saw the guy who pushed me, and . . .
I'm *furious!*" I exclaimed with gritted teeth.

"Okay . . . Okay . . ." said the medic as he raised two hands in a
defensive, *okay, crazy lady* motion.

I really was mad. And it was utterly frustrating when I teared up
because I was mad. Just then, I saw a very familiar and very comforting vision running toward me, arms flailing, bellowing at everyone.

"Fio," I said, with a great sigh of relief.

"What the hell happened, Lane?" he screeched, with the force
of a foghorn. "I heard someone fell onto the tracks on the police radio, then a buddy called from the department moments later saying
they thought it was you! Good God, you scared me." He pulled me
into a careful, one-armed hug as he sat down next to me. He took a
good look at me and nodded sagely. "You're crying. You're angry."

I started to laugh. "Only you, Fio . . . Yes, I'm ticked off, and
damn these tears!" I said, half-chuckling, half-crying.

Fiorello turned my face to him with a gentle finger under my chin. "First, are you all right? Are you hurt?"

"I just banged up my knee and shoulder, but nothing's broken and no stitches needed or anything."

"Good. Secondly . . ." Here, he paused and looked even more intently into my eyes. "Why *exactly* are you angry? Did you see who did this to you?" He really was omniscient.

"Didn't you say that over the police radio the report was that someone *fell* onto the tracks?"

"Yes. But you're not *someone*, Lane. You were pushed, weren't you?" His eyes looked stormy, and his fedora was cocked at a rakish angle.

"Yes. I *know* I was. It was the same guy, Fio. The same guy who pulled me into the shadows. I looked up after I fell, and he was smirking at me. And that horrible, sarcastic, mocking smile actually ended up helping me," I said, with a self-deprecating grimace. "I got so mad; I was *not* going to let him finish me off like that. I ran to the center of the tracks between the trains."

"Good. Good, Lane. We'll handle this. The police aren't going to be much help, because I think they still believe you fell, and I doubt the tourists around you saw anyone, they never do. But I believe you. My buddy on the force will get a sketch from you on that guy. Can you do that? Describe him in detail?"

"Yes. Absolutely, Fio."

"I need to see this guy, and I'll get the description into the right hands. When I hear something, I'll let you know. Now, let's get you home."

My knee was starting to feel very tender and stiff. So, in spite of the fact that I wanted to get to work and be part of whatever Fio had in mind, I absolutely needed to get off my knee. Fio took me home in his car. I spent the ride replaying over and over again that sickening gesture from the man who tried to kill me. Instead of a hushing finger to the lips, he held a gun. The silver of the gun had glinted in the lights, and the bloodred scroll on the handle matched the blood on my knees.

CHAPTER 5

Aunt Evelyn and Mr. Kirkland were waiting for us on the side-walk, Kirkland with his arms folded across his chest like an imperi-ous king and Aunt Evelyn piercing every car that went by with her steely glare. Fio had called, so they knew the details already and I didn't have to go into them all over again. I eased myself out of the car, and although the day had been chock full of surprises already, the most surprising of all happened next.

I looked up at all those stairs ahead of me and practically groaned. Mr. Kirkland strode over with a scowl worthy of Fio, picked me right up like I weighed about ten pounds, and carried me up all those flights of stairs. I was utterly stunned.

I looked up at his face, and a funny feeling of déjà vu stole over me. Kirkland looked fearsome, yet he gently set me down on the bed in my room. I looked up at him as he put his hands on his hips just like Valerie.

"Are you all right, Lane?" he barked, with a demanding, gruff voice.

"Yes, Mr. Kirkland. I really am. My knee is just very tender."

"*Hmph.*"

"Thank you for carrying me up all those stairs," I said.

"You're welcome," he said gruffly, and turned around and left.

Aunt Evelyn refused to entertain me going back to work for at least a week. My knee and shoulder were fine, but I have to say, the next couple of days they were very sore. No high heels this week. The good thing was that I was just badly bruised, no twists or sprains. I had a lot of visitors, including the police artist who was a buddy of Fio's. He was quite talented, and after I had described the man and adjusted his drawing, it was very accurate; he captured the arrogant, leering attitude perfectly.

Valerie came by every day, and she also brought me my tattered purse and notebook, which had gone flying through the air when I fell. The police recovered them and had them sent to the mayor. Thank God both my purse and notebook had landed in the trench beneath the train, sparing them from annihilation. I pawed through my bag immediately and got my hands on my precious scarlet book from my parents. It was like me: banged up, but not too damaged. I sighed a breath of relief. I would be keeping that by my bedside from now on.

One day, I leafed through my parents' notebook. I loved this book; it was full of notes and charming little letters from one parent to another. Matthew to Charlotte, Charlotte to Matthew. A few clippings, many photographs and postcards of things they'd done and places they'd visited. When I came into the picture, they moved to Rochester, Michigan, and stayed put other than their business trips buying books for the store. But there were a few mementos from that time, too. Mostly many little notes to each other that were inside jokes where the actual meaning was lost on me. But it was always fun looking at them, even though it felt like someone else's family, someone else's life.

The spring was in full bloom; however, today was surprisingly cooler, like the ghost of winter wanting to make a last farewell. I was talking with Aunt Evelyn by the glowing fireplace in the parlor. After we chatted for quite a while about insignificant yet entertaining day-to-day things, I got up the nerve to ask her something that had been on my mind a lot lately. With a knowing smile on my face, I asked, "So . . . were you surprised by Mr. Kirkland's remarkable burst of energy when he carried me up the stairs, Aunt Evelyn?"

She let out a very unladylike guffaw. "I could tell he gave you quite a shock, Lane! Your eyes were as big as saucers. I've never seen you more stunned in your life!" She kept laughing, and it caught hold of me, making me laugh, too.

When we finally stopped laughing, I asked again, "But really, didn't he surprise you as well?"

"Well, Lane, I've known him a very long time. And one thing I've learned: He feels very deeply about a few people in this world. And for those people, he would leap over mountains if they needed him to. And, Lane . . . you're one of those people."

I was shocked. I mean, I sort of had a soft spot for the man myself, but he wasn't exactly demonstrative. "I am?"

"Yes, dear. You are." I let that sit and took a thoughtful sip of my tea.

Aunt Evelyn tilted her head thoughtfully and nodded once at my notebook lying open on my lap. "Lane, I've noticed that you've been reading your journal from your parents a lot lately. With all you've been through, is it bringing back memories from your past?" she asked, with a furrowed brow.

"You know, I hadn't thought about it like that, but I suppose it is," I said as I caressed the binding of the deep red journal in my hands. "When I look at it, I feel closer to them. Closer to the world I came from, even though I don't remember much. Sometimes, though, it feels like this album is about some other family or distant ancestors. We're related, but from a different world.

"But you know," I continued on, warming to the subject, "I remembered the old Brownie camera that was a constant companion to my mom and dad. And I've always loved this one photograph my mother took of me and my father outside, sitting on a dock with fishing poles in our hands."

I circled my fingers around and around on the moss green velvet of the soft, cushy chair I was curled up in, watching the alternately light and dark patterns my fingers created in the material.

"Aunt Evelyn?" I asked, on an impulse. "What exactly is that lavender notebook of yours?" Her eyes looked slightly downward, and I blurted out, "I mean, I shouldn't have asked. That's your private business. It just . . . It reminds me of my journal."

She was quiet for a while, then she smiled a very small, thoughtful smile. "Actually, it's funny that you should bring that up at this particular moment."

"It is?"

She calmly laced her fingers together and said, "Yes. It is my most prized possession. I think you might find it intriguing. And possibly relevant to what you're working through. I have often found that art has a special way of being a support system to life. I think that I would like to share it with you. How's your French?"

"Not too shabby. I can read it better than I can speak it."

"Excellent. Pour us some more tea, and I'll be right back." I did as I was told as I heard her climbing the stairs to her bedroom. She brought down the lavender volume, caressed the silk cover once, and handed it to me.

"What is it, Aunt Evelyn? Is it something you put together, or is it from someone else?"

"It's quite old, from when I was a young girl. You'll just have to read it for yourself, and then we'll talk about it someday." She remained standing as she picked up her cup of tea. "I hear my canvas calling. I think I'll go and paint a while, Lane. Do you need anything else?"

"No thanks, Aunt Evelyn." She smiled with a glimmer of sadness in her eyes, and I wondered if this book was the source of that sorrow. She turned and made her way up to the attic, the stairs creaking in their familiar way. In a few moments, Bach drifted down. Her favorite.

The well-worn pages had been turned many, many times. There were a few slight water stains on the front cover, but it was still in wonderful condition. Inside, it reminded me of my own notebook. It was full of intriguing quotes about life, nighttime, magic, and courage. I turned to one slip of paper that seemed to be written directly to Evelyn.

My tiny darling friend, I am so happy to see you today. One may have a blazing hearth in one's soul and yet no one ever came to sit by it. Passers-by see only a wisp of smoke from the chimney and continue on their way.—ML

Every one of the quotes was written by ML or about ML. Who was ML? I flipped to a page where Evelyn's own but youthful hand had written a cluster of notes that read:

He's so brilliant, so immensely sad, and something in me wants to help heal him. It physically hurts to be around him.

Why can he see such beauty that he can create deep, poignant images, but he can't see that beauty in himself?

Today we looked around the village. The houses are quaint and beautiful—he seems enthralled with them. And his painting of cornfields! There is something reaching out in this painting that you would think would be boring. But it is so, SO much more!

It's like part of ML's heart was meant for a natural place like this. His good, good heart just wants to serve people, to help them. But there is something in him that can't do anything by halves. I worry that he scares the very people he longs to help. But I like him a lot! I hope that he knows that.

I put the book down, thinking about the beauty and the sorrow of the words. I loved the young Evelyn's use of exclamation points and her earnest questions of how to help this troubled man. Even then she was extraordinary. It seemed ML might have thought so, too.

I was tired, and the rain was making me sleepy. I curled my legs up into the deep chair and laid my head down on the soft arm. I yawned, my eyes closed readily, and I drank in the warmth of the fire as a rumble of thunder rolled through the city and through my dreams.

I was in the midst of a field in the middle of the night, walking on crisp grass in bare feet, the air soft and cool on my skin. The sky was a deep blue. There were millions of stars, even the highlights of the Milky Way, but the most remarkable thing was the beautiful, deep blue that seemed touchable. And in the sky, vaporous, curling clouds hung low, beckoning to me. I had never seen anything so inviting in my life. I wanted to wrap myself in the deep blue and misty white as though it were a cosmic blanket.

I lifted into the air—what a delight to feel the air around me and not to be tethered to the ground. To be able to control my flight, going higher and higher, twisting and enjoying the airy freedom of being suspended without hindrance or contraption. The clouds were coming closer, and just as I drew near, I stopped flying and let myself linger in the clouds, curling my back into them, feeling the cold, tingly, crunchy mist like millions of minuscule snowflakes, an embrace from the heavenly cloud. I let myself slowly drop toward earth, and then I did it all over again for the sheer thrill of being wrapped in sparkling night and clouds.

Something below caught my eye. I looked down. There were three men holding shotguns that gleamed in the moonlight. I willed myself to blend into the dark sky. What could they possibly be hunting in the middle of the night? I started to make a slow descent to get away from them, to find cover. I was exposed and vulnerable.

It looked like they were going to go in the other direction, but as I softly alighted on the ground, the last one in line saw me, and I suddenly realized . . . they were hunting me. *A light glinted in that third hunter's eye as they and their horrible guns turned toward me and started a slow, deliberate procession toward me. I ran.*

Then everything started to swim with confusion. Flashes and images drifted in and out: a girl in a yellow sweater, Roarke's face, which quickly morphed into my mystery man's face, then the oily man who was laughing at me as he pushed me onto the train tracks. I was falling. As I turned and looked at him one last time, in midair before I hit the tracks, he slowly pulled out the silver gun. His lips came close to the gun, and I expected the hush gesture, but this time he kissed it. His black eyes locked with mine as he steadily leveled the barrel at me, put his finger on the trigger, and pulled.

"Lane! Lane! Wake up!" said Mr. Kirkland, shaking me roughly.

"What? Stop that!" I said irritably.

"*Hmph.* You were making quite a fuss. You sure you're all right?" He eyed me doubtfully. None of that sincere, *worried about you* look on his face from a few days ago when he carried me up all the stairs.

Just a look that said, *Shake it off, Missy.* The dream started coming back to me, and I was actually quite relieved that someone had woken me up at that particular moment.

"Uh, thanks, Mr. Kirkland. Sorry I bothered you. Just having a bad dream."

"Yep, that was pretty obvious," he said, and slumped into the chair opposite me, folding his long legs and putting his clasped hands across one knee. I must have looked surprised that he took a seat, because he went on to say, "Ah, well, I don't mean to bother you, either, but . . . do you mind if I have a seat?"

I straightened my face and said, "Oh, sure! Please." Knowing he was a man of mission, I waited for him to talk.

He looked around like maybe he was thinking of what to say or gathering the courage to say something specific. Then he looked right at me and said something completely unexpected. "Do you want to talk about your dream?"

"My dream. You want to talk about my dream?"

"Well . . . only if you do. Seems to me, Lane, that you've been through a lot in your life and an extra helping of trouble these past weeks."

"So, Aunt Evelyn has kept you abreast of the situation. The man in the shadows?" He nodded. "The threat against Fio?" Nodded again. "Roxy?" He nodded yet again. "She certainly has been thorough," I mumbled.

"Yes, she has." *Oh, he heard that.* "She doesn't keep me in the dark about much. What I want to know from you is two things. First, what's the deal with the silver gun?"

My eyes must have bugged out, because I had never, ever told anyone about that dream before. I shook my head. "How could you possibly know about that dream?"

"I heard you just now as you were waking up. You said, 'He's got the gun—the silver gun.'"

"Oh, well, I guess that explains it," I said, mildly annoyed. "I was dreaming that the man who pushed me onto the train tracks pulled a silver gun out of his coat."

"Did it have a red scroll on the handle?"

"How did you know that?"

His eyes shifted side to side. "Oh, you said something about something red . . . a scroll . . . while you were dreaming."

"Hmm," I said, not too sure about the complete veracity of his statement.

"Have you had a dream about that gun before? Because you said, 'He's got *the* gun.'" He bent further forward, intently watching me.

"All right. Yes, Mr. Kirkland," I said resignedly. "I've had dreams about it ever since I can remember. I always wonder if I saw it at the movies when I was younger and it stuck with me," I said, trying to laugh just a bit, trying to make that suggestion a possibility. But I already knew that there was no fiction to this gun. The detail I could conjure of the curving lines of the sharp, bloodred scrollwork was effortless and crisp. I swear I could almost feel the weight of the gun in my hand. No, I now had proof that the silver gun existed, and at some point I had seen it up close, probably held it. What could possibly be the connection between me and that gunman?

"Lane?" he asked, after I'd been silent for a few moments.

"The guy who pushed me onto the train tracks had that exact gun."

Mr. Kirkland had been drumming his fingers thoughtfully on the arm of the chair, but in that instant, he froze.

"Lane," he said, suddenly urgent, leaning closer to me, almost face-to-face. "You have to be absolutely sure. What exactly did the gun look like? Don't confuse it with your dreams. What did the man's gun look like?"

I told him every detail I remembered. But why the urgent interest? He was carefully mulling over all this as I scrutinized him closely, trying to figure out what was behind his questions. His gaze locked onto mine, and a wall came down behind those light blue eyes, blocking my prying gaze.

"Lane?" he asked, in a tone that made it sound like he'd come to a decision. "I don't believe in coincidences. We'll keep watch. We'll figure it out." He had clearly decided not to let me in on what he was really thinking and was covering it over with the fatherly statements of, *It'll be fine, don't worry about it.* "Now I have to go get dinner started. Making spaghetti, not as good as Fio's surely, but still good."

He stood up, with his long legs making snapping noises as his knees straightened out. I had not one single idea how old that man was. One minute his bones were snapping and crackling, the next he was carrying me up four flights of stairs with the ease of a prize-fighter.

I smiled at him, letting him think I didn't see behind his subterfuge. "Thanks, Mr. Kirkland. Sounds great. Perfect." And then he was off to his domain.

I sat in wonderment trying to figure out what had happened for us to have turned a corner of openness. That was, by far, the longest and most interesting conversation we had ever had together. And it was good. He was hiding things, but I was okay with that for now. I was hiding things, too.

Suddenly, Mr. Kirkland came bounding in with his rain gear on and said, "Hey, Lane! The sauce is simmering on the stove, the bread is in the oven, the salad is in the refrigerator. I have to go out for a while; why don't you and Evelyn have dinner whenever you like? I'm not sure exactly when I'll be back." And before I could answer, he bounded out the door.

Later that evening, Aunt Evelyn and I were enjoying our dinner in the cozy kitchen. The storm hadn't let up yet, and the kitchen was delightfully warm and homey, the kind of room that invited you to come in and stay a while. The spaghetti sauce was excellent; Fio would have been proud.

Just as we were finishing up, we heard a commotion on the back porch off the kitchen and laundry room. There was a clatter and pounding on the steps up to the back door, then Mr. Kirkland's voice. But what was he doing? The only description I can give it is that he was crooning softly . . . to something. Well, as softly as he could get with his gruff voice. And in he came with a large bundle held securely in his arms: a big, floppy, furry . . . puppy.

Aunt Evelyn knocked over her glass.

CHAPTER 6

If you don't have a dog—at least one—there is
not necessarily anything wrong with you, but
there may be something wrong with your life.

—ML

Mr. Kirkland was proud as any proud papa could be. In his arms
was an extremely large puppy that was gnawing on anything he
could get his teeth on, which, at the moment, was Mr. Kirkland's
collar. He had big puppy paws and legs that the rest of his body had
yet to grow into. He was about five or six months old and already
had to be fifty pounds. He was a wiggling mass of happy-go-lucky
German shepherd puppy.

I dove over to the pup. I was a sucker for dogs, well, most animals, that is. He was soft, and his black muzzle, big brown eyes,
and perky ears drew me like a magnet. Mr. Kirkland and I looked
at each other. Then, as a team with the puppy, all three of us looked
at Aunt Evelyn with goofy grins on our faces like little boys saying,
Can we keep it?

She groaned.

We named him Ripley. We petted him, brushed him, and gave
him something to eat. Aunt Evelyn sat at the table just shaking
her head with a bemused smile on her face. She loved animals, but
she'd never had a dog of her own before.

"What were you thinking, Kirk?" she asked Mr. Kirkland, with
a resigned look on her face. "Why a puppy, and why right this second? In the rain?"

"Well, you see, a friend of mine at the Humane Society told me a group of gorgeous shepherd pups had been dropped off, and they had one left. I figured that with everything that's been going on lately, it couldn't hurt to have a little more protection around here."

Ripley chose that particular moment to spy his tail, cock his head to one side, and go dashing around in circles trying to catch the tantalizing bait.

"Mm hm," said Aunt Evelyn skeptically.

The next morning came with bright sunshine, a fresh, clean scent in the air, and . . . a puppy barking. Breakfast was a do-it-yourself affair, as Mr. Kirkland was fully occupied with Ripley. I have to say, he had never looked happier. Evelyn smiled and winked at me.

I heard the unmistakable, obnoxious five honks from Fio's car, saved just for me. Lucky me. I kissed everyone, including Ripley, good-bye and headed out to the car. I waved at Ray, the driver, and jumped in the back. My knee still had some pretty bruises that were turning a lovely puce, but I felt great, and I was anxious to get back to work. Plus, Fio had promised that we would talk more about the case.

Fiorello, who knew that anger was behind my tears at the train station, also knew that I abhorred people making a fuss over me. So, as I slid into the backseat, we chitchatted about the day and then started right in on our normal routine of him dictating instructions. What was conspicuously missing from this agenda was my time with him going over the case. And there was a strange fifteen-minute slot first thing in the morning that had been blocked off.

He ran out of steam and looked up, way up, as we were passing under the early morning shadow of the Empire State Building. He smiled to himself and muttered something about getting to the top again soon.

It really was remarkable. I'll never forget the race six years ago, in 1930, between the Chrysler Building and the Empire State Building to be the tallest in the world. It looked like the Chrysler building was surely going to win out at seventy-seven stories. And it did. For about three months. Until the Empire State Building was topped with the final tower and spire.

Almost every day we'd go down to Fifth Avenue to watch in awe as the behemoth was being erected. The men would walk and dance and sing along those dizzyingly high metal beams. The riveters had their own rhythms and dances. It was hard to tear your eyes away from them as they'd toss red-hot rivets to each other, sometimes seventy-five feet away. But those buildings were more important than that. Because on one horrible fall day in '29, the lively sounds of the Jackhammers, drills and riveters from the construction happening all over the city suddenly ceased. Leaving only an eerie silence floating through the streets. It was like something had died. The construction of these two spectacular buildings reminded all of us that we could still build and dream.

I turned a glaring eye to Fio. "All right. So. Fio. What's with the small talk and no morning meeting? You promised we'd have a little chat about the case."

He raised an eyebrow. "*The case*, Lane?"

"*Ehhh* . . . yeah. The case. You know, the developments of the past couple weeks."

He looked at me with a pitying, sardonic smile. "You read too many books, Lane."

"Yes, I do. But that doesn't change anything. What's going on with the schedule this morning?"

He looked shifty. His eyes started darting about, and he looked out the window again. I could tell he was trying to scrounge up something to distract me. "Fiiiooooo?" I said, in my best *out with it* voice.

"Well . . . we have a meeting, as usual," he said, still not looking me in the eye.

"With whom?"

"Well, it's just someone in the office," he said, and then pretended to suddenly have a very consuming issue with the cuff of his suit coat. Well, if it was that difficult for him to spill it, then I was just going to wait. I was not about to force it out of him.

Turns out, I should have put forth the effort. We walked into the office, and lo and behold, *Roxy* was sitting quite comfortably at my desk. At. MY. Desk.

She smiled up sweetly at me, and I pursed my lips and raised my eyebrows. "Why, hello, Roxy. Helping out, are we?"

"Ahhh, yes. Yes, I have been, just while you were gone. Here you are, Mr. LaGuardia, the notes you requested about the legislature regarding the new parks," she said as she handed him quite a hefty pack of papers.

"Thanks, Roxy! That was really efficient, very quick of you," he said, a little too enthusiastically. He regarded me, with my lips still pursed, and backed up a step. I cocked my head at him and smiled, trying unsuccessfully to make it look like I wasn't baring my teeth at him.

"Thanks, Roxy, for helping out while I was gone," I said, which I really did mean. I wasn't vain enough to think the whole office would come to a standstill without me. But *Roxy?* What was wrong with Val? I thought my bad morning meeting had ended, but apparently it had just begun.

"Uh, Roxy, let's have that meeting you requested with Lane right now. Let's go into my office," said Fio. *A meeting with Roxy? Well . . . how nice.*

Roxy and I pulled up chairs to Fio's desk. He sat down behind his, adjusting some papers and rubbing the space between his eyes with a thumb and forefinger as if, perhaps, he was catching the headache that I was enduring at the moment.

"All right, Roxy. Did you have something you wanted to tell us?" he asked, turning his attention to her and clasping both hands on his desk.

I turned to look at her and, with a bit of satisfaction, saw a bead of sweat appear on her brow. But she took a deep breath and boldly said, "Well . . . I've been thinking about everything that's been going on lately with Lane and the fact that she's attracted such deviant attention from some kind of bad character . . . and I've been wondering if maybe she should work from home or maybe work in a different department."

And the penny dropped. *That little, scheming, devious . . .* She was after my job. At the very least, she was finally figuring out a way to get me out of the way. That was the only way to do it, too, I'll give her that: play on Fio's concern about my welfare. All the words I would have said came tumbling out at once, effectively choking me, I was so livid.

Luckily, Fiorello came to my rescue. He had shot me a wary

glance that bespoke his concern that I might possibly be about to throttle her. I was deeply considering it, especially when Fio took a quick look out the window and she winked at me.

He started in at a rapid pace. "Well, Roxy, dear, I appreciate your concern for Lane. I really do. But I think that would be taking things a bit too far." Her shoulders slightly slumped, and she pouted in defeat. She looked at me and rolled her eyes when Fio looked down at his paper. I winked at her.

"Is that all you wanted to convey, Roxy?" asked Fio, looking up at us with an oblivious smile, as he had mentally checked this meeting off his list and moved on.

"Well, yes. I guess it is. Thanks for letting me meet with you. I'll get back to work."

After she closed the door and I heard her footsteps walk away, I said, "What was *that* all about?"

"Lane! Not so loud! The office is used to hearing me bellow, but not you," he said while shifting a little farther away in his chair and pulling on one ear.

"Sorry," I said, in a much more mellifluous voice. "It's just that she always gets under my skin. I'll work on it."

"Oh, she means well, Lane. Besides, she types like lightning!" he said, with a happy pat to the papers she'd just handed him. *Oh, brother.* I rubbed my temples, my headache not abating one iota. He'd changed gears to work mode like a flick of a switch, as usual, so I went out to my desk.

There was a pink card from Val waiting for me, saying welcome back and that she was treating me to lunch, which helped ease the headache just a bit.

From that point on, a few weeks passed in relative peace. Valerie and I worked hard, we went out to lunch, she had a couple more dates with Pete. I saw Roarke frequently, as he was consistently in Room 9, the famous press room, covering Fiorello's escapades. We'd had a drink and got caught up with each other. The blonde from Copioli's didn't take, but that wasn't a surprise. Roarke was a lone wolf at heart, always seeking the next big story. Roxy and Lizzie remained their irritating selves. You'd never have known that Lizzie and I had a long, pleasant chat that one day.

The weather was gorgeous as we pulled into the true summer. I loved summer in New York City: deep blue skies; the beach; street fairs that sprinkled the city with greasy food, stalls of jewelry, fun music, and brightly colored scarves every weekend. The whole city was outside, eating at the cafés, walking along the water, and exploring Central Park. The energy was palpable, festive.

One sultry day at work, we were not working at our best as the heat became intense. Despite my efforts to keep my black fan spinning air directly at me, I could feel my hair getting curly in the humidity and sweat trickling down my back. Roarke came in to see a few friends and get some updates for an article he was working on about Fio's Summer of the Pools. Ten were to be opened in ten weeks, along with many new modern parks and playgrounds. Fio believed that if you cared for families, the city would grow. He even made his dream come true and opened the High School of Music and Art. He'd enjoyed music his whole life. He was quite the trumpet player, and he even led a few orchestras in the city as guest conductor. He knew firsthand the profound effect art had on a person and on society.

Roarke appeared out of nowhere and perched on my desk. "Hey, Lane. Do you think you can leave a little early today? I have something I want to run by you, and I found this great new place down on the water. Want to go get a drink?"

The idea was more than tempting. I could hardly focus on my work at hand, it was so hot, and Fio had left early to have a meeting about the new Randall's Island sports complex that was opening soon. I'd been working plenty of overtime to balance out leaving early.

"Done! Let's get out of here." I grabbed my bag, and we practically skipped out the door, relieved to get into the comparatively cool air outside. At least the air was moving.

We sat at a little round table covered in blue mosaic tiles. I ordered a Floradora: gin, framboise, ginger ale, and lime. Roarke thought that was an excellent idea and ordered the same, and we shared crab cakes. We were close to the fish market, so the seafood was fresh and delicious, not to mention pretty cheap.

"This is absolutely beautiful, Roarke. Great idea. You can coax me to leave work early any time," I said, with a smack of my lips as I popped the last bit of crab into my mouth.

He chuckled and dabbed his mouth with his napkin. The sun glinted brightly off his blond hair. With his golden brown eyes and tanned skin, he looked the epitome of summer. Behind him, the river was strewn with millions of bright sparks of sunshine. I could hear a little band playing on the streets below, something with a cheerful, island flair.

Laying his napkin aside contentedly, Roarke took one last swig of his drink and looked me squarely in the eyes. "Lane. I have something I want to talk to you about. I want your thoughts."

I also took one last drink as our plates were cleared from the table. I nodded and said, "All right, Roarke. Shoot."

He lowered his voice and leaned in toward me. "I've been talking with a buddy in the NYPD. I got a copy of the sketch from the police artist of the man you described, the man who threatened you and Fio on the night of that fire. The same man who pushed you onto the tracks."

"You . . . *What?* I didn't tell you it was the same—"

"Yeah, yeah, yeah," he said, with a dismissive wave of his hand. "I figured that out all by myself. Remember? Investigative reporter?"

"I should have known better," I said, with a droll look on my face and a long, resigned exhale. "So? What's the scoop? What have you discovered?"

He took a deep breath, cracked his knuckles mindlessly, and said, "I know who he is." And who he was could not be good, judging by the look on Roarke's sober face.

"Out with it."

He leaned in and brought his voice down to a low whisper. "He's Danny Fazzalari. More importantly, he's the hired gun and nephew of a mob boss. Well, *the* mob boss. *Louie Venetti.*"

CHAPTER 7

The fishermen know that the sea is dangerous
and the storm terrible, but they have never found
these dangers sufficient reason for remaining ashore.

—ML

My blood drained right to my toes, and a prickly sweat broke out on my temples that had nothing to do with the heat.

"Louie Venetti," I whispered, with a squeak. I cleared my throat. "Better known as Uncle Louie? One of the most notorious gangsters in New York, who earned tens of millions from the slot machines in the grocery stores that Fiorello has been taking down? *That* Louie Venetti?"

"Yes." He looked around and ordered us another round of drinks, this time something more medicinal.

"What do you think that means, Roarke?" I asked, my mind running a mile a minute.

"I've got some theories, but I'd like to hear anything that comes to your mind about why you've been a target."

"Well, it would be obvious that . . ." I cleared my throat again and lowered my voice even further. "It's clear that Louie would have a major grudge against Fio, and I'm an easier target than he is. And I'm someone he cares about. Fio's made that known to enough people."

"Yes. 'Grudge.' *That's* an understatement," said Roarke.

"And he certainly got a message across to Fio. But then again, it's been quiet for a bit. Has Fio stopped something or begun a new phase of one of his projects that would take the heat off Louie and make him think he got the message loud and clear?" I asked, processing out loud.

"Huh, that's a good point. Something has definitely changed, since there were two attacks close together, whereas it's been quiet for a few weeks. Definitely something to consider. It could be as incidental as the whole swimming pool mania. Fio's been running around opening one pool after another, not to mention the park openings and Randall's Island coming up. He hasn't had time to pound any slot machines with his sledgehammer," he said while stroking his chin in concentration.

Just then a barge drifted by and blew its horn. I jumped a mile and nearly knocked over my drink.

"Whoa! A little jumpy, are we, Lane?" said Roarke while straightening the things I'd knocked askew.

I gave him a dirty look.

"Anyway," he continued, oblivious to risk and danger. *My* risk and danger. "I've got an informant who has something that I think you and I can check out. He says he's been running errands for Venetti's gang and he overhears things, see? So, he owes me big time for something I helped him with, and he told me that something is going down today in the Meatpacking District." I groaned. "They're having some kind of meeting, and we might find it interesting."

"Are you out of your mind? The Meatpacking District? And who exactly are *they*, and what is the *it* that we might find interesting?" I asked, with exasperation. Patience was not my strong suit, and all these unidentifiable pronouns were about to drive me to jump into the river.

"It's not a meeting with Louie or anything, but I think with Danny Fazzalari."

"So, we're supposed to overhear some dubious conversation and then what? Call the police and tell them . . . what?" I could not see the logic.

"Well, I don't know, but my informant is supposed to be there as well, and he often carries messages to and from these guys. So, if they're having a meeting and we can identify the participants, or if we're even luckier and overhear part of the conversation, and then on top of that, if we can get a copy of the message . . . it might really help us get a lead on this case." Those were a lot of *if*s.

"Aha!" I said, nice and loud. Now it was his turn to jump out of his seat. "You said *case*. Fio thought I was being overdramatic calling it a case, but it is," I said triumphantly.

And with that revelation, my bad attitude about the whole thing capitulated. I'd be damned if I was going to let some scumbag tinker with my life and make me fearful of the shadows. No way was I going to just sit around and do nothing about it.

"I think you're right. We can do it, Roarke."

Roarke gave me a big, sly, approving smile. "That's my girl."

"Let's not rush in without thinking it through, but let's do it!" And I slammed down my glass in determination.

"Roarke, I think we rushed in without thinking this through," I said in a whisper as we drew near the slimy building in the Meatpacking District, which, by the way, carried all the odors, images, and carnage that the name implied. I'd never been over here before, and I slipped my hand into Roarke's as we slunk down a close alley toward our meeting place he'd set in advance with his informant.

My heart about stopped when we heard a loud crack echo through the tight alley. It could have been a window opening, breaking the seal. We both stood stock still as we strained our ears. After several long moments, we took one more tenuous step and stood sandwiched together between two brick walls with refuse and liquid things I didn't want to think about swirling around our feet.

The window that we had come close to was high, but Roarke would just about be able to see in if he stood on tiptoe. It was open; maybe the informant had cracked it so we could overhear what was going on inside. All I could hear at first were muffled voices. Then Roarke's hand tightened on mine as we heard the determined, clipped steps of someone's shoes making their way across a tile floor, closer and closer to the window we were directly under.

This part here further suggested that perhaps we hadn't thought this through. We were dead-ended in an alley, tightly hedged in on all sides but the one we came in on. The window we were eavesdropping through was over our heads, but if someone were to check the window and even just slightly tilt his head down, he would most definitely see us.

Roarke whispered closely, "My informant figures we'll be quite safe, since who would bother to look out the window?"

Suddenly, we heard something shift above us. *Someone* was bothering. Right this second. We ducked down in the narrow alley. I huddled up to the brick wall, willing myself to be invisible like you do in a bad dream. I held my breath as someone wrenched the window further open. Then came the reassuring sound of someone's steps walking away.

We both slowly looked up. Low voices drifted out. I could only make out every third or fourth word. Then the voices raised, and so did the hairs on my neck as I heard *my name*.

"What do you mean Lane knows? Knows what?" said a very angry, high-pitched male voice that I knew in an instant was Danny's. The guy who tried to kill me.

"Well, I'm not sure, I'm just the messenger. I'm just giving you the note. Sh—" said a nasally, fearful voice that must have been the informant's. But something or someone had cut off what he was going to say next. Was he about to say *she* or someone's name that began with *S-H?*

Then a couple of steps sounded, and a third voice addressed Danny in a low murmur. Just then, Roarke spied something in the window, a small piece of white paper. He slowly raised his hand and took down the paper, using careful, delicate movements. He brought it down as the voice was still murmuring. He opened the paper so both of us could read it. Written on it in sloppy writing was one word: RUN.

Roarke and I locked eyes at the same moment we heard loud footsteps decidedly coming toward our window. In one fluid movement, I turned around and we ran down the alley toward the light. Puddles splashed, things skittered in front of me. I ran like hell. I could hear Roarke behind me, *right* behind me. Before we reached the end of the alley, a gun fired.

We were rocked in our shoes for one horrifying second. We realized it came from inside the room and we weren't hit; we kept running. We swerved around the corner to the right. There were workers all over the place, but we stood out like an ink stain on a white shirt. With me in my bright yellow dress and Roarke in his navy pinstriped suit with white shoes, neither of us was exactly blending in.

We bounded up the street, trying to stay close to other buildings. Just as we thought we might be clear, we saw them: two guys who had *gangster* written all over them. One was Danny. As I turned my head to look back at him, I saw him smile that awful smirk, and the sun shone off the deep shine of his black, slicked-back hair. They started chasing after us.

"Roarke, run!" I yelled.

I had an idea. I ran ahead and took a left going north toward the docks on the west side, Roarke running right after me. I never ran so fast in my life. My sides hurt, my legs burned. But when you're literally running for your life, those are very minor inconveniences.

I heard the clack of our pursuers' shoes on the pavement, urging me to keep going. Neither of them yelled; they just ran relentlessly on after us. *Come on, come on, where are you? Ah, there!* When I saw my target, I got a final burst of speed. I heard a funny grunt of a laugh as Roarke figured out my plan.

Just ahead was a bevy of at least twenty navy sailors making their way off their ship in port, heading out for some fun for the evening. I ran right toward the biggest guy, waved enthusiastically, and launched myself right into his surprised but receptive arms. I looked back at my shocked pursuers, turned to the stunned sailor, and planted a gigantic kiss right on his lips. He responded with vigor, and it had the reaction from his mates that I'd hoped: They all cheered. I could hear Roarke laughing behind me.

The sailor let me go and set me down carefully. I brushed my hair back, and I said as loudly as I could, "Ah, well. Welcome to New York!" They all cheered again, and we all walked happily toward Broadway. Roarke and I were careful to stay in the middle of the group of laughing, shoving, playful sailors.

About twenty feet away, I spotted Danny and his partner. They had steered clear of the sailors. He was not smiling now. Danny touched his hat in a sort of salute to my efforts, but then slowly raised his hand in a small gesture of a gun, shooting at me. He softly blew the imaginary smoke off his fingers; an unimaginative gesture, but frightening nonetheless. Then he readjusted his hat, did an about-face, and walked away.

Up at Broadway, Roarke and I said farewell to the sailors and wished them a fantastic night of fun, then hailed a cab uptown. Inside the car, my heartbeat started to get back to normal, and I rubbed the back of my neck, easing the tension. "Roarke, do you think they killed your informant?"

He'd obviously been thinking along the same lines. He held his fist pensively against his lips and was slowly shaking his head. "God, Lane, it's my fault."

"No, he was in this with or without you, Roarke. He was already mixed up with those people." I told the driver 80th between Lexington and Park Avenue. I figured a drink at my place would be safe and a good idea all the way around.

Our ride took a while in the rush-hour traffic, but the drive turned out to be cathartic. As we pulled up to our brownstone, Roarke had started to relax a little. We got out and made our way up the steps toward the front door. Just as we got to the top, Mr. Kirkland swung it open with Ripley by his side.

Roarke let out an involuntary, "Whoa! He's getting big!" to Mr. Kirkland's delight.

Ripley had most definitely gotten bigger. Those paws of his were still a bit large for his body, though, so I knew he'd grow even more. The dog was impressive in stature, color, and intelligence. And at any sign of a possible threat to us (postman, milkman, anyone who dared to knock on our door), he took a powerful stance, and one look told you he meant business. But Ripley was also affectionate. There were many times when I'd be helping wash dishes at the sink, and he'd come up behind me and lie down against my heels. Right now, I could tell he had his guard up. But when he saw me, and he obviously remembered Roarke, he let his tongue loll out of his mouth and gave an affectionate *woof.*

Roarke and I sank onto the couch in the parlor, utterly spent.

"Well? So, where are we exactly with this fabulous lead of ours?" I asked.

"First, I have to call my buddy at the NYPD and tell him about the shot fired. Find out if anyone was really hurt or if it was meant to scare us off. What else did we find out?" he asked me, like a professor asking his student.

"Well, someone told your informant to give that particular message to Danny. And, by the way, that most definitely was Danny. Did your guy ever tell you who he was working with—the person who sent the message?"

"No. Besides, I'm positive he didn't know who was who, just that we might be interested. Probably heard your name come up, and he knew that you and I are friends. Figured we'd be plenty interested at that. And he was cut off just as he was about to say something else. He might have been about to say *she*."

I nodded vigorously. "I know. I thought the same thing. It could be a woman he was working with. Or he might have been about to say a number of other things. But whatever it means, they think I know something. Maybe it *looks* like I might know who this other person or boss is? The main thing that we've discovered lately is that my assailant from the shadows and from the subway is Danny, and he has powerful links to the gangster world, Uncle Louie in particular. But that means I was some sort of target even before today."

"It all depends on who my informant was working for. There are so many things going on here. Maybe someone who sees the whole picture realized we learned a vital clue. It just doesn't mean anything to us yet."

"And it can't be the silver gun; Danny has it."

"What silver gun?" *Damn.*

There was something ugly and menacing about the gun that kept haunting my dreams. I wanted to keep it a secret. The more I talked about it, the more it gave the nightmare credence. Too late now. I begrudgingly filled him in on the gun.

"So, okay, what have we learned?" I asked as Roarke stroked his chin with his thumb and forefinger.

"Oh, we've learned quite a lot," he said, with an intense flash of his golden eyes. "These people are against you knowing what you know, they are willing to kill, and they are more concerned about you than about giving themselves away. It'd be smarter to just leave you alone if their main aim is a political move against Fiorello. But for some reason, Lane, you are right in the middle of it all."

CHAPTER 8

What would life be if we had no courage to attempt anything?

—ML

Roarke notified the police about the gunshot. However, they went to the building in the Meatpacking District and didn't find anything out of place. Roarke hadn't heard from his informant since. It was possible it was just a scare tactic against him or us, but deep down, we believed the worst.

Soon after the Meatpacking District debacle, Valerie and I had lunch at our favorite diner. She was telling me all about her latest date with Peter and how her clumsy side had come out as she'd tripped on the sidewalk and kicked her shoe twenty feet down the street.

Her laughter was even better than the story. She always got me laughing, and I sighed happily as I took a sip of Coke. I hated to break the light moment, but after I took a couple of bites of my sandwich, I told her about what Roarke and I learned during our escapade. I left out some of the more lurid details of our adventure.

"You *what?*" she yelled. Apparently, I left in too many. Even in the booth, she had her hands on her hips looking like an indignant mother hen.

"*Shhhhh!* Val, keep it down!" I grimaced. At least she hadn't blurted out Uncle Louie's name. The entire diner would have come to a standstill. That man's name was equivalent to a grenade in the room.

I rubbed my forehead, something I was doing a lot lately. "Val, I'm sorry! I know it was dangerous, but it was the only lead we had.

No one is talking to me about what the police know, and I can't figure out why these people are targeting me."

"Can't you let the police do their own investigation?" she asked.

"Yes, but I'm not convinced they're taking all this seriously. Don't forget they still think I fell of my own clumsy accord onto the train tracks. And what kind of evidence do we have that *anything* untoward has been happening? It all just looks like a bad set of coincidences."

"Well . . ." she said begrudgingly, slowly taking her hands off her hips. "You do have a point. And if it were me, I'd want to do something, too. But honey, the Meatpacking District?" I just nodded in a repentant sort of way.

"*Unh . . .*" she murmured. Now it was her turn to rub her forehead. "What am I going to do with her?" I was pretty sure that was a rhetorical question.

After we got outside, we started to slowly walk back to the office. We were almost to the steps of city hall when we heard sirens. Several fire trucks were coming in our direction. We instinctively looked around and saw smoke coming out of a tenement building a few side streets away.

"How much you wanna bet Fio's on his way?" I asked.

"Are you kidding? That's no bet! Of course he's—" She never got to finish her sentence.

Right at that moment, Fio came dashing out of city hall, looking wildly around with a manic smile on his face. But his car and driver were nowhere to be seen. His eyes pounced on the nearest vehicle: a motorcycle with a side car attached. He pounded down the last few steps, leaped into the side car, and yelled, "Go, go, go!" to the widely grinning officer in the driver's seat. As they took off, he bellowed to all of us struck dumb on the sidewalk, "I am not a sissy!"

Val and I had to hold each other up, we were laughing so hard. God, I loved that man. I looked up and saw no fewer than a dozen reporters, including Roarke, laughing and scribbling furiously. Two photographers had caught the moment and were jabbering away, figuring out who got the best shot.

I just had to follow Fio, so I looked at Val and nodded in the direction he drove off, asking her without words if she wanted to come along.

"Oh, yeah. Wouldn't miss it."

We weren't the only ones; Roarke and a few other press guys went along with us. We arrived at a tenement building that had been in the process of being torn down. Someone had decided to make it go quicker. There were thick black columns of smoke puffing into the sky. We couldn't get too close, the smoke was so bad.

I spotted Fiorello standing over by the fire chief. Then he walked farther off, taking in the whole scene. When we were still a hundred feet away or so, a man in a black suit and hat came right up to Fio, roughly bumped him in the shoulder as he passed by, and surreptitiously handed him a white envelope.

I started to pick up the pace, as I wanted to see that envelope, and I just knew it was not a gift of goodwill. But then we ran into a pack of firefighters and couldn't dodge around them. I jumped pointlessly up and down a couple of times to get a better view. When we could finally make our way around them, Fio was still about fifty feet away from me, standing by himself in deep consternation.

A tall firefighter with his coat off, but suspenders and fire pants still on, went up to him. The fireman bent his head down to talk with him, nodding earnestly as Fio replied to whatever he said, and walked away. There was something very familiar about that lean, muscular frame. But how could I be sure? With their gear on, the firefighters all looked so much alike.

So many questions were flooding through my mind that I had trouble organizing my thoughts. I finally got over to Fio, and my main thought, my main concern, was this dear man in front of me. His face was ashen, but his usual resolve was right behind the shock that he'd incurred from what he'd been handed.

"Are you all right? Fio!" I shook his arm, as he hadn't looked me in the eye yet.

He nodded and wrinkled his nose, saying, "Yeah, thanks, Lane. All right, it's about time we had a chat. Meet me back at the office in an hour, and we'll have that talk. Got it?"

"Got it, Chief."

Finally.

An hour later, I was waiting in Fiorello's office with two iced teas for us. I was completely impatient and jumpy. He came in, went directly to his desk, and sat down.

"Thanks for the iced tea, Lane. So . . . down to business," he said, clasping his hands on his desktop. "First things first. What did you see today at the fire?"

I got the feeling he was trying his hardest not to tell me anything I didn't need to know. "Fio . . ." I started, not wanting to play games.

"Lane, dear, I need to know what you saw. Humor me." His eyes were intent, and it was clear that he, too, was not in the mood for games.

"All right. Here you go. I saw a guy in a black suit come up to you, bump you pretty roughly, and hand you something in a white envelope. Then a firefighter, tall guy without his coat on, came up and talked briefly with you, then walked away. I think he was the same man who came barging out of your office the other day—the one that you said you couldn't tell me anything about."

He blinked. I sipped my tea.

"You evidently have excellent vision," he said. He massaged his chin in deep thought, probably weighing what he could really tell me, what I'd figure out on my own, and how little he could actually get away with without me giving him a hard time. It took a while to decide.

"Okay, Lane. I am still not at liberty to tell you anything about that gentleman. And really, Lane, if I could tell you, I would, but it's absolutely imperative that I do not. Can you live with that?"

"Of course, Fio. I understand," I said, with a sigh. "How about that envelope? Are you all right?"

"Well, given what happened with you the other night, I think this is something you should see." He handed it to me. I read it.

I blinked. He sipped his tea.

"What does this mean? *Be careful, Little Flower, or someone might fall down a well.*"

"Oh, the well part is just gangster talk for someone disappearing—permanently. I didn't recognize the guy who handed it to me; it was so fast, and then he quickly blended into the crowd. I think it was just another threat, might even have been the same guy who shoved you in the subway, Danny Fazzalari. It happened so fast I didn't get a good look at him. Did you see him?"

"I was pretty far away. It could have been him, but I was blocked by a group of firefighters and was jumping up and down just to catch glimpses of you. He had the dark hair, hat, and black, shiny shoes."

Fio grumbled, "The exact description of about ninety-five percent of the gangsters."

"I know," I said dismally. "How about his voice, though?" I asked, with sudden inspiration.

"He only said, in a singsong voice, 'Here you go!' and walked off. But now that you mention it, it sounded higher and slightly squeakier than I had expected." Which was ironic, coming from the squeakiest, screechiest man around.

"That's him, Fio. I think you just met Danny Fazzalari. Look, just promise that you'll take some extra precautions, okay? Like maybe another bodyguard or something?"

He made a face like he'd just been offered a squid and peanut butter sandwich.

I laughed out loud. "Aw, come on! It can't be *that* bad!"

"It is. But all right. I'll get a couple more guys on the force to make more rounds and whatnot. Satisfied?"

"For now!" I said as I went out the door to my desk.

After our talk, I needed some time to gather my thoughts. I worked on some filing, I put some folders together for a press conference, etc. When I finished, I took a deep, satisfied breath and packed up for the night.

There weren't too many of us left in the office, but I said some good-byes and headed to the stairs. I didn't mind not having an elevator; I would go out of my way to take the stairs beneath that beautiful rotunda any day. A few press guys were walking down, too, and at the rear of their little pack, was . . . *him*. My God, I had to figure out his name. I walked right behind the group and gave him a half smile, trying to convey telepathically, *What the hell are you doing here?*

He was pretending he didn't know me. Great. Always a boost for a gal's confidence. I mentally shrugged, and just then, my foot slipped and his hand shot out and steadied me. After the electric shocks running up and down my spine weakened a bit, I wittily said, "Thanks."

"Sure, love," he said, without directly looking at me. But he did leave his hand at the small of my back a little longer than strictly necessary, the heat of it lingering with me the rest of the way down.

When we reached the lobby, before I could turn to say something, *anything*, to him, three Tammany policemen hailed him over and started bantering loudly like guys do after work when they can start to play. I stole one last glance back at him as I walked out the door, but he didn't look back.

So, I decided to go for subtlety. I stalked him.

I casually waited outside in the nearby park, wanting to catch one more glimpse of this elusive guy. He and his pals walked out, obviously heading toward McNally's, the nearby pub. A couple of grubby street urchins peered at them from the street corner. These street kids were still pretty prevalent despite a big increase in child services, and tended to blend in with the scenery. Most of them were dirty, underfed, ill-treated, often pickpockets and thieves, and heartbreaking. The guys were not in uniform, and the kids must have been very young, because most urchins kept a wide berth between themselves and the police. And streetwise kids can sense a policeman a mile away, uniform or not. The men mostly ignored them, but one of them took an annoyed swipe at their outstretched hands. My stalkee slowed so that he was at the back of his group and casually passed a couple of coins to the kids. Then he did something stunning: He playfully mussed the curly, grubby head of the littlest kid and smiled at him.

I was quite satisfied with myself, as I had learned a few crucial things from my stairway encounter and stalking spree. One, my mystery man still smelled great, but he must not have been able to get a full shower after the fire, because there was a definite tinge of barbecue; it *had* been him at the fire with Fio. Two, he was a part of the Tammany crew. And three, between the clamor of nicknames and back-slapping, his buddies had called out enough for me to deduce the mystery man's name: Finn Brodie.

* * *

As I took the subway uptown, I ruminated on a variety of topics, from the distracting Finn Brodie, to the fact that I was hungry, to the fact that the woman in front of me held a teacup-sized dog that had a fancier wardrobe than I did.

At 59th, a large rush of people started to push off the crowded train, so I stepped out of the door to let them pass. I was annoyingly jostled on every side, when I was suddenly jerked around with the force of someone yanking my handbag right off my arm.

With everything that had happened recently, I had reached my limit. All I can say is, something inside me snapped. I yelled a furious, "That's it!" I took off running.

I actually caught up to the guy pretty fast, as he hadn't counted on my reaction. If I hadn't been running so fast, I would have yelled a lot more. That silence proved to be an excellent tactic for a sneak attack. He had just turned his head with a cocky look back when I leaped and tackled him right to the ground.

He wasn't a huge guy, just a teenager, so he hadn't gotten his man shoulders yet. As he sprawled on the ground, I straddled his back, grabbed one arm, twisted it behind his back, and shoved hard. I grabbed my purse back and said a hardy, "Hah!"

I'd only had the guts to wear trousers to work a few times, but thanks to Hollywood actresses Marlene Dietrich and Katharine Hepburn, who had been making trousers more acceptable, especially with professional women like myself, I had tried them out a few times. I got a few disgusted looks from people who clearly thought dresses and skirts were the only appropriate attire for ladies, *but* . . . my trousers saved the day. A dress would have encumbered my tackle.

By this time, the people who had seen the kid steal my purse and then watched as I went pelting off after him arrived at the scene. Until the police came, I wasn't about to let him up. Several people clapped, and more than a few were asking me if I was all right, behind big grins. The police arrived, and over traipsed a very amused, very tall friend.

I blurted out, "Pete?"

He laughed. "Val didn't tell you I was on the force?" I gaped at him. "I guess she didn't."

"Well, I'll be . . ." I said.

He smirked down at me as I sat on top of the miscreant and nodded down at my hands, which were still holding the thief's arm behind his back, his mortified face against the cement. Pete said, "If you like, I think I could take it from here, Lane." I leaned down and whispered something to the mugger, and then Pete helped me up.

I gave my statement to Sergeant Pete and his amused friends on the force. One of them asked me out on a date; I cracked up as Pete swatted the guy away. Afterward, I decided to just walk home, and Pete decided to accompany me. At this point, I did not mind a uniformed bodyguard.

As we strolled uptown, he asked me, "So, what did you whisper to your young assailant?"

"Never underestimate a woman."

"Definitely not *this* one," said Pete, to no one in particular.

I chuckled.

Where Val was soft and pliable, he was a rigid, stiff wire. Peter was pleasing to look at, but as he strolled with his hands clasped behind his back, his posture was like a carefully studied caricature of a casual stance, which made it anything but casual. After a long pause, he said, "Lane, you know, if you ever want to talk with me about everything that's been going on, I would be happy to help you in any way I can."

"Uhh . . . Did Val say . . . ?" I stammered.

"No, no, she hasn't said much of anything," he said, with a smile and a shake of his head. "But from what I can gather, she's worried about you, and knowing your job and the situations that have been happening with you . . . You've got a lot going on, Lane." *Yes, yes I do, indeed.* "Let me ask you this: Do you believe in coincidences?"

"I haven't given it much thought, but as of late, I don't think I do," I said as I viewed the darkening sky and the glowing skyscrapers around us. I loved nighttime; the city was magical. My stomach growled as we passed a trattoria. The aroma of garlic, olives, and tomatoes wafting out was unbearably delicious.

"Do you think your purse-snatching today has any relevance or connection to the other events?" he asked, in his best investigative voice. How had I not seen it before? He was so clearly a policeman, with or without his uniform.

"Let me think. I didn't recognize the thief. If it was a random purse-snatching, he could have just been waiting at that popular stop for a perfect situation, or he was on the train with me and I just didn't notice. However, if he was part of something bigger and they were targeting me, it was pretty well-thought-out. Do you think that kid has any links to Danny Fazzalari? The guy who pushed me onto the subway tracks?"

"I can check on that. Is there anything else that you should tell me about?"

"No, I think I'm good."

He looked like he darn well knew that there were things I wasn't telling him; I must've had a suspicious look on my face as I thought of my escapade to the Meatpacking District. I'd have to work on that.

The next day dawned hot, dark, and rainy. When I didn't have to go anywhere, I loved the rain. When I had to be somewhere in the city, it wasn't so fun. So on came the boots, the umbrella, and the raincoat with rain hat.

I felt slimy as I entered city hall. Fio had picked me up in his car, but even the walk from the car to the office drenched us both. After I dried off and took off my boots, I spotted Ralph going into the coffee room.

"Hi, Ralph. How are you doing this morning?" I asked as I poured a hefty cup of coffee and braced myself for Ralph's fast and furious onslaught of information.

"Hi, Lane. Good, good, how you doin'? I had a great night, met some fun people. Oh! I found a new coffee shop—"

I figured I had better barge into his ongoing monologue if I was ever going to get my question in. "Hey, Ralph!" I yelled, a little too loudly in my fervor to be heard. In response to his startled look, I moderated my voice. "I wanted to ask you something. Val told me that you helped with interviews when Roxy and Lizzie were first hired. I've been trying to, you know, figure them out a little.

We don't always get along, and I was wondering if there's anything that could help me get to know them better." I gave him a coaxing smile, almost out of breath from spurting out all those sentences quickly enough that he couldn't interrupt me. "Any ideas?"

"Well, let me think, let me think. Type like lightning . . ." I rolled my eyes. "Both have been in the city for several years, but didn't grow up here."

"Do you know where they grew up?"

"Oh, I don't know. Somewhere way out in the country, I think. I can't remember." Which was completely unhelpful, because most Manhattanites figured anything outside of Manhattan was way out in the country somewhere. Could have been anywhere from Queens to Yonkers to Idaho.

"Let's see, I don't remember much about their parents, either. And nothing too interesting like hobbies or something."

"Hobbies?" I questioned.

"Yeah, you know, something you could do together."

"Oh, right! Well, it was worth a try. Thanks, Ralph. I appreciate it."

"You know, it's funny you asked me about them."

"It is?" I said, with something akin to a dire foreboding.

"Roxy just asked me about you last week. Then Lizzie asked a couple of questions about Valerie. Maybe you guys will be friends after all!" he chirped, with genuine hopefulness, as he took his coffee and turned to the door.

"Yeah," I said rather sickly, "that'd be gr—" And he was off and running out the door.

Just then, across the office, I saw Roarke come in, looking avidly around. He nodded at me to follow him. As we drew away from the main cluster of desks, he said in a low voice, "I heard from my pal in the police department that they found conclusive evidence that the fire where you first met"—he mouthed *Danny*—"was definitely arson."

"Well, that's not that big of a surprise," I whispered.

"That's what I thought, until the guy says to me that they can actually link the fire to Danny."

"You mean really link him? As in handcuffs and arrests?" I asked.

He saw the hope written on my face and was slightly crestfallen as he said, "Well, no, they know that it was him, but the proof is a bit circumstantial. Not enough to make an arrest. But it gets more interesting, Lane." He looked back over his shoulder at the door between the coffee room and offices. He whispered, "They also found something else at the fire." He paused, building my anticipation. "They found a woman's scarf, and there's one corner of it not scorched. It's *bright yellow.*"

"Roxy's?" I whispered. "Wait a minute, does she have a connection to Danny?"

He nodded, as he could see I was getting the picture. "My guy said that they've had suspicions that there was a mole of sorts in the mayor's office, and they narrowed it down to one of the women in Fio's secretary pool. Nothing big, but you know, people hearing things before it's officially declared from city hall, etc."

"Well . . . she could be a mole, but Roarke, what if she's more than that? What if she's Danny's lover?" He'd been thinking business angles, not personal angles.

His brows shot up in surprise. He nodded and smiled, bringing out his dimples. "Oh, yeah, that could definitely be the case, Lane."

CHAPTER 9

It is with the reading of books the same as with looking
at pictures; one must without doubt, without hesitations,
with assurance, admire what is beautiful.

—ML

By the afternoon the rain had stopped, having thoroughly washed
the city clean. The sun was peeking out, casting great shafts of
golden light through watery clouds. I left work by way of the bus
uptown. It smelled so good outside; I really wanted a quick walk in
Central Park to think and enjoy the clean, summery scents.

It was a typical, crowded bus. I had a seat by the window, and an
elderly woman next to me rattled a box of mints in her purse. I was
currently reading a new novel, *Gone with the Wind*, but the book was
enormous and completely impractical to bring to work. So today I
pulled out *The Strange Case of Dr. Jekyll and Mr. Hyde.* Thinking of
these books and Aunt Evelyn, I planned to read more of her lavender journal from the mysterious ML.

At 60th, the lady next to me got up to leave and someone else
took her place.

"Hi, Finn," I said, not looking up from my book.

"How . . . But . . ." he stuttered.

"I spotted you at 42nd."

He looked to the front of the bus and nodded forward, like I
should do the same. That was rather ominous. I followed his lead
and stared out front.

Hardly moving his mouth, in a small voice, he said, "You're being
followed." I swallowed and nodded slightly. He said, "Follow me."

I did some quick calculations of my situation. I had met a lot of unsavory characters recently, but Finn? If he'd wanted to hurt me, he could have already done so several times. Fio knew him and had some sort of relationship with him. That was good enough for me. For now. And on top of that, visions of the man on the subway with the nose hairs swam into my mind at that precise moment. Yeah, I'd take Finn.

At the next stop, we both got up slowly to move toward the front of the bus, making it look nonchalant as we gave our seats to a young mom with a baby. As the bus pulled up to 79th, a popular stop, we stepped aside to let out dozens of people and let on dozens of people, and just as the driver was about to close the doors, we quickly squeezed out. The doors shut firmly behind us, and the bus took off with cars honking, urging it on its ponderous way in the rush-hour traffic.

I was pretty sure we had ditched whoever was following me, but just in case, I didn't want to go home; I felt like public, busy places were better. I turned toward Central Park and the Met.

I walked up the famous, wide steps of the Metropolitan Museum of Art, where many tourists and New Yorkers paused and rested or met up with friends. I walked right in after looking back out of the corner of my eye to see if Finn was still with me. He was. I saw a minuscule smile pull at one side of his mouth as he shook his head.

Once in the main entry hall, I walked toward the section with ancient Roman statues. I circled around several large pieces, and after tailing me for a bit, Finn made his way over.

"Do you like this piece?" he asked me, sounding like any other British stranger who wanted to share in another's artistic experience.

"I have no idea," I said. He laughed. When Finn laughed, his smile was completely genuine, not affected or self-conscious. It felt like liquid gold running through me, a contagious happiness.

I smiled and looked again at the marble statue of a youth who was on that engrossing cusp between childhood and manhood. It astounded me that such a hard, cold material could be sculpted with such soft smoothness; the curls atop his head were perfect and intricate. "I like looking at the sculptures, but I really just like this area of the museum. Ancient art that still speaks, the cool feeling of the air, and the fantastic high ceilings."

We walked through several other parts of the museum, not talking much, but enjoying being side by side, looking at beautiful things. Occasionally, our arms would press up against each other as we stood side by side, making my spine sizzle.

We strolled up the main staircase and stood at the railing overlooking the entryway of the Met. I felt Finn draw close, and I looked up at him slowly, my heart throbbing. He put his arm up over me on a column, and he leaned his head down toward mine. His eyes were dark, and I thought he was going to kiss me. I wanted him to kiss me. But with a few quick blinks, he cleared his head.

"Lane," he said, in his deep and slightly whispery voice that held that British accent that was so tantalizing. Or was it Irish? "You were being followed by someone who is linked with Danny Fazzalari. I'm fairly certain you know who he is and who *he's* linked to?"

"I know who they are," I said, my voice hardly above a whisper.

"I can't . . . I'm not supposed . . ." He leaned down a fraction of an inch closer. "Look, there are even more players in this than you know about," he whispered intensely, his eyes trying to tell me more than he really could.

"Finn, what . . ." But before I could get my question out, he gingerly put out his hand, and with one gentle motion, stroked my hair, his right hand sliding down my face and letting the strands slip out of his grasp. It was excruciating and heavenly at the same time. He looked at me, both of us with so many questions behind our eyes. But he said only, "You have to go, love. We can't be seen together. Too often." He smiled a one-sided, crooked smile.

I whispered, "When we were dancing in Little Italy and you left, why did you say you were sorry?" But he stopped my words, cupping my jaw with his right hand, his thumb gently covering my lips.

"Oh, no you don't, Lane. Not that question." Then, as he started to back away, he smiled a devilish smile that simultaneously made my heart melt and brought my hands to my hips.

"Oh, yeah, Mister. *That* question," I said, in mock indignation.

But he backed away farther toward the stairway and smiled a real smile, one I found extremely appealing. From my roost up on the landing, both hands on the railing, I watched him walk through the lobby down below and out of the building, trotting quickly down the steps outside.

I had a lot of questions. I was being followed by someone linked to Danny. So, was Roxy or one of Danny's guys following me now? And was Roxy too obvious of a villain? In novels, it was the least suspected person. So what the hell did that mean? Ralph? Lizzie? Val, for cryin' out loud? And I didn't want to think about this, but Finn was following me, too. Why? I had to consider all the possibilities. But I knew one thing for sure from experience: You could not survive distrusting everyone. You had to make leaps of faith sometimes.

Finn knew that I understood about the gangsters' involvement, so his comment about the fact that there were more players meant that I needed to worry about the gangsters *plus others*. Great. The only other big player that could compete with the gangsters was Tammany. I had to talk with Roarke about any other thoughts or leads involving them. I needed to call him and get him to come over for a little chat.

Roarke was able to stop by after dinner, and I decided that I wanted Aunt Evelyn in on the discussion; two birds with one stone, so to speak. So we gathered at the pine kitchen table and I set out a snack for us all. I chose vanilla ice cream and my absolute favorite: Sanders hot fudge poured liberally over the top. It was a Michigan thing. Great candy company and great name; I had always wished it would be discovered that I was a long-lost heir to the Sanders legacy. I wasn't really a sundae fan, but Sanders hot fudge? It was more delightful than you could possibly imagine. Roarke had two helpings of the thick, smooth, caramely fudge while Aunt Evelyn and I finished up our own. Mr. Kirkland sat down at last, and I decided to dive right into the meeting I had called.

"I have a friend who is very connected and who knows all about our case, all the *incidents* that have been happening lately. He knows that some of the events are linked to Danny Fazzalari and Uncle Louie." Mr. Kirkland flinched at Uncle Louie's name and muttered something indescribable. Aunt Evelyn's eyes narrowed keenly.

Roarke's shoulders were braced, like he had his guard up, antici-pating what I could possibly be leading to. "Okay. Your contact is up to speed," he said, urging me on to my point.

"Well, today he said something that I need your opinion on. He said that there are even more players involved than we know about."

"Others?" exclaimed Roarke. Then, under his breath, he said, "As if Louie wasn't enough."

"*Mm hm,*" I said, scraping the bottom of my bowl, waiting to see where their line of thinking would take them.

"I've got a thought, Lane," said Aunt Evelyn, with her arms crossed and leaning on the table. "I was talking with Ellie last week, and she and I have come up with a couple of people we should take a look at."

"You briefly mentioned her last week. Which Ellie is this, Aunt Evelyn? Do I know her?" I asked.

Roarke dropped his spoon in a surprised clatter. "Eleanor?" he exclaimed. Mr. Kirkland chuckled. "Not . . . You mean the first lady? Eleanor Roosevelt?"

I whipped my head toward Aunt Evelyn. "What? All this time I thought Ellie was some little old lady from the art gallery meet-ings."

Aunt Evelyn tut-tutted and made sounds like, *Don't be ridiculous.* "Eleanor and I have been dear friends for ages; I've always called her Ellie. I brought her up to speed on some of this, and of course you know she and Fiorello are very close, so it was only natural. After talking through quite a list of people and discarding the ones in jail or dead or without the wherewithal to pull something like this off, she and I think that there are two men who are worthy of looking into from Jimmy Walker's old Tammany crew. They were disgusted by Fiorello's new direction and could still be compelled to take vengeance on him. Donagan Connell and Daley Joseph."

"Okay," said Roarke, ready to get down to the business of in-vestigative reporting. "What makes them stand out, Ms. Thorne? I thought Donagan was in prison, and Daley Joseph, well, wasn't that maniac institutionalized when they found out what he did to those two . . . eh . . . fallen women?"

"Prostitutes, Roarke. Hookers. Say it like it is," said Aunt Evelyn. Roarke choked on something, and she absentmindedly patted him on the back. "What makes these two suspicious is that they seem to have disappeared, whereas most of Jimmy's other crew are still in prison, have moved away, or have decided to try to make it work with the new administration.

"Those two were particularly vicious and absolutely devoted to Jimmy, but even more devoted to their self-promotion. We should at least find out where they've been hiding to rule them out."

I looked at Roarke. "All right," he said. "I'll do some digging around. See what I can come up with," he said, taking copious notes on his notepad. I noticed Mr. Kirkland and Aunt Evelyn looking at each other and him nodding to her.

I said, smirking a little, "Do you two have something to share?"

Aunt Evelyn's head whipped around to me rather guiltily. "No. Nothing. Mr. Kirkland and I have just been discussing this, so he knows about all of it. Would anyone like a little more ice cream?" She was blabbering, unsuccessfully trying to cover up something. I looked at Roarke, and we shared the exact same expression: a disbelieving cocked eyebrow. He looked at me, and we both shrugged at the same time.

"Sure! I'll have more, Aunt Evelyn," I said, pushing my empty bowl toward her.

"Me, too," said Roarke. "Say, Lane, since we're *not* getting things out on the table . . ." Mr. Kirkland coughed, or was it a laugh? "How about telling us who your contact is?"

Damn, I thought I'd maneuvered away from that topic. As Evelyn handed me my second helping, I quickly put a huge spoonful of ice cream in my mouth to give me a few extra seconds to think. Aunt Evelyn stared me down, fully engaged.

"Uhhh . . ." I began.

"Let me guess," said irritating Roarke. "Is it the serious, intriguing man you danced with at Copioli's?"

I put my face in my hands and muttered, "Oh, bugger."

Aunt Evelyn perked up further and said with great interest, "Copioli's? Intriguing man?"

I gave Roarke a withering look, and he beamed even more broadly. If he'd been seated closer to me, I would have kicked his shins under the table. "Well, actually, yes."

Grinning and looking like a complacent, self-satisfied cat, Roarke said, "I thought so." He licked the last bit of hot fudge off his spoon in triumph.

"*Grrrrr,*" I said. Mr. Kirkland chuckled.

"So, out with it, Lane," said Aunt Evelyn.

"All right. I don't know much about him. But I saw him the day I was pushed onto the tracks; he actually helped me over to a bench." That sobered everyone up quickly. "His name is Finn Brodie, and I ran into him on the bus today. He told me that someone whom he knew to be connected to Danny Fazzalari had been following me, and he helped me get off the bus and lose him. That was when he told me about the fact that there are more players than I know about."

Mr. Kirkland wasn't chuckling anymore. He put his elbows on the table and asked, "Do you trust him, Lane?"

I took a moment to gather myself. I thought about our all-too-few moments together: our dance, our walk through the Met, his eyes, his smile. "I do, Mr. Kirkland. He's a mystery, but I think he's on the right side. The first time I saw him, he was coming out of Fio's office." That raised three sets of eyebrows. "Fio says he's working with him on a special project. But other than that, Fio's been avoiding my questions about him, which makes me even more curious, of course."

"*Hmph!*" exclaimed an indignant Aunt Evelyn. "We'll just see about that!" Poor Fio.

Just then Ripley came over to the table. He'd been patiently waiting on his rug by the door, and he finally couldn't take it anymore. He skulked over to us and suddenly grabbed the bottle of fudge in his large mouth and skittered away in a clatter of paws on the wood floor.

"Ripley!" yelled Mr. Kirkland and Aunt Evelyn simultaneously as they both ran from the table.

I looked at Roarke. "Meeting adjourned!" I said as I happily finished the last drops of my sundae.

* * *

The next morning, I was up in my room getting ready for work when I heard Fio come crashing through the door, screeching, "Good morning!" I quickly zipped up the back of my sleeveless light pink dress. I put on my little white bolero jacket and swirled on a coat of pink lipstick. I heard voices coming from downstairs and just knew that the trap Aunt Evelyn had set for Fio would be profound and impossible from which to extricate himself. I didn't want to miss one second of the show.

I made my way to the table, which was laden with two big platters of scrambled eggs and biscuits. Aunt Evelyn had just invited Fio to sit down and was watching him like a cat watches a mouse just about to enter its ambush. "So, Fiorello, dear, how is your breakfast?"

"Wonderful, Evelyn, tell Mr. Kirkland thank you very much."

"I was wondering, Fio, what can you tell me about a man you're working with named Finn Brodie?" Fio froze his fork midway between the plate and his mouth.

He slowly raised only his eyes to Aunt Evelyn and said meaningfully, with a touch of menace, "What did you just say?" Perhaps the man *did* have a chance.

My eyes switched to Aunt Evelyn to see how she'd maneuver. Her eyes squinted in a strategic, calculating glare.

"Finn Brodie, Fiorello. We would like to know more about him. We"—she looked pointedly at me, and I tried to sustain an innocent look on my face—"all have a vested interest in him. Is there anything you can tell us about him?"

Fio looked around at me, Aunt Evelyn, and finally, Mr. Kirkland, who joined us and was grinning while he drank his hot coffee. Fio swallowed, dabbed his lips with his napkin, and chuckled.

"Well, well, well. Isn't this little ambush fascinating," he declared. Aunt Evelyn just smiled, saying without words, *Yes, isn't it?*

"Okay, dear friends. What can I tell you about him? Let's see. Nothing. I can tell you nothing about him."

Aunt Evelyn put a determined elbow on the table and propped her chin in her hand, leveling a piercing gaze at Fio. His bravado of a second ago started to run like a frightened deer, his eyes shifting back and forth, assessing a possible escape route.

"All right, let me ask you this, Fio," I said. "I'm thinking you can't tell us about Finn because it would compromise something, probably that special project of yours." At this point, three sets of eyes turned to me.

Fio started to sputter, "But . . . you . . ." And then gave in. "Yes."

"Look, Fio? The main thing I want to know is, can he be trusted? Is he playing on the right side?"

Fio's face softened. His mouth remained serious, but his eyes smiled, and he replied, "What I can tell you, Lane, is that *I* trust him. It's complicated, and I truly cannot talk about him with you all, but I have taken him into my confidence, if that helps."

It didn't look like it helped Aunt Evelyn at all, but it helped me immensely. She changed the subject with a slightly aggrieved air. "Well, Fio, maybe you can answer *this* question," said Aunt Evelyn. "We are also wondering about two of the old Tammany crew: Donagan Connell and Daley Joseph."

"Why on earth would you ask about those two?" he asked, with great disgust.

"Well," began Aunt Evelyn, "we've been thinking through possible suspects, who could have the power and mental acuity to be behind all these events. Ellie thought that—"

"Eleanor?" Fio cut in.

"Yes, of course, dear. And she brought up these two, how they stood out to her because of their devotion to Jimmy and the fact that they have been off the map, conspicuously so. She felt that if we could locate them, we'd find some leads. What do you think?"

He squinted in concentration, bringing his fist to his mouth as he thought through the possibilities.

"The fact that they've fallen off the map did come to my attention. However, it was some time last year, and I figured they just disappeared, gone to wreak havoc on another unlucky part of the country," he said sarcastically. "But given our current circumstances, those two do have a flair for such things. But I thought Danny Fazzalari was our prime suspect. What happened to him?"

I took up the conversation. "He's still in the middle of it all. But it's so complicated. There are several things going on at once, from a calculated purse-snatching to a potentially deadly shove onto the subway tracks and the threatening message to you from Danny at the fire. . . . I'm just not sure Danny is capable of all that. Maybe. But on the other hand, it can't hurt to think about other possibilities."

"*Hmph.* True, Lane, true. And those two characters are a whole different league of bad, that's for sure. I had been hoping that they would be locked away, but no such luck," said Fio.

Aunt Evelyn inquired, "What can you tell us about them, Fio, that might shed some light on this?"

"Donagan is a pretty predictable gangster. Big guy, narcissistic ego that's written all over his face. You look at him and you wonder if he's wearing makeup, which is incongruous with his tough-guy appearance. He's Irish, but doesn't have much of his brogue left, and has nappy red hair. Oh, and he has a bad scar on his left arm from his wrist to his bicep and one on his face. It pulls his lip down on one side. I heard he'd gotten out of jail through a legal a loophole.

"His narcissism fed off of Jimmy Walker and the lifestyle he'd created: the galas, the opening night performances on Broadway, The Casino . . . Donagan would have a different model or movie star on his arm every night. So, yeah, he's upset with me, all right."

"And Daley Joseph?"

"I find him to be difficult to talk about," said Fio, in a very uncharacteristic fashion. I'd never heard him *ever* find anything difficult to talk about. "He's a psychopath. Criminally insane."

He let that sink in, then Fio went on, "He should have been locked up with the key thrown away, but with his mental issues, the court went too easy on him. And there wasn't enough allowable evidence of his brutality to get him properly convicted. He was sent to a medium security mental hospital, but clearly it looks like he escaped or they let him loose."

"What brutality?" I asked, dreading the answer.

Fio looked down and said with a pained voice, "He tortured and killed two prostitutes. It was disturbingly cruel and intentional. Yet he'd had no known past with either prostitute or prostitutes in general for a motive anyone could figure. It was one of the ugliest, most disgusting crimes I've ever seen."

"You gave a good description of Donagan, what does Daley Joseph look like?" asked Aunt Evelyn.

"Ah, there's where it gets even more interesting," said Fio, with his face clearing. "He's more than one person."

"What do you mean?" I said.

"He has two known personalities, but I suppose there could be more. I've never seen him in person, just through courtroom sketches and whatnot. When the side of his personality called Joseph is coming through, he wears a black suit or tux with crisp white shirt and black tie. He is educated, slick, sophisticated. Overweight, big around the waist, balding head, but he wears a hat most of the time."

We all nodded, getting a good idea of what to be looking for.

He went on, "Joseph is cunning, but not the brutal one. He's more of a businessman. Very educated, extensive vocabulary, and even knows a few languages." He took a drink of his tepid coffee and looked like he was mustering up courage to continue.

"And then there's the personality called Daley. He's gruff, sloppy, always has stains on his untucked shirts. He usually wears a grimy brown hat that looks like he sat on it. He smokes a cigar all the time." I sat back in my chair, horrified. "Oh, and I almost forgot. Whatever his personality is, his most disgusting and prominent feature is the abundance of stiff, black nostril hairs that stick out of his nose."

The room swooped a little, and I rested my head in my hands. All the primal fear that had oozed into me that day in the subway came flooding back in a torrent.

"Good heavens, Lane, are you all right?" said Aunt Evelyn as she reached out her arm and took hold of my shoulder.

Fio stopped talking, and the coffee cup that he was about to raise was frozen in midair. "Lane?"

"I saw him. I saw Daley Joseph." No one moved. "At the train station, Fio. That's the guy I saw on our way to work, watching us, remember? And when I turned around and caught his eye, he laughed."

CHAPTER 10

Great things are not done by impulse, but by
a series of small things brought together.

—ML

The next day at work, I was at my desk when Roarke beckoned to
me from the office door, nodding to meet out in the hallway. I took
a look around, and everyone seemed occupied as I walked over.

His face was like death warmed over. "Roarke, are you ill? You
look awful!"

He didn't parry my outburst; that's when I knew something was
very, very wrong. "Lane. I have to make this quick. A body washed
up in the East River late last night. Some early morning fishermen
found it." He looked at me with an intense stare.

"Oh, my God, your informant?" I asked, with a sinking feeling.
He nodded.

"And . . . they found a press badge in his pocket. From the water,
they couldn't make out hardly anything, but . . . I'm sure it's one of
mine he must have picked off me for insurance. I already talked to the
police about everything I know." He looked about ready to pass out.

"Roarke, you better sit down. Did you sleep at all last night?
How did you find out about this?"

He shook his head, at the sitting down part or the lack of sleep
part, I wasn't sure. His voice strained, he said quietly, "I need to
get my head wrapped around this. This case is getting more complicated by the moment. I've got a cousin who lives out of the city. I
told my bosses I'm taking a leave for vacation. I've never taken even
a day off, so it's not like they could argue with me."

"But Roarke, I . . . well . . . I don't want you to leave," I said, realizing how much I liked his presence and the safety and consistency of our friendship.

He smiled for the first time, just a little. "I'll miss you, too, Lane. It'll be all right, it won't be for long. This will give me time to check into something that's been nagging at me. I've got this hunch. I'll send you a telegram if I figure anything out, okay?"

I looked up at him, worried. I had this feeling he might be jumping out of the frying pan into the fire. I bit the inside of my lip.

He kissed me lightly on the cheek. Then he leaned down and whispered in my ear, "Stick with Finn, Lane. I don't get his involvement yet, but he obviously cares a lot about you. He'll keep you safe. I gotta go, I'll write soon!"

The surprise at hearing Roarke extol the virtues of Finn just about knocked me off my feet. In my staggered silence, Roarke chuckled and ran down the stairs. At least in hearing Roarke's laugh, I felt encouraged that he was all right. But still . . . the frying pan or the fire?

That night, I dreamed of eyes, but not Fio's this time. First they were Finn's dark eyes, looking deeply into mine, trying to tell me something. But then they transformed into the dead, watery eyes of Roarke's informant. I woke up with a start from the creak of a floorboard sounding right above my head. It wasn't unusual for Aunt Evelyn to paint at night, but what *was* unusual was the lack of other sounds. Usually she had music playing softly or I could hear her pacing. This was one creak, then it stopped. After a long pause, it happened again. I wanted to go downstairs to the kitchen to get Ripley, but it seemed awfully far away. The sound was directly above me in the attic studio.

I reached out for one of the sturdy brass candlesticks that were on a little shelf by my nightstand. I quietly walked up the stairs to the fourth-floor studio. It just had to be Aunt Evelyn. I mean, it would have been ridiculous for a burglar to come up here; everything of obvious value was downstairs, not to mention the difficulty of getting all the way up there to the top floor and out again. I was willing the steps to not creak or groan as I ascended. Luckily, I knew them like the back of my hand, and by stepping on each stair in just the right place, I avoided making any noise.

I was almost to the top. There was no door up here, just an open, airy space for Aunt Evelyn to work. I held my breath as I reached the top step. The window was open and the night wind was blowing in; the moon cast striking shadows in its white light. Maybe she'd left the window ajar to air out the studio and a raccoon got in or something.

Just then a shadow shifted over in the corner. A shadow much too large to be a raccoon's. A man was going through some stacked paintings. I cautiously backed out into a hidden niche in the stairway, and then at the top of my lungs, I yelled, "Ripley!"

The guy jumped about a mile. I kept to the side so he couldn't see me in the deep shadows of the stairway. I saw a flash of a knife in the moonlight as he swiped in startled fear from side to side. Already I could hear loud, deep barking and large paws flying across the foyer and up and up the stairs, every second getting closer. The guy clearly understood what was coming for him because I heard him swear elaborately, then he grabbed a small painting from the floor, and before I could yell at him to drop it, he ran to the window.

Ripley made it to my side, and I yelled ridiculously, "Get 'm, boy!" Ripley snarled and barked like a hell hound. The man leaped out the window, landing hard on the roof below that jutted out from the third floor, cussing in pain and anger.

Ripley was barking his head off at the window. I made my way over to him, taking a firm grip on his collar so he wouldn't jump out. "Good boy," I said, patting the raised hackles of his fur. "Good boy."

Just then Mr. Kirkland ran in and skidded to a halt. "What the hell is going on?" he bellowed.

Aunt Evelyn rushed in right behind with her nightgown billowing as she ran to us. "What on earth?"

"I heard something up here. I thought it was you, Aunt Evelyn, but the light wasn't on, so I came up, and I saw a man rifling through your paintings there on the floor." I was panting from all the excitement and from telling them the tale so quickly. "When I saw the man, I backed over to the stairs and yelled for Ripley."

They both looked down as one at our huge German shepherd, whose ears and furrowed brow were still perked, still on guard duty.

"Ripley!" said Aunt Evelyn with immense affection. "Very, very good dog!"

As he patted Ripley's big head and back, Mr. Kirkland said gruffly, "That's my boy, good boy." Ripley sat down, very pleased with himself and with the attention. Finally feeling off duty, he let his big tongue loll out of his mouth.

Sirens rang out, coming down the street fast. Aunt Evelyn said, "We'd better get dressed. I called the police as soon as I heard you yell for Ripley." We all went our own ways, getting dressed as quickly as possible. I pulled on a pair of trousers and was buttoning my blouse when I heard pounding on the front door.

Mr. Kirkland and I made it to the door at exactly the same time. He swung open the door to two stern, worried, angry men.

Simultaneously, Pete and Finn yelled, "Lane!" Mr. Kirkland jumped back, about to seek Ripley's assistance once again. Pete and Finn looked at each other with a wide variety of emotions racing across their features.

I exhaled with a big huff. "Do you two know each other? Finn, this is Valerie's boyfriend, Pete." The mutinous look on Finn's face disappeared to be replaced by just plain anger. "You both better come in." They looked at each other once again. Pete had Finn in height, Finn had Pete in muscle. They sized each other up. They did seem to know each other, but neither looked too happy about the other's presence. They resignedly came in. Pete motioned to the other policemen who had come along that he'd be taking point on this.

The five of us sat at the kitchen table, and Mr. Kirkland started pouring cups of coffee. Ripley went over to Finn and cocked his head at him as if he'd known him in the past and was trying to recall from where. Finn smiled and rubbed Ripley's back and neck.

I started the conversation. "Ripley there actually saved the day." Mr. Kirkland beamed and nodded smartly.

Pete said, "All right, so I hear there's been an intruder. First of all, are you all right?"

Aunt Evelyn, not wanting to be left out, jumped in with, "Yes. Thanks to Ripley and Lane's quick thinking to call for him."

Finn, not missing a beat, said, "Lane's quick thinking?" When he was angry, his accent was more Irish than British. "Lane, you did not go and confront a burglar, did you?" Pete turned a frosty stare on me as well.

"Well, I didn't know it was an intruder," I said indignantly. "I heard something above my bedroom. It woke me up. I didn't hear Aunt Evelyn's usual music when she's in her studio, but the floorboards creaked. Sometimes she leaves a window open to air out the paint fumes. I went to check to make sure a raccoon hadn't gotten in." Finn squinted his eyes at me like he was trying to decide if that was the whole truth. Pete rolled his eyes, and a smile was tugging at his lips despite his best efforts.

Pete cleared his throat, back to all seriousness, and asked his next question. "So, when you checked out the studio, what happened?"

"I made it up the stairs and stood to the side at the top. I could hear movement up there, and by now I was sure it wasn't Aunt Evelyn, but then again, I wasn't sure what it was. The window was open, and in the dark I saw a large figure of a man in the corner by Aunt Evelyn's stacked paintings. I slowly backed farther into the stairwell so he wouldn't see me."

"What exactly made you think it was a man? Did you see him well enough to describe him?" asked Finn, Pete nodding.

"He was much too large and broad-shouldered for a woman, but other than a trench coat, I couldn't see anything but his form. That's when I thought of Ripley. I *knew* Ripley would be up there quick as a flash, causing a ruckus, and scare the guy into leaving."

"Damn it, Lane!" exclaimed Finn. "What if he had a gun and you scared him into shooting the area where you were standing?" His dark gray-green eyes looked black, and the muscles in his jaw were tensing. I couldn't help but admire how his short-sleeved shirt was nice and tight around those biceps. My preoccupation and obviously unbothered stance at his anger made him close his eyes, rub his forehead once, and then hold his mug of steaming coffee rather tightly.

"Well, he'd been pawing through the paintings and hadn't been carrying anything in his hands. And I was about twenty feet from him and around the corner," I said.

Pete asked, "Did you see anything else that would be helpful to know?"

"One last thing," I said. "I don't know if it was what he was looking for, but he *did* take a painting. It was a small one, and he grabbed it right before he dove out the window. Aunt Evelyn, I think it was that little one you did of a rolling field, with a little town in the middle."

Aunt Evelyn blinked once and sat back in her chair. She was curiously silent, which really caught my attention. Pete hadn't noticed, but Mr. Kirkland had. He said in his gruff but gentle voice, "Evelyn, was that painting meaningful or valuable to you?"

She exhaled in a quick spurt. "Of course it's not valuable, Kirk. I was trying my hand at a replica of an old friend's work. So, it was meaningful to me. But only to me, so I don't think it will shed much light on what he was trying to find. It's all just my own work up there. Our older, more valuable paintings are down here, in the parlor." She said that, and it was an honest reply. But the way she swept her hair away from her face made me think she wasn't telling us everything.

Just as we were about to wrap up our meeting, a loud horn honked from the front of the townhouse, succeeded by a concussive bang of the front door being shoved open, with immediate hollering.

Fio had arrived.

The five of us said a collective, *Oh, boy*. Ripley greeted Fio's shouts with some joyful barking, inviting him to play. Aunt Evelyn yelled to him, "In here, Fio! We're all in the kitchen!"

Fio was just barely dressed; he had his pants on, but his night-shirt had been tucked into them. His usual hat had been left behind, and he had two different black shoes on. His yelling came to an abrupt halt as he came into the kitchen and saw all five of us standing up to greet him by the table. None of us said one word.

Fio stuttered out a circuit of all our names. "Lane . . . Evelyn . . . Mr. Kirkland . . . Peter . . . Finn?" The last name was said with an obvious question mark. Which made it dawn on all of us at once: Why exactly *was* Finn here, and how did he know about the police call?

Aunt Evelyn cut to the chase. "I am very aware of *why* you're here, Finn." She gave me a pointed stare. I blinked. "But, if I may ask, how did you know about our dilemma?"

Pete cut in with a disgusted curl to his lip. "Because . . . he's a detective."

In the midst of jaws dropping and general gasps of dismay, I blurted out, "But you had on a fireman's outfit."

Finn looked at me with a one-sided smirk. "You saw that?"

I crossed my arms in front of my chest. "Oh, yes I did," I said.

Fio took a good look at us, figured out how to take charge, and began barking out orders. "Finn? It's probably time you've headed off to your other, er, ah, affairs."

Finn glanced at me again with a hesitant look on his face, then looked back to Fio, and with a quick nod, said, "Yes, sir." Then he headed out the door.

"Peter, did you have a look around the room where the intruder came in?"

"No, sir, I'll get right on that. Ms. Thorne, would you take me to the studio, please?" asked Pete as he picked up his pad of paper, ready to take more notes.

"Of course, Peter. Come with me," said Aunt Evelyn as she led him upstairs.

"Mr. Kirkland, nice work with Ripley, he's a beaut, isn't he? And could I bother you for a cup of strong coffee?"

"Absolutely," said Mr. Kirkland as he stood up to pour him a cup.

"And that leaves you, my dear," he said to me as he sat down with a getting-down-to-business, elbows-on-the-table stance.

"Yes . . . me." My head was swirling with thoughts, from the intruder and what he could possibly have been looking for, to Finn and his "other affairs," to more about Finn and why Peter would have an inherent dislike of him, to how I suddenly felt exhausted.

"Lane, let me just say that I realize your unanswered questions concerning Finn have to be frustrating."

"Yup."

"I know, but it's dangerous for you to even know Finn by name. And it's patently clear that you know each other better than just by name . . ."

I had nothing to say to that.

Fio cleared his throat, trying to find another tack, when we heard Aunt Evelyn and Peter coming back down the stairs. Mr. Kirkland had been at the kitchen counter listening to Fio and me, then he joined us back at the table, handing Fio his coffee, as we all reconvened.

"Peter, what did you find?" asked Fio.

"Lane was right. The thief took a small painting of Ms. Thorne's. One painted by her, approximately fifteen inches square with a black frame, not valuable in Ms. Thorne's estimation."

Fio asked, "Evelyn, is there anything else you can think of that would help us figure out this puzzle?"

We all looked at Aunt Evelyn. I could tell she was considering the situation, but it struck me as odd that I couldn't tell if she was trying to think of why a thief would want that picture, or if she was prevaricating.

"Evelyn?" Fio repeated.

Startled, she looked at us all as if she had no recollection of how she'd gotten back down the stairs so suddenly. "Oh, yes. Sorry, Fio. I'm just trying to figure out why on earth someone would want that painting or if he'd come looking for something else, was thwarted, and just took whatever he could. It's just so odd."

At that point, the other policemen came to the door and Pete went over to talk with them. We busied ourselves with our coffee, each of us lost in our own thoughts and fatigue.

Pete came back to the kitchen to make a last report. "The only other piece of evidence we found is a bit of torn fabric from a dark coat that was caught on the roof just below your studio window. We'll have the neighborhood police on the lookout, with a man posted for just this block, watching your house in particular. For now, let's make sure your windows are locked, and I don't think there's anything more to do here tonight. If you think of anything else, just let me know."

"Good work, Peter," said Fio. "Evelyn? Let me know if you can think of any other reasons for the robbery. Or if anything else comes to mind. Mr. Kirkland? Thank you for the coffee and for watching over our dear girls here," he said, making Mr. Kirkland smile but also slightly roll his eyes as if the two of us just might be beyond him.

"Lane? I'll see you tomorrow. Get some sleep if you can. The morning will be here before you know it. Good night, everyone." And with one last pat to Ripley, he headed out the door with Peter.

The three of us remained at the table, not quite ready to go back to bed.

"Evelyn," said Mr. Kirkland, with a pointed look at her. "Are you all right? I know this is very disturbing, having our home invaded. You look very preoccupied. Is there something you need to tell us?" He always seemed to have her number.

"I do have some thoughts, but nothing of substance yet," she said, with her mind still ticking away. "I just can't work my mind around why an intruder would go up to my studio." She shook her head, trying to clear her thoughts. Then she looked at me and took a deep breath and let it out as she studied my face. "Did Fio tell you more about your friend Finn?"

I shook my head. "No, just what we talked about the other day, that he can't tell me the whole story yet. And that it is somehow dangerous for me to even know Finn's name, let alone . . ."

She pursed her lips. "Yes, let alone . . ."

Despite myself, I started to laugh. "I can't help it, Aunt Evelyn. He's been at the right place at the right time a lot lately. I don't know what's going on, but he's *got* to be a good guy."

"*Hmph*," grunted Mr. Kirkland. "Well, I think we should keep our eye on him. Pete doesn't seem to care for him, and that doesn't make sense if Finn's on the right side."

Which made me uncomfortable, because that thought had run through my own mind when I saw how Pete had divulged that Finn was a detective. I'd never seen Pete be the slightest bit disagreeable. But when he talked about Finn being a detective, he looked like he'd just gotten a whiff of trash in August.

CHAPTER 11

He sat down on a bench after the police call to Evelyn and Lane's home. Things were getting very complicated. But he could handle it. They just needed to stay in the dark until he figured out the final game plan. He thought about that first day he'd finally infiltrated the notorious gang. It was a strategic triumph for all his efforts. It had all finally paid off. Until he realized more was at stake than he'd planned. He hadn't planned on meeting Lane.

He started to play back in his mind those mere minutes that would change his life.

They were walking toward 77th. It was a glorious spring morning, but it was all he could do not to be overwhelmed by the presence next to him. He'd been around some vile creatures in his past, but this *man*—if you could call him that—was, hands down, the most sinister. There were slight subtleties in faces, details that came together in figuring out who a person really was inside. If you knew how to see through the mask, you could read or manipulate anyone. Unless he was a psychopath.

This man walking along next to him fit that description, and on top of it all, he was actually two people. Few really knew this, but he'd just figured it out yesterday when he saw the rare transformation. Two evil personalities that made up one diabolical being. *Great*, he thought, *a psychopath with two personalities. Brilliant.*

He'd never worked with someone like this before; there was a terrifying element to it. The constant changing, never knowing who you were going to get, making him that much more deadly. Slippery and lethal, like a moray eel trying to devour you, and no matter how hard you tried, you couldn't get your hands around its throat.

They were walking past the Butterfield bakery, the cozy scent of bread wafting out making him think incongruously of his grandmother and the back porch of her home that he used to visit as a child, where the rolling hills were endless and deep green.

The man next to him made that signature gurgling clearing of his throat and said, "Not much farther now. I want to see what you think, what you pick up on." He just nodded his head and looked determinedly forward.

The morning rush hour was in full swing, thousands of colorful people heading off to their day. Up ahead he saw a bobbing black hat of someone short in stature, his arms working busily as he walked quickly, occasionally waving hello to people. It was definitely the mayor. He looked back to his left and saw a slight nod of affirmation that this was indeed what he was supposed to be picking up on.

Beside the mayor was that assistant of his, practically running on red high heels and writing furiously as the mayor's instructions left his mouth. They followed them down the couple of flights of stairs into the subway station, keeping back quite far, yet still able to watch them. They walked casually, slowly, and saw the mayor talking to many people, saying good morning, giving a message to some member of the family and whatnot. The assistant continued taking copious notes.

The mayor walked over to where he had decided to wait for the train. He must have ceased giving orders and directions, because the aide's pen finally stopped its furious pace. She flexed and pointed her foot like she was working out a cramp. Her legs were gorgeous in those red high heels. She turned slightly toward them, drawing her brown hair behind one ear, and looked at a young mother with a couple of kids who had bumped her. She smiled, her red lipstick making her smile even more vibrant and contagious, but it was her eyes that made him take a quick breath.

What was it? They weren't an exotic color, just sort of bluish.

Yet there was something utterly alive about this girl, like she was capable of just about anything and enjoyed everything. He'd seen her before, a few times, but maybe he hadn't actually seen *her*. She was captivating.

Then his partner, for lack of a better term, slowly moved a few inches toward the girl. He had an involuntary, repulsive reaction to this grisly man drawing close to her. She looked up, and her radiant face turned to a travesty of what it was moments ago. The rosiness of her cheeks paled, her eyes grew wide, and fear rippled through her. The joy was gone. His own left hand made a fist, and his right moved back to his gun in one fluid reflex. He heard a disgusting grunt come from his left that was supposed to be a laugh; a grotesque noise that meant he recognized her fear and was amused by it.

Just then the train roared in, and the girl turned abruptly to it while he and his partner disappeared into the dark shadows, back toward the exit. They left the station, walking farther downtown along Lexington Avenue.

"So, what do you think? What are your thoughts?" he asked with his greasy drawl as he pulled over to a corner to take some puffs of his cigar. Today he wore a white shirt that was covered in stains, and a dirty brown hat. His face was pudgy and mean, vacant of any human warmth or kindness. Then there was his defining feature: long, bristly, black nose hairs that poked straight out of his nostrils like a scrubbing brush had been shoved up there. It was almost impossible not to look at them, but he'd actually seen someone beat to a pulp for staring.

"Yes, it's possible. LaGuardia has a gun in his car, but he doesn't carry. And he isn't careful to have guards with him everywhere he goes. The only tricky thing about him is that he has no reliable daily routine. His meetings are at all hours, and sometimes he takes the car, sometimes the subway, sometimes the El on Second or Third. . . ."

"*Mm hm. Mm hm,*" said the man around his chewed cigar, which was dripping a slimy piece of blackened paper at the mouth. "But what about the tasty treat who was with him? Do you think we could use her to get to him?" He grinned like he particularly liked the idea. The nausea was almost overwhelming.

He steeled himself. "Possibly. She's young and with him a lot, but other than that, I don't know if she's a person of interest."

"We'll see, we'll see. . . ." said the oily voice, with an accompanying chuckle.

He tried to keep the fox from seeing his real thoughts. If he played it too nonchalantly, the predator would see right through the lie; yet if he sensed his personal interest in the girl at all, he'd sink his teeth in and never let go.

"We'll meet again next week and talk through more details. You'll hear from me by the usual means," he said as he scratched a bothersome spot just under his grimy hat brim. "Oh, and uh, Finn? Don't think for a second I didn't see your reaction to little Miss Red Lipstick. Oh, yeah, I saw it. It better not get in the way of your duty, boy. Do you understand?" He made that repulsive gurgling in his throat again.

"Got it, Daley."

CHAPTER 12

I would rather die of passion than of boredom.

—ML

After the fireworks of the burglary, the Fourth of July came and went in reasonable peace. Aunt Evelyn, Mr. Kirkland, and I took Ripley down to the East River walkway, where we could see the Macy's fireworks. The barges went down the East River to about 36th Street, but up around 84th Street along the river, there was a wonderful view, and it was not quite as crowded. Plus, the distance helped muffle the firecracker pops and booms so that dogs weren't as bothered.

At work on the fifth, we had a boatload of things to do as we prepared for the Randall's Island grand opening the following day. We kept up a tiring pace, even more so than usual. The entire office was a flurry of activity, enduring an epic heat wave as the temperatures soared over a hundred. Even Lizzie and Roxy didn't have the time or strength for dirty looks or caustic comments, and poor Ralph could scarcely get in any flirting time with us. Once in a while I'd catch him grabbing a coffee, looking longingly at all the women of the secretary pool.

I was really missing Roarke. I hadn't heard a word from him. We'd seen so much of each other lately, and I wanted to fill him in on the burglary and bounce some ideas off him.

As I was pondering this, a messenger bounded into my office carrying a telegram. Since it was later than usual, I thought the telegram office would have already closed. I looked up at the young, dark-haired messenger, then I looked at my watch. He replied to my quizzical expression, "Yeah, I know, miss. We're usually closed already, but we got the message just now, and they wired us saying they'd pay extra to get it to you right away. I was on my way home anyway." He plopped the telegram into my hands and ran off.

I opened the yellow paper carefully. It read:

IN MICHIGAN STOP ON WAY BACK STOP
FOUND CNXN STOP WATCH OUT FOR
RANDALL DAY STOP HOPE TO BE THERE
IN TIME STOP TELL FLOWER TAKE GUN STOP

I had no idea Roarke was in Michigan. What could be there that would be a connection? Maybe a Detroit gang connection to Uncle Louie? The Purple Gang fizzled out a few years back. Maybe the notorious Detroit Partnership? Randall Day meant, of course, the opening day of the arena on Randall's Island tomorrow. There could be thousands of people in attendance; the arena held thirty thousand. Could he mean a possible assassination attempt? If Roarke had clear evidence of that, he'd surely be talking with the police. Or . . . Roarke did have dramatic tendencies.

Well, I had nothing to go on, but I could at least give Fio the warning. He was still in his office, so I went over and knocked on the door.

"Come in!"

He was writing and mouthing words to himself, presumably working on his speech. "Mr. LaGuardia?" It never failed to feel strange calling him that formal name as I was always careful to do at work. At least when other people were around. Mostly.

"Yes, Lane?" said Fio without moving his eyes from his text.

"Sir, I just received a telegram from Roarke, and I think you should see it." That got his eyes to look away from his consuming speech.

"I thought I hadn't seen him in a while. Didn't you say he was on vacation or something?"

"Sort of. I think he was visiting family, but he also said he'd had a hunch about the events that have been going on here. That's all I know, except this." I handed the telegram to him.

"Bring my gun, eh?" he chuckled. "Good grief. Well, we don't have any evidence that we can take to the police that offers anything like direction or purpose," he said, mulling over the problem. "If Roarke had found some information about a bombing or something catastrophic, he certainly would be talking with the police. So we can assume it has more to do with me specifically, I think, and mustn't be anything too dramatic. We'll keep a wary eye, Lane."

"I was thinking along the same lines," I said, nodding.

"All right, Lane, let me know if anything else comes to mind. Have a good night, get some rest. We'll see you early tomorrow morning!" He'd already moved on to more pressing issues.

"Okay, Mr. LaGuardia, see you tomorrow," I responded, with a wave as I went out the door and closed it quietly behind me.

I practically ran into Lizzie. I bit back a loud yell. "Where'd you come from, Lizzie? You made me jump out of my skin!"

"Sorry, Lane," she said while nervously fingering her long ponytail.

"That's okay, did you need something?"

"Yes, actually, I do. I've been waiting to get you alone to give you this. I found it on the floor near my desk. I thought I had dropped it, but when I picked it up and read it, I . . . I didn't know what to make of it. I don't know what it means, but it sounds strange to me." She suddenly became nervous and jittery, like she was going to hyperventilate, and I did not want to deal with *that*. So I led her to a chair and had her sit down.

"All right, Lizzie, take it easy. Let me see it." She handed over a rectangle of creamy linen paper that looked like it should be a thank-you note to someone for a birthday gift. The letter was written in a neat hand in perfect cursive lettering.

> *Please reconsider, darling! It's not the right timing, and there are too many lives at stake. It won't work with the plan. Think of me, think of the big picture. There will be too many children there, it won't have the right effect. Just wait and be patient. Trust me, please.*

The paper had been crumpled, like perhaps it had only been a first draft.

"What do you think it means, Lane?" asked Lizzie.

I put my hands on my hips as I considered the troubling words and took a good look at the girl nervously twitching in my chair. "I'm not sure, but I'll give it some thought. You're acting str—, not like yourself. What makes you think that it's something dangerous? And is it Roxy's writing?" I already knew it was Roxy's writing. I'd seen her precise script enough times, but I wanted Lizzie to confirm it.

"Yes, it's hers, all right. I don't know what it means, either, but the part about children, the lives at stake . . . made me concerned. We've been working so many hours lately; we haven't had time to talk like we used to do. She's still acting weird, not wanting to chitchat or anything." Which I had noticed, too, now that I thought about it. Roxy would even choose to sit by herself over lunch sometimes or just disappear for breaks instead of hanging around picking on everyone. It made me nervous.

"Okay, let me think about it," I said while pocketing the note. We said our good nights, and I made my way home.

It was my favorite time; the city was cloaked in her nighttime apparel. At the bottom of the steps of my townhouse, I could see that the household was asleep but the little golden light in the living room had been left on for me, its warmth glowing out the front windows. I loved the front of our brownstone, with the bumped-out front window topped and bottomed in green copper, the mullioned windows on all four floors, with small, curved attic windows at the top. The steep front steps led up to a large, red front door flanked by a tall, skinny side window, with Ripley on the other side wagging his tail.

Ripley had taken to sleeping by the front door as a sort of sentry, and I saw his stalwart form behind the side windows well before I came up to the front door. He always knew when any of us was due to arrive home. He'd be sound asleep or in another part of the house, but then suddenly and quietly get up and go to the front door to look out the side window. Sure enough, the homeward-bound traveler would round the corner within a couple of minutes. He lifted his big head and pricked his ears in greeting as I walked up the front steps.

I quietly went in, gave Ripley a big hug, and smiled as he let out an enormous yawn. I got the message: I was home late, and I'd better get to bed. I made my way up all those stairs to my soft blue and white room with the tiny candle lamp beside my bed, beckoning me to come and rest. It looked enormously inviting.

I got ready in a jiffy, and as I got into bed, I picked up the scarlet journal from my parents and started to gently turn the well-worn pages. There was a first love note from my dad to my mom when they were probably my age now. There were several pictures of the three of us when I was little, and one that I loved of us with Aunt Evelyn. *Huh.* If she was in the picture, who took it?

Several pages later, there was a small postcard from a lobster restaurant they went to in Maine. There was a tiny note next to it that said, *The best dinner! Blueberry pie was amazing!* I flipped to a matchbook from a Parisian hotel and a few photos of my mom and dad looking young and chic. It was hard to imagine these two sophisticated people were the same parents from Rochester, Michigan.

Wait a minute. Michigan. *No, it can't be.* That niggling feeling I'd been having returned in full force. Why was Roarke in Michigan? And more importantly, why was he acting so secretive? I rifled through the book some more, just knowing that I was going to find something interesting and I'd know it when I saw it. I turned to a page that opened easily because it was one of my favorites that I looked at frequently. There was a photograph of my mother in a long white dress and fur stole outside of some dazzling restaurant. I took a closer look. Yes. This was it.

Right behind my mother, I saw the side of a face that made my heart skip a beat. *No. It can't be.*

But it was—Uncle Louie. Directly behind her. Not with her, exactly, but he looked like he was in her party. Someone's hand was on my mother's shoulder, and her other hand was flung out to the right in an elegant pose, her eyes intently looking at the camera—at me. At the top of the photograph was the bottom half of the restaurant's name on the famous sign. It could only be one place: The Casino. My mother had been in New York City at Jimmy Walker's Casino, *with Uncle Louie.*

And that hand on her shoulder. I looked closer. I'd seen that hand a million times. It had served us scones this morning.

The next morning dawned too early to interrogate Aunt Evelyn about my mother's presence in New York and her close proximity to Uncle Louie, one of the most notorious of all gangsters. I had a hard time sleeping with the intense heat and the bickering thoughts milling around my mind, but I managed a couple of hours. I got out of the house by about six and started to make my way to Randall's Island.

The city was just waking up, but there were still many people out and about already. The morning always held a different air about it, a quiet, peaceful, heavier feel. Like the city was trying to wipe the sleep from its eyes to prepare for the busy day ahead. The early dog walkers were up and out, paper boys were making their deliveries, merchants were hosing off their storefronts and sidewalks. I saw many familiar faces as I made my way east, then took a bus uptown to the walking bridge that led to the island.

I was just a couple of blocks away from the bridge when someone came up right next to me, walking in step. I had been looking out for him, so he didn't startle me.

"Roarke!" I started to yell, ready to give him a hearty hug, but tightened up my voice and my posture when he made a small gesture with his hand and a quick shake of his head to keep me walking straight.

"What's going on? Are you okay?"

He remained silent but picked up the pace. I took a good look at him and saw dark circles under his eyes; his usually well-brushed and shiny blond hair was darker, and he looked, overall, like he'd been sleeping in a barn or something. Considering his dapper and sophisticated tastes, that must have really cost him something. But instead of enlightening me about his trip and his cryptic telegram, he added more questions to the pot.

"What's been going on here while I've been gone? I've been getting this feeling that I've only collected a few pieces to a very complex puzzle."

"That's what everyone keeps saying," I murmured. "Roarke, you're killing me! You're really going to make me wait longer?" I said, with an exasperated tone.

Instead of bantering back and forth like we usually enjoyed doing, he just said, rather tightly, "Just fill me in, Lane."

"All right." I couldn't deny a growing sense of urgency and alarm in the air. It had been gnawing away at me all night, and it was becoming more and more tangible, something I could almost touch, yet remaining just out of reach. I quickly filled him in on the burglary and the note that Lizzie gave me yesterday with Roxy's writing.

"My God, you've been busy," he said while rubbing his tired face like he had an invisible washcloth. "Tell me again what Roxy's note said." I told him.

"She's got to mean today, this opening. Something's going down, and I don't like the sound of it. And there's one more thing," I said. He groaned. "I was looking through an old photo album from my parents last night, and I found a picture of my mother that I've looked at a thousand times, but this time I took a closer look. She was at The Casino. Here in New York City." Roarke abruptly stopped walking and looked at me.

"What?" he said, his eyes turning dark and sober. "That was a really high-rolling place. That doesn't sound like the typical hang-out for a couple of bookstore owners."

"I know, and that's not the kicker," I said, starting to get more and more edgy. "Uncle Louie was in the photograph right behind her."

"*Oh, shit.* We've got to get to Randall's Island. Now." He took off running. I'd never be able to keep up, but I ran after him, my own sense of mounting fear propelling me forward. Something he found in Michigan had clearly just been confirmed. He outpaced me, and I lost sight of him.

Around another corner, with a painful stitch in my side, I saw a young paper boy making what looked like the last delivery in his bag. I ran up to him, panting, and told him I'd buy his bike from him. I thrust several ones at him, and it was obvious he thought he'd gotten the far better end of the deal, since a brand new bike cost about seven dollars. I was wearing a black skirt suit with a jaunty little red scarf at my neck that matched my shoes. Luckily, the hip-hugging skirt had a little give with its flared hemline. I hiked it up a bit, threw my leg over the bar, and raced off with the wind throwing my hair off my face.

I made much better time despite trying to pedal with high heels. I biked my legs off across the walkway suspended over the East River that joined Manhattan to the little island. Up ahead, I saw that Roarke had gotten the same idea, having commandeered a bike as well from another lucky kid. His bike had playing cards woven into the spokes of the wheels, and I could hear the buzz of the cards whirring around. He was still outpacing me as we biked north along the island, past some sort of factory or plant, and under another bridge, and at last I saw the arena, my thighs burning and sweat trickling down my neck.

At the entrance to the arena, the only people around were the setup crews. I thought I caught a glimpse of Roarke running up ahead, having ditched the bike, with his eyes scouring the area for . . . something. Anything out of the ordinary, I supposed.

On the bike ride over I'd had time to give some thought to this predicament. Something was linking all this together. The letter from Roxy pointed to here and now, with thousands of people expected. If Uncle Louie was involved, he was well-known for scare tactics, including the use of explosives on buildings—and people— that were in his way.

Those two points alone were enough to bring out a cold sweat. I tried to find a policeman around to notify, but they hadn't arrived yet. The only thing they would be preparing for would be the normal protocol for high-profile guests like Fio. And Fio wasn't due to arrive for two more hours; he'd probably be at home still or city hall.

I ran around to the other side of the stadium, hoping to cover ground Roarke hadn't canvased yet. I rounded the smooth corner of the massive building, and up ahead I saw a thin man with a shining black head of hair, smoking a cigarette. He flicked the remains down on the ground and looked around in nervous agitation, his mouth working, licking his lips. It was Danny. I ducked into a doorway to get out of sight and then peeked out to take a careful look.

I was just about to start walking cautiously in his direction to see if I could get a better look at what he was doing when a hard arm wrapped around the front of my shoulders and pulled me back into the doorway. A hand clamped down on my mouth. My hands went up to pull down the strong arm, and just as I was about to give a mighty kick behind me into his shins or, better yet, up higher, a whispery voice said in my ear, "What are you doing here, love?"

My hands stopped pulling and I stopped the kick from happening, relaxing into him. He let go of my mouth but kept his arm around my shoulders, and I felt him exhale. I twisted around to look him in the face. His eyes looked tired, and his five o'clock shadow had grown to a distractingly sexy, scruffy morning shadow. Apparently no one had slept well last night.

"Finn, listen," I said quickly. "Roarke just got back from Michigan. He said he found a connection to what's been going on here. But first I filled him in about the events here: the burglary, and then last night I found an odd letter from Roxy to someone about not rushing into some event here today. Something big, something bad. And since things just aren't exciting enough, I also came across a photo of my mother taken here in the city with Uncle Louie right behind her."

"Oh, shit."

"That's what he said. So we've both been running around here looking for anything out of the ordinary, when I spotted Danny up ahead."

"I know. I saw him, too. In fact, I saw all of you and couldn't figure out what you were doing. You have the most uncanny ability to get yourself in the worst—" I was about to roll my eyes at him when he cut off and pulled me back tighter into the doorway. I heard footsteps. I felt Finn's arm reach back behind him and heard the gun's safety click off.

"Yeah, I got it figured out, quit worrying," said Danny's high-pitched voice. "I put it where they'll never find it. And this is going to do the trick. My other ideas were child's play, they said. Well, they'll take me seriously now. No doubt about it." I heard another voice but couldn't make out the words. The footsteps had stopped, and Finn and I were holding our breath. His arm clamped tighter across the front of my shoulders, every muscle taut and at the ready. Then the footsteps started up again, taking them farther away from us. The safety clicked back into place.

I swiveled around again to face him. "What do we do?" I whispered.

"Come on," he said, taking my hand and leading me out of the doorway in the opposite direction of Danny. We slunk along, trying to stay close to the side of the arena.

Finn pulled me over and put his hands on my shoulders. "Look, stay here for just a moment. I'm going to make sure Danny isn't backtracking." I started to shake my head vehemently, and was just about to say, *You are* not *going to go gallivanting off and keep me out of it.*

But he closed his eyes for a second and moved his hands to my head. "I'm not trying to keep you out of this, Lane. Look, I'll run around to the other side, and you can keep an eye out on this side for Roarke, all right?" That same smile was playing around the corners of his eyes. I couldn't help but smile back at him, grudgingly, realizing he had read my thoughts perfectly.

"All right. Go, I'll watch for Roarke." He quickly and cautiously went back the way we had come.

I walked just a little farther on, watchfully scanning the area. If Danny was here, who else was? And what *exactly* had he put where no one would find it? Inside a corridor that looked like it led to the interior of the stadium, I heard the sound of agitated voices. They started getting louder, and I could hear Danny's familiar voice.

Danny was arguing with someone, then I heard a scuffle break out. I tried to see farther into the corridor, but it was too dark. Suddenly, Danny yelled, "Hey! Hey! What do you think you're doing? Drop it or we'll . . . Hey!" Then he and his scrapping partner took off running after whatever miscreant he'd been yelling at. It sounded like they went dashing into the belly of the arena.

Then, from up above, I heard another familiar voice. It was Roarke's. I looked back behind me, where I'd just been standing with Finn. There was a temporary upper walkway for the construction crew that was basically a small, makeshift bridge from the arena to a walk along the water. Roarke was up there, running from the arena toward the water. His voice was filled with more terror than I thought possible. "Oh, God, oh, God."

Oh, no, we're too late.

Roarke carried a bundle in his arms and was running with all his might toward the water. You only run with that much terror when you're carrying one thing. I started to run away from the water, but something caught my eye back under the walkway.

It was Finn. My God, he didn't see Roarke. He didn't see the bomb.

I ran toward him. "Finn! Look out!" He looked up at Roarke's running form and understood the situation in an instant. Roarke heaved the bomb into the water and dove backward. I turned back to Finn, only twenty feet away now, locking eyes with him as we ran toward each other. "Finn!" I screamed as the explosion rocked the ground out from under me.

CHAPTER 13

One must work and dare if one really wants to live.

—ML

I woke up coughing and spluttering. My eyes fluttered open, but it was just as black as if I hadn't opened them. An ocean of old, secret fears came cascading down on top of me in a single, horrifying wave. The cold, dark water. The long, agonizing swim up the endless tunnel toward consciousness. The claustrophobic feeling of being trapped. I started to kick and scream when I felt two strong arms come around me and gently but firmly force my head against his chest.

"Lane! Lane! I'm here. You're not alone. I'm right here, love." He kept his arms tightly wrapped around me while I tried as hard as I could to stop gasping for air, to control the fear that was ripping through me.

I finally started to feel other sensations: the softness of his shirt against my face, the firm, strong muscles of his chest, the warmth. His heart was racing, and I let that sound absorb into my mind. I started to concentrate on the in and out of my breathing. After a while, a huge shudder ran through my body, and then I could relax. He took one hand and stroked the back of my head. Over and over, not saying anything. I rested my hand on his chest.

We were both sitting on the ground. His back was leaning up against a wall and I was sitting in front of him, leaning up against him. "Where are we? What happened? How are we going to stop Danny?" I asked, trying to get up.

"Hold on, Lane," he said with a soft chuckle, pulling me back down toward him. "Don't run off just yet. We may be in a predicament ourselves, here. The debris has us a bit trapped, but it's not too bad. I just can't clear it from here without bringing more down. I think it best we wait for some help. Clearly, Roarke found the explosive that Danny must have set."

"I overheard him say that he'd put something where no one would find it. Apparently it wasn't that good of a hiding place. He really isn't the sharpest knife in the drawer, is he?" I remarked.

"I'm certain it wasn't supposed to go off yet; Roarke probably hit a trigger when he grabbed it. Bloody lucky he got it to the river."

"Do you think they can get us out of here pretty fast?" I asked quietly, not liking the feel of this stifling darkness. "I'm, ah . . . not very fond of dark, confined places."

"Don't think about it, Lane. It shouldn't be long for them to get us out. It won't take heavy equipment or anything." He stayed quiet for a while, still stroking my hair.

"Lane," he said. "What happened?"

I was quiet for some time. I'd been asked that question ever since the accident, when kids would wonder what happened to my parents. I made up all sorts of stories, not wanting people to really know. Everything from fantastical pirate kidnappings and fights with tigers to plain old illness. I hated reliving it.

But there was something therapeutic about thinking it through, here with Finn. A feeling that if I could work it through this one time in this darkness, it might not have as strong a hold on me. Like when you have a piece on the piano and you know if you could just conquer this one, terribly difficult measure, the rest would melt into place.

I took a deep breath and dove in. "Well, I don't remember much, really. Except the music—I always remember the music. 'Without You' by Nora Bayes, 'Pretty Kitty Kelly,' 'When My Baby Smiles at Me,' even 'The Love Nest,' which was so scandalous back then," I said as I smirked into the dark.

"Anyway, when I was ten, my mother and father and I went ice skating on the lake in our little country town. I remember my dad's tan barn coat and scratchy red wool mittens. My mom had on a long, dark gray coat with a brilliant blue scarf. The whole town was out, just enjoying a normal winter day. My dad had a habit of racing around the far edges of the rink. He must've been a hockey player or skater at some time in his life." I heard a soft sound from Finn, like he was smiling.

I took another deep breath as I reached the part of the story that I dreaded. "After we'd been there a while, my father was still racing around, and my mother and I decided to chase him. We raced to catch up with him, and just as we were about to reach him at the outer edges of the rink near the middle of the lake, there was a loud crack and then screaming. I was instantly in the water. I never felt anything like it. The cold was so fierce, so painful, it just sucked the air right out of me. I could barely move; my clothes and skates were pulling me down. And then . . . everything was just black." Finn had grown perfectly still, his hand resting on the outside of my arm.

"After feeling like I crawled through a heavy, thick darkness and finally made it to the top, I opened my eyes, and I was in the hospital. The first face I saw was Aunt Evelyn's. When my parents went on various trips, she would come and take care of me. We were very close, even then."

I started to talk faster, as I wanted to get the rest of it over with. "But I couldn't ask about it; I'd never been so tired. After a couple of days waking up for a drink of water and going right back to sleep, I was finally able to stay awake for more than a few minutes, and I heard the news of what had happened. My parents both died, along with one other man from town. I had been in a coma for several days before I'd first opened my eyes. Occasionally, my heart still does this fluttery thing, and I have to be careful of getting pneumonia, but other than that I am none the worse for wear. I don't even remember how I reacted to the news of my parents, that part's still a blur.

"I came to live with Aunt Evelyn; I don't have any other relatives. Mr. Kirkland and Aunt Evelyn gave me what I needed—space and some silence. Slowly, very slowly, life here began to be normal."

I dreaded what Finn would say. But he surprised me. He said nothing; I felt the soft press of a kiss on the top of my head, and his hand began stroking my hair once again. I relaxed into his chest, letting my head rest on him.

After several minutes of just lying there, I asked quietly, "Do you have any brothers or sisters?"

I felt his body tense a little, like I had asked some kind of forbidden question. "You don't have to say anything, Finn," I offered quietly. "I sometimes wonder what it would be like if I had someone here with me, who helped me remember my parents. Someone who shared my past, who would make that home in Rochester seem more real, more like a real home," I said, thinking that thought for the thousandth time.

His body relaxed as I talked. This darkness was a place of confidences. I let the silence roll on, and it wasn't uncomfortable. I subconsciously nuzzled the side of my face further down into his chest, feeling an inner chill despite the intense heat of our cave.

He broke the silence with a soft, "I have one brother. Sean."

"Is he older?"

"Younger. By two years."

"Do you stay in touch?"

"No. No, we don't." And whatever past he had, those small words held a mountain of pain, disbelief, and sadness.

"Are your parents still in the UK?"

"Yes, same house I grew up in. I don't really keep in touch with them, either." He seemed embarrassed by that, and I felt bad for opening old wounds.

I thought he'd leave it at that. But after several more minutes he must have felt the darkness prompt him, and he forged on. "Sean, my . . . my brother . . . and I were close when we were little kids. But something changed. He changed. The four of us hadn't been the family of the ages or anything, but pretty close. Then, when we were teenagers, Sean started to turn . . . devious.

"Once, I think we were about thirteen or fourteen, he took a girl's bicycle and threw it into a stinking marsh. He'd convincingly blamed it on the local bully, and the boy was whipped by his father for it. And once the deed had been done, Sean realized there was an opportunity to gain even more than that luscious brutality on an innocent boy. He retrieved the bike, cleaned it up, and brought it back to the girl. He was a hero.

"I tried to talk to my parents about it, but they couldn't see Sean's deception. They only saw his big, innocent eyes. Not the eyes that turned harsh and mocking as soon as they looked away." His voice burned with bitterness.

"He became a master of manipulation. But he always stayed true with me, even talked of his exploits in a self-deprecating way, like he was not being as bad as it looked, just having a little fun. He even had my back several times over insignificant boyhood issues that came up." It seemed like this was a big mystery to Finn; he was still working it out, and part of him wanted desperately to believe that some truth he had found was not really the truth.

"And then something happened, didn't it?" I asked, knowing there had to be more.

He sighed raggedly. "Yes. Sean eventually found a woman he wanted to marry. By that point I knew there was much more to Sean than met the eye, and I was anxious about the marriage. I knew it was something that he was working on, like a business venture or a manipulation, versus love. His fiancée and I had been friends for years, and I tried to talk with her about Sean and my concerns while trying not to look like the jealous brother. But she remained steadfast; she wanted to marry him. So she did."

"And you loved her," I said, very softly.

He was quiet for a long time. "I thought maybe I did. But she wasn't right. She wasn't . . . She just wasn't." And he left it at that.

I had no words, so I tilted my head and kissed his neck, giving me a feeling as warm and familiar as the sun baking my skin at the beach.

CHAPTER 14

The beginning is perhaps more difficult than
anything else, but keep heart, it will turn out all right.

—ML

I suddenly heard scraping and digging noises, then a loud, "Lane? Lane! Are you in there?" *It was Roarke!*

I yelled back, "Yes! We're okay! We're in here! Can you get us out?"

"Oh, God, thank God." And then a large window of light suddenly broke into our cave of darkness, making me squint in its harsh brightness. It was the most glorious thing I'd ever seen. Roarke's head peeked into the hole he'd created.

"Roarke! Are you okay? We saw you with the bomb!"

"Who the hell is this *we* you're talking about?"

I turned to Finn and said with a smirk, "He's all right, he's just grumpy." Finn chuckled. We could hear more rocks and debris being moved. We inched over to the light as best we could and started moving little bits. Quite quickly, we made a hole big enough for me to squeeze through. I squished myself out and threw my arms around Roarke's neck.

"I'm so glad you're all right, Roarke! I can't believe you found the bomb!"

Roarke was scowling a scowl worthy of Fio. "Yeah, and I almost killed us in the process, Lane!"

I had started removing more debris on my own, making a bigger exit for Finn to come through. "So? Who's in there with you?"

I was so elated to have him alive and to be out of the dark that I didn't care one iota that he was being surly. Despite sounding like he was peeved that he hadn't been my only rescuer, he had begun to open up the hole with me. Finn's hand came out. Roarke took it and heaved him out.

Finn brushed himself off, looked at Roarke, and then looked at me. Then, smacking Roarke's back with great vigor, said, "Well done, Roarke. Well done. And uh, thanks for digging us out, as well."

Roarke turned to me. "This is Finn, huh?"

"Uh, yeah, Roarke, this is Finn." Roarke looked mutinous and suspicious, like an eight-year-old who wasn't getting his way.

But then a couple of sirens sounded and were rapidly coming near, forcing us to pull it together. Finn said, "Roarke, did Danny take off? Are there any others around?"

Roarke quickly responded, "As soon as the explosion went off, Danny jumped in his car and sped off. It looked like there might be a couple of other guys with him in the car. I haven't seen anyone else yet. The cleaning crews were on the other side of the building, so they might not have known what the explosion really was. There really isn't that much damage. Nothing that can't be cleaned up in a couple of hours. I don't think we have to cancel the opening."

"How did they know to come over here?" I asked, looking at the police cars coming closer.

"I made a call to Fio right before I met up with you, Lane," said Roarke.

Just then, two police cars pulled up with a black sedan right behind. Pete leaped out of the first squad car, only to be beat by Fio and Val out of the sedan. They all pounced at once.

"My God, are you guys okay?"

"Jesus, Lane, what is with you?"

"*What* happened?"

These questions, among some mild swearing, were all peppered on us at one time with increasing volume. The three of us must have looked so shell-shocked that they all shut up at once. Concern replaced their looks of outrage as we were ushered over to the squad cars with gentle care. I gave Roarke a quizzical look, and he raised his eyebrows in an *I know* salute. I looked at Finn and saw him shrug and give in to Fio's attempt to put an arm around his shoulders, hunching down to receive it.

Val had her arm around my shoulders, and she whispered down to me, "Really, Lane, are you all right? I know it was more than a construction issue. Having you, Roarke, and Finn in one place, with an obvious disaster? That is *way* more than a coincidence. Are you hurt at all?"

"No, I'm actually fine." I relayed to her as quickly as I could everything that had just happened. She shook her head in disbelief as I talked.

"I have no idea what to say. But I brought you an extra set of clothes from the office."

"How did you know . . . Never mind." I put my head on her shoulder, and she gave me a one-armed hug as we walked along.

She smiled. "Well, it doesn't take a brain surgeon to know that you are a master at getting yourself into scrapes. *And* that you wouldn't be caught dead running home to change and possibly miss something."

I laughed and took the towel she gave me, rubbing my face to clear off some of the dust. I took a quick inventory. A couple more bruises and scrapes, but nothing serious—the usual.

"Hey, Lane, I think someone's trying to get your attention," said Val. I looked, and Finn was on the sidelines of the circle of police, motioning me to come over. I walked toward him.

"Lane, I've got to go," he said, looking at me with an apologetic expression. But then his face took on a hard, stony look. "I've got some things to attend to."

"You know, Finn, we've got to talk soon. *Really* talk."

He looked down at me, taking a minuscule, restrained step closer, and said softly, "I know. I want to. Things are . . . complicated right now."

I hated that word. *Complicated.* My face must have clearly told him my thoughts, because he said with an even softer tone, "No, Lane. It's not like that. I want to tell you everything, but I can't. Not yet. But I will. I really will." He paused, and I looked up at his dark gray-green eyes with crinkles at the corners, his worried brow, that tantalizing jawline. "Can you trust me, Lane?"

I took a breath and let it out slowly. "Yes."

The rest of the day didn't stray too far from the original plans. The cleaning crews were recruited to pick up the rest of the construction mess. A few hours later, the crowds started rolling in. Roarke had given our statement to Peter, and additional police presence was called in. No other threat was discovered, so they decided to keep the attempted bombing quiet until they could figure out what had really gone down. A diver was sent into the river to see if he could find anything that would help the investigation, and an APB on Danny was issued. The new arena was opened with all the pomp and circumstance.

Late in the afternoon, my work was finished, and I was dog tired after a full day on my feet and wrangling Fio to all his appointed venues. I had one last issue that needed wrapping up. I found the press guys in a huddle down by the entrance to the new field. A couple of them saw me coming and elbowed Roarke before I could get there. He strolled over to me.

"Roarke, you want to grab dinner? I *really* need to know what you found out in Michigan." I looked up at him in earnest, willing him to see how deeply I needed know what was going on.

"Let's go now before I get roped into covering another story tonight. Besides, I'm dead on my feet. I've gotta get something to eat, then go to sleep."

"Yep, I'm right with you. Wait a minute, how are you so clean, and how did you get new clothes? You even shaved!"

He grinned. Val had brought me my set of emergency clothes from the office, which consisted of a pretty generic cream dress with fitted sleeves and ruffled cuffs, but I doubted that Roarke had a best buddy who would do that. I self-consciously put my hand up to my hair, which would once in a while issue forth a hidden piece of dust or cement. Roarke looked like he'd gotten a full shower and time at a day spa with a beautifully cut tan, double-breasted suit complete with white shirt and light blue tie. So infuriating. Roarke looked closer at my face, licked his thumb, and made like he was going to spit-clean my chin.

"Cut that out!"

We went to a little bistro on the east side, Firenze. *Small* didn't quite describe the place. Try *itty bitty*. But it was private, dark, and they served very good food that we could afford.

We ordered and then shared a bottle of cheap wine and a loaf of buttery bread. I was famished and ate half the bread and drank my whole glass of wine before I felt the hunger pangs abating. It hit me that only three years ago, we wouldn't have been able to order this wine. It was hard to believe that Prohibition ended such a short time ago.

Roarke broke into my moment of delicious food-induced reverie by diving right in. "So, I've had this feeling lately. Like there was something that we weren't seeing in these circumstances that have been happening, and if we could just get the key to the puzzle, it would unlock the mystery. And Lane, my dear? I believe *you* are part of that key."

I gulped down the big bite of bread that I'd just bitten off. "I have to admit, I've started feeling like I'm in a spotlight of disaster." Roarke laughed out loud. It felt good to see him laugh with his dimples in full force; it had been a while. It erased some of the strained lines on his brow.

Our salads arrived and we immediately started eating, both of us understanding that right now, first things first. The salad was covered in a light dressing of fresh lemon juice, olive oil, and big grains of kosher salt and pepper. It was delectable.

"Okay, continue on, D—" I said, cutting myself off.

"You were *not* about to call me Dimples," he said, utterly offended.

"No! I would never do that," I said vehemently. I would *definitely* do that, especially after not much sleep and this much wine. I quickly made something up. "I was about to say Doc. You know! Doc Savage."

"*Hmm . . .*" he said, rubbing his chin, looking like he was caught between being unsure if I had just come up with a masterful cover-up and feeling gratified that I was comparing him to the famed man of adventure. He gave it up, probably settling on the latter. "Well,

I've never heard you talk much of your past, but I knew you grew up in Rochester, Michigan, and that your parents died under suspicious circumstances."

I put my fork down and took a sip of crisp white wine. "Suspicious circumstances? It was an accident while we were ice skating."

"Well, I asked Evelyn about it, and she told me that it *seemed* like an accident, but at the time, there were rumors and innuendos that suggested foul play."

"*What?* Foul play? How could someone engineer a hole opening up in the skating rink of a lake, exactly when we were skating by?" I exclaimed, with extreme skepticism.

"I agree, but there it is. I wanted to know more of the story and why you were being targeted. So, I went to Rochester, Lane. But first, I went to Detroit."

"Detroit? What did you find there?"

"First, I found great shopping and restaurants." He laughed again. "There's this great department store called Hudson's; the Fox Theatre is incredible. A lot of fun. Lots of life, with people pouring in to be part of the auto industry, you know? Then I found an old contact of mine who had moved to Detroit a few years ago. And I had one question for him: Did the gangsters in Detroit have any links to Uncle Louie?"

I stopped chewing and murmured, "We're going to need another bottle of wine."

"*Mm hm.*" Roarke nodded. "This is the deal. He said that there was one young guy who came to mind who used to live there, but moved to New York several years back. He was a cousin or something of Uncle Louie's; had a big mouth and bigger ego. Kept mouthing off about his connections that would make him powerful. Most guys thought he was getting too big for his britches. But he did, in fact, move to New York City. And he does work for Uncle Louie," he said, in tantalizing tones.

"You've got to be kidding me. Danny?"

"Yes. Danny Fazzalari used to live in Michigan. But it gets even juicer. I then went to Rochester and got a haircut. Worst cut of my life, by the way. You owe me!" I laughed; he hadn't quite looked his normal self. Definitely the cut.

"*But*, as you know, the best place to check out the scoop on rumors and gossip is at the barbershop. I made up some story about a distant cousin who used to live there, trying to get in touch with her, her name is Lane. . . ."

"Nice."

"Thank you. I got a lot of silence at first. But I put on my puppy dog face, told them funny family stories, and eventually they cracked. Well, they cracked after we left the barbershop and I bought the guys a couple rounds at the pub."

Our entrées arrived, and we took a few moments to inhale the aromas that were making my mouth water: the butter, lemon, and parsley over the delicate fish; Roarke's steak, medium rare with spices over the top and dripping in juices. Oh, man. We both had wide, goofy grins on our faces despite the heavy topic of conversation. Another sure sign of our fatigue and the copious amount of wine.

"So, after we had a *few* rounds of beers, the guys started talking. They told me about the skating incident. It was tragic, but nothing more than a horrible winter accident until two things happened that started a rumor. One, there were a couple of interesting characters who came around the neighborhood asking questions and saying that they were there to help your Aunt Evelyn go through the house and get things in order."

"What do you mean by *interesting?*"

"Oh, *very* interesting characters with trench coats, unsmiling faces, and broad shoulders."

"But Roarke, that sounds like federal agent–type people or . . . gangsters."

He nodded in agreement. "And they were asking the townspeople questions about enemies that your parents might have had, any mysterious things that might have suggested foul play. Most people thought it was routine questioning, but it was enough for people to start wondering about it. The only thing the police ever found of interest was a light coating of black dust around the part of the rink on the lake where the crack opened up. But nothing else." Roarke took another sip of his wine without taking his eyes off mine before he went on.

"Then the second thing. Do you know anything about that other person who died in the accident?" he asked.

"No. Not a thing. I don't even remember hearing the name, and if I did, I didn't know it. I knew most of the people in the town, but not everyone. I was only ten."

"His name was Rutherford Franco. He had a wife and a daughter. The wife, Daphne, was a big Hollywood dreamer and the Twenties had absolutely fed into her desire for fame and fortune. She stood out in Rochester because she'd prance around that small town with fur stoles and long gowns, making up stories about her friends in Hollywood and how she was about to get her big break.

"When her husband died, she went completely off the deep end. She blamed the whole town for his death, was a nut case about being disgraced. The townspeople tried to talk with her, to help her see that they weren't looking at her any differently and that she wasn't disgraced, but she'd have none of it. One day, she just up and left. Left her house, took her daughter, Louise, and disappeared."

I took a drink of water and let that news sink in. I had never known anything about the other tragic loss that happened that day. Another girl had lost a father.

"So, what does this mean," I said, trying to summarize. "Let's see. Danny has a history with Detroit, and he has been targeting me along with Fiorello. There is something probably fishy about the death of my parents and something definitely fishy about that other family and where they disappeared to. We need to find out where they went and what was going on with those suspicious characters who were asking questions."

"Lane, why don't you talk with Evelyn about it and see what she says about your parents? I'll tackle some connections who might know more about Danny. How can we find out about that woman and daughter who left? It might not be anything, but it feels like there is *something* here that links everything together. We just have to keep digging."

"So, when we were heading to Randall's Island, what made you feel the situation was so urgent?"

Roarke put a sugar into his coffee and stirred it, looking at me with somber eyes.

"There were a lot of questions raised in Michigan, enough that I wanted to warn Fio to be careful. The Randall's Island opening has been widely publicized, so it seemed like a good target. But on top of that, when you told me about your mother's picture with Uncle Louie nearby, and knowing his penchant for using explosives, plus that strange note from Roxy about a major threat, I just had to get there and see with my own eyes."

"Yeah, I was thinking along those lines myself. What exactly did you find in Michigan, Roarke?"

"Before I got into journalism, I worked with a construction company out in Pittsburgh. We used explosives to take down old buildings or just make bigger holes in less time." He sighed and ran his hands through his hair. "When it's extremely cold out, explosives can leave traces of fine black dust. Like they found at the lake. Lane, I don't think it was an accident. I think your mother and father were murdered."

CHAPTER 15

Paintings have a life of their own that
derives from the painter's soul.

—ML

Roarke's declaration had made me question everything I thought
I knew about my parents. In the days following the incident at
Randall's Island, I resumed my normal routine, but something was
missing. What had my parents been involved with prior to Rochester, Michigan? The photos in my journal took them all over the
world. I'd assumed that they were just having fun while collecting
the books that my father would sell in his bookstore one day.

But just like that photograph at The Casino, now that I was looking more closely, every once in a while I'd spot a photo that would
have a prestigious character in the background. Like Uncle Louie.
There were a couple of millionaire bigwigs, a few high-profile poli-
ticians, and a movie star or two. It didn't make sense. What on earth
were my parents doing? I had no one to ask except Aunt Evelyn.
I had a sneaking suspicion that she knew more than she was telling me. Even though I needed to talk with her, I found it difficult
to bring up that subject. It was never the right time or right place.
And, to be honest, there was a part of me that didn't know if I really
wanted the answers.

One evening, I walked in the door and heard Aunt Evelyn upstairs in her studio. But the music was extremely loud, and I heard
a lot of stamping around. I laughed to myself. What was she doing?

I went up the stairs into the loft at the top. There was Aunt Evelyn, dancing around in front of a huge canvas. Some Chopin was

playing so loudly I almost had to plug my ears. I hated to interrupt her, but I also didn't want to scare her. I cleared my throat very loudly and gave a stomp to get her attention.

She turned to me in delighted surprise. Today her hair was down, cascading down her back, making her look more like she was in her thirties instead of in her fifties. She looked like a fortune-teller from the circus, with a long, flowing skirt that went down to her ankles and a top with short sleeves, and all of it was spattered with colorful speckles of paint. Her smile lit up the room.

"Lane! I'm so glad you're here! I was hoping you'd come home early. I want to show you something." After she carefully lifted the needle off the record on the Victrola gramophone, she came over and took me by the hand. We walked over to the giant canvas. "It's something new I'm trying. Painting to *music*," she said, in a rapturous voice. "I was just talking about it with Diego and Juan. I'm not sure what they thought about it; they weren't very chatty, but you know men. . . ."

Diego Rivera was a close friend of Evelyn's. He was one of the elite artists whom Evelyn knew; he'd had a magnificent exhibit at the Museum of Modern Art five years ago. He also did an enormous mural at the Detroit Institute of Arts that I was dying to see. The Rockefellers commissioned him to do a mural in the RCA building in '33, but being a revolutionary at heart, he put in a picture of Lenin, and that *did not* go over well. The mural was destroyed when he refused to change it. However, because he depicted American life so well, he was the first inspiration for President Roosevelt's WPA program, which gave hundreds of artists the ability to find work. His friend Juan DeFelipe wasn't as well-known as Diego, but was clearly talented, and they formed the delightfully blind-to-status bookends of Evelyn's typical friends. Diego was from a wealthy Mexican family and enjoying great success. Juan was from a low-rent neighborhood up in Washington Heights, he and his wife eking out a living as two young artists.

I loved the art that was so popular right now: the mixture of the human form standing alongside machinery, yet proportionally bigger than the machinery. A visual reminder that technology was nothing without humanity. And the materials and colors? Luscious.

From the elevator doors and the Cloud Club in the Chrysler Building to the lobby at Radio City Music Hall, we didn't just look at art, we got to *walk through* works of art on a daily basis.

After Aunt Evelyn rubbed her paint-flecked hands on a rag, she said, "So, this is what you do: You listen with all of your being to the music, feel it as deeply as you can, here in your soul." She clasped a hand to her heart. "Then you look at the colors on your palette and you just let go! Painting what you *feel*, not worrying about the form or the design, just what the music is telling you to do, letting the music move your body as well as the paint." She turned her bright face abruptly to me. "I want you to try!"

My response was feeble. "Oh . . . Aunt Evelyn, you're the painter. I'm more of a writer . . . I like to read. . . ."

"Don't be silly, Lane, this has nothing to do with painting ability, it has to do with passion and enjoying a new experience. *And* . . . I already bought you a canvas!" She ushered me to the opposite side of the room to an enormous, six-foot-by-four-foot white canvas. I took a good look at it, and I had to admit, it was very tempting. I was most definitely not a painter, but I was an expert at enjoying new things.

"Let's do it!" I exclaimed.

"Wonderful." She practically squealed with delight, clapping her hands. She looked like a little girl. "Go and change into something you can get paint all over. But make sure you feel good in it."

I ran down to my bedroom and found exactly what I wanted. I had an old skirt of my mother's that was shorter than Aunt Evelyn's, coming to my shins, but flowing and bohemian with reds and oranges. I threw on a tight, black cotton camisole that had a couple tiny holes in it and raced back upstairs.

Aunt Evelyn was putting on a new album. "All right, Lane, first, we're listening to one of my favorite nocturnes by Chopin, No. 12 in G. Now, take a few deep breaths and let go of everything from the day, the last few weeks . . . everything."

"Okay."

"Now, I put out a whole slew of colors for you on a few palettes, and I kept out a few big jars of paint, too. There are several brushes, but I also think you should feel free to use your hands. This is an experiment for all your senses. While we're painting, I have a new piece of Chopin's—well, not new to the world, of course, but new for me. I've only heard it once, but it's powerful. Are you ready?" I nodded, very excited about the whole thing. "It's his Polonaise in A-flat major, and I'll let it play over and over until we're done."

She put the thick, shiny record on the Victrola. The piano opened up and was bold, rich. I took a deep breath and just listened for a few moments. I took the midnight blue and mingled and swirled it with white, took the biggest brush and painted a huge swath across the large canvas. I took more deep blue and moved and swayed the deeper color on, remembering my dream with the blue night and the misty clouds. I used a rich black and painted the bottom with large strokes. The marchy, quick notes of the music entered in, and it felt like bright yellow.

The music was loud, all-encompassing, filling the room and making me feel like I was on a lone cloud, just me and my colors. The slower parts of the music rolled in; I took a bluish purple color and let my hand dip into it slowly, feeling the coolness ebb up and over my fingertips, my fingers . . . and I laid my hand on the canvas and moved it in a languid, fluid motion, feeling the canvas and letting my hand go where it wanted.

More marchy, strong tones came, but they were underscored by a softness I couldn't describe, and at times it was almost heart-breaking. I dipped all my fingertips into a soft yellow, buttery color, raised up on my tiptoes, and let my fingertips dot and sprinkle the top portions of the canvas, back and forth all over. I dipped my fingers back into a light aqua, raised up again, and repeated the process over and over, my fingertips dotting and sprinkling the canvas with bits of color.

Then deep scarlet, midnight blue, black. Drips flecked my bare toes and my face. A last, slow dip of my hands into the black. The cool, smooth paint coming up and over my fingertips, my fingers, my knuckles, over my palms . . . Back to the canvas.

I let everything I'd been feeling for the past weeks and years overflow onto the canvas. With one final stroke of black mixed with crimson, I was done.

I was smiling broadly, exhilarated and refreshed. It was utterly amazing. One of the best experiments of my life. I spun around to Aunt Evelyn, having completely forgotten she was there.

She was sitting on the floor, looking at me with an intense stare, smiling with closed lips and deep eyes. After a few moments of silence, she said, "You know, Lane, I picked this piece by Chopin on purpose. He was from Poland, a country constantly at war, fighting people who wanted to oppress them for centuries. His nocturnes are velvety and divine. But some of his music, like this polonaise, can be militant and strong. Yet there is this profound beauty and joy that pervades his pieces. It's rich, complicated, and ultimately victorious. My dear, you have a similar fight in your life. It will take hard work, faith, and passion to overcome."

I sat down on the floor next to her as I wiped my hands on a piece of cloth. "*Hmm*. You may be right," I said, with a great, weary, but satisfied exhale.

She brought her hand under my chin and up, patting the side of my head, then gently bringing my head down to her shoulder. "You will be victorious, Lane. Without a doubt. My friend ML told me once, 'Great things are not done by impulse, little Evelyn, but by a series of small things brought together.' *That* is how your journey will work out, Lane."

I sat up, crossed my legs, and faced her. This was the moment I'd been looking for. "Aunt Evelyn. I think it's time you talked with me about my parents."

She slowly nodded. Then she sat up and crossed her legs, facing me head-on. "All right, Lane. Your parents did own a small bookstore in Rochester. But before that . . . they were intelligence agents in the war."

"I . . . What?"

"Yes. They were both very intelligent; languages had come easy for your mother. She was a rarity, as she had gone to college. Most women didn't. They were both recruited, and met on the job."

"Well, what does that mean? How many people know? What were they involved in? Who—"

"Hold on, hold on," she said, in calm voice. "I don't have a lot of answers for you. They didn't fill me in on all their doings—they weren't allowed to. I was aware of their work, and that made it all the more imperative that I help them as much as I could. But what I do know is this: They were your parents, first and foremost. They loved you so much, Lane."

"I do know I was loved. I remember that clearly," I said, with a smile. "But I've always struggled with feeling like I wasn't part of *their* story, a bigger story. And now that they had this other life on top of everything I did know, a life based on deception . . ." I shook my head pensively, unsure about this new knowledge. It reminded me of a time I walked across a rope bridge at the park. It was unstable, swaying in the breeze, and it was easy for a foot to slip through the holes.

"Lane, they were good people who loved you like nothing else in their lives. Their career was important even though it was also deceptive. Their life with you . . . That was real. That was true."

I let that sink in. I wanted to believe that. Of course I loved them. But . . . did I trust them?

CHAPTER 16

Love always brings difficulties, that is true,
but the good side of it is that it gives energy.

—ML

The next night I went out dancing with Ralph and his friends as planned, but after several partners, I escaped to the bar.

So, my parents were intelligence agents. Huh. That was a lot to process on top of everything going on as of late. My thoughts went to Finn and how he had an amazing ability to be there right when I needed him: in the subway, at Randall's Island. . . . Where was he now? Someone bumped my elbow at the bar, and I looked up with expectation. It was a new friend named Tucker. I'd danced with him a couple of times. I tried hard not to look disappointed; he was a great guy.

"Hey, Lane, you up for another dance?" He smiled shyly; he was very cute. His strawberry blond hair and blue eyes framed a ready smile. He was probably in his early thirties. I think he said he worked for one of the businesses on Wall Street. Something in finance. He was good-looking, had a stable job that didn't involve guns, nice guy, good dancer. But he wasn't Finn. But then again, Finn was very regrettably not around.

"Sounds great, Tucker." He took my hand, and we walked out onto the dance floor. It was nice. We talked about his job, he asked me about mine. He made me laugh. I started to relax and found him interesting. I was finally enjoying myself.

As I was singing along to the song, I said, "This is a great song,

Tucker." He smiled like he was hiding something. "What?" I asked, suspicious.

"Well . . ." He was *really* trying to hide a smile now.

I chuckled, knowing what he was going to say. "Spit it out."

"The song is 'The Way You Look Tonight.'" He started to crack up in earnest now.

"Aw, shoot. I always get it wrong."

"But, Lane, you weren't even *close*. 'To wave a book in sight'?"

"I can't help it. It's a chronic problem, apparently," I said, with a self-deprecating smile.

After that dance, a slower song came on, and he looked at me intently. "Do you . . . want to keep dancing?"

"As a matter of fact, I do," I said, and took a tighter hold on his hand as he pulled me closer. He smelled nice. I was thinking of a date gone bad a while ago and laughed to myself.

"What?" asked Tucker, smiling down at me.

"I was just thinking of a date that didn't go so well once," I said, wrinkling my nose.

"Really? What went wrong?"

I laughed again. "It was an awkward night all the way around, but the *pièce de résistance* was when he went to kiss me good night. . . . Well, he missed."

Tucker laughed. "He missed? What do you mean?"

"I mean, he leaned in slowly and kissed my right nostril." We both laughed, and I laid my head on his shoulder. The soft music was very inviting and pleasant.

"Lane?"

I looked up. "*Mmm hmm?*"

"Can I give it a try?" I looked into his blue eyes; his face had become serious and intent. I nodded.

He held me a little tighter. And slowly, slowly, he brought his lips down to mine. They were soft, firm. . . . It was a good kiss.

"Nice shootin'," I whispered as I smiled up at him. We kept dancing.

Tucker walked me home, holding my hand as we enjoyed the night, listening to the sounds of the city and chatting about the upcoming week. The lights sparkled, and the sizzle of a summer thunderstorm was in the air. We made plans to go to Central Park and have a picnic the following week.

After Tucker gave me a gentlemanly peck on the cheek, I walked into a sleeping home, dark except for the light in the living room and the small one in the kitchen left on for me. Aunt Evelyn had gone out to the Hamptons for the weekend to visit a friend. Mr. Kirkland was home, but he always retired early. He had his own apartment in the basement of the townhouse.

I patted Ripley, and he lay back down at the door to keep watch. I walked to the back of the house to the cozy sitting area by the kitchen with a large window overlooking the patio. I got a glass of water and plopped down in the cushy love seat, putting my feet up. A rumble of thunder softly rolled through the air. Goosebumps prickled my arms and neck as I reveled in that favorite sound. It was magical, dark, and . . . lonely. Damn it.

I liked being alone, but that was quite different from being lonely. A flash of lightning lit up the sky and was slowly followed by another low rumble in the distance. I set a couple of candles on the coffee table in front of the couch and retrieved my book. The rumbling thunder was slowly getting closer, louder.

There was a knock at the door.

Ripley barked just once, softly, and then made some whimpering noises that let me know he recognized the visitor. I ran to the door, the book still in my hand. I tugged it open without looking out the window, and my book dropped to the floor.

"Lane, can I come in?"

I opened the door wider. "Sure, Finn."

I took him back to where I'd been sitting in the nook just off the kitchen, asking, "Do you want something to drink? I have a nice bottle of wine I've been waiting to open."

"Sure, that sounds good." He took off his dark gray suit coat, laid it across the back of a kitchen chair, and loosened his dark red tie. I took down the bottle, got out the opener, and handed them to him. He started to uncork the wine while I got down two glasses. Another low rumble of thunder sent that special, unearthly static through the air.

I had no idea where to begin with Finn. What did you say to

someone who was such a mystery? You've shared secrets. But not a meal. You've shared deep emotions and fears. But not a coffee. You've kissed his neck and been held in his arms, but have not held his hand at the theater. You know so little. Then again . . . That loneliness and that feeling of constantly looking for something, someone. *Hmm.* Maybe I knew a lot.

I set down the glasses on the counter. Finn put down the bottle of wine, and we stood there looking at each other. Another rumble, a flash of light from behind us in the window. His hair was slightly damp from the first drops of rain. His eyes were dark and intense. He had rolled up his sleeves, revealing his muscular forearms. My dress from the evening of dancing matched the sky, a sleeveless dark blue with a deep, square neckline and ribbons crisscrossing down the back.

"Lane, I . . ."

I walked over to him and stopped about three feet away. I looked into his eyes, searching, looking for the real him. He did his own searching, deep into my eyes.

He walked over slowly, never taking his eyes from mine. He took the back of my head with his hand and slowly, slowly, then quickly the last inch, brought his lips down to mine. My heart leaped out of my chest, and my hands went up around his shoulders and then his neck as his arms brought me close.

We pulled slowly apart, our foreheads touching for just a moment. He gently took my head into his hands, looking deep into my eyes, searching every inch of my face, and said in a whisper, "Damn."

We went over to the couch, taking the glasses and wine with us. The light of the candles created dancing shadows on the golden walls, and the rain started to come down in earnest, showering and slapping against the windows and the patio. Ripley lumbered in to visit and said a loud *raaow* as he yawned.

"Hello, big fella, did I visit too late for you?" Ripley grinned up at Finn and then sank down beside us with a thump.

I took a deep drink of my cabernet and leaned back into the love seat, crossing my ankles on the coffee table.

I tipped my head and looked at him thoughtfully. "So, what have you been up to, Finn?"

He looked at me, hesitated a moment, then said, "I've tried to stay away, Lane. It's not a good idea to be with you. It . . . puts you in danger." There it was again—sometimes his accent was more Irish than English.

"Can I ask you something?" I said softly. He nodded, a wary look in his eye. "Are you English or Irish?" Which brought an abrupt laugh from Finn. It hit me again how his face could look so serious, yet when he laughed, he was even more handsome, as it lit up his entire countenance.

"I just said that my presence could put you in danger, and *that's* the question you have for me." He silently laughed as he took another drink. "Well," he continued, "I'm both, really. My mother is Irish, and my father is English. I was born in Ireland and lived around London since I was ten."

"When did you come to the States?"

"I wanted to be part of the up-and-coming police force in New York City that I'd heard about growing up. Scotland Yard wasn't too keen on my Irish background, so it made the decision easy. I moved here, started from the bottom, and worked my way up in the force." There was a lot more to his story, by the look on his face. I wondered about that errant brother of his, Sean, and if he had anything to do with Finn coming here. But tonight wasn't the time for going into it. Not yet.

I decided to cut to the chase. "Why now, Finn? Why tonight?"

"Here I thought we'd get to know each other better," he said, with a knowing smile.

I raised my eyebrows at him. *First things first.*

"Yes . . . tonight . . ." he said, contemplating his answer. "Let's just say that the job I'm working on is coming to a head. And there are critical pieces to the picture that I'm just flat-out missing. I think that *you* have those pieces, love."

"And that's why you came tonight. That's the reason."

"Oh, I think you know that's not the only reason, Lane," he said, in a deep whisper with his brow knit in consternation.

I decided to take Finn into my confidence and tentatively try out a couple of the new things I'd learned about my parents. "I talked with Aunt Evelyn about my parents, Finn. She said that they were working in intelligence during the war."

He'd been taking a drink of wine, but quickly put his glass down, giving this his full attention. "Intelligence? What exactly were they doing?"

"I really don't know. That was pretty much all she said, that when they had work to do, she would come and babysit me. So they weren't on vacation or hunting for books for their shop when they were traveling like I'd thought, but working for the government. The book shop was probably a great cover."

Finn was surprised, yet I could tell I was supplying some substance to his puzzle, as he started to nod like he was just beginning to get glimpses of the big picture. But before I could talk through my own reservations and questions, yet another knock came at the door. Ripley ran ahead of us, but once again started whimpering.

I turned to Finn. "Busy tonight, huh?"

"Grand Central," he muttered, in a slightly aggravated voice, as we went to the door. I had to admit I wasn't thrilled about being interrupted, either.

I reached the door, and it was Peter. I have to say, I answered with not a lot of hospitality. "What are you doing here, Pete? It's almost midnight!"

"Nice greeting, Lane, but this is—What is *he* doing here?" he exclaimed.

"Would you two stop with the pissing match already?" My vulgar language had the desired effect: They both shut up and calmed down. Pete looked disconcerted; Finn hid a smile behind a fake cough.

"That's better. You'd better come in out of the rain, Pete. Come on."

I decided it wasn't a good idea for Peter to see our romantic back room with the wine and candles, so I led him to the parlor and put on a couple of lights, and we all sat down.

"Lane," Peter began, "I wanted to notify you, Evelyn, and Kirkland before it hit the newspapers. A body has been found."

My eyes darted from Finn to Pete. "Who?"

"Danny Fazzalari."

"Oh, no," I said, thunderstruck. "He's been the main suspect."

"I know," said Pete. "And it was definitely a hit. Gunshot to the forehead and several in the chest. And, uh . . . he was found naked."

"Oh," I said, with my brows lifting in surprise. "So, a woman probably killed him."

Pete blushed heavily. Finn nodded and said, "Seems like a decent possibility. Most hit men don't bother to take a guy's clothes off."

My brain was working at a fast clip, putting things together, shifting them around in new ways. "So. Danny's been our main suspect. He's definitely the one behind me being pushed onto the tracks"—Finn clenched his jaw—"the bombing, and maybe even the break-in here at the townhouse and the purse-snatching. But someone didn't want him in the way or didn't like what he was doing. Someone obviously *more* powerful than Danny, who happened to be Uncle Louie's nephew." I whistled, wondering who would be that bold. And stupid.

I turned to Pete, looking him full in the face. "I've been talking with Aunt Evelyn about Tammany people, and we all know they have plenty of motive for all this. Have you looked into Daley Joseph and Donagan Connell?" Finn grew very still, I noticed.

Pete looked at me, aghast. "Lane, how do you even know those names? They're two of the most despicable lowlifes ever to come to New York City!"

I put my hands up in mock defense. "Trust me, it wasn't me. Aunt Evelyn talked with Ellie, and by Ellie I mean the first lady, Eleanor Roosevelt, and together they thought that the disappearance of those two was very conspicuous and that they fit the type of criminal who could be behind all this. Plus, after Fio described Daley Joseph, I realized I had seen him. So they're definitely on the scene now."

Pete stayed quiet, reflecting on what I'd said. I heard Finn mutter incredulously, "Good Lord . . . *Ellie*."

Then Peter said, "I haven't looked into them . . . *completely*," and he gave Finn a very enigmatic look. "But they have come up in conversation. There have been rumors of them around town. And having them anywhere nearby is never a good thing."

We couldn't come to any more conclusions, but I thanked Peter for coming by and told him we'd let Evelyn and Kirkland know. We ushered him to the door while he made it clear that he was not happy about the fact that he was leaving alone. Too bad; Finn and I had a few things to finish up.

We went back to the kitchen but didn't sit down. The romantic feel to the night had been usurped by the urgent and dangerous business at hand. We simultaneously took the last drink from our wineglasses, set the glasses down on the table, and turned to each other as if we'd rehearsed the motions.

I knew what was coming. I just knew it. Finn said, "Lane, I have to leave for a while." Yeah. That was it.

"I know, damn it," I said. I paused a few long seconds and looked at him squarely. I took stock of him and the situation. Then stalked slowly toward him.

"I know about your job, Finn," I purred. He looked at me, stunned and a little fearful, his eyes darting side to side. I decided to dive in; I felt reckless and rascally. *"Mm hm*. I figured you out. I know you have to go. . . . I know I'll have to trust you . . . even when I don't see you for a while . . . maybe a long while. . . ."

"Ah . . . you're making me nervous, Lane," he stuttered as I came inching toward him like a tiger, my eyes trying to devour him, taking in every detail of him: his almost-black hair, his dark eyes, fair skin, lean body, muscular arms and shoulders.

"Mmm hmm. I don't like the situation. But I know you. I *know* you," I said, a few inches from him, putting my hand on his chest, and suddenly, the realization of what I was saying dawned on me. I meant it; I *did* know this man, and I was becoming more certain of just how much I felt about him. As I searched those dark eyes, he looked more vulnerable than I'd ever seen him look. His handsome

face was open, honest. I wondered if he'd been that honest, that bare, before with anyone else.

This time he wasn't slow. He took the last step toward me in a flash and kissed me not gently, but with passion and urgency.

"I'm sorry, Lane. I had no idea it would be like this. *No idea . . .*"

"I know." I smiled, and he kissed me one last time. Gently. Sweetly.

Then he left.

I was wide awake, and I knew there was no chance of sleeping for quite a while. I decided to go up to Aunt Evelyn's studio. I put on a few of the lanterns and walked around the warm room, looking at the pieces she'd been working on. I ran my hand over one of my favorite frames, black with deep cutouts along the edges. It perfectly highlighted the subtle black lines within the piece and made it deeper, richer. I sat down and gazed at my Chopin painting. Perhaps it didn't look quite as bad as the dog's breakfast. It was growing on me. The colors spoke to me. I fell asleep on the floor beneath it, on a pile of tarps.

I was walking along a dark parking lot outside the city. A few street-lights glowed eerily here and there. I heard footsteps echoing off the pavement. I knew that they were coming after me. I tried to run and hide, willing my own steps to be silent. I finally found an impression in the wall of a building and pressed far back into the corner. I waited. Around the corner came the glint of a silver gun with a red scroll on the handle. A shadowy figure in a trench coat pointed it right at me. As the face came into the light, first it was the same demented lady in the bright green hat of my old recurring dreams grinning down at me, then she turned into Roxy, then it was Finn, then it was Danny. He smiled, he raised the gun toward me, and fired.

I woke up to Ripley licking my face. My heart was racing, and I hugged that dog like he was a furry life preserver. He just let me, sitting still, solid, secure, and reassuring shepherd that he was. I must have been making some amount of noise for him to come all the way up here, or maybe it was that sixth sense that dogs had that let them know when you were upset. He rested his head on my shoulder like he was reciprocating the hug, his ears tickling the side of my face. "Thanks, Rip." I heard a deep rumbling noise in his chest.

The dream left the lingering feeling that I was being hunted. But why? Maybe I was getting closer. Closer to something hiding in the dark.

CHAPTER 17

I am always doing what I cannot do yet,
in order to learn how to do it.

—ML

The next morning came all too quickly. If you could feel dark circles under your eyes, I could feel mine. Fiorello would be picking me up, but not coming in for breakfast, so it would be just Mr. Kirkland and me this morning. Aunt Evelyn would be returning from the Hamptons later in the day. I wore a summery, white, short-sleeved sweater over a brown linen skirt. Comfort was key today. I wore a cute little pair of sandals that were dark brown with white polka dots. They still had a heel, but not ungodly high. A woman has to make concessions.

I tapped down the stairs, my mind foggy as I tried to sort through the many emotions and factors of yesterday. I joined Mr. Kirkland in the kitchen. The pine table had a new yellow rose on it, and there were two place settings with steaming hot tea already there. That man was a godsend.

"Good morning, Mr. Kirkland. Ripley." Mr. Kirkland muttered with a gravelly voice something akin to a good morning as he stood at the sink slicing strawberries. Ripley was next to him, leaning up against his legs. I sat down at the table with a hefty sigh and started dumping sugar and cream into my tea.

Something about my sigh made Mr. Kirkland turn around, knife and strawberry still in hand. "How was your night last night, Lane? I thought I might have heard a knock at the door at some point." His gray hair touched the collar of his gray, short-sleeved shirt. His longer hair was very unfashionable for the time, but was so fitting for him. His large hands tenderly held the strawberry, but I could just as easily see them hoisting the lines on a huge sailing vessel. He wasn't handsome, but he was definitely attractive, with a tanned and deeply lined face and light blue eyes . . . and he was completely unaware of his craggy good looks, which made him that much more interesting.

"Well, I have some news," I began. "Peter came by to let us know that a body has been found. Danny Fazzalari."

His eyes took a keen interest, but his expression didn't alter a bit—serious, taking it all in, mulling it over. "And what does Finn have to say about that?"

I dropped my teaspoon into my cup, splashing the tea. "Pardon?"

"What does Finn have to say about that?" he repeated, intently looking at me.

"Why would Finn have something to say about that?"

He smiled. "Because, whenever there is bad news affecting you, my dear, Finn is sure to turn up." Then he turned back around to his sink.

Honestly, this family of mine is obnoxiously omniscient.

"Well, funny you should say that," I said, with a wry smile. "He did stop by last night."

Mr. Kirkland barked out a laugh. "Ha! Bet Peter loved that!"

"*Mm* . . . Sure did," I murmured. "Finn is tricky to figure out. He wasn't too happy about Danny being killed. By the way, it was execution style, bullet to the forehead and a few more in the chest. Danny's been our main suspect, and yet the style of the killing suggests someone quite powerful. Powerful enough not to be afraid of the repercussions of taking out Uncle Louie's nephew. Plus, he was found naked."

"*Ooh.* Lady killer."

I nodded.

Mr. Kirkland said provocatively, "*Hmm.* I wonder how Uncle Louie feels about that."

I hadn't thought of that. If Uncle Louie was behind it, if Danny had done something to provoke his powerful uncle, then he'd obviously be fine about it. However, and that was a big, fat *however*, if someone else did it, Uncle Louie would be a terrifying enemy. We both silently mulled over the possibilities.

Fiorello and I drove to work. I filled him in on Peter's news, but he had already heard. Neither of us talked about Finn. I was very tired, and the morning was a tough one to get through. I drank my share of coffee at the office. Lizzie wasn't in today, but Roxy was. She had the same dark circles under her eyes that I had. In fact, she looked so regular, so much more approachable, that I actually tried to strike up a commiseration conversation with her in the coffee room.

Even with dark circles, she looked cute. Her shiny blond hair was beautifully styled, and her curvy shape was highlighted by a tight white skirt and tighter light pink, short-sleeved sweater. Oh, what I would have given for cleavage like that.

"Hey, Roxy, how are you? I am *so* tired today. This coffee better pack a punch."

"Really, Lane? Do I need to come in and do your job for you again?" she said, with dripping sarcasm and contempt. *That* woke me up.

But I had learned from Val: Don't take the bait. Do *not* take the bait. I stifled a yawn. "Whatever you say, Roxy. See ya later."

Wasn't worth the fight.

For lunch, Valerie and I decided on a nearby park that had dozens of café tables. We bought sandwiches, bags of chips, and a couple of Coca-Colas, and found a table. It was warm, but not humid for a change. Val had on a light blue dress, her golden brown hair in a matching headband.

"So, I ran into Peter this morning on the way in to work, and he told me he delivered some news last night."

"He sure did," I said, unwrapping my sandwich and getting settled. "That's something, isn't it? I can't get over it. That slick, disturbing guy is gone."

"It *is* crazy. But I want to talk about something else," she said, quickly swiping away the darkness of Danny. "How was the walk home with Tucker last night?" Good heavens, Tucker seemed like a million years away.

"Why the blank face? It looked like you were really enjoying your time with him, Lane. And he's a really nice guy."

"Oh, we did have a good time together. He's great."

"Oh, no, not the *he's great* comment," she said. "What you really mean is, *he's a nice guy, but not for me.* Lane, I know you have a thing for Finn, and I have to admit you had some really romantic times with him, but I also know you've been so lonely lately. When you were dancing with Tucker, that lonely look was gone. You looked happy."

Her green eyes were so earnest. She always wanted the best for me. "I was happy, Val. We made plans for next week, a picnic in Central Park."

"You did?" she exclaimed, with great delight. "So, you really did like him?"

I hesitated, not sure why I wasn't being completely honest with her. Maybe I was questioning the same things about Finn and our relationship. But when I was with him . . . I made a mental note to send a message to Tucker that I couldn't meet.

"Did he kiss you again? I saw him kiss you on the dance floor." I blushed, giving myself away entirely.

"He did! And you liked it!" she practically yelled.

"*Sssshhhh!* Val!" *What have I done?* But just then, all thoughts of Tucker and even Finn, for that matter, went flitting out of my mind like a dry leaf in the wind.

"Hello, ladies, would you mind if I joined you for a moment?" asked a very deep, commanding voice.

He took my breath away. I coughed, then plastered a formal smile onto my face, and said, "Of course. Have a seat, Mr. Venetti."

In all his mobster glory—expensive, perfectly tailored, double-breasted black suit, black shirt and white tie, shiny black shoes, black fedora with a white feather in the band, and three bodyguards surrounding us—our guest for lunch was none other than Uncle Louie. He was in his late sixties with graying black hair slicked back, an old scar down the side of his face by his ear from someone's knife, deep brownish-black eyes, and enormous gray and black eyebrows that looked like tremendous caterpillars. If you've never been around a gangster, I mean a *real* gangster, you've never understood raw power.

But in my job with Fiorello, a job that never failed to educate me, I had also learned that although they were ruthless killers, many gangsters appreciated three things: money and therefore good business, courage, and respect. However, there were also those who were incapable of appreciating anything. Full of a vacant sort of evil that had raped and pillaged their humanity, they had an irrational, ravenous look in their eyes that meant they'd just as soon shoot you where you stood as listen. I took a good look at Mr. Venetti, assessing which camp he might lie in.

I didn't see the crazy camp. I took one more moment, then looked him straight in the eye and said with great care, "Mr. Venetti, I'm very sorry for the loss of your nephew."

He raised his massive eyebrows and pursed his lips as he looked deep into my eyes, doing his own assessment of my sincerity. One side of his mouth went up about a quarter of an inch, and I took that as a dramatically positive response.

"That, Lane, is what I've come to discuss. With Miss Pelton as well." He nodded a greeting to a very wide-eyed and shell-shocked Val. "His demise came to my attention last night, but he'd been missing for a few days. I heard that he had caused you some harm lately, is that true?"

I simply nodded.

"Once I heard what he was involved in, I disapproved greatly and told him so. But whoever is controlling the situation had more of a grip on him than I thought."

I asked, "You disapproved, sir?"

"I know what you're thinking, Lane. I have to admit that having Fiorello, and you, out of the way would achieve *some* ease for me. But the bottom line? I am a businessman," he said as he lit the end of his cigar. He gave three slow, intentional puffs, which gave me time to kick-start my heart again after his distressing words: *you, out of the way.* "And Danny's tactics that pinpointed you—and

I can only assume they were meant to try to persuade Fiorello to leave office—would not have improved business for me. Fiorello is bringing money back into the city. When the city has money, I have money. Despite the fact that he hates my slot machines, I have other things I can . . . focus on. Do you understand?"

"Oh, yes, I understand," I said, willing my voice not to shake. I cleared my throat. "So, if you don't mind my asking, why come to me directly with this?"

"I didn't always like my nephew's . . . eh, shall we say, style?" His three goons chuckled. "But he is—*was*—my nephew, and *no one* touches"—puff, puff of the cigar—"my family."

His eyes suddenly transformed into black, serpentine orbs. I rubbed the goose bumps that had popped out on my arms. I had no doubt he meant it, through and through. "Secondly, I don't need the police attention, so I wanted to notify someone that neither I nor my organization is responsible for this. Lastly, I want your boss and his policemen to help figure out who did this. I think we would all benefit from finding out the ones in control here."

He was powerful, all right. He wore a strong cologne, and every inch of him was covered in expensive fabrics made by top-notch designers. But it was more than that. His essence radiated his ruthlessness. Especially his face; his olive, Italian skin was etched with the lines of a sixty-five-year-old who had built his empire on the broken lives of others.

Yet . . . and yet . . . there was something that was magnetic about him. There was this weird kind of respect I had for him. I was fighting a battle within myself, between loathing him and liking him. *How is that possible?* Part of me hated him, and the other part hated myself for liking him.

"All right, Mr. Venetti, I will relay the message to Mr. LaGuardia." He stood up and nodded to his guys, gesturing that he was ready to go.

"Thank you, Lane and Miss Pelton, for your time," he said as he rose and tipped his hat to us.

"Ah, Mr. Venetti?" I asked, on a sudden hunch.

"Yes?" He turned back to us, surprised.

"Do you know of a Donagan Connell and Daley Joseph?"

"No. No, I don't, Lane." *Puff, puff.* "Good day." He casually sauntered away, his hand elegantly placed in the pocket of his suit coat, the three bodyguards walking after him.

Valerie and I paused for a long time, watching them walk away down the park path. They were such an incongruous sight amid all the cheery lunchers in the park. I looked at Valerie. She looked at me. A long, awkward pause ensued.

"Uh . . . chip?" she asked, offering me a potato chip.

I cracked up. "Yeah, how exactly do you follow *that?*" She finally looked more like herself and less like a trapped animal. We both took a tentative bite of our sandwiches and tried to digest that outrageous conversation.

"One thing for sure," said Val, "beyond a doubt, he knows Donagan Connell *and* Daley Joseph."

Chapter 18

Your profession is not what brings home your
weekly paycheck, your profession is what you're
put here on earth to do, with such passion and such
intensity that it becomes spiritual in calling.

—ML

As the summer progressed, I needed to buy a few new clothes with some of my money I had scrimped and saved. Of course, over the past several years, money was a lot tighter than it used to be. But I could afford a couple of new things here and there. We all got really good at being resourceful. I think artists are exceptional at this. Like Aunt Evelyn.

Sugar was at a premium, so Mr. Kirkland had been raising honeybees on our roof. He grew all sorts of vegetables and herbs, too. He harvested so much honey and so many vegetables, we were able to give out quite a bit through the neighborhood. For women, stockings were getting more and more rare. We'd even get hand-me-downs and re-darn the seams up the back to make them fit us. Sometimes in the summer, we would put pancake makeup on our legs and draw narrow lines up our calves to make it look like stockings.

The Depression had hit the city hard enough, but the rural and small towns of America were hit the hardest. That was another reason I loved my job. It felt satisfying to be able to help people in a concrete way, something that was worthwhile and purposeful.

Finn was true to his word; it was like he'd dropped off the face of the earth. I'd seen Tucker at a few dances over the last week. He didn't seem put out at my note canceling our trip to the park, but he didn't ask me to dance, either. One day I ran into him when I was doing some shopping on my lunch break.

"Hi, Tucker!" I said, honestly happy to see his easy smile. "How have you been?"

"Great, Lane, good to see you." And it looked like he meant it. "How's your job been going?"

I remembered the gist of my nice enough but abrupt note to him and felt a guilty blush creep into my face. "It's been crazy as usual." Which it definitely was. "But good; I love it." And suddenly, I was dead tired. My arms and legs felt like a ton of bricks, and I yawned.

He laughed. "I guess it *is* crazy! You know, you might not have time for a picnic, but would you want to go to the Met for a glass of wine at the rooftop gardens?"

Anywhere but the Met; it reminded me too much of Finn. "Well, I'd like that. What would you think about trying The Boathouse? They just put in a small outdoor café by the rentals. Want to go after work?"

"Sure. That sounds great. How about I meet you in the lobby at your office at about six?"

"Six is perfect. See you then," I said, and we both went our separate ways.

He met me at city hall, and we made our way uptown, making small talk that was cheering and comfortable. He really was easy to be around. We talked about the new Hollywood musical *Show Boat* and the latest songs by Bing Crosby, Billie Holiday, and Fred Astaire.

We got up to 79th and Fifth Avenue and walked into Central Park by Cedar Hill. Everything was verdant and smelled so good. We started meandering along on the paths that led to The Boathouse. We passed through the quaint little Glade Arch and then saw several ducks at the duck pond. Then The Boathouse came into view. It was a favorite place for New Yorkers to come and enjoy the pond and the sight of the rowers rowing their boats languidly along. The café was outside just off the rental area, and we sat down on the tall stools.

I'm not sure why people find rowing romantic. Rowing is hard and frustrating. I couldn't row a boat in a straight line to save my life. I started to tell Tucker some of my thoughts on the matter.

". . . to save my life. Then you're stuck on a pond with lots of other onlookers. There's no room for a private, cozy chat. There's the constant danger of falling out of the boat, then the matter of possibly knocking the other boaters with your oar. . . ." At this point, he was cracking up.

"I see you've given this some thorough thought, Lane."

"Yes, yes I have." I took another sip of wine. The cold sauvignon blanc tasting of icy grapefruit was delicious.

"And what are your thoughts about the gondoliers who sing to you?" he asked, with a mischievous look.

"I'm not sure I get the hats." He laughed harder.

"And the singing. Why is a total stranger singing to you while holding a really long pole in an impossibly narrow boat something that makes you want to fall in love?"

We were wiping tears away from our eyes. "Well, Lane? You've made an excellent case, and now we are going to test that case if it kills us. Let's go. Get up!"

"What?"

"You heard me. We are getting a boat." He took me by the hand and practically dragged me over to the boat rental shack.

"Aw, do we have to?" I whined, sounding like a sulky teenager.

"We sure do," he said, with a glint in his eye and a great big smile.

My dark pink dress with pleated skirt and matching little hat wasn't the typical sailing outfit, but I was game for just about anything. He was first into our questionable vessel. I didn't like the look of the rocking he was causing. I stepped in with the help of the rental guy. The boat rocked violently with my step, and I sputtered, "Whoa!" as I got my balance and sat down too quickly, smacking my butt hard on the bench.

Tucker was smiling with a *See? Isn't this fun?* look on his face. He rolled up the sleeves of his shirt and took the oars. His strong shoulders had no problem with the oars. I hated oars. They never did what I wanted: They slip, they fight you, one little tiny inch off and you're going cockeyed, *grumble, grumble, grumble.*

We got out to the middle of the pond and then stopped, bobbing in the green water. A couple of swans were swimming along as gracefully as only swans can do. You could hear chatting and laughing from the other boaters floating across the water. Only one gondola was out, and the gondolier was making his way closer to us. I could hear him singing an Italian love song.

"And why are their pants so short?" I asked. Tucker chuckled.

"I kind of like it out here after all. There's a little breeze, totally different surroundings for a change. You can hear the wind rustling the leaves in the trees. It's nice," he said, with a contented smile.

I smiled back. It *was* nice.

"Are you sure it's not romantic, Lane?" He leaned closer to me, looking intently into my eyes. He whispered, "I want to tell you something, come closer."

I leaned closer to him, trying hard not to make the boat rock too much. "Yeah?" I whispered back.

"Little closer." I edged closer and leaned in until I was a few inches from his face.

"The dark circles are gone from your eyes, Lane. It's good to hear you laugh. Have you been laughing enough lately?" he asked, with a genuine look of concern on his furrowed brow. His strawberry blond hair took on red highlights in the late, golden sunshine. I could just start to see the blond stubble on his cheeks, which made his face look even nicer.

His statement and question surprised me. I softly said, "I'm not sure. I guess it's been a while." Which made me a little sad; I love to laugh.

"You need to laugh more, Lane. You need to be happy more. Not for other people, just for you," he said, still talking softly. I looked into his blue eyes and paused, taking in what he had said. He leaned in the last few inches and kissed me gently. His lips were warm and soft.

He leaned back, smiling just a little. "I've wanted to do that again for a while."

And that's when one of the oars slipped and sank into the murky green water. I hated oars.

* * *

After going in circles a few times and trying to use our hands to propel us in a forward direction, laughing more and more, we were able to flag down the gondolier and let him know that we needed another oar. He brought us one, and we made our way back to shore.

We walked slowly back to my house. It was dusk and once again my favorite time in the city. He took my hand, and I thought of our last date. And how that had ended . . . with Finn.

We were both lost in our own thoughts, neither speaking. Tucker suddenly pulled me aside a couple of blocks before my house, right by my favorite flower stand.

"I'm not ending it like last time," he said, then took my face in his hands and gave me a surprising kiss that was not-as-gentlemanly as the last time. "Let's get together again soon, Lane. Maybe a gondola ride next?" he said, with his open smile.

After I got my breath back, I said, "Thanks, Tucker. It was fun. It was good to laugh." He nodded, still smiling, but with his mouth closed. He put his hands in his pockets and turned 180 degrees to walk in the opposite direction.

A large bunch of summery roses, bright yellow tipped in fiery orange, caught my eye. I bought them, then slowly walked the last couple of blocks home, letting my thoughts run through the afternoon. I liked being with Tucker. I ran down the list of his virtues: He was a nice guy, he had a stable job, he was a good kisser, he was around. . . . But still . . .

I turned down 80th, which was all townhouses, no restaurants or grocery stores, and therefore darker than the avenues. A cat meowed from the top step of a townhouse on my side of the street. It broke my deep thoughts, and I looked up to see a large man with a black suit, white shirt, and black bow tie coming straight toward me. What made my heart stop was when I got a good look at his large, repulsive face. Daley Joseph.

CHAPTER 19

As we advance in life it becomes more and more
difficult, but in fighting the difficulties the
inmost strength of the heart is developed.

—ML

When he saw the recognition dawn on my face, he gurgled a grunt
of amusement. He was bearing down on me like a freight train, and
with one meaty hand, he grabbed my throat, pushing me against a
wall. My flowers dropped to the sidewalk. I tried to scream, but no
air would escape my pained throat. My feet were practically lifting
off the ground. I tried to kick out, but it was equal to a child kicking
out at a heavyweight champ.

"Joseph, do you really think that will help our cause?" drawled a
very familiar and hoped-for voice.

But my mind reeled, as he didn't say what I wanted him to say
and didn't goddamn do what I needed him to do! The hand at my
throat loosened suddenly and let me drop to the ground. My knee
hit the pavement where my roses lay crushed and falling apart. I
couldn't speak; my throat felt like I had eaten hot coals, and I was
gasping, with my hands around my neck. I had never felt fear and
rage like I felt at that moment.

I looked up at Finn, searching his face for anything remotely like
what I'd felt from him the last time we saw each other. I saw something, a flicker, then a flat wall of emptiness.

"Mr. Joseph, shall we leave her your message? We may be getting some unwanted attention soon," said Finn.

"True, my friend, true," Daley grunted. The *my friend* almost made me vomit. The revulsion this man brought out in me was primal. I knew the game, I knew the choices, but my God . . .

Gritting my teeth in hatred, filled with anger and determination not to be ruled by the terror of this travesty of a man, I savagely rasped, "What's your *fucking* message?"

"Huh," he grunted. "I like her moxie." A muscle twitched in Finn's jaw. "Well, sweetheart, tell Fiorello the big one is coming. Unless he gives up his office, he'll have the blood of thousands of New Yorkers on his hands. Oh, and one more thing. If he doesn't give up his office by tomorrow morning, we'll throw in a little press incentive by happening to mention that little bomb blast at Randall's Island that you so neatly swept under the rug. Got it?"

"Got it," I rasped through my gritted teeth, getting to my feet, clenching my fists. I was careful not to look at Finn again.

"Come on, we need to get going," said Finn.

Mr. Joseph gave me one last grin and tucked an old cigar into his mouth, and then they strode leisurely away, turning down Lexington. Like they hadn't a care in the world.

I walked in the other direction; my house was only about ten houses away. It felt like ten miles. The searing rage was melting, the nausea rising. I threw up in the street a couple of houses away, which made my throat feel like it was on fire again.

I was just about to the bottom of my steps when I heard, "Hey, Lane! There you are! Peter and I have been looking . . ." Her sentence died on her lips as Peter and Valerie came up to me. My legs gave out, and Peter caught me as I started to slump.

"Jesus, Lane, what happened?" said Peter.

Val took over, hands on her hips. "Pick her up, Pete. Aunt Evelyn will know what to do. Let's move it!" I loved Sergeant Val right then. I had no more to offer, and I needed someone to take charge for a while.

He muttered as he picked me up, "Jesus, every time I come over here, some new drama. I bet Finn's inside, too. And Roarke. Maybe even *Eleanor*."

At the mention of Finn's name, my heart tightened and a lump formed in my throat, threatening tears, but they didn't overflow.

When Val threw the door open, I was shocked to see that Pete's mutterings had been pretty accurate. Fiorello, Roarke, Aunt Evelyn, and Mr. Kirkland were sitting in our front room. They had been talking, but as they turned to greet us, their pleasant chatter turned dead quiet.

Aunt Evelyn was on her feet in an instant. "Lane, are you all right?" I nodded miserably, and thank God, Val was still in charge. Hands still on hips, she started dictating orders and pointing at everyone.

"Pete, take her to the little couch by the kitchen. Mr. Kirkland? I think Lane could use some tea, heavy on the honey. I think her throat has been injured. Aunt Evelyn, bring us some comfortable clothes for her, please. Fio, stop flailing your arms and get Roarke to come into the kitchen. We all need to talk once we take care of Lane."

I actually started to smile to myself. I heard several obedient *yes, ma'ams*, which amused me, as Val was all of twenty-three years, like me. I poked Pete in the chest and pointed to the bathroom instead of the couch.

Everyone quickly and obediently followed orders. I changed clothes and freshened up. We all regrouped in the kitchen. Some at the pine table, a couple on the love seat, and the others on stools at the kitchen counter.

Mr. Kirkland spoke up first after I got a few giant swigs of tea down. "How are you feeling, Lane? Can you tell us what happened?"

My throat felt much better already. I was still pretty raspy, but it wasn't on fire anymore. I relayed what had happened to my stunned audience, ending with the audacious threat that Mr. Joseph had sent to Fio. After a moment, everyone started locking eyes with everyone else. Mr. Kirkland looked at Aunt Evelyn. Peter looked at Val. Fio looked at Roarke. I rubbed my aching forehead.

Val said quietly, "So, Finn was there with Daley Joseph? And he didn't help you?"

Peter's eyes darted to Fiorello. "See? I knew it! He's been bad before, he's bad now. I tried to tell you, Mr. LaGuardia." His fists were clenching and opening, clenching and opening.

I stayed quiet. I thought about saying things like, *But he did stop him from choking me. . . . He had this look on his face for one fleeting second. . . . I know it looks bad. . . .* But it all sounded stupid and like the things an insipid heroine says in a cheap melodrama. The fact remained, I didn't *exactly* know what Finn's involvement was, and only time would tell.

I squeaked, "Can I ask you something?" They all nodded. "What were you meeting about when we came in?"

Mr. Kirkland and Aunt Evelyn looked at each other and raised their eyebrows as one. Roarke said, "Yep, time to get all our cards on the table, folks." He was smiling his good old, closed-lipped smile with the dimples showing.

Aunt Evelyn took up the line of conversation. "Well, Kirk and I have been talking about the case." I smirked at Fio and mouthed, *See? Case.* He smirked back and shook his head. I saw him sigh with relief. I felt the same way. It slowly felt like this horrifying night was getting back to normal.

"And we've been thinking about why Lane has been targeted, besides the link to Fio. Such as being pushed onto the tracks, but also the mugging in the subway a little while later, as well as the theft at the house."

"*Attempted* mugging," I rasped. Roarke laughed. Valerie closed her eyes and shook her head.

"And we came up with a theory that we wanted to throw out to you," said Fio. "Roarke, can you fill her in?"

Roarke said, "Sure. I got back to Detroit this week, Lane. It was a last-minute visit, but I got the chance to ask around some more at the casinos. I finally found an older guy who was a blackjack dealer back when all that happened to you and your family when you were ten—in 1923.

"He remembers a woman who started to hang out with the gangsters. Remembers her because of a few things. One, she was hanging out with this certain gangster who was close with the formidable Uncle Louie, and when Uncle Louie came to town, one took notice. Two, she had long, light blond hair and a couple of other great . . . ah, eh . . . assets. And three"—he looked pointedly at me—"she had a kid, a young girl. She would sometimes bring the poor thing to the casinos while she hung out with the guys. They had the waitresses look after her."

"My God," Val breathed. "Roxy." Roarke nodded.

He went on, "That's what I'm thinking. And if Uncle Louie was around, then it could have very neatly happened that Danny was around. Maybe when Roxy was older, like seventeen, they took a liking to each other, and he brought her out here to New York City."

I asked, "So, why would that make her target me? It seems like there have been so many events, yet there could be a dozen reasons they all happened, and one of those reasons could simply be coincidence."

Aunt Evelyn broke in, "That's where Mr. Kirkland and I come in with our hypothesis." We all looked at them.

"I have been a collector of art. And our family, including Matthew and Charlotte, Lane's parents, has been known for owning valuable works of art and books, of course, for their shop. We are wondering if Roxy and Danny got wind of this and were hunting for treasure. Lane has her notebook that she carries with her from her parents. Perhaps they were trying to get at that for clues about anything valuable here."

Peter, in true policeman form, asked, "So, do you have many valuables here that could continue to make you a target? And Lane, do you still carry your notebook with you?"

I shook my head and replied, "No, after I almost lost my purse in the subway and in that mugging, I've kept it here. I can't replace it."

Aunt Evelyn replied, "And I can't think of anything of value that would stand out to others, things that could be stolen and sold easily. There *are* valuables, but things that are important to me and, like I said, difficult to sell to make an easy buck."

Roarke spoke up. "Lane, if you don't mind me asking, whatever happened to your parents' property and home furnishings after they died? You surely don't have them all here."

Aunt Evelyn piped in. "Well, Lane was so young when the accident happened, we didn't think it would be a good idea to empty out her childhood home back then. There is a couple that lives next door, and they've maintained it over the years. Most of the bookstore stock was moved to the house. We sent a truckload of books to local libraries, but the special ones were taken to the house in Rochester. Mr. Kirkland goes back every now and then to check on things."

"You do?" I blurted out. "I didn't know that."

Mr. Kirkland shuffled bashfully and said, "Yep."

Fiorello had been silently taking it all in with his hands twined together, working his fingers as his mind worked on the puzzle pieces. "So let me get this straight," he said, after he cleared his throat. "Roxy has a shared past with Lane from Rochester. She may have found out about and decided to get her hands on the valuables left behind from Lane's parents, which would explain the burglary and purse-snatching. It still doesn't explain why they would want to do her harm, like the push into the subway. Perhaps she also has a personal motive. Then, there seems to be a political motive somewhere in here. There's the Randall's Island incident, but we still don't know what that was supposed to achieve outside of just creating mayhem. Maybe forcing my resignation or something. In addition to that, we have tonight's developments. A clear connection with Daley Joseph, and he, for certain, has made it clear that he'd like to get me out of office."

The room gave a collective inhale of breath as we prepared to face what that might mean. "Daley Joseph and presumably his partner, Donagan, came out with a direct threat to me and my office. We will talk about Finn's involvement later, but for now, we need to think through the threat and all that implies. First, is this threat a viable one?"

Peter and Roarke both nodded their heads with an air of absolute conviction. Peter said, "Daley Joseph is more than capable of doing the harm. I'm wondering what exactly he has in mind for that kind of attack and what kind of manpower and finances would be needed to pull it off. And what about the mob? Have we discounted their involvement?"

Valerie and I involuntarily looked at each other and then, as one, at Fio. After that lunch with the unexpected meeting with Uncle Louie, we had gone together to tell Fio about it. But after that, we hadn't talked about it with anyone.

Pete, Roarke, and Aunt Evelyn all said an accusatory, "What?"

Fiorello took ownership of that one and said, "Well, right after Danny was killed, Val and Lane had a surprise visit at lunch from . . ." He must have belatedly realized how everyone was going to react, because he winced. "Louie Venetti." The whole room erupted.

"Uncle Louie!"

"You had *lunch* with Uncle Louie?"

"Oh, my God, you've got to be kidding me."

Roarke just laughed. Pete gave a disparaging look to Val as he shifted a few inches away from her, garnering a look of bewilderment from her. I looked over at Fio and said with my eyes, *Do something!*

Obligingly, he said, "In all fairness to Lane and Val, I asked them not to share that with anyone. Even the police force, Peter. If word started getting around that the mayor's aide had a meeting with Venetti, it would have caused a press frenzy and all sorts of difficult things to maneuver." He then filled them in on what Uncle Louie had said that day.

"If we can trust what he said, I believe they're not part of this. At least, not at the moment. And speaking of tricky things to maneuver . . . Roarke, do you have any suggestions on what to do about Daley's threat of the press scandal he'll release tomorrow regarding the attempted bombing at Randall's Island?"

"*Hmmm* . . . yes, I'm sure we can do a late run tonight. I'll call the boss. He loves a good late night story from Hizzoner." I smiled to myself at Fio's nickname from the press and city officials. Tucker continued, "I think we should keep it low-key and cool. Danny did a schlock job of it. It wouldn't have done the kind of damage that it seems Daley Joseph is talking about, so why'd he do it? Anyway, I'll put some thought to it. And I'm sure you'll want to make your own statement, so I'll get that from you when we're done here, Mr. LaGuardia."

"Thank you, Roarke. And now, what about my leaving the office of mayor?"

"No," I said, simply but indignantly.

"Oh, Fio, don't be ridiculous!" exclaimed Aunt Evelyn, amid a general violent murmuring of objection. He smiled his LaGuardia smile that reminded me of Lou Costello, clearly pleased.

"Plus," said Roarke, "I think he'll move on whatever he has planned regardless. I have a buddy who was unlucky enough to run into both Mr. Daley and his alter ego, Mr. Joseph, on a couple of occasions. Lane, from what you've described to me, the day you first saw him on the subway platform, you saw Daley. He's a disgusting slob, wears stained, rumpled clothing. Tonight you saw Joseph. Just as deplorable, but thoroughly clean, always a white shirt and black suit. Both are criminally insane personalities, but where Joseph was able to control himself when Finn talked to him and he let you go, Daley wouldn't have. He wouldn't have cared about the consequences. He's unpredictable and lacks control, the animal-torturing kind of guy," he said, with a curl of derision to his lip. "He takes pure pleasure in harming others. It will be *his* personality that will do the destruction; Joseph handles the business. And whatever he has planned, Daley will be salivating over the possible mayhem it will cause. There is no way on God's green earth that he will stop what they've put into motion. So, Fiorello, it's pointless to resign."

A pause stretched out as we all considered what tomorrow would hold.

"Damn it, Mr. LaGuardia!" Peter suddenly exclaimed. All our heads snapped to look at him. "Why didn't you listen to what I said about Finn months ago? He cannot be trusted! Look what could have happened to Lane tonight! He did nothing!" said Peter, clenching his fists as he launched to his feet.

"Peter, sit down," said Fio kindly, but with authority that wasn't about to be pushed around or disrespected. "I did give what you said thorough consideration. But there are elements to this that you know nothing about. And you'll have to trust me, that I've made my decisions with great care."

"I'm sorry, Mr. LaGuardia. It's just that the guy is always in the wrong place at the wrong time, and something about him just puts me on edge." He sat down and scooted closer to Val, but I could tell she was still stung by his quickness to remove himself from her side at the first glimpse of conflict.

"Lane." Fio looked over to me. "What was your take on what happened tonight, as far as Finn is concerned?"

"Well, there's no question that he could have stopped him from hurting me at all," I said, trying hard to stay focused on the business at hand versus how it had *really* affected me. "But he also didn't egg him on, he certainly didn't look pleased, and it was Finn's words that urged Joseph to let me go." Aunt Evelyn shivered. "I didn't talk to Finn directly at all. I was so angry at the whole thing."

Fio asked, "Angry? Not scared?"

"Oh, plenty scared. Never so scared in my life. Daley Joseph is revolting. And evil. I can't even begin to describe what he's like in person. I don't know what Finn is doing, exactly, and I guess only time will tell what's happening with him."

"That's it?" said Peter, back to his obstinate tone of voice. "That's it? You're just going to shrug your shoulders and pretend that Finn is fine, just happened to be there, doesn't do a damn thing to help, and you're all just *fine* with that?"

Mr. Kirkland said in his gruff voice, "Now, Pete, you'd better start getting yourself under better control, son." Peter was way out of line.

"I can't stand it anymore. I can't be part of this. You're all being played. It's not Danny and Roxy that you have to worry about, it's Finn! Finn Brodie! I just . . . I just can't do it." He turned to Valerie. "I'm sorry, Val. I'll see you some other time." With that, he took up his things and left.

Val was looking crestfallen and yet more than a little angry. She was in no mood to take charge anymore, so Aunt Evelyn did. "All right then, everyone. Roarke, you work on something to handle the press tomorrow concerning the Randall's Island issue. Also, try to ask around about people Daley Joseph would work with to handle this threat. Mr. Kirkland and I will talk more about the valuables in our family and see if we can figure out any leads in that vein. Fio, prepare yourself for a press onslaught and think about how to handle Daley demanding your resignation. Valerie, I think you should stay the night. Lane might need some extra help tonight, and it will be good for you both to be together. Now, it's late, and I think we should all be heading toward our tasks and to bed."

I smiled wearily. I was so tired. But I spoke up with a thought I had. "Actually, I have one more thing to bring up."

Roarke stopped in his tracks as he was heading to put his coffee cup in the sink. Evelyn said, "Oh, dear."

"It's not that bad! Sheesh. It's just something that keeps piquing my curiosity. When Uncle Louie, eh, dropped by to see Val and me"—I smiled sheepishly—"on a whim, I asked him if he knew Daley Joseph and Donagan Connell. He said no, but Val and I are certain that he was prevaricating. Any thoughts on that? Anything come to mind about a connection between the gangsters and Daley's crew, maybe back when Jimmy was mayor?"

Roarke and Fio both shook their heads as they rolled around the possibilities in their minds. "Not that I can think of," said Fio. "But I think that would indeed be something to look into. Roarke? Keep that in mind while you're digging around."

"Sure thing, Mr. LaGuardia."

Everyone left, and I slowly made my way upstairs with Val's supportive arm around my waist, another hot tea, and a dutiful Ripley, who had been sent up with us, apparently to give his own vote of confidence. I had to admit, I did feel ten times safer with his bigger-than-life presence by my side.

Val and I got ready for bed, and despite the relative warmth of the night, it felt so good to cozy down into the thick covers of the bed. We were quiet, staring at the reflections of the city lights on the ceiling, listening to the hum of the nighttime noises.

"How's your throat, Lane? Does it hurt to talk?" asked Val.

"It's much better, but I can tell there'll be bruises tomorrow. I may need your help with makeup. But the tea and honey are making my throat feel fine."

"Are you okay?" she asked, in a deeper, quieter voice. I knew she meant Finn.

"*Hmmm.* Still thinking about that one. I was shocked to see him with Daley. And . . . he's come to the rescue so often, right at the exact moment I needed him. But not this time, not really. After Joseph let go of me, I kept blinking, over and over, trying to make the image I was seeing make sense. Then I saw something in Finn's eyes. Just . . . this flicker. And I didn't bring it up with the others because it sounds naïve, but I'm sure I saw this flash of the real him. But then it went away and there was just a frightening, blank look in his eyes. But that flicker was enough."

"Peter really hates him. He's never said why, just that he thinks we shouldn't trust him."

"Yeah, he made that pretty clear tonight." I paused for a while. "Val? Are *you* all right?"

"As you said, still thinking about that one," she said, in an attempt at humor, but I could hear the disappointment in her voice. "Pete's look was so accusatory when he found out about Uncle Louie. I mean, you're not even dating Roarke, and he just stayed quiet until Fio told the rest of the story."

"Well, actually, Roarke wasn't exactly quiet. He laughed," I said, laughing out the word.

"Yeah. It was such a stunning moment for everyone. Can't you just imagine all the images going through their minds? The two of us sitting with Uncle Louie, for crying out loud, having a quaint, civilized *chat*."

"I know. What we must have looked like! You and I, our eyes had to be big as saucers when he walked up. And his bodyguards!"

"They were something, weren't they? Big as doors. Like being surrounded by trees with legs."

"With suits on," I gurgled as the laughter overtook us. It felt such a relief to laugh. The stress and confusion of the day started to release their tight grip. After we stopped laughing and took a couple of deep breaths, I said, "I had a sort of *date* with Tucker today."

"What?" she exclaimed, sounding excited. "How'd that happen? How'd it go?"

I told her all about it. Running into him, the walk through the park, the wine, laughing about the rowboats and gondolas. I even told her about the kiss. I also told her about his comment about how I needed to laugh more. Did I? I couldn't quite shake that thought.

"Do you like being with Tucker, Lane?" she asked.

"Yeah. Yeah, I do. He's easy to be with, fun, we laugh together. . . ."

"Buuut . . ." she said, prompting me to go on with what I wasn't saying.

"There's just something about Finn, Val. I feel . . . *alive* with him. It's powerful." I turned to her to see a wide smirk through the blue moonlight in the dark room. I returned her look with a withering, droll look of my own. "And it's not just because I'm lusting after him with everything I've got." She laughed. "I don't know. It's so complicated; I guess I'll just have to wait and see how things play out." I yawned.

"Yeah. Because you're *so* good at waiting."

"Shut up, Val."

"Night, Lane," she chuckled.

"Night, Val."

CHAPTER 20

Let us keep courage . . . and make
distinction between good and evil.

—ML

The next morning, we were up early. My neck was just a little
bruised, not too bad, considering. So after she helped me with some
cover-up makeup, Val ran home to change, and we met up back at
the office. We made sure we got there almost an hour before the
usual time. We had no idea what was going to happen; we hadn't
heard what Fio and Roarke had planned. And I could only imagine
what Daley Joseph had up his sleeve.

Turns out, I underestimated Joseph, even in my imagination.
However, I also underestimated the savvy and cunning public rela-
tions that Fio and Roarke exhibited.

The press conferences were brilliant. A calm, cool, and collected
Mayor LaGuardia answered every single reporter's question with
the absolute truth. Fio had released a late night statement to the
press; they were always ready for him to give them a good story.
The front pages of two major newspapers had accurate articles. Two
other minor newspapers were pretty inflammatory. After the fabulous and calm press conferences, they notified the mayor's office
that they'd be printing retractions the next day.

We at least knew which papers Daley might have influence over,
and we could follow up some clues along those lines. The negative
point being that he followed through on this first threat with the
press, which further strengthened the validity of the big threat involving thousands of New Yorkers.

In the late morning, I decided to go for a short walk. My throat was still sore, and I needed time to think and be by myself. I went outside, and since it wasn't lunchtime yet, the city was lively, but not hectic with the hustle and bustle of the lunch hours. I thoroughly enjoyed the peace as I walked slowly along the paved paths across from city hall. I bought a hot tea from a vendor and sipped it, letting it soothe my throat.

Of course, my thoughts were back with Finn. I didn't know *exactly* what he was doing, and I had to admit that it was frightening to see him look so blank. But the fact remained, I still trusted Finn. Right now, I would do anything to talk to . . .

And he was there.

"My God, Finn, how do you do that?" I said softly. He was standing a few feet away under an expansive sycamore. Worry was etched into his brow. And something else. Something making his jaw clench. I walked over to him.

"Are you okay, Lane? It took everything I had not to come to your house last night. But I knew everyone would be on alert, and I didn't want to draw more attention to you if I was followed."

There it was. That same look that had just barely flashed in his eyes last night. The look that let me know what was going on. I nodded slowly. "I'm all right, Finn."

"Lane, I . . . I didn't know he had that planned. He didn't tell me. But if I'd jumped in, he would have known my feelings for you, and that would have been even more deadly."

"I know, Finn," I said earnestly. I saw the battle in his eyes and written in turmoil all over his face.

"Lane, I will never—ever—let him touch you again." Then I recognized the emotion I was seeing in his eyes. Absolute fury.

"I know that, too."

"I wish we were back on your couch, Lane."

"Me, too."

He let out a breath, his clenching shoulders and jaw relaxing just a bit. "I have to go," he said, after he looked at me a few moments longer.

"See you soon?" I asked, smiling a little.

"Yes. You will," he said, with grim determination. He started to walk toward me, like any other stranger would, mastering his demeanor, nonchalantly looking past me. I did the same, but just as we passed each other, he brushed my side and softly pressed my hand.

The following day in the late afternoon, a slightly worse-for-wear but beaming Roarke came into the office, dimples showing and everything. "Hey, Roarke! Nice going on the press coverage and conference. Fio loved the photos. As always." I beamed right back at him.

"Thanks! It was fun," he said, with a devilish grin.

"What do you make of the other papers and Daley's connection with them?" I asked. "Does that bring anything to mind, any leads?"

"Actually, yes, it does. And that's one of my reasons for dropping by. Feel like doing some sleuthing, Lane?" he asked, eyes already glossing over at the anticipation of more adventure.

"Sure! I can take off. I got here early, and things have slowed down considerably. Want to get a bite to eat on the way so we can talk about said sleuthing?"

"You got it, Lane!" He took my arm, and we made our jaunty way to the diner across the street. I hadn't had time for lunch, and I was starving. My throat was a tiny bit tender, but I was dying for a cheeseburger and fries.

After I ate about half of my burger, I asked, "So what does the sleuthing involve today, Roarke?"

"Well, I found out that a buddy of mine—"

"Wait a minute, another buddy? How many buddies and informants do you have? How do you have the time?" I asked.

He laughed. "I know, I know. Anyway, this guy, Steve, works at a coffee shop near the *Gazette*'s main offices. You know, the paper that had especially lurid details of how the mayor's office was crooked?" I nodded and raised my eyebrows appreciatively. He went on, "Well, he keeps tabs on the interesting goings-on at the *Gazette* for me. Let's just say that their less-than-veracious headline yesterday wasn't the first time I thought they were fishy. So, after the papers came out, Steve kept his eyes open. He noticed a heavyset guy with black suit and white shirt coming out of the main building. That wasn't that remarkable, but what *was*, was the two enormous, gorilla-sized men on each side of him. All three of them came into the coffee shop, sat at the bar, and ordered coffee and six pieces of pie, two each. The main guy was smirky, but what really set him apart was his face. It was Daley Joseph."

"The nose hairs," I said, shuddering. Roarke laughed, but he hadn't met Daley yet. After you met him, there was no room for humor. "You don't understand. There's something twisted in him. He's . . . *disturbing.*"

He abruptly stopped laughing and said queasily, "Yeah, that's just what Steve said. Disturbing. Anyway, he overheard the guys talking about a small office on one of the back streets of SoHo. They mentioned a firehouse right across the street and that the building had a water main problem today. So I talked to another buddy at Ladder 13—shut up, Lane, yes, another buddy—and he knew exactly what street that was on. I got the address. You want to go check it out?"

He looked delighted with himself. If it had even been Uncle Louie, I would have been more inclined to go. But I had had enough of Daley Joseph to last a lifetime. "Uhhh . . . I'm not sure," I stammered, my hand subconsciously going up to my throat.

"Oh, God, Lane, I'm sorry. I wasn't thinking about what you'd been through. What an idiot. I'm sorry."

I smiled at him. "Cut it out, Roarke. No big deal. I'm a big girl. If I don't want to go, I won't go." I paused. "I don't want to go."

"Well, before you say no completely, let me give you all the details and let me know what you think. It isn't Daley Joseph's office, it's someone he's working with. I'm wondering if it's an explosives expert or demolition guy or something."

"In SoHo?" I asked skeptically. SoHo was a prime fashion area, not exactly where you'd place a construction office.

"It's on the edges of SoHo," he said, in his defense. "And they mentioned that there's some knockout who is there a lot. They didn't mention names or descriptions, well . . . at least any *helpful* descriptions. . . ." He cleared his throat and blushed. *Oh, brother.*

"Anyway, it's too juicy not to check out. But I'm happy to go by myself, just let me know any thoughts you have."

"Well, you're right, that does pique one's interest. Maybe the knockout is Roxy," I said ruminatively. "Huh. If it's not Daley's office, I'm in!" He smiled, looking like a sly fox.

And I suddenly felt like a chicken being led astray into the conniving fox's den. I had flashbacks of the Meatpacking District all over again. This time, it wasn't so sleazy and slimy with disgusting substances flowing and skittering around my feet, but when Roarke said *edges* of SoHo, what he really meant was *not* SoHo. He meant Chinatown.

"Aw, Roarke, this isn't SoHo!" I argued, with a disgruntled look on my face. People flooded the streets with innumerable vendor wares and tentlike structures attached to the fronts of the buildings, flowing onto the already clogged sidewalks. My vision was assaulted by thousands of colorful banners up and down the buildings. It was extremely crowded, making it almost impossible to navigate because you couldn't see very far in front of you or over your head. There were some delicious scents floating around, but then you'd suddenly be assaulted by strange odors, not to mention the shocking sight of dozens of headless chickens, ducks, and other disturbingly unidentifiable critters hanging from hooks in the front of restaurants.

We located the building just off the main thoroughfare, and sure enough, there was a run-down firehouse across the street, just like Roarke's source had said. The office we were looking for was a tiny affair with greasy windows. On the outside pane of the door, it read, SCHMIDT BROTHERS, but nothing about what exactly the Schmidt brothers did. From what we could see, there was a secretary inside.

We went inside, making the bells on the door jangle harshly. Sitting at the desk was a woman who was most definitely not Roxy. She had a giant, towering hairdo coming straight off the top of her head, dyed a very artificial orange that clashed wildly with her long, green dress from circa 1900. Her makeup was caked on, with shocking blue eyelids and about a gallon of eyeliner and mascara. Her nails were so long they started to curve downward like claws and were painted bright pink to match her lips. She was paralyzingly vivid, and had a weird air of the film *The Bride of Frankenstein,* which had come out last year. My eyes kept trying to blink the color away.

Then my eyes traveled downward to where she displayed the biggest . . . um . . . Let's just say that when those guys had been discussing the "knockout," they hadn't even come close to doing her assets the justice they clearly deserved.

Roarke and I were making a valiant effort to drag our eyes away from her bountiful display, and I said, *"Ahh . . . ehhh . . ."*
Roarke came up with, "Hi. *Uhhh . .*" *Nice. Real nice secret agents.*

I was suddenly overcome with a Southern accent, which seemed to appear out of nowhere when I was trying to be covert. "Hello there, ma'am, my name is Bobby Drake, and this here is my fiancé, Mr. Dudley P. Richardson."

Dudley gave me a dirty look. He must have felt compelled to also be Southern, because he answered in a slightly less exaggerated accent than mine, "Hello, ma'am. How are you today?" He held out a friendly hand as he tipped his hat.

The lady must have liked my Dudley's looks, because her guard, which had been up when we first entered the room, was now completely discarded. She held out a too-friendly hand that squeezed his with an energy that screamed, *Meet me out back.* I didn't think it was possible, but she wanted to further enhance her cleavage, so she took a deep breath that threatened to overwhelm her already precariously buttoned dress.

She batted her eyes and blushed beneath her very orange makeup, saying in a nasally Brooklyn accent, "Why, hello, Mr. Richardson, how can I help you?" Since she was completely ignoring me, I was given the time to look at everything in the office. There were a few dusty photographs on her back shelf, and other than that, a lot of staplers, pencils, calculators, etc. Typical office paraphernalia.

"I was wondering if the Schmidt brothers are in today. I have a friend who does business with them, and he recommended them highly," said Roarke, with a hopeful look toward the back office.

"Oh, no, they're not in right now. Should be back in a while. Are you here for an estimate?" she asked, with the *here* sounding like *heeya*.

"Ahhh, yes, an estimate. Do you think they'd have time to fit us in?" he said, hoping that she would give us some more information that we could work with.

"Well, that's a tough question. They have a lot going on this next month, but I think after that, they should have more openings. What exactly would you like to have done?" she asked, getting out a notebook.

"Well, ah, the usual. I think just the regular job would be plenty," Roarke tried.

She gave us a queer look, and I thought she had us, but she said, "Sssssso, you want a septic tank put in? Huh, you two look like city types, not country. You have a country house or sumthin'?"

Roarke sounded relieved. "Oh, yes, in Long Island. Do they go out that far? And also, do they do other construction jobs? We may be doing a whole remodeling job, and we'll be looking for help."

"Oh, sure, they do everything. Have every tool imaginable." She took on a conspiratorial tone, and with a proud look on her face, she said, "They can even do demolition. They're always talkin' about how much they love tearin' stuff down and how they like to blow things up." She laughed like a proud mama. "Like grown-up little boys!"

I wasn't laughing, for two reasons. One, I paled at the fact that these guys liked to blow things up. Two, I had just spotted a guy who looked like a weasel coming up the walk, followed by two brawny men whom I immediately recognized and whom I was pretty sure would recognize me. I had seen them around the offices with Finn, and I was certain they were part of the Tammany Hall crew.

Roarke saw the look on my face and started to make sounds of leaving, but the secretary had also spotted them and was telling us to wait. We hastened to make an exit and narrowly made it out the door before she could lay her claws on Roarke to forcibly stop him. However, we came to an abrupt standstill just outside. Roarke and the small, weasely guy came face-to-face—well, face to chest. They backed up and let us out first. We thought we were home free, but the secretary came bouncing out after us, wanting to make sure that we officially met the Schmidt Brothers. I tried to keep my face down so that the big guys couldn't look at me too closely.

Just when I thought my heart couldn't possibly race any faster, Finn walked by. He walked past and stopped at a newspaper stand just a few feet away, out of view of the Schmidt brothers. It took everything I had not to turn and look at him.

The short one, who seemed to be the leader, was directly in front of me. He was talking with Roarke, and the secretary was rapturous that she had caught us in time. Roarke was doing a fine job talking up our Long Island home and even had a great line about his reference to the Schmidt brothers from an acquaintance he'd met at a club, a Don Wilson Somebody.

The threesome was an unusual little group. The two big guys must have been twins, as they looked almost identical. The smaller, weasely guy didn't have their brawn or height, but something about his narrow eyes and pointy nose was definitely a blood relation to them. I thought we were doing swimmingly, when the big guy on the left suddenly lowered his gaze and took a good look at me. I kept busy adjusting my skirt and dodging his glance.

But then he said, in a muffly sort of voice, "Hey, Boss! That's Lane. That Lane girl. *You know.*" He said the *you know* with great emphasis. I really didn't care to be this famous. Weasel stopped in midsentence, his head jerking back like he'd been slapped.

He stammered out, "What the . . ." and I tried out something I'd been wanting to test for a while. You know how all the women in movies try to go for the slap on the face of the man who just made them angry? And the guy *always* sees it coming, and he grabs her wrist before she can slap and then gets that maddening grin? I hate those scenes, once again proving that I see far too many movies.

Anyway, I stepped up and made a big show of drawing my left hand back for a mighty slap, and I could tell Weasel was going to react just like I expected and grab my wrist with pompous aplomb.

But before he could, I quickly stepped with my left foot and drove with the power of my right shoulder and right fist as hard as I could into his unsuspecting stomach, resulting in a great big, "Oooof!"

It took everyone by surprise as he doubled over, giving Roarke and me a precious couple of seconds to scramble away. I did have one quick moment when I looked back at Finn and we locked eyes. He was outright laughing, trying unsuccessfully to hold up a newspaper to shield himself. My smile matched his, and I raced away with Roarke, blending into the thronging crowds of Chinatown.

After we felt like we had put enough distance between us and the Schmidt brothers, we slowed down and started evaluating what we had learned. We were so out of breath, it took us a few minutes to gather ourselves. We were now in Little Italy.

Chinatown butts up against Little Italy, and it always takes me by surprise to see such vastly different cultures colliding. Within view were many restaurants, green and red awnings, no more strange critters in the windows, several shops with tasty-looking pastries, and many men and women enjoying a chat in their native tongue outside on the stoops. Roarke and I found an unoccupied one and sat down to rest.

"Well, that was refreshing, Roarke. We should do this more often."

"Oh, yeah, I know how to show a girl a good time," he said, dimples showing.

"Yeah, and if you play your cards right, Chesty LaRue back there would love a little alone time with you, Dudley."

He groaned. "Thanks for the excellent name, and what's with the Southern accent?"

"I have no idea. It just comes out," I said resignedly.

"Well." He let out a big breath of air, finally getting his breathing back down to normal. "I think that those guys are definitely involved with Daley Joseph, and they look good to me to be the ones who could handle some kind of bombing attempt or something along those lines. But how did that guy know you?"

"I've seen those two bigger ones around the office. I think they're part of the old Tammany guys. I saw them talking with Finn once." I paused, letting that soak in. "He was there today. Finn."

"Yep, over by the newsstand. I wonder if he was there keeping tabs on the Schmidts or on you. He looked pretty pleased at your getaway plan, Lane. As was I. Did you see that at the movies or something?"

"Ha! I wish! I always get fed up with the women who predictably go for the slap. It was just a little something I've been working on."

"Nice. I think you deserve a reward. How about I treat you to a cannoli?"

CHAPTER 21

Normality is a paved road: It's comfortable
to walk, but no flowers grow on it.

—ML

The cannoli had been delicious. I ate two, in fact. And two days later, I was still thinking about manufacturing a way to go get another one. Roarke put out some feelers to keep track of the Schmidt brothers, but just like the void of cannoli in my life, there was a dearth of activity with the case. However, just after lunch, I received a special delivery via messenger. It was a note promising some action:

> *I have a great favor to ask of you, Lane. A job.*
> *It's a bit risky, but I know you can handle it. And*
> *God help me, I can't seem to keep you out of trouble*
> *anyway. Meet me outside Charlie's Club at nine p.m.*
> *Wear something sophisticated and sexy. Thanks, love.*
> *—F*
> *P.S. I know your overactive imagination will think*
> *this letter could be a trap. So to prove to you I am*
> *who you think I am, Mambo Italiano will always be a*
> *favorite. —F*

I chuckled at the *overactive imagination* line, because that had been *exactly* what I was thinking. But what kind of job could he be talking about? And, wear something sophisticated? Charlie's wasn't exactly a fancy place. Of course I would do it, but it was one of the most ludicrous letters I'd ever received. And that should have been a premonition.

I arrived at Charlie's Club at nine o'clock on the dot. I had trouble deciding what to wear, but landed on a basic black dress with a *V* in front and back. I didn't have any cleavage to speak of, but the closely fitting dress highlighted, let's just say, *my* best asset. And of course I had on a beautiful pair of black heels with toes peeking out, nails painted in dark red to match my red lipstick.

I was waiting just outside when Finn walked up. He was wearing a crisp, expensive-looking black suit with a deep blue tie and a handkerchief in his suit coat pocket. The cut highlighted his broad shoulders, tall frame, and tight waist. He walked up and let out a huge *whoa* of an exhale. "Wow, you look beautiful."

"Why, thank you. You don't look so bad yourself," I said, with an appreciative grin.

"Nice maneuver the other day. Where'd you learn *that*, love?"

"Oh, just a little something I've been working on."

He narrowed his eyes. "You watch a lot of movies, don't you?"

"Sure do," I said, with a smirk.

"Thanks for taking me up on this job tonight." He offered his arm, and I took it. We leisurely walked along the block toward Charlie's.

"Your note was pretty unusual. What exactly do you have in mind tonight, Finn? I don't think that Charlie's requires a sophisticated and sexy dress code, by the way," I said skeptically.

"Yeah, well, if you thought the note was unusual, just wait." *Uh-oh.* "This is the deal. The men you met the other day—I'm sure you and Roarke figured out that those three are the Schmidt brothers. The big ones you've seen around your office, right?"

"*Mm hm,* I saw them talking with you in our lobby once."

"Right, well, as you could also probably tell, those three aren't exactly geniuses; they're more or less the worker bees for their operation, because whoever is in charge is not telling the Schmidts any details. A smart move on their part. There's someone who's leading them, working out all the angles and execution. And he's the one who could be the weak link in figuring out the threat to Fiorello

and the city. Daley Joseph has been in and out of their office, but
with everything we *do* know, we don't know when and what they're
planning, other than explosives being involved. There's a guy coming tonight to Charlie's who I think can give us the clues we need.
However, I think he won't respond to me. I think he needs someone with your"—he looked at me appreciatively up and down with
a sly smile—"skills."

"So you want me to go up to a total stranger and say something
like, 'Gee, ever work for a psychopath with diabolical nose hairs?'"

"Might be a little too direct."

"I'm taking suggestions. . . ."

"Well, I'd approach him like all men want to be approached: Ap-
peal to his ego."

"Ah," I said, nodding sagely on the outside, nervously twitching
on the inside. *What have I gotten myself into?* "How did you know
he'd be here tonight?" I asked.

"Oh, I have my sources."

"You, too?" I murmured exasperatedly, thinking of Roarke and
his legion of informants.

"What was that?"

"Oh, nothing."

"Well, turns out this guy and his friends have a thing for the kind
of music being played tonight, and it's pretty hard finding this kind
of band in Manhattan."

"What kind of music?"

"Country."

"Country music," I said flatly.

"Country music. Deep, Southern, country music."

"Oh, boy."

We walked into the bar. It wasn't a club, it was a bar. I blurted
out my first question: "One more time. *Why* did you tell me to wear
something sophisticated? I should be wearing blue jeans and a plaid
shirt."

"Love, it's still Manhattan. You know this is all we wear. You'll
see. *And* the men you'll be approaching will appreciate your outfit
much, much more than jeans and plaid. Trust me."

Inside the *bar*, there was a band already on stage just wrapping up. Sounded more bluesy than country. They finished their last song and started removing their equipment as Finn came up and handed me a beer. I just could not see how this night was going to pan out. The bar was smoky with bare lightbulbs poking out of the walls here and there, all in all a very dark room except for the stage. But Finn was right; despite a couple of random cowboy hats, most of us were wearing work clothes or dressy, New York–style outfits like my own.

Finn stood slightly away from me so we didn't look like a couple. As the next band was getting up on stage, a group of three men came in and stood in front of us. Men were so intriguing. I really only saw these guys from behind at first, but I could tell instantly who the leader was.

All three had on suit pants, dress shirts, and ties, but had left their suit coats and hats at the coat rack. They were all slim, pretty well built, and looked like businessmen. But the leader had this confident air about him. And the three together were very interesting to watch. They had an appealing camaraderie, and there was a certain powerfulness about their postures.

The leader of the band was about ready to begin, and he put on an enormous white Stetson hat that matched his white suit. They started an upbeat number that was pretty toe-tapping as I sipped my beer and tried to come up with a savvy way of starting a conversation with these guys. Then the second song crawled into existence. It was an impossibly slow song, with caterwauling lead vocals and syrupy steel guitar, and it was completely, utterly, shoot-me-now depressing. I backed up to Finn, who was still behind me.

"You are an awful, awful man," I said.

"Enjoying the ambiance, my dear?" he said, enjoying himself.

"You owe me *big*," I groaned. The song went on and on, like they do.

As the beers kept flowing, the guys' inhibitions started lowering. The leader remained pretty stalwart, but his friends were shimmying, toe-tapping, and elbow dancing to the merrier tunes. At the depressing songs, they all sat down and put their elbows on the table in a dejected sort of way, nodding their heads empathetically with the droning lyrics about unfaithful women and nitpicky wives. I was going to need something stronger than beer.

I went up to the bar and ordered a scotch. I really don't care for the fiery liquid, except when Aunt Evelyn hands out her restorative beverages. But in this case, it seemed necessary. For a couple of reasons. The barkeep was a huge, beefy man sporting blue jeans with a white denim shirt. He was in his fifties, probably, and winked at me as he set down my glass of scotch.

As I held the cool glass in my hand, the leader of my three guys came up and put his elbows on the bar, ready to make an order. I was about three feet away. I rolled the cold shot glass between my hands. I watched the guy, his strong hands clasping his glass. He looked up and caught my eye. I gave him a small smile and held up my glass in a *cheers* motion.

He came over to me and clinked my glass, and we both downed our drinks with only a slight watering of my eyes as the fire hit my throat and my gut. He rested his elbows on the bar once again. I turned back to the bar as well, now only inches from his elbow.

I decided on taking Finn's advice. "You're the guy in charge, aren't you?" I said, with what I hoped was a beguiling tone.

He clearly enjoyed my compliment. "Yeah, you could say that."

"I thought so. I've been watching you," I purred, and I walked away to the other end of the bar.

His eyes grew dark, and a look of desire stole over his face. He took the bait and came over to me. "Can I get you something else?"

"Sure, I'll have another," I said, nodding to the barkeep. There was no way I was going to drink another one. "Thank you. I'm Julia," I said, offering my hand.

"Lyle," he said, taking my hand in his. He grasped it warmly, smiling, with a look on his face that said he knew he was handsome. And he was, with his dark hair and blue eyes. But he was almost too good-looking in an artificial way, too up front and overly aware of his good looks. A little of Lyle went a long way, and I found myself wanting to back up.

I decided to stay along the same lines I had been going. I turned around with my back to the bar, elbows resting on it. I regarded his buddies, and as he turned around to look at them with me, I flicked my wrist, deftly pouring my scotch onto the floor, then pretended to down it. I said, "Yep. I bet, whatever you do, *you* are the boss." He nodded, loving my praise, gobbling it up.

"Yeah, those two?" he said, nodding toward his buddies. "They're all right, but I pretty much tell them what to do and"—he snapped his fingers—"they do it!"

"And let's see, I bet you work with other powerful people in the city, don't you?" I asked, trying to fawn over him.

"*Mm hmm,*" he replied, saying without words, *Oh, do go on!* I smiled broadly and inched just a tiny bit closer to him, hoping his alcohol had done its work.

It had. He continued on a lovely, self-absorbed route. "Oh, yeah, Julia. In fact, I work with a coupla major players in the city. Things are gonna be changin' around here real soon. I got a big, big job coming up." I tried to wrangle my face into an expression that didn't say what I was really thinking (*He's such an ass*), but reflected that I was extremely impressed. His tightly pulled-together composure was losing the battle with the copious amount of alcohol he had consumed. His eyelids were getting heavy, and his speech was starting to slur. He started calling me *Chulia.*

"Really, Lyle? A big job?" I said, with wide eyes. *Please, please, please keep going.*

"Oh, yeah. Big time. It's gonna make my career."

"Really, Lyle? What do you do?" I tried to sound innocent and naïve, willing him to divulge that crucial piece of information that I was hunting for.

"Oh, let's just say I organize people and . . . big events in the city."

"Really? Can you bring a *friend* to this next big event?" I asked, coyly nudging his elbow with mine.

He chuckled, loving the fact that I was practically throwing myself at him. "Oh, honey, this next big event isn't something quite up your alley," he said, giving me an all-knowing smile. "It'll be shpectacular, but, uh . . . something you'd want to see from the shidelines."

"The sh—sidelines?" I asked, with an engaging smile, prompting him along.

"Yeah. In fact, let's just say the best seats will be in Manhattan. I'd stay out of Queens August tenth, Chulia." My stomach lurched. Hot damn, that was it.

CHAPTER 22

Keep going, keep going come what may.

—ML

Finn was casually leaning up against a railing, watching us. I could see the strain on his face. I was pretty sure he'd decided that this wasn't such a good idea after all. I guess having me near a guy like Lyle was very different in theory versus reality. It was catching up to me as well. I didn't think I could keep this up much longer and was trying my hardest to think of a good exit plan, but not coming up with anything very promising.

Lyle was just about to get a little uncomfortably close, his breath sending out waves of alcohol, when a presence made itself known behind me. But it wasn't Finn; I could still see him about twenty feet away, and his face had a horrible, *oh, shit* look on it. I looked up and saw . . . Peter.

"What on *earth* are you doing here, Lane? And with this creep," he practically yelled. I was pretty sure it wasn't a good idea to call Lyle a creep. I cringed, knowing full well what was about to happen.

"Lane? I thought you said your name was Chulia." But before I could say something cunning, like, *Yes, Julia Lane at your service,* Peter's insult made its way to Lyle's fuzzy brain. "Hey, pal! You can't call me a creep! Whadaya think you're doing?"

Friends from both parties of Lyle and Peter started to form ranks around their comrades. Finn only had eyes for me. In fact, at the moment, *I* only had eyes for me, as I really, really, really wanted to escape. The men were all flexing their muscles and their fists.

The music slowed down and stuttered to a stop as the band noticed something happening and wasn't quite sure what to do about it.

But before anything could get out of hand, we all heard the unmistakable *chook-chook* of a shotgun being cocked. Everything, everyone froze instantly.

The massive barkeep actually had *two* shotguns, one held in each bulky arm. "Is there gonna be a problem here?" he rumbled from a deep throat.

Everyone's arms relaxed, fists went down, faces tried to look innocent, and everyone shook their heads in a uniform, *Of course not!* I took my cue, ducked down, and ran toward the door. I saw Finn follow, and I didn't look back. I went right out the door, turned left toward a main avenue, and hoped Finn would catch up to me.

He did, of course. I wasn't running, but I was walking at a rapid pace. I hadn't looked back once. I just wanted space between me and Lyle. And country music. I heard footsteps come up behind me and felt an arm come around my shoulders to pull me close as we kept up our pace. I bent my head to his shoulder in greeting for just a moment. He was so solid, so warm.

In a guilty, apologetic voice, Finn started talking fast. "I'm sorry, Lane, I shouldn't have asked you. I just saw how you've handled everything lately, and then when you slugged that weasel guy, I just let it get out of hand. . . ." He stopped walking and looked at me. "Wait a minute," he said, his eyes narrowing. "You're laughing! You got something!" He started to walk again, keeping his arm around my shoulders. "You're absolutely incorrigible, Lane." I could feel his chest shaking with mirth.

"Well, I did get something, Finn. But that Lyle is really something else."

"Oh, yeah, you could say that again."

We made our way down side streets and avenues, making plenty of turns to make sure we weren't being followed. "Did you know Peter was going to be there tonight?" I asked Finn.

He hesitated for a minute, tensing. "No, I didn't know he'd be there."

"Do you think it was coincidence, or was he following up on some lead or other?"

"He and his buddies didn't look like they were ready to work."

"Frankly," I said, in a pained voice, thinking of the gut-wrenchingly awful song, "it's hard to imagine anyone going there on purpose."

Finn laughed. "I know exactly what you mean."

He looked down at me and said more softly, "You really do look beautiful, Lane. Do you want to get a coffee? Then I have a couple of friends I'd like us to go see later. Would you feel up to that after our little adventure?"

"Sure, that sounds great. But, ah, no more alcohol." I rolled my eyes.

"Yyyes, do you drink scotch often, love?" he said, with the lift of an eyebrow.

"No. Only when necessary. And tonight it seemed utterly necessary." I cocked my head to the side as I remembered something I hadn't thought of in years. "My father used to drink scotch on the rocks at night once in a while. I loved the decanter that we had in the library."

"Seems like it went down quite easily," he said, with a smirk in his voice.

"Yep, sure did," I replied, with a smack to my lips.

We came to a small mom-and-pop diner and went in. We slumped down into a booth, ordering two coffees and two slices of warm blueberry pie with vanilla ice cream. It made me think of that little postcard in my parents' album about the place in Maine.

"Okay, so out with it. What did you and Lyle discuss that made him look at you with such enchantment?"

"Were you jealous, Finn?" I asked, vastly interested in his reply.

"Most definitely."

"*Hmm*," I replied, fully enjoying his answer. "Well, he wasn't enchanted with me."

"Oh, sure . . ."

"He was enchanted with himself."

I filled him in on the big job Lyle was working on, and Finn's smiling eyes grew serious and intense as I got to the point. "I asked him if he could take a date to this next big job that sounded so interesting. He was plenty pleased that I asked, but said that the better seats were on the sidelines; the best seats would be in Manhattan. I had started to think that he meant the target would be *in* Manhattan. But then, he said that I should stay out of Queens. On August tenth."

Finn had been in the middle of taking a drink of coffee, and he slowly put the cup back onto the table, not taking his eyes off mine.

"Queens. August tenth. Good Lord, Lane. They haven't even told the Schmidt brothers an exact date. They're trying to keep it as quiet as possible, for the least number of foul-ups. Nice work."

"Thanks." It was new and a bit of a thrill to feel like we were a team. "But, Queens is a pretty big place. Any ideas about where? And what they're planning?"

"Nothing too solid yet. But our meeting later tonight may prove to be enlightening. It usually is," he said provocatively.

Our pie came, and I had worked up quite an appetite. The warm, gooey center was delicious, and the cold vanilla ice cream was melting into the pie. Finn and I both looked up with gratified smiles on our faces. The cold linoleum table was smooth to my fingertips as I made figure eights with my middle finger on the table. We finished up our coffee and pie, then started walking toward our next rendezvous.

"So, where are we going?" I asked.

"To see a couple of friends," he repeated. We walked uptown and came to an old, Italian hole-in-the-wall restaurant. It was late, and it looked like the place was cleaning up for the night. But when we entered the dark interior, friendly waiters pointed to the back, where we were obviously expected. We went to the back and around a curtain.

"Well, look at what we have here!" I said, sauntering over to greet Fio and Mr. Kirkland.

"Good evening, Laney Lane!"

"*Grrrr.*" Which made him smile broadly.

"Have a seat, you two, and we'll get down to business. Would you like some coffee or something?" I said no thank you.

I mumbled to Finn, "Maybe another scotch *will* be required." I heard Finn's low laugh behind me.

"Mr. Kirkland and I have decided that it's high time we all got our cards on the table, so to speak," said Fio. "Again."

"Mr. Kirkland . . ." I said, realizing that something I'd been ruminating on for a while now was looking to be true. I started to feel that the joke was on me, that I was the only one not in on some big secret. I was not fond of that sensation. My face must have revealed that sentiment, because Fio started talking faster and took his grin down a notch.

"Lane, I think things are coming to a head, and I'm guessing we all have some information. So, we need to get it all out in the open. I figure that you might have several things that we are in the dark about, and there are a few things that you need to know as well." I looked at Finn questioningly as we both nodded in response. Despite them being very courteous, the air felt like it had the slimmest edge of them treating me like a little girl. I was not a little girl.

I decided that I'd like to take the reins back for a moment. I sat down, crossed my legs, put both hands on my thighs, elbows out, and leaned forward like I was about to give them a pep talk before the big game. "Excellent. Here's what I know, *gentlemen* . . ." My eyes were flashing and sparking at each of them in turn as I spoke carefully and firmly. "First of all, Fio, you and Finn Brodie, here, have been working together for at least the past year to keep tabs on the Tammany Hall crew and clean up the corruption of the NYPD. Of course, Finn is undercover posing as what, a dirty cop?" I enjoyed the fact that Fio's jaw dropped open and Finn didn't move a muscle except for a long blink that spoke volumes.

I carefully looked at them, scrutinizing their faces, trying to determine if they would be honest with me about some questions I had. Finn and I had never spoken about his involvement as an undercover cop, and I wasn't sure how he would feel knowing that I knew what he did. There were a lot of dark parts to undercover work, and I couldn't imagine how hard it must have been to be thought of as a dirty cop.

"I have a question, though. Finn, how is it that you've been reporting to Fio, yet he didn't know you were working with Daley Joseph?"

"Well, it started with Commissioner Valentine, initially," Finn replied. Lewis Valentine had indeed worked hard to clean up the corruption in the NYPD. "To seek out which cops were corrupt, someone clean had to look corrupt. It only took a few whispered notions to get it out that I might be dirty. I would report to Valentine, and in the meantime, Daley and Donagan showed up. They had always worked with dirty cops, so my job turned into undercover work with them. Fio, in conjunction with Valentine, had asked me to keep him posted on any Tammany dealings, but he didn't know about Daley and Donagan. I'd told Valentine about their interest in the mayor, but we didn't notify Fio until much later because we didn't know enough information."

I nodded thoughtfully, a lot of the pieces falling into place.

Another thought occurred to me. "But what was the deal with dressing up as a fireman?"

Finn shot a glance at Fiorello, who had a pleased smile plastered onto his face. "Well . . ." he began, with a funny roll to his eyes, "Fio wanted me to get a feel if Tammany had infiltrated the fire department as well. He had the fire chief set up a few times where I filled in at certain departments. That day you saw me, I had seen Danny approach Fio, so I wanted to be sure he was all right."

Fio chipped in, "I had Finn everywhere! Then, when you started getting into trouble, I had him keep an eye on you once in a while, too."

I looked at Finn with a smirk. "You had your eye on me, huh?"

"Oh yes," he replied with a devilish smile that made my face turn pink.

I kept going, beginning to enjoy myself immensely. "So, Roarke and I found the guys who are probably the ones who will execute Daley Joseph's plan of some kind of explosion: the Schmidt brothers. And from our little expedition tonight, we found out from the Schmidt brothers' boss that the big event will be"—I paused for effect, making them draw in a little closer—"in Queens, August tenth."

Finn spoke up with a smirk, "Yes, gentlemen, Lane is quite resourceful. You should have seen her the other day. Sucker punched one of the Schmidt brothers."

"What? Those huge guys?" asked Fio, with his screechy voice.

"Well, no," I admitted. "Just the little weasely one."

"Bah!" barked out Mr. Kirkland.

"So, you've been busy, Lane," said Fio, with a father's look of being distraught with a troublemaking daughter.

"Oh, yeah, plenty busy," said Finn, in his delicious accent.

"All right, so I laid my cards on the table, now let's hear yours," I said, pointedly nodding at Fio. "Oh, wait," I said slowly, pretending that I had just remembered one more significant thing. I decided that now was the time for my final bombshell. "One . . . thing . . . more."

Mr. Kirkland quietly said, "Oh, hell."

"I still don't have all the details, but Mr. Kirkland . . ." I nodded at him and looked him right in the eye. "I know you were friends with my father. Close friends. There is a lot to your past that I'm sure I don't know, but . . . I *do* think you were involved in espionage in the war. With my parents."

CHAPTER 23

Don't lose heart if it's very difficult at times,
everything will come out all right and
nobody can in the beginning do as he wishes.

—ML

Everything came to a standstill. No one moved, no one spoke, and no one breathed. I was quite sure Finn had not known that part, about Mr. Kirkland's involvement. Well, not that I had put it all together, exactly; I was making an educated guess. A supremely cocky guess.

Fio looked from me to Mr. Kirkland and back again. "Espionage, Kirkland? It seems to me like we have even more cards to get out on the table than I thought. I wish Evelyn were here to help us put some organization to all this."

As he spoke these words, she came sweeping into the restaurant, eyes beady, ready for battle. She had her get-down-to-business attire on, no whimsical or flowery bohemian skirt tonight: crisp, dark red skirt and starched white blouse. Her black hair was up in a full bun at the nape of her neck. Even with her conservative attire, she had an exotic air blended with a somewhat fearsome countenance. The men all rose to greet her, but she hushed them all down and took her place at the table, opposite Fio.

"From your shell-shocked expressions, gentlemen, and from your gratified sneer, Lane, I take it that you just blasted them with your knowledge of your parents, Finn's role in all this, and anything else juicy that you came up with recently." It was my turn to look baffled. *How did she do that?* I quickly brought her up to speed. She merely nodded at my information, but there was a wicked gleam in her eye.

She briskly continued her organization of the meeting. "I knew you'd be getting your cards on the table, as you enjoy saying, Fiorello, so I had to look all over for you, since I was not invited. I'm sure it was just an oversight. So, here I am. We need to hear from each one of us. Kirk, I think you should go first to give us some background, then we'll end with Fio so we can see how each of these threads makes up the tapestry of our case." We were putty in her hands, ready to do whatever she asked. "But to give you more time, Kirk, and since your mouth is still open . . ." He shut it precipitately. "Lane, dear, how did you know about Kirkland's involvement with your parents? How did you find that out?"

"You just told me," I said, with a wicked grin. Fio shook his head. "Well, I've been thinking more about my parents, and I've been studying their journal. They were innately interested in strategy and survival; teaching me to be intuitive; thinking and analyzing the nuance of any situation. Even in the games we played, it was just how they were wired. So, once I learned they'd been involved in intelligence, it all made sense. Then I took a good look at that picture of my mother with Louie Venetti. I think it's *your* hand on her shoulder, Mr. Kirkland. You also seem heavily involved in the details for the Rochester house. Invested. It seems like that would be someone who cared a lot for my parents, not just me. And someone had to have taken that favorite photograph of me, my parents, and Aunt Evelyn. It makes sense that it was you."

Mr. Kirkland opened his mouth like he was going to say something, but quickly closed it again.

"In some ways, all the secrecy seems ludicrous, but then again, we've never been the normal, traditional family," I said, sipping my coffee.

"*Pfffft,*" said Finn. I looked at him with my brow lifted, saying, *Do you have something to add?* He just gave a quarter inch of a devious grin and looked away.

After a long pause, Aunt Evelyn looked at Mr. Kirkland like that was his cue to get a move on.

"Okay," said Mr. Kirkland as he cleared his throat and shook his head just a little, like he was getting the cobwebs cleared. "First of all, Lane, we wrestled and wrestled with how much to tell you as you grew up. We figured you could handle it, but then again, we weren't sure if any of the information would actually put you in danger.

"You're correct about my, uh, business in the past. I worked with your father before and during the war. We worked on several assignments together and became good friends over time. He and your mother were already a team. We worked well together. Some of the information is classified still, but some of our missions were to investigate and recover stolen art and national treasures. Our government started to hear of wealthy families in Europe who tried to flee their country with the help of some sort of agency, only to discover their bank accounts drained. All the while, we were gathering intelligence. Being bookstore owners was the perfect cover.

"When Charlotte discovered she was pregnant, they went to Rochester, Michigan. They had no roots there, it was a quaint, unknown town, and they could make a fresh start. Matthew had a friend who had recently moved there, so he'd had a chance to get a feel for the little town. In our work, we had discovered the beginnings of a new gang responsible for all those massive thefts. Matthew and Charlotte felt like they couldn't retire completely; there was so much at stake. After you were born, they would take a couple of missions here and there. That's when Evelyn would come out to take care of you."

Mr. Kirkland's brow was knitted with concern and anxiety. But with the last few sentences, his face cleared of the darkness, and he held a reminiscent smile.

"I never saw your parents happier than when you arrived on the scene, Lane. Here it was a vastly different lifestyle than they'd ever experienced, and yet it suited them perfectly. We eventually did retire. That's when I came here with Evelyn; she and I had been friends for a long time. I came just to visit, but then the back garden needed a lot of work, and Evelyn couldn't cook to save her life. . . . A routine started that never ended. But I did visit your parents a couple of times every year."

It was my turn to be shell-shocked. I mean, I had guessed at some of this, but to hear the details was another story altogether. With little to go on, I had been throwing darts in the dark, making the best supposition I could. I was going to need some time to mull this over.

I guess I had become used to not knowing my past. True, I had felt an odd void, like my life had been kick-started when I was ten; that I had suddenly existed with no preamble. But to abruptly know the bigger story that I had been part of was a very strange feeling. Something akin to finding out you'd been adopted after two decades of thinking otherwise. And speaking of a bigger story . . .

"Mr. Kirkland, I think it's time to talk about the silver gun."

Finn looked at me. Evelyn and Fio countered simultaneously, "What gun?"

"*Er . . .*" Mr. Kirkland mumbled, making me wonder if he'd suddenly turn back into that old, shy, murmuring butler.

I filled them in on my longtime dreams of the silver gun with the red scroll, only to see it realized in Danny's hands.

All eyes turned to Kirkland, whose face held a visible argument in deciding whether to be forthcoming or to keep to himself as he had for the past decades.

"All right," he said, in an aggrieved growl. We all sat back, ready to hear the tale. "Back in the war, Matthew and Charlotte and I discovered a gang that was behind most of the major art thefts. It was a group who called themselves the Red Scroll Network. The leader was Rex Ruby. He was vile and incredibly intelligent, and he created a deeply complex network of theft, extortion, prostitution, every crime you can imagine."

"So the silver gun was his?" asked Finn.

"Yes. Rex loved symbols and mystery and puzzles. His megalomania knew no bounds. He had two silver guns made with the red symbol of his network on the handles. They never, *ever* left his possession. They were one of his trademarks."

"How would I have a memory of the gun?" I asked incredulously.

"Matthew and I finally tracked him down. A long time after they moved to Rochester, we finally had solid intelligence on where to find him. We most definitely found him, and we most definitely killed him."

"But . . ." Fio urged.

"But we only found *one* of the silver guns on him. Matthew and I decided to keep it quiet that we only found one. Those guns must have stood for something in his organization—everything did. Everything had deeper meanings, and Rex gained in status and power as the mystery of those guns increased. We didn't want word to get out that one was missing. We wanted the myth of the guns to die with Rex. Matthew kept the gun, Lane. I'm guessing that you probably found him looking at it one day. But after your parents died, I never saw it again. It disappeared. Anything's possible."

"Regardless," said Evelyn, putting everything together, "Danny definitely had one, and that means that this is all connected. The silver gun is pointing to the people behind the threats."

"And," I added, "if Danny's dead, who has the gun now?"

I was mulling over this vast amount of information: Kirkland, my parents, Rex Ruby, the Red Scroll Network, New York, Rochester. "Wait a minute," I said, with urgency, as something else monumental occurred to me. "Mr. Kirkland, were you *there*—in Rochester—the day my parents died?"

All eyes turned to me, then to Mr. Kirkland. Except Finn's. His eyes remained on me. We exchanged a knowing, dark look. Mr. Kirkland took a deep breath, and I had my answer before he said it. "Yes, Lane. I was there."

I closed my eyes as several images ran through my brain at once: my mom's blue scarf, my dad's red mittens and red coat. . . . Wait a minute. I thought I remembered a *tan* barn coat. My dad's face as he turned back to us, reaching out . . . the cold water . . . a hard arm around my waist, dragging me toward the light.

I raised a hand sharply. "Wait. Mr. Kirkland, when you carried me up the stairs the day I had been pushed in the subway, it felt like déjà vu. You . . . Were you actually *there* at the skating party?"

He nodded, his eyes grave and dark, the lines on his weathered face deeper than usual. "Yes."

"Did you . . . did you dive in and save me?"

I heard a sharp gasp from Fiorello. "Yes, Lane," said Mr. Kirkland softly, with the kindest eyes I'd ever seen in my life.

Before the lump in my throat could overtake me, I had to ask one more thing. "Mr. Kirkland, my father was shot, wasn't he?"

"Yes."

CHAPTER 24

I am still far from being what I want to
be, but with God's help I shall succeed.

—ML

I shut my eyes as I tried to tease the details of that awful day to the surface. My father *had* been wearing his tan barn coat, but as he turned to my mother and me, a swelling red stain seeped out from the chest of his coat.

I said quietly, "I remember him turning back to us before we went into the water, and a red stain coming through his coat. What exactly happened that day?"

"Well, I was there at the party," began Mr. Kirkland, looking into the past, telling a story that he didn't want to tell. "I had come to visit you all. Your father had been doing his skating thing, where he zipped around the perimeter of the rink. I remember laughing as you and Charlotte started to chase after him. You had just about caught him, on the farthest part of the rink out into the lake. There was a loud crack, and at first I thought it was the lake creaking, but then I saw your father stumble and turn to you, and I knew it was a gunshot, maybe two in close repetition. Then I realized it *had* been the ice as well; a huge hole opened up. You, your mother, your father, and another man who had been nearby all fell in. I raced over and jumped in. You had been the last to go in. I found you and pulled you up. You were the only one I could save."

"But I don't understand, someone shot my father *and* the ice broke apart? That doesn't seem possible."

Mr. Kirkland bit his bottom lip in thought. "I know. We could never find more evidence to piece together what really happened, but when I went back to the scene later in the day, there was a fine black powder along the edges of the broken ice, suggesting an explosive." He paused for a moment and then went on, "Your father was shot, but I believe he was not the only target. The explosion could have been to cover the shot fired or to intentionally take out all of you, I don't know."

I said, "Roarke thought the same thing. He heard about the fine black dust on the remaining ice. But we didn't know about the gunshot."

Fiorello's eyes were the epitome of empathetic love and understanding. His son and daughter were lucky kids indeed. "Lane, dear, are you all right? This is a lot to hear in one sitting."

"You could say that again," I said as I rubbed the back of my neck. "Okay. Well, we will have to talk much more at length about this. But right now, is there something that might link this to what is currently going on here, in New York? Roarke found out about that other man who was also killed: Rutherford Franco. His Hollywood-crazed wife, Daphne, went to pieces afterward, and she and her daughter disappeared."

Evelyn piped in, "You know, I seem to recall a mental hospital in Rochester, Michigan; maybe we could check that out."

"Good idea," said Finn.

"Given the timing of them in Rochester and their link to New York, plus Daphne having that platinum blond hair, I think that there is a strong possibility that the daughter is Roxy." I filled them in on the specifics Roarke had discovered.

Finn spoke up after a long, contemplative silence. "There are multiple motives here, and I have an idea on how they all might come together. Donagan Connell and Daley Joseph work together, but Donagan's been all but absent the last couple of weeks. He calls in orders and writes messages, but he's not around. On the phone the other day, I overheard Daley talking to him about *her*. Daley didn't sound too happy about that *her*, but he didn't discuss it with me, either. I'm wondering if this woman is Roxy and if she and Donagan have formed a kind of partnership. That would account for his absence if he's been more . . . *involved* with her. Personally and businesswise. So, if Roxy really is Rutherford's daughter and she *is* behind some of this, maybe her personal motive could be to get back at you, Lane. In her mind, she might think that your family caused the death of her father."

I felt guilty and angry at the same time. I had been ten years old at the time, so why get back at me? Then again, ever since hearing of that man's death from Roarke, I felt somehow guilty and remorseful that there was another child who had lost a parent that day.

Finn went on, "And if she joined forces with Donagan and Daley, she could kill two birds with one stone. Get back at you *and* help them get Fio out of the picture. Danny worked with one or all of them. One of them has that silver gun. And God only knows what that means."

"What do you mean, Finn?" asked Evelyn.

I supplied, "He means, the gun points to the threats here in New York City. But if that gun really is Rex Ruby's, it could point to a whole lot more. It could mean that their gang is getting back together."

We wrapped up our chat, discussing possible targets in Queens. We knew it would be big, it would be highly visible, and it would cause the most damage possible to the city and to Fio's career. We decided to give it more thought, do some digging, and see what we came up with. We had just under ten days. Fiorello said he'd see me at the office the next day, while Mr. Kirkland and Aunt Evelyn graciously left Finn and me to walk home together.

It was after midnight. The air felt fresh and sweet. The buildings shimmered, the moon was almost full and a brilliant white, there were scores of people milling around going to restaurants, going out dancing, just walking around despite the late hour.

It reminded me of something I read by a friend of Aunt Evelyn's, Hulbert Footner, who was working on a book about New York City. He'd brought over a chapter, and he had the best description of the city I'd ever heard. He and a friend had stepped out of the Astor into the middle of Times Square and they stopped to enjoy the scene before them. There was a phrase he'd said, about the way that you could see something ninety-nine times, but on the hundredth, be "arrested by its magnificence." What a way to say it! He had such a poetic way of writing about the city. I couldn't wait to get my hands on the book when it came out.

Personally, I was more partial to the parts of the city outside of Times Square, like the small section heading up to the Upper East Side, where we were now. But that part about how the city would capture your imagination at unsuspecting moments—it was perfect.

"You're smiling, Lane," said Finn, looking down at me and taking up my hand as we started to walk. Those familiar, warm shocks went up my arm. "What are you thinking about? How are you doing with everything we just discussed?" He tried to sound nonchalant, but anxiety seeped through the background of his voice.

"Oh, I was just smiling because I love living here." I looked up at the buildings and the moon. I told him a little about that chapter by Hulbert Footner.

"I never thought about it that way. He's right. It's like a living thing," he said.

He was right. It wasn't the hectic nature of the city that invited you to jump in, it was the life itself. A living thing that had the capacity to invite you to be part of it.

"So . . . how long have you known?" asked Finn.

I knew what he meant. "Well, I wasn't sure for a while. But you kept popping up in the right places at the right time."

"But, how did you know—I mean really *know*—that I wasn't playing on the wrong side? Like Peter thinks. He has reason to think that way, Lane. I mean, the whole point of my role is to look dirty. Not that it takes much. Only a whisper of corruption, and a reputation is lost. It will take so much more to get it back. I've fought with myself for a while about doing this kind of work and about being with you. I . . . I am so far from perfect."

He was going down an old, despairing path. I blocked the path. "I don't care about your perceived reputation. Valentine will be sure to fix it. And I know you're not perfect, Finn."

"You do?"

"Of course. You're not perfect. But you're good. There's a big difference."

"I've done things I wish I hadn't," he said, stopping me, releasing my hand. He turned my shoulders so we were face-to-face, forcing me, or perhaps himself, to confront this head-on.

"I know. I can tell," I said, my eyes searching the gray-green of his.

"How can you see the things you do, Lane? You see things that other people don't."

I stammered, "I do?"

"Yes, you see beauty and humor and color. And you see people, deep down as they are. Things that they try to hide. Things that go right by others, but you take the time to see, to really *see and feel*."

I drew closer to him and touched his lapel, feeling the black fabric, listening to the cars and chatter floating by, smelling the hint of roses from the stand nearby mingled with coffee from the bistro and the smoke of a cigarette, enjoying the golden windows peeking into the darkness above us . . . every piece of the night.

"What happened with you and Peter? Can you tell me?" A light breeze ruffled his dark hair, and his eyes were intense with reflection, looking into the distance at a story, at a memory riddled with what-ifs and if-onlys.

"All right," he said softly and firmly, having come to a decision. It felt like he was making a sacrifice, like he knew this could change everything. As we started to walk along, I glimpsed his stony countenance. He seemed ready to get it over with. "Well, it was a few years ago. I was working undercover, a position I'd taken only about a few months prior. I had been sent to check on a prostitution ring that had sprung up. I pretended to be someone, uh . . ."

"Looking for some action?" I supplied.

He coughed. "Ah, yeah. When I arrived at the place that was supposed to be the . . ."

"Brothel?" I contributed.

"Good God, Lane, how . . . ? Never mind. *Anyway,* I got to the place and met with the owner, told her the services that I'd require, and that I'd want to set something up for a party we were having the next week." He winced. I wasn't too thrilled with that part, either.

"We fixed a date for the party, and I left. When I came out, I ran into Pete and his date. They must have been coming home from a Broadway show or something. The . . . *ahem* . . . brothel was just east of Times Square. He saw me and recognized me from the department, but he obviously decided I was not there on business. A look of absolute loathing went across his face. Then . . ." His voice cracked. I braced myself.

"Then . . . someone inside must have made me. Maybe it was seeing Peter, who was a pretty well-known cop. Maybe I'd given myself away somehow, I have no idea. But two guys came to the windows and started shooting. Peter and I dove at his date and the other people outside. We shot back and ended up nailing the two shooters. In the end, we took down the brothel and gambling ring that was associated with it."

In the silence that ensued, I prepared for the worst. "Peter's date?" I asked, just above a whisper.

"She was shot in the cross fire. Died the next day."

"Oh, God," I said, feeling the awful weight of that admission. With things like that, you torture yourself, thinking if things had only happened just a few seconds earlier or later, if he'd only made that meeting the day before, if . . . if . . . if . . . It was agony.

"Pete never forgave me. The head of the department even talked with him, told him about the undercover business. But it didn't matter. He sees something in me that is *not* good, and he cannot forgive me. He still thinks that it wasn't really official business, that I was there for my own lecherous purposes." He had bared his teeth with a snarl when he said *purposes*, repulsed by the idea.

I let us think in silence for a moment, but I guess I let the silence extend too long. He stopped me abruptly, turned me to him again, this time more forcefully, and said, "Lane, you don't think—"

I stopped him just as abruptly and put my fingers over his mouth. I could feel his soft lips and the rough stubble from the late time of the day. "No. No, Finn." I said clearly, without hesitation. I smiled just the tiniest inch. "I told you." I took my hand off his mouth and laid it on his chest. "I know you. The real you." His eyes looked into mine, longingly and with something that was achingly hopeful. I reached up with both hands on either side of his face and kissed him.

We walked home holding hands, letting the time and the silence ease away the stressful enormity of what we'd both learned that night.

Our sense of urgency was growing, and the evil air that was developing in the case was overpowering. We had to figure out exactly where the threat was going down and how, and try to stop them while keeping them in the dark about Finn's real role. Over several hours and many cups of coffee in our kitchen, Finn and I came up with a plan. Things were complicated in this tricky case, and it was a risky plan. But it was the only thing we could work out that helped us have the upper hand . . . and all come out alive.

At least that was the goal.

CHAPTER 25

... and then, I have nature and art and poetry,
and if that is not enough, what is enough?

—ML

Despite the ongoing, urgent investigation, we still had our own, regular routines as a week passed by. In the midst of great uncertainty, it felt good to enjoy simple dinners at home with Mr. Kirkland, Aunt Evelyn, and Ripley. Val ended up having a talk with Peter that cooled things off with their relationship. Work was interesting as usual, but nothing out of the ordinary. Roxy and Lizzie were their same, irritating selves; no new development with either of them. In fact, they were up to their same old, juvenile antics. Who knew? Maybe we were wrong about Roxy, and maybe my involvement really had been coincidental . . . Maybe.

Finn was working long hours undercover again, so we waited. Our plan we came up with was something that couldn't begin until the perfect moment. We needed their side to make a move for the game to start. Then we were going to use a dangerous resource to help us. You know the saying, *the enemy of my enemy is my friend*? We'd put that to the test.

While the days were moving inexorably closer and closer to August tenth—only four days left—it also felt like things had slowed down. There were fewer leads despite the fact that we were all checking on possible threat zones in Queens. The police were keeping an eye on the Schmidt brothers and Lyle, but nothing out of the ordinary was happening. A consistent, nagging thought pulsated on the edge of my mind. It was like trying to remember a word, but no matter how hard you try, it remains just out of reach.

So, in order to keep us distracted from the nerve-racking uncertainty of what the next four days would hold, Valerie and I decided to take Ripley on a picnic to Central Park.

As I was packing up our picnic items, I decided at the last minute to throw in a kite and, on a whim, Aunt Evelyn's lavender notebook from ML. It was beautiful and tempting, like a perfect poem that lingers in your mind for weeks, popping into your consciousness at the slightest provocation. I wanted Valerie to read it.

After seeing a bigger pile than I had planned on, I brought down one of Mr. Kirkland's rucksacks from the attic. Valerie was bringing lunch; I was bringing everything else. As I put my things in the rucksack, a small object at the bottom of the bag caught my attention. I reached in and pulled out a pawn piece to a chess set. It was black, scuffed, and worn. I liked the heavy feel of it in my palm, so I pocketed it and piled in my books, blanket, and kite.

Val and I met in between our two homes and then headed west to the park.

"I brought a kite!" I said excitedly.

"You are like a little kid, Lane," said Val, her green eyes lighting up.

"And I hope that never changes," I said, with a grin.

She laughed, throwing her golden brown head back, and said, "Me, too, Lane! Me, too."

It was pretty hot out, so I was glad I'd decided on my little shorts outfit. The navy shorts had two white stripes, top to bottom on each hip, and a line of five cute brass buttons from the waist on either side. My white canvas shoes and ankle socks showed off my legs. With a short-sleeved, V-neck blouse, it was a variation of the sailor suit. I couldn't quite bring myself to wear one of those jaunty little sailor hats, though. A little too cute for me. "Val, I love your light green shorts!" She always looked fantastic in light green. She turned to me with a smile. "Thanks! I actually took a pair of trousers and cut them down and sewed in a cuff." I smiled to myself as I remembered that only a little more than ten years ago, a woman was arrested in in Chicago for wearing a swimsuit that didn't have the required leg covering. Progress.

We decided on a place by the obelisk, Cleopatra's Needle. There were lovely picnic areas, plus it was near the Great Lawn so we could fly the kite. We spent an easy day reading, talking, snacking, and just enjoying each other's company. I think Ripley enjoyed the day, too. He'd curl up right next to our blanket, and once in a while, he'd allow us to use his sturdy sides as a headrest while we read our novels.

I put my book down and closed my eyes, soaking up the sun on my face. Ripley's breathing was slow and steady underneath my head.

"Val?"

"*Mm hmm?*" she replied drowsily.

"I brought something to show you," I said as I sat up and pulled out the notebook. I didn't tell her who it was from or what it was about, not that I really knew myself.

She picked up the notebook and started to browse through it. "Oooh, it's French," she said, like she had just found a really juicy pear and was ready to devour it. She read several pages, leafing through the well-loved volume, looking at the different sketches of Aunt Evelyn's and the many notes. Then she asked the question that was definitely my first question: "Who's ML?"

"I don't know. But isn't he something? I mean, the way he describes his setting, wherever he is, is so beautiful. And yet there is something tragic about him, isn't there?"

"Yes," she agreed. "Do you think he's a young man? Do you think Evelyn might have had a crush on him?"

"Huh, it's funny, but I have this idea that while he was actually young, his soul was old. No, I don't think a crush is the right word, plus I think Evelyn was quite a young girl at the time. But her feelings for him seem to be very earnest," I said as I rested my chin in my hand and pulled a few strands of my hair behind my ear.

"Oh, and there is such a . . . a . . . longing in him. It's like I can almost *see* it," she said.

I looked over at Val and her kind smile as she twirled a lock of her hair around her finger. She said, in deep thought, "He seems sad. But his words can be so hopeful despite that."

I smiled, glad that I had shared this with her. "All right, time for some lunch," I said, with my stomach grumbling an exhortation.

Val started unpacking her picnic basket. She brought chicken salad sandwiches, potato chips, Cokes, and The Best Chocolate Chip Cookies on the planet. Val knew they were my favorite and made them for me as much as possible. She told me once that they had a lot of butter, vanilla, and all brown sugar, but I had no idea why that made them better than others. All I knew was, they were *good*. Like magic.

As we finished off our feast, I said, "*Ahhh* . . . what a great day!"

I could hear her chuckle. "You know? I think it's going to get even better. I was just thinking that I have . . . a little headache . . . so I think I'll let you stay here and just enjoy your day."

"*What?*" I said, sitting bolt upright. "What are you talking about?" My outburst made Ripley get up in expectation, happily wagging his tail and looking around.

Then she smiled and pointed over to the trees about fifty feet away. Leaning up against the crabapple tree was Finn. He waved and motioned to ask whether he could come over. I have to admit, my heart skipped a beat. He had on tan trousers and a white polo shirt. I waved him over.

Valerie was gathering up her things as he came over. "Val, you don't have to leave, I was just coming through the park and saw you two."

"Ha! Sure you were!" She laughed, which made him grin sheepishly. He knelt down and gave Ripley a good welcome, rubbing down his back and patting his great big head. The rubdown made Ripley's tongue loll out of his mouth and one of his ears bend down a little. He was *not* the picture of a valiant protector that I knew him to be.

Val stood up, beaming. "I'll leave you two the rest of the Cokes and cookies. Have fun!"

"Cookies?" asked Finn eagerly.

"Oh, not just any cookies, The Best Chocolate Chip Cookies on the planet," I said, slightly sad to have to share them.

"Oooh! Look at that look on your face. You don't want to share!" he said, reading me loud and clear with a great big smirk.

"Nope."

"Ha! Valerie left them to *both* of us. You *have* to," he said, and I grudgingly gave him the bag. After taking two more.

"What have you two been doing?" he asked, extending his long legs and leaning back on one arm. "Oh, my God! These *are* good!" he said, looking down at his cookie like it was about to speak to him.

"Told ya. Now give me the bag back." He laughed and grudgingly gave me the bag back. After taking two more.

I leaned back, stretching my legs out to match his. I noticed his eyes skimming up and down my bare legs. "Oh, we've been talking, had lunch, read a while. It's been a great day," I said as I looked up at the passing clouds and took a deep breath. "What have you been up to?"

"Actually, it's the first day in . . . months, really . . . that I didn't have to be somewhere," he said, in a sort of bewildered way.

"*Months?*" I exclaimed. "How can you do that?"

"What do you mean? I do it all the time," he said.

"*Hmm,*" I murmured contemplatively. "I may have to do something about that." Finn was taking a good look around at the deep green trees, the guys playing baseball up ahead, and Cleopatra's Needle to our left. He rubbed his right knee and thigh.

"Your leg bothering you?" I inquired.

"What? Oh, no. No, just an old injury." He said it in tones that plainly meant he didn't want to talk about it.

I paused for a few seconds, keenly aware of his bright eyes. Something about that particular injury made him look wary and sad. I slowly raised my hand to my lips, not taking my eyes off his, kissed my hand, and laid it on his leg. I leaned closer to him, feeling my hair fall softly over the side of my face. I whispered, "I'm sure I can help you with that."

"Oh, I just bet you can."

After a long and spicy kiss, I said, "All right, I have an idea. Come with me." I stood up, put our things back in the rucksack, and offered my hand.

"Where are we going?" he asked as I helped haul him up.

"How about that way?" I said, pointing vaguely southwest.

Finn took up the rucksack after I folded the blanket and stuffed it in with our remaining Cokes and cookies. I got Ripley's leash, and we walked in the direction I had pointed.

We eventually came to Turtle Pond and the enormous statue of the Polish King Jagiello. He looked fierce with two magnificent swords drawn and crossed over his head, and I wondered what he was like in real life five hundred years ago. His statue was going to be part of the Polish pavilion for the upcoming World's Fair, but had a temporary place to stand and regard us New Yorkers right here. If he liked it, he would come back after the fair. I hoped so.

I looked up at Belvedere Castle and said, "That way! Have you ever been up there?"

"No," he said, completely predictably.

I steered us toward the path that led up to the old fort, which was sometimes used as a weather station. At the entrance to the stone castle, there was an emblem of a griffin that looked dragonish, and I placed my hand on it, feeling the warmth from the sun. "This is the dragon's house."

"Dragon?" he asked.

"Of course." I chuckled. "Aunt Evelyn always told me stories about the dragon that lives here and watches over New York. His room is that highest circular window up there. I've tried to visit, but the door is always locked." I traced the griffin with my fingertips and then touched the gray flagstone, feeling the rough, cool texture.

"Well, certainly," said Finn, nodding seriously, looking up at the top window. "Everyone knows dragons like the nighttime. Plus, they tend to be shy, contrary to public opinion."

I laughed. "I had no idea you had such a thorough knowledge of dragons. What else don't I know about you?"

"Oh, let's see, I like to ice skate. I hate mustard. Birds make me nervous."

"It's their beady eyes, isn't it."

"Yep. And their feet. I love the thought of sailing at night. Well, for that matter, I love the beach at night." And didn't that conjure all sorts of enticing images. "And that ribbon candy at Christmas.

It's a favorite of my grandma's, so I love it, too." He looked down at me and grinned with a perplexed sort of smile. "What are you thinking about?"

I had to restart my brain after I got stuck on dreaming of being on a beach with Finn at night. "Oh! I mean, wow, excellent list. I will have to keep those things in mind." Smooth recovery.

After a quick tour of the dragon's castle, enjoying the soaring view over Turtle Pond and the Great Lawn, we found ourselves at one of my favorite parts of the park: the top of Cedar Hill.

At the crest, the sweeping green hill coasted down below us with large rocks scattered about from ancient glaciers. At the bottom of the hill was another perpendicular path, and beyond that a big, open area where you could picnic or play ball. Tall buildings flanked the lush green space spreading out before us, framing the park with modular mountains.

"Let's go sit over there," I said, wanting to relax for a moment. We went over to a large gray boulder peeking out of the ground, gave Ripley some water, and got out the last two Cokes. The sun was warm on our faces and had heated the smooth rock we sat upon. People were scattered all over the place, colorfully dotting the landscape, yet it didn't feel crowded. Down below us, somewhere under a canopy of pine trees, a small jazz band performed with upright bass, drums, and sax.

"This is wonderful, Lane." I watched his satisfied face. "It's so full of life," he said.

After a while, I got up and nodded my head down the path. "Come on, I have another idea."

I took him down to the base of Cedar Hill, past the jazz band (I threw some coins into the bass case), aiming for the lawn of Cedar Hill. But I loved the old bridge just to the south of it, so we went through there. It was called the Glade Arch, with wildflowers growing in profusion around the sides of the banks. Instead of going under the arch as I usually did—I had no idea what made me do it—I veered right toward the path that led over the top of the bridge. We stopped at the railing and looked around.

I had my hands on the railing, and Finn came up behind me, putting his arm around my waist, looking over my shoulder. He brought his face close to mine, and my heart was fluttering with desire. He whispered in my ear, "Lane, today has been . . ."

I turned my head a fraction closer to him. "It's not over." He bent his head and softly kissed the side of my neck, making my knees turn to jelly. I turned into him, and his lips found mine for a kiss full of heat as my arms circled his waist.

"But don't think that kiss will distract me from my next plan for us," I said.

"Oh, really?" he asked, still so close I could feel his breath on my neck. I take that back. He could *most definitely* distract me.

He took my hand and started to pull me away from the railing. "All right, Lane! Let's go—" He cut off his statement as he saw me and what had to be a horrified look on my face. The world started to bend and twist, I was so astonished, but I grabbed his arm, and he caught me around the waist.

"Finn! Do you see this?"

"What? You look like you've just seen a ghost."

"I think I have. This scroll in stone here, on the bridge . . . Is it at all familiar to you?" Along the railing, there were small diamonds with a sculpted scroll in each one. The scroll was a diamond shape with loops at the four corners, then a small cross in the middle of the diamond with fleur-de-lis at the four points.

"No. Can't say that it is. Why? Is it familiar to you?"

"Yes, I dream about it all the time. It's the same scroll on the silver gun."

"Bloody hell, that gun has a lot of history."

"Yeah. You can say that again. That cannot be a coincidence. Can it?"

He nodded as he thought about it. Then he shook his head with a worried, furrowed brow. "No. I don't think it's a coincidence."

"Well . . . let's not think about it right now. The day is too beautiful. I've got an idea," I said as I grasped his hand.

We walked down into the grassy area of Cedar Hill. I tried to shake off that image of the scroll and the gun. It was beginning to take on a life all its own, with a more profound history than I ever could have guessed.

We got down to the open grass, and I brought out my kite. Finn looked at the colorful fabric and smiled. He said softly, "I haven't flown one of those in about twenty years."

"Doctors highly recommend flying a kite at least once a year," I said knowledgeably, successfully shaking off the feeling of ghosts nearby.

"Oh, really? I'll have to remember that."

I unfurled the long, curling, red tail of the kite while Finn expertly attached the crossbars to my brightly colored flier. I was momentarily distracted by those arms of his and almost got my kite tail in a knot. We got it all together, and the wind behaved perfectly. Not too strong, but it definitely got a hold of the kite. Finn had the string winder and let the kite up, slowly walking backward, letting out more string.

"This is nice," he said, with a calm look of satisfaction. We took turns flying the kite, and after quite a long while and two near misses by the large sycamore trees that loved to snatch at my kite, we decided to sit in the grass and finish off the cookies. I wanted to stay for weeks, I was having so much fun. I wondered where the rest of the day would lead.

That was right when Roarke showed up.

"My God, do I have a beacon attached to my head?" I asked indignantly. Roarke was mystified, and Finn cracked up. "Is it really *that* easy to follow me?"

In unison, Roarke and Finn said, "Yes."

"I ran into Kirkland, and he told me where to find you," said Finn.

"I ran into Valerie," said Roarke. I rolled my eyes.

"Anyway, I'm sorry to, uh, bother you guys, but I have a lead about Roxy's mother," said Roarke. "Lane, do you think you can come with me? I think she'd respond better to a woman."

I pulled Finn over to the side as he said, "Well, actually, I have to get going anyway, Lane."

I wanted to continue my afternoon with Finn, but then again . . . Roarke's lead about Roxy's mother was tantalizing.

"From what Roarke found out in Michigan, she sounded like a wreck," I said, feeling weirdly responsible.

"Yeah, I know," he said softly. "Lane?"

"*Hmm?*"

"Be careful, love."

I cocked my eyebrow. "Of the lead? Or of Roarke?"

He laughed out loud. "Both!" Then he said softly, "Thanks for a great day, Lane. It was the best I've had in a long time." He kissed me quickly on the cheek and left us.

"So, how do you want to handle this lead, Roarke?" I asked. His eyes shifted left to right as he shuffled his feet. "Wait, does this one lead us to the Meatpacking District or Chinatown again?" I asked warily.

"No. But it may be worse," he said, suddenly much more serious.

"Worse?" I asked, with a skeptical turn of my head.

"Well . . . Roxy's mom, Daphne Franco, is on Blackwell's Island."

"Oh, no. Here we go again."

CHAPTER 26

I put my heart and soul into my work,
and I have lost my mind in the process.

—ML

We took Ripley home, and I changed into nicer clothes: a respect-able, below-the-knee navy skirt with white blouse and a red and violet scarf at my neck. I needed something cheerful to go to that dark place. It was really called Welfare Island. After the prison and the workhouse got to have such a horrible reputation for violence and drug trafficking, the city changed the name of the island about fifteen years ago. Then last year, in '35, the prison was moved to Rikers Island, so now Welfare Island was home to only the elderly and the infirm. But somehow, the name Blackwell still stuck for many of us. Maybe that name fit the semicreepy feel of it better.

You could only access it via Queens, so we stopped and picked up Roarke's car. When we were on our way and going over the Queensboro Bridge from Manhattan into Queens, I finally asked him, "Um, where exactly is Roxy's mom on Blackwell's Island?"

"Oh . . . the hospital," he said.

"Aw, Roarke! Are you kidding me? Metropolitan Hospital?" I whined. "Just like Chinatown all over again."

Metropolitan Hospital's official descriptor was *lunatic asylum.* Fantastic. Call me a scaredy cat, but you put a prison, a workhouse, and a lunatic asylum, not to mention a smallpox hospital, on one dinky island . . . I broke out into a cold sweat.

"It's okay, Lane." Roarke chuckled. "Would I really take you somewhere that was unsafe?"

"Are you *really* asking me that?" I said flatly.

"Sheesh, it'll be fine. Look! We're almost there!" Like I was going to be excited by that.

Once into Queens, we took the bridge that led to Blackwell's, right by the towering white and red factory smokestacks that also kindled warm, fuzzy feelings. We went down Main Street (the only street that went down the middle of the narrow island) and drove up to the hospital with its infamous octagonal tower.

"So, how did you locate Daphne?" I asked.

"Well, a buddy of mine—shut up, Lane—checked into a few ideas I had. I wanted to see about the time frame when Daphne and her daughter, Louise, may have come to New York. I had him check out a platinum blond lady hanging out with anyone associated with Venetti's crew, with a daughter in tow. It took a while. I've actually been checking this out since that first trip to Michigan. I think this is the right woman. We'll find out," he said, with an air of *for better or worse—and it's probably worse.*

We walked up the front steps and talked with the receptionist about a Mrs. Franco. That was definitely not Roxy's last name, which was Loughlin, but it was the last known name of that man in Michigan who had perished in the lake accident, along with my parents. *Daphne and Rutherford Franco . . . daughter, Louise Franco.* I tossed around the names in my mind, trying to hunt for clues, small shreds of memory, anything.

Roarke came up with some story to get in to see her, batting his wonderful eyelashes and bringing the dimples out for the receptionist. She was done in. We went up to the third floor, through several doorways, and down a few hallways, and believe me, I was memorizing the way back out.

Inside, the hospital felt like any other hospital—with additional locked doors. It was clean, not too dark, and filled with the smell of antiseptic and the sound of nurses and aides chatting away. However, I felt uneasy. It could be my admittedly overactive imagination, but it was difficult walking through there. I longed to get back outside and would have been quite happy to swim across the East River to Manhattan if need be.

We got to Daphne Franco's room, and the interior was not what

I expected at all. It was a sunny room with fancier bed linens and curtains than I thought strictly necessary. And an elegant woman of about fifty was lying across the bed in a carefully crafted pose, wearing a plain, white robe. I could easily imagine a silky negligee and fluffy, feathery boa wrapped around her neck. She had a melodramatic arm across her brow, as if she were fighting off a fit of the vapors.

"Hello, darlings," she drawled, in a trans-Atlantic accent, like a movie star.

"Hello, Mrs. Franco," replied Roarke. He had said that he needed my help, that maybe Mrs. Franco would respond better to a woman. But after one momentary glance at her . . . not a chance. It was going to be Roarke all the way.

He looked over at me, and I cocked my eyebrow at him, muttering under my breath, "Go for it, Loverboy."

He looked confused. Honestly, men could be so naïve. So I mouthed the word *watch*. I meaningfully nodded to Mrs. Franco, walked one step closer to her, and clearly said, "Good afternoon, Mrs. Franco, how are you today?"

She didn't acknowledge my presence in so much as a blink. Her eyes were plastered onto Roarke. I turned back to him and said out loud this time, "See?"

I turned back and took a more thorough look at Mrs. Franco. It's very helpful watching someone when they aren't aware of you. You can see things in their eyes and their facial features that you might be blind to when they are actively engaging your attention.

She was staring at Roarke hungrily, which made him nervous in the extreme. Her blond hair was brushed, but it looked like it needed a good cut, and it had lost its luster. She certainly was well-rounded, like Roxy. She kept pursing her lips, trying her best to look like a Hollywood starlet. Yet there was also something else. Her face looked like there was something lurking just beneath the surface. But there was a nice, tight and shiny veneer over the top. Covering what?

Roarke stammered out a question. "Um, Mrs. Franco, we were wondering when you came to New York City." She looked at him with a dubious expression, so he continued. "Ah, you see, I'm a reporter, and I'm doing a story on, uh, people who might like to be famous actors."

"*Like* to be actors?" she said, with disdain.

"*Are* famous actors," he amended. She brightened right up and started chattering a mile a minute about her promising career; how she was cooped up in this hotel while her agent was working on the deal of the century for her; how all the top directors had heard of her, etc. We nodded our heads enthusiastically.

"And so you got to New York . . . when?" he asked again.

"Oh, let's see, not long ago, I think it's been just a couple years, about 1926, I think." Which was a decade ago.

"Uh-huh," said Roarke, making a show of taking down notes. I wondered how he would frame the next question. "And . . . did you come with any family?"

"Of course not. I came here for my *career*," she said importantly.

Roarke pretended to check his notes again. "Um, it says here that you came with a little girl. Would that be your daughter?" he said, with a smile and dimples. No dice.

"Why do you want to know about *her?*" she demanded, with a curl to her lip. And the veneer slipped just the tiniest, scariest little bit. My eyes flashed to Roarke. He didn't glimpse the monster beneath the mask; he kept going.

"Oh, nothing at all, the fans, you know," he said, with a conspiratorial wink. "They just love stories with moms and their daughters. Really makes the stars stand out," he said, with a knowing smile. She took the cue.

"Oh, yes, of course! Yes, I came with my . . . daughter." But she couldn't help herself, even for the fans. She still said the word *daughter* with less than love. Far less.

"But you know, just between you and me, Louise was always a useless burden on me. She was always so selfish. And then when she was about sixteen, she started hanging out with these guys, one in particular. He was actually pretty good-looking, but I think she was loose," she said, with derision. "Why else were they hanging around?"

"This one guy, do you remember his name?" Roarke slipped in smoothly.

"Oh, something like Dennis, David, Daniel . . . something with a *D*."

"Danny?"

"Yes, I guess. That sounds right," she said airily, like she was quickly becoming bored not talking about herself. The veneer was tight, locked firmly in place once again.

Then I made my fatal error. I should have kept my mouth shut, but I spoke up innocently, with a lighthearted smile, and asked, "So, before New York, where did you come from, Mrs. Franco?"

Her head slowly turned to me like it was on a mechanical swivel. She looked directly into my eyes, deep down into my soul, making my flesh crawl. Her pupils dilated. And the veneer came crashing down.

Her face was suddenly a mockery of what it had been a second before. Her skin became taut, with the tiny veins in her face coming to the surface of her papery white skin. Her nostrils flared; she squinted her eyes and bared her teeth. "You!" she snarled.

I jumped, ready for her to pounce, but she stayed put. Roarke took a defensive step toward me with his arm out.

"You came back, huh?" she said as her lips curled into a cruel smile. Then she raggedly whispered with her teeth bared, "Want me to finish the job now?"

"Oh, my God, it's *her*," I gasped, my knees wanting to give out.

"Lane!" said Roarke, rushing close.

Then she cackled like a witch, to some inside joke known only to her . . . and she wouldn't stop. She just kept cackling and cackling. I had to get out of there.

"Roarke," I said, desperate to get the message to him. "We have to go!" The cackling kept going relentlessly on and on, with grating insanity. He didn't say one word. His arm went around my waist, and he hauled me out of there for all he was worth.

We were moving fast, and the distance was starting to clear my head. My feet started to make better purchase on the shiny floors. We hustled down each corridor, and I had never been more elated to see an exit in my life. We could still hear the now-distant maniacal laughter.

"Lane, what the hell was that?" demanded Roarke as we burst

out the front door and ran down the front steps, making our way to the parking lot. I was panting as we ran out, trying to get as much clean, unsullied air into my lungs as possible.

"My God, Roarke. I remember her! I've had nightmares about that woman ever since my parents died. She came to the hospital where I was recovering and leered over me with that demonic smile. She was wearing a green hat," I told him. I was out of breath, but not wanting to stop our fast pace.

"You remember her? Well, she certainly remembered you. I think we have our answer. That was definitely Roxy's mom, and there is *absolutely* a link between that family and you."

"Yeah," I panted. "Yeah, I know."

Suddenly we heard the clip of shoes behind us. I looked back, and about twenty feet away was the weasely Schmidt brother. The one I had sucker punched. And he had a gun pointing right at us.

CHAPTER 27

A great fire burns within me.

—ML

Roarke spotted him at the exact instant I did, and we both stopped dead in our tracks, putting our hands up, breathing hard from our run.

"Huh. You don't look so tough now, chicky," he said to me as he slowly strolled closer. Was that *boring* line the best he could do? Really, you'd think New York thugs could do better. I suppressed an eye roll, since that gun was still pointing at my chest and coming closer.

"So, you find what you were looking for here?" he asked, nodding toward the hospital entrance.

I said, "Oh, yes, thanks. Roarke's aunt is here. We were visiting for her birthday." Weasel looked confused, like I had thrown a wrench into his plan. I fought the urge to speak with a Southern accent.

Roarke said convincingly, and at a quick pace, "Poor Aunt Trudy has been here for about two years. She's doing really well, though. I think it made her day that we stopped by, Lane. Really. Thanks for coming with me."

Weasel's gun lowered a few crucial inches, and he wrinkled his nose in what I think was an attempt at deep thought. From behind Weasel came a loud voice that yelled out, "Hey!"

I knew that voice.

At just that moment, three policemen came running toward us. Weasel made a mad dash into an alley.

I was still using all my mental faculties to process what had just happened, so I let Roarke handle talking to the police and thanking them as they walked us back to our car.

We didn't waste any time chitchatting before we started up the car and got the hell off that abysmal island. Even the smokestacks now looked warm and friendly in comparison. I desperately wanted to get home and take a hot, hot shower. I felt almost as grubby as when I had that run-in with Daley Joseph.

After I got home, showered, and went down to our warm, homey kitchen, I felt like myself again. Mr. Kirkland was prepping mashed potatoes to go with the roast beef that was slowly roasting in the oven; delectable scents wafted throughout the house. My mouth watered. I was suddenly ravenous, which surprised me, because at one point this afternoon I was pretty sure I'd never have an appetite again.

There were some oatmeal cookies (without raisins—they really ruin a good cookie) in the tin, so I helped myself and made some tea. I filled in Mr. Kirkland on our strange visit to Metropolitan Hospital, including the part about the mystery lady with the green hat from my dreams. I still couldn't believe that I had finally put a real person to that dream. And I wasn't entirely sure that that was a good thing.

Mr. Kirkland had taken it all in, nodding from time to time. It was pleasing to watch his long, capable fingers deftly peeling the potatoes, cutting them up, and putting them into a large pot of water. I perched on a stool at the kitchen counter, sipping my tea, outlining the etched fleur-de-lis on the mug with my finger over and over again. Aunt Evelyn was upstairs in her studio; I'd fill her in when she came down. Slow, jazzy piano music floated down from upstairs.

There was a knock at the front door. I told Mr. Kirkland I'd get it; I had a feeling I knew who it would be. Ripley and I got to the door at the same time, and I opened it. Finn was standing there with worry etched into his brow, looking just about ready to break the door down.

"Thanks for distracting Weasel," I said casually, my arms crossed in front of me, leaning up against the door jamb.

"Wh . . ." he stammered. "I better come in."

It was still warm out, but the day was getting dark, and heavy clouds had rolled in. The entryway was dark and shadowy, but a warm candle in a hurricane globe had been lit and the flames danced on the walls, making it an especially inviting alcove. The music from upstairs was still going, and suddenly it felt like we were in the middle of a lonely jazz club. Just the two of us.

"How did you know?" he asked, his brow still worried.

"Well, I know your voice pretty well, and let's just say I had a sneaking suspicion that you might not trust Roarke's abilities to . . ."

"Keep his nose, actually, *your nose,* out of danger," he supplied.

"Exactly." He'd changed into a dark blue oxford shirt, open at the collar, arms rolled up a couple of times, that made his shoulders and arms look very nice. His eyes were black.

"What did you find out?" he asked. I filled him in on Daphne. He picked up on something I had not wanted to admit yet, to myself nor anyone else. He took a step closer, touched my cheek with his palm, and let his thumb come around my chin lightly, like a wisp of air. "When you remember her from your nightmares . . . do you really think that when you saw her face hovering over you when you were a child, she . . ."

"Yes. I do. I think she intended to kill me when she came to the hospital after the accident, but something prevented her. I don't know if she was in on the whole thing, but her raw look of insane hatred . . ." I shivered.

He reached out and put his arm around my waist, pulling me to him. I laid my head on his chest, the top of my head just touching his jawline.

We slowly, slowly swayed back and forth to the piano music. I had no idea what that song was; I'd never heard it before, and have never heard it since. It would be decades later that an artist would come out with a song called "Come Away with Me" that came close. Very close.

"I have a question," I said.

"*Mm hmm,*" he said, not moving his head, his cheek now resting on the top of my head. I didn't risk moving an inch, either. I had never been held like this before, never felt such a perfect fit. It was like our bodies were made for each other. And there was another feeling—what was it? I couldn't figure it out.

I murmured contentedly, "Is Finn your full name?" I could feel his chest vibrate with a little laugh.

"That's funny you should ask. Is Lane *your* full name?"

"Oh, no, don't change the subject. Is it Finnegan?"

"No."

"Phineas?"

"No."

I was already running out of ideas. "Ffffinster?"

He laughed. I loved the sound of his laugh, and I could just imagine the crinkles at the corners of his eyes. I loved those crinkles.

"Finster? Really?"

"Sorry, it's all I got."

"*Hmmm* . . . Well, I don't usually divulge my secrets, but in your case I'll make an exception."

"Thank you."

"It's just Finn. Finn Brodie." When he said his full name, I could hear the Irish loud and clear.

I was smiling to myself. The music kept going, as I was willing it to never stop. We kept swaying, closely locked together.

"So? Your name, love. Is it Elaine?"

"No."

"Delaney?"

"Isn't that a street?" I asked.

"I think that's Delancey. In Greenwich Village. Is it Delaney?"

"No."

"That's all I got. Oh, wait . . . I know what it is."

"No, you don't."

"Yes. I do."

"Finn . . ." I said very, very softly. "I'm worried about the plan. If we can really pull it off."

He took a deep breath and said, "I know. I'm not that fond of it, either. But it *will* work, Lane. I know it will." I pulled my head away just enough to look up at him, still tightly entwined, our noses almost touching, a hair's breadth apart.

"Finn . . ." I whispered. "Are you *sure?* I can do it, but . . ." He bent his head down, his lips melting into mine. I held his hand tight, not wanting to let go. I felt his arm tighten around my waist. We danced there for a long, long time.

CHAPTER 28

"Sir, you wanted to see me?" he asked, decidedly concerned about this unusual call for a meeting. He was repelled by the man, but he did need more information, so he hoped it was worth it. Plus, you never, *ever* ignored a call from this man. The room was dark red, with bookcases all around and ferns in tall, brass plant stands scattered about. The room contained a layer of stale cigar smoke that made it look like a London fog had rolled in.

"Yes, come in, come in," he said as he pointed to the much lower seat on the other side of the desk in front of him. He folded his hands on top of his grand desk and smiled without warmth as the younger man came in and sat down. "Is the plan in place?"

"Yes, sir, it is."

"Does she suspect anything?"

"No, nothing."

"I've had my eye on you, you know."

"Good."

"I've heard how you have a thing for her."

"It's all part of the plan."

"You do understand that she knows too much already. And you know what that means," he said, with an evil lift to his eyebrow. He had a cocky look in his all-knowing eyes. His expensive suit reeked of cigars, alcohol, and cheap perfume from his *acquaintances* whom he liked to keep. His short, orange hair had a nappy texture, and it made the top of his dangerous head look like a rusty steel wool pad.

"Yes, I know what it means. We'll have to kill her."

"That's right. Can I count on you, Brodie?"

"Yes, Mr. Connell."

CHAPTER 29

I am convinced that there will be a time when,
let us say, I will make something good every day.

—ML

The next day, I was upstairs getting ready for work when I heard
the usual: the door slamming open, the joyous barks of Ripley, and
the screechy greeting of Fiorello. In stark comparison to the emotional roller coaster of the day before, it felt good to hear the normal
parts of my everyday life. And the aromas. I could smell freshly
baked biscuits, and I licked my lips at the thought of butter and
honey on them. After last night's roast beef and mounds of mashed
potatoes, I thought I'd eaten enough to last me the week. However,
one always had room for Mr. Kirkland's biscuits.

The bellowing downstairs had stopped completely, so I figured
Fio had discovered them as well. I finished buttoning up my deep
purple dress with elbow-length sleeves. I slipped on my black high
heels and headed downstairs.

On the way down the steps, I saw a little picture Aunt Evelyn
had painted of a cottage. It always reminded me of my home in
Rochester, and I remembered a fuzzy dream of that place from the
night before. Maybe a trip back there would be in order soon.

Everyone was seated at the table, clearly enjoying the biscuits. I
must have had a desperate look on my face as I scanned the table,
because Mr. Kirkland chuckled and handed me a whole new basket
full of steaming biscuits.

"God bless you, Mr. Kirkland," I said. Fiorello smiled at me
while chewing.

"While you're all eating, I have a lot to fill you in on." So I did. Apparently they had become used to my little adventures, because everyone just listened attentively to my story about Blackwell's Island. No gasps, no wide eyes.

Aunt Evelyn spoke up first and said insouciantly, "I assume it was Finn who made the distraction and called the policemen over? I can't say I blame him for following you both. You do tend to get into quite a bit of trouble."

"*Hmph,*" I muttered.

Fiorello summed up the situation. "So, now we know that Roxy and her mother have some kind of motive in all this, but we need more evidence for their involvement with Daley and Donagan. I think it best that we keep an eye on her at work, Lane."

Aunt Evelyn visibly shuddered. Then she turned to Mr. Kirkland. "Do you remember Daphne and Louise from your visits to Rochester?"

He shook his head, confounded. "No, you'd think they would have stood out. But when I was there, I mostly spent time with Matthew in the barn making furniture, cutting wood. . . . Or, when I was making more frequent visits, when you were just a baby, Lane, we'd have family dinners together, just the four of us. We figured that with our past it would be best, even in that small town, to have me keep a pretty low profile. And as time went on, I only came out to visit once a year or so. It was the only time I felt off duty. So, I wasn't always looking over my shoulder." He said that last part with piercing, deep regret.

"Kirk," said Evelyn, with a hand on his shoulder, "there is nothing you could have done to save Matthew and Charlotte. You did all you could."

"No. I'll never believe that. I wish I could," he said. And he slowly, almost painfully, got up from the table and left the room.

I looked at Aunt Evelyn. She said, "It's all right, darling. I'll talk with him. You two go off to work."

I looked to Fio, and he nodded. I picked up my notebook and bag and gave Ripley a good rub and kiss on the nose before we headed out the door.

"Lane," said Fio. "You're doing a good job handling all this. If I can help at all, or Marie—she's offered many times to have you out to the Bronx house just to relax. Please, please, let us help if we can. All right?" I smiled and nodded a big affirmative nod.

"Then, let's go. We have work to do!"

And we were off! He was happily shouting out orders and tasks for the day. As always, my hand scribbled furiously, and I looked forward to my day ahead. We walked down the steps to the 77th Street subway and stood on the platform. It was a particularly crowded rush hour, all sorts of people on their way to work, and we were jam-packed.

The train pulled into the station, and suddenly I had that prickly feeling like someone was watching me. The hairs on the back of my neck rose, and I looked around as best I could. The doors of the train opened, and a flood of people came off, and a flood of people wanting to get on started to push forward.

I felt a rough hand pull my arm back, and I came up against Daley Joseph. His foul breath spilled over my face as he whispered in a sick, singsong voice, "I'm watching you. And I have a surprise waiting for you." He abruptly let go of my arm, and at just the right moment, he shoved me into the crowd getting on the train.

"Fio! Fio! There he is!" Fio turned quickly around and just barely caught a glimpse of Daley as the door shut and the train jerked hard as it started to move. Daley smirked and touched his hat in greeting to Fio.

"Daley Joseph," Fio said, with reverent gravity. "What did he want?" he asked, his face curious and taut.

"He caught my arm and said that he was"—I gulped—"watching us and that he had a surprise waiting."

"That can't be good," he said, his face pale.

"No. No, it can't."

We made our wary way to the office, both of us deciding maybe we should have a police escort to and from work after all. I turned to him as we raced up the steps of city hall. "Seeing him in person is eye-opening, isn't it?"

"Sure is. And in light of all this, let's keep an eye on you know who today. I want to make sure we are aware of any of her movements and if she's up to something that might give us another lead, okay?"

"You got it, boss," I said.

But when we got up to our offices, Roxy was nowhere in sight. Instead, we were faced with a very worried Lizzie and Ralph.

"Mr. LaGuardia . . . Lane. It's Roxy. She hasn't shown up for work today, and I know she's not sick or anything. I just saw her last night. We always let each other know if we won't be in the office. And nothing! She's just not here," said Lizzie.

I looked at Ralph, wondering if he had anything to contribute, but he was evidently just moral support for Lizzie. He kept bringing her things to calm her down, and one time tried to put a comforting arm around her shoulders, but she kept shrugging him off.

Fio said, "All right, Lizzie. Let's give her the benefit of the doubt. Maybe she's just late. If she's not in by eleven, why don't you and Lane go to her apartment and see if she's sick or if anything is wrong. Okay?"

Lizzie took a shaky breath and tried to smile. "All right, Mr. La-Guardia, sounds good. I'm sure you're right, she's probably just late. Maybe she had a doctor's appointment or something and forgot to tell me. Thanks. I'll keep you posted."

"You do that, Lizzie."

It really bothered me, though. Roxy was never, ever, late. I was utterly frustrated and filled with anxiety that we let her slip right through our fingers. I wondered darkly if this was our little surprise from Daley.

The minutes slowly ticked to eleven, and still there was no word from Roxy. So Valerie and I offered to go with Lizzie to see if Roxy was home ill or if she had possibly left a note there. Plus, I wanted to check out her place for more clues. Lizzie tried her darnedest to go by herself, but let's just say that there are times when Fio is absolutely immovable in his decisions, and there was no way on earth that he would let her go without three of us at least. In addition to Val and me, he sent a jubilant Ralph to be our supposed bodyguard.

Lizzie was exuding contempt, and she rolled her eyes so much

I was worried she'd go cross-eyed. But Valerie, Ralph, and I were impervious, as we were excited to be able to go, for our own separate reasons. We got to Roxy's little place, a top-floor apartment of a large brownstone. We rang the bell, but there was no answering buzz from her apartment, so we buzzed the landlady. She came to the door, and after we explained our reason for being there, she offered to take us up herself to make sure Roxy was all right.

We walked up the three flights of stairs, and the landlady unlocked the door. Roxy's apartment was neat and orderly in the extreme. The bed was perfectly made, and the dishes were all clean, not a single dish or cup sitting in the sink. Roxy was not there, and wherever she went, it looked like she meant to go. There were clothes missing from her closet, and her luggage was gone, along with toiletries from the bathroom.

Valerie and I exchanged knowing looks. Lizzie and Ralph looked shocked and confused. Lizzie exclaimed, "But, why didn't she tell me she was going away? And for how long? I mean, we're best friends!" She sounded outraged and close to tears. I knew she was worried, but the tone of her voice was incredibly grating. I looked at Val and made a face that said I couldn't take much more of her. Val mouthed the words, *I know.* Ralph tried putting his arm around Lizzie again, and this time she let him. He looked exceedingly pleased.

Just as we were getting ready to leave and were on our way out the door, I saw a lone hat on the kitchen table. I had seen it when I came in, but now I realized that it looked oddly out of place. *Why?* I didn't bring it up, but there was something significant about it.

"All right, well, it looks like she meant to leave. Maybe we'll get a telegram later that will explain. Maybe she got a call during the night from a sick relative or something," I said, trying to sound convincing. It worked for Lizzie; she almost smiled. We all went back to the office and tried to work the rest of the day, but it was hard to concentrate. We only had three days left until August tenth.

I finally went home and as I opened the door to our townhouse, I heard Mr. Kirkland humming in the kitchen. I greeted Ripley, put my things down in a heap, and went to have a chat in the heart of the house.

"Hey there, Lane. How's your day?" greeted Mr. Kirkland with his gruff voice.

"Very . . . interesting," I said uncertainly as I sat on a stool at the counter.

"Oh. Interesting good or interesting bad?"

"Not so good," I said, and brought him up to speed on Roxy's disappearance.

"Hmm," he grunted, ruminating on the possibilities. "I'm with you, I don't think she's on a spur-of-the-moment vacation."

I nodded and started munching on a bowl of hot popcorn that Mr. Kirkland handed me.

"You know," I said, "I've been thinking. It seems like everything is coming to a head. And I've got something to tell you and something to ask you. Which do you want first?"

He looked wary. But then the old spy always did like a challenge. "The ask."

"All right," I said, licking the salt off my lips and grinning, fore-telling that this was going to be a doozy. I took a big breath and told him about the plan that Finn and I worked out. All of it.

"You want to ask *who* to do *what?* And then you'll . . . *what?*" he asked, his voice louder than usual and a little squeaky in disbelief.

"Yep. You heard me," I said calmly. "Just think about it. I know it's risky, but hundreds or even thousands could be in danger. It's time for risk. My question is, will you go with me when it's time?" A spark in his eyes told me he was well-pleased that I asked him and that I had my answer. I smiled broadly.

I hopped down from my stool and grabbed a couple of beers from the fridge. I uncapped both and handed him his. He took a long swig and before he was finished, I quickly said the statement part of my twofold talk with him.

"Now the tell. Mr. Kirkland, I know you can't forgive yourself for not stopping the hit on my parents. But from what I know of my parents, they would want you to forgive yourself for *them*. It's what you would want if the situation was reversed."

He slowly lowered his bottle of beer to the counter. His gray hair looked debonair in the golden kitchen light. He took in a deep breath, his powerful chest increasing in size. Once again a seafaring image came to mind. He looked at me, searching. Then made a quick, determined nod of his head.

He cleared his throat and said, "Well, if we're going to go through with this plan of yours, I have a few things I want to show you. And I want to give you something of your father's that you should have. Come on." He called for Ripley to come, too, and I followed them outside onto the patio.

That night I had a significant dream for the first time in a long while. I had been willing my subconscious to help me figure out these damn puzzle pieces; we were running out of time. But every single night I had been disappointed. Not this time.

The white sand spread out before me and the sea wind whipped through my hair and pushed hard against my body as I walked toward the water. I could taste the salty air on my lips, hear the cry of the gulls and the pounding, rolling surf. The waves were beautiful and blue, calling to me with white foam cresting at the tops as they creamed over onto the smooth, wet sand.

Up ahead there was a couple walking toward me. The wind dashed their clothing around and their faces were obscured from the blowing sand and bright sunshine. As they drew near, I started to feel fear run its finger up my spine.

The man was tall and was wearing a hat tilted down, hiding his face. The woman was clearer. She had light blond hair and gorgeous curves. They stopped right in front of me. I was frozen to the spot. The woman's face kept changing from Roxy to her mother. I stared at the man. He slowly looked up. It was Finn. My heart stopped. He looked me right in the eyes and then looked pointedly at Roxy. She had a black hat on top of her little head, and wore a startlingly bright scarf tied at her throat.

I sat bolt upright in bed and gasped. *Oh, my God.* I yelled out to no one in particular, "Damn it!" I raced out of bed and ran downstairs to Mr. Kirkland's basement apartment. I knocked on the door loudly, unafraid of waking Aunt Evelyn; she needed to hear what was up, too. He came to the door disheveled and bedecked in his pajamas, but his eyes sparked with alertness. And he was holding a revolver. Okay, then. I guess he was prepared.

I told him what I realized from my dream. "It's not Roxy we have to worry about. We have to execute the plan *right now*." Aunt Evelyn must have heard me running down the stairs, because she was waiting for us in the kitchen. I filled her in on the deduction my dream provided, and she agreed. Luckily, it was already six in the morning, so we could get to work immediately.

I ran back upstairs. I put on my best black suit with pencil skirt and extra wide red belt. I threw on my favorite red heels and quickly brushed out my hair, pulling one side behind my ear. Quick stroke of eyeliner and mascara, and crisp red lipstick for courage.

My jaw was set with determination as I looked in the mirror. I took from the top of my dresser a few crucial items for the day. I fingered the black and pearl dagger that Mr. Kirkland had given me yesterday, its weight perfectly familiar and easily handled. Like I'd had it forever.

At the threshold, I turned back and took a careful look around at my comfortable blue and white room: the white chair in the corner by the window where I whiled away many an hour reading novels, my blue and white bedspread, the dark dresser with the glass knobs. With an odd feeling of finality washing over me, I wondered when I would return.

Or if I would.

CHAPTER 30

I must continue to follow the path I take now.
If I do nothing, if I study nothing, if I cease
searching, then, woe is me, I am lost.

—ML

Mr. Kirkland flagged down a taxi, and we headed for the West Side. He had on a black business suit, complete with fedora, and I could see the bulge of his holster and gun. He looked like a different man.

We hardly spoke. It was now about quarter to seven in the morning. I figured the household would be up; I was hoping he'd understand the early hour. We needed as much time as we could get.

The butler answered slightly wearily; we were obviously the first visitors of the day. But he ushered us into the parlor and told us to wait; he would retrieve us. We stood around a glamorous parlor full of dark burgundy couches, an ebony grand piano, an enormous fireplace I could have walked into, and hundreds of silver frames all over the place featuring family members and a number of famous people.

After a quick pause, the butler retrieved us and ushered us through the house to a dark and regal office. I looked back at Mr. Kirkland. He nodded his head slightly.

I stepped in, walked right over to his humongous desk, and said, "Mr. Venetti, I know who killed your nephew, Danny. We have a plan, and I was wondering if you might consider working with us."

Later, I headed to work, and Mr. Kirkland went back to the house. The deadline of the big threat was only two days away. We had to find the target. I wanted to shout to the world that I knew who was behind all this, but we still needed evidence. Who would listen to a hunch and a dream? Plus, if we jumped in too soon, they would know we were on their trail, and it would be much harder to find the target. We needed the element of surprise.

Roxy still didn't show up at work. Ralph was unusually quiet and kept to himself, which was alarming in and of itself. I didn't see Lizzie, but heard she had come in early that morning and then left to go to the post office and do some other office errands. We all were trying to do our work, but the tension in the office was palpable. Even to those who didn't know what was going on, there was something in the air that kept everyone at a quieter volume, waiting, watching.

Later in the morning I grabbed a quick coffee with Valerie, then walked a package over to the courthouse. As I dropped off the package, then headed down the long set of steps outside, I ran through the details of the evidence and clues one more time, and something dawned on me. I might know where to look for a lead. Maybe back at the Meatpacking District, we could at least take a look around. But I needed to get a message to Finn.

I found a cop who was willing to take a message to Detective Finn Brodie for me; my job as aide to the mayor had its perks. Hopefully the message would get to him. Just as I was lamenting not having some kind of phone that I could carry with me or even the ability to send smoke signals, for God's sake, I heard a familiar voice and absolutely rejoiced.

"Roarke! I could not be happier to see you. I need a partner." I quickly told him about checking out the factory where we'd overheard his informant talking with Danny.

"Yeah. That's a good idea. Can't hurt," he said.

We took the crosstown bus west to the Meatpacking District. We crept up to the same building that Roarke and I had scoped out that memorable day. The streets were still slimy, and I was grateful that I had chosen closed-toed shoes. We went down that tight alley and to that same grimy window. It was open just a crack, and we listened intently. I heard knocking like a shoe being rapped on the ground and the unmistakable *"Mm! Mm! Mm!"* of someone with a gag, trying to call out. Roarke and I looked at each other, half in victory, half in fear of, *What now?*

A disgusted voice suddenly rumbled right above us, "Oh, no, not you again." Then a blinding pain struck my neck and head. Everything went black.

I woke up with my head resting against a man's chest. For an instant I was deliriously happy that it was Finn. But then again, it wasn't quite right. But he did feel good, and I felt a hand rubbing my back gently. I looked up and saw that it was Roarke. Then everything came rushing back to me. I tried to sit up, but my head pounded with a monumental throb, and I almost passed out.

"Whoa there, Lane," said Roarke. "Take it easy." He gently brought me back down to his chest. We were lying up against the wall of a barren room. I quickly looked around and saw that there weren't any windows except up near the ceiling. It was getting darker outside, maybe five or six o'clock.

"What happened?" I whispered, trying to keep my fragile head as still as possible. I gently probed around my scalp and didn't feel any blood, but I had a painful egg sprouting off the back of my head. "Ow!" I exclaimed. Make that *very* painful.

"Well, as you can tell, we were discovered," he said ruefully. "After they incapacitated us both, they dragged us to this room. They hit me over the head as well, but being that I'm a lot bigger than you and therefore harder to carry, I guess they wanted to make their job easier and just make me more compliant. I was able to get back here on my own. They slumped you over one of their shoulders, and . . . we're here."

"Have you scouted out the room yet?" I asked.

"Well, Lane, I wasn't sure you were going to wake up," he said tersely. "So I've been right here."

"Oh, Roarke. I'm so sorry I got us into this," I said as I patted him on the chest.

"I'm sorry. It's just the stress of it all. But really, they thumped you on the head, and the thud . . ." His voice went lower. "It was awful. You really had me scared."

I carefully nodded against his chest. I didn't want to talk about it, but I was plenty scared, too. His arms felt warm and safe. I wasn't budging any time soon. In fact, I must have fallen asleep, because I woke up to Roarke shifting around and whispering my name.

"Lane, I think they're coming. Wake up. Are you all right?"

"Yeah, I'm good. Actually, I do feel better. I think I'll try to sit up a little higher." At first I was very woozy, but then my balance equalized. My head was still hurting, but the raw throbbing was going down. The sky was completely dark now. Time was short. Day after tomorrow was The Day—August tenth.

Two guys came in looking big, dumb, and mean. They had looks on their faces that meant business, and they were shaped like meat loaves. The extra meaty guy wearing a dark brown suit came at Roarke, and I got the slightly less beefy guy in navy. There was absolutely nothing in their eyes. Emptiness. Like machines doing their duty. All they said was, "You have a trip ahead of you. You can do it the easy way or the hard way, see?"

Yeah, that was obvious. "We'll take the easy way," I said quickly.

"We have a hood and a gag for each of you, then we'll lead you to your vehicle." They went ahead, and we complied. I hated gags. I was a gagger. It took immense concentration to breathe through my nose and not retch. I got the rhythm of it and tried to stay pressed up against Roarke.

The two meat loaves bound our hands behind our backs and then led us out of that room and through many hallways. I could hear the echo of our footsteps, but nothing else. They put us into some kind of van or truck and the engine started up. I strained my ears as best I could and paid attention to any possible detail that might give a clue to where we were going.

I could hear traffic and an occasional siren, and we took plenty of turns. Since the Meatpacking District was on the mid to lower West Side and it was clear we hadn't gone through a tunnel or bridge yet, we were probably making our way across town or maybe uptown. We finally got to a bridge. I could tell because we went up an incline and the tires made a different noise, like we were on a different kind of pavement.

Then it hit me. I could feel the familiar *thum-thum, thum-thum* of the seams in the cement. If I had a hundred bucks, I'd bet it all that we were going across the Queensboro Bridge. *Please, not to Black-well's Island, please, not to Blackwell's Island.* But we kept going for a while after that, so we were definitely not going to Metropolitan Hospital, unless the Meatloaf Twins were bright enough to trick us and backtrack in their driving. I was pretty sure that wasn't going to happen. So? We were in Queens somewhere.

CHAPTER 31

Mr. Kirkland finished up his pot of chili with a few tosses of Tabasco Sauce. It was late, but he'd had a long day, and Evelyn was working hard on finishing up a piece in her studio. It was late for Lane not to be home already, but she sometimes met up with a friend for a drink or something after work.

He went over in his mind everything he'd taught Lane the day before. She was a quick learner, and he could tell she enjoyed it. The biggest shock was her delight in the dagger he gave her. She took it, enjoying the feel in her hand, and it had suddenly brought back a long-forgotten memory to her.

"Oh, wow, I remember that. It was my dad's," she said, with a pleased smile.

He nodded, happy that she remembered.

"Oh, wait!" she'd exclaimed. "I can do this, watch!" And she'd taken the dagger handle in her hand and flung it at the nearby tree. It unsuccessfully hit the trunk with a thump, clanging to the ground.

"Shoot! Wait, really, I can do it!" He had been shocked into a stunned, horrified silence.

"Wait, Lane, you shouldn't . . ." But she'd picked it up again, this time with the blade of the dagger in her fingertips, and flung it with power and precision to the other tree on the other side of the patio. And like a dart, it had shot across the space with a satisfying *thunk* into the wood and stuck fast.

She faced him with wide eyes and a satisfied grin.

His reply was weak and insubstantial. "Uh. Okay."

"My dad taught me that. We worked for hours in the woods whenever we went camping. He loved that I had great aim. Not too shabby after all these years."

They'd worked for hours on handling the dagger and on some defensive strategies. Chuckling to himself over that time with Lane, he sat down on a stool and uncapped a beer for himself. He picked up the paper and started reading.

Later on, Evelyn came down looking satisfied and refreshed like she did when her painting had been a success. Her dark hair was cascading over her shoulders, and her eyes were bright. She fairly skipped over to the counter and took the beer he held out to her.

"Kirk, it smells great! Chili was an excellent idea. Perfect."

He smiled at her. Their friendship had always been solid, changing and deepening over the years, but always very secure. Especially meaningful in a world that was continually shifting and unreliable. He scooped them each a bowl and took some fresh, sweet cornbread out of the oven. They sat down and started eating their simple dinner. The sky was dark, the lamps a cozy golden.

"So, where's Lane? Has she eaten already?" asked Evelyn.

Mr. Kirkland stiffened; more time had passed than he'd thought. "What time is it?"

"Why, it's already nine thirty. Time really got away from me upstairs, and—" she said, and then stopped herself midsentence when she saw his troubled face.

"What?" she asked, with mounting fear.

"She hasn't been home yet," he said urgently.

"Oh, dear."

Normally, they wouldn't be worried, but given the circumstances and the deadline of Daley's threat . . . They immediately rang up Fio. He had no idea where Lane was; he had been in meetings out of the office all day. She had looked a little tense that morning and deep in thought, almost to distraction. But with everything going on lately, that was hardly unexpected. They all decided to casually check around, and if she ended up coming home, they would call him back.

What followed was a sleepless, miserable night.

By the next morning, they were convinced that things were definitely amiss. But they didn't have anything to go on. And who could they trust? Valerie didn't have a phone to call, so Fio would find out from her in person this morning what she knew. No one knew exactly how to reach Finn since he'd been working deep undercover trying to flush out Daley and Donagan's plan, but they would try.

During the day, Mr. Kirkland took Ripley for long walks to all of Lane's regular haunts. Aunt Evelyn got in touch with some of Lane's other girlfriends. No one had seen her.

Fiorello went to the police department, but Finn was out for the day, working. He'd send him a message later. Val had heard nothing from Lane, and she looked desperately worried. They didn't speak directly about it, but he knew she understood something was wrong. She had seen Lane at the café for coffee the previous morning, but not since then. Just like Fiorello, Val had been out of the office on errands or in meetings most of the day. She'd figured she and Lane just hadn't crossed paths.

Finally, late in the day, Fio left the office and decided to try to find Roarke. He went over to the press station and asked around for him. No one had seen him that entire day, and he was supposed to do a couple of interviews earlier. Roarke never missed an interview. Fio asked a few more pointed questions that he had been considering, but the reporters didn't have anything interesting to say. However, one man pulled him aside. "Mr. LaGuardia, I've been hearing some rumblings of a new gang or something. And there's one madam out in Queens who seems to keep coming up. Might have something to do with this. Her name's Lady Red."

Fio had his driver immediately run him over to Evelyn's.

He burst in the door, as usual, and Evelyn and Kirkland pounced on him, as they had been anxiously awaiting his arrival.

"We need to talk," he said. "I've found out some things. And Roarke is missing, too."

The lights of the city were backed by the dark nighttime sky before Valerie finally looked up from her mound of work. She rubbed the back of her neck, the tight muscles aching from the nonstop hours of the past week. Plus, she had to admit, she was keenly worried. Roxy had never shown up the past couple of days. Lizzie was obviously distressed, and then she called in sick, her throat raspy and raw on the phone. And suddenly, the deadline for Daley's threat was tomorrow. The hours were running out, and they weren't any closer to finding the target.

Most importantly, Lane hadn't shown up for work. Every time a visitor came to the office, she'd look up instantly, anxiously searching for Lane. At every loud thump or noise, she'd jump a mile. Her nerves were shot.

"Hey there, Val," said a quiet voice from behind. "You have a headache or something?"

Valerie turned around and saw Ralph standing there, brows knit with concern. His very lined forehead was even more deeply lined than usual. At his question, she realized she'd been rubbing her temples while she had been deep in thought. "Oh, just thinking," she said.

"Yeah, I can't stop thinking about Roxy and how she's just disappeared," he said while he perched on the edge of her desk. His usual wide smile was closed-lipped, and his eyes were shifting back and forth like he was trying to decide between two difficult choices.

"You okay, Ralph?" asked Val, with a tilt of her head.

"I, um . . . I'm just worried, I guess. Seems like there's a lot going on here, like a tension in the office, you know?"

Val nodded, but it looked like he had more to say. "What is it, Ralph? You're not saying everything."

He shook his head as he thought about it. "I just . . . I'm not sure I ought to say . . ."

She gave a harsh, self-deprecating laugh. "I know what you mean. I feel like there's something I need to figure out, and I just can't put it together. How about this? How about you tell me what things don't make sense to you, then I'll give you my pieces to the puzzle, and we'll see what we get." She grinned, trying to prompt him along. She *had* to find out what he wasn't saying.

Ralph nodded his head, having made his decision. "All right. It's been bugging me for a while. I'm afraid I might have made a big mistake. I've been going over it and going over it, and at first it didn't seem like a big deal, but somehow . . . I just feel like it might be, after all." He looked guilty. Her stomach dropped.

"Ralph, you better spit it out. *Right. Now.*"

He suddenly looked like a frightened rabbit. Then he spit it out all at once, in one giant sentence on high speed. "Okay, it's like this, a while back, Lizzie came to me and said that she and Roxy were trying their hardest to put their past small-town images behind them and that they were scared no one would take them seriously here in the big city if people knew where they came from. See? It's not that big of a deal, right?" he asked, still nervous and shaky.

"Ralph. What exactly did you conceal and from whom?" she asked, deadly serious.

His eyes widened. "Well, you see, it's all in their records, I didn't falsify documents or anything. But a few people have asked about them, just in passing, you know, so I told them what Lizzie said to say."

"You mean you lied."

He gulped. "Yeah, I lied."

"What *exactly* did you say?"

"Well, Lane asked about them a while back as well as Roarke. And then that Finn guy. I didn't think anything about it; it was just a conversation in passing. You know."

Her gut was doing a little dance, and he still hadn't said the punch line yet.

"Ralph!" she yelled.

"Okay! I told all of them fake places. Roxy is really from North Carolina, and Lizzie is from Michigan."

"Michigan? Where in Michigan?"

"Rochester, I think. Rochester, Michigan."

"Oh, my God. Rochester," she said, just barely above a whisper. "Is Roxy's real name Roxy?"

"Yeah. I think it's Roxanne. But . . . but Lizzie's real name is Louise. Louise Franco."

Finn nervously sat at his humdrum desk, which was a drab green that had been painted approximately thirty times. The top middle drawer had been touched up so many times it was impossible to shut completely, making it appear to be grinning with the under-bite of a bulldog. He had a lot of paperwork to do, but he couldn't focus on that to save his life. There was too much going on. And tomorrow was the deadline for Daley's threat.

He had to admit, Donagan Connell and Daley Joseph were turn-ing out to be more than the average thugs. Cunning, smart, knew how and when to keep quiet. Most didn't. They kept their cards close to their chests, no matter what angle Finn tried. How could he focus on typing reports? He had put on a brave face for Lane, and the plan really was a plan that he had faith in. But it was risky. If there was any way not to involve her, he would do it. Gladly. But she was already wrapped in everything too tight. She had to be part of it to get her out of it. Alive.

That night when they danced in the foyer of her house to that sexy piano music . . . He'd never forget her face, so full of life, laugh-ter, wonder. He'd never met anyone like her before. Her intuition constantly startled him; they'd make eye contact, and instantly he'd know she was thinking exactly what he was thinking.

Just like that first time he really saw her on the platform to the train. He still felt the same way: She was the most *alive* person he'd ever met. She wasn't beautiful in a cover-of-a-magazine kind of way. Which was what took him off guard. In many ways, she was average. Average height, brown hair, blue eyes. But there was some-thing about her eyes and smile that made you want to just keep looking. And her body was lithe and sexy to the point of distraction. In the park that day, when she'd kissed her hand and put it on his thigh that had been aching from his old injury, he had thought he'd burst into flames right then and there. And he really did believe her: She saw something worthy in him, which was something he'd given up on a long time ago.

He wanted to mentally kick himself in the ass. He was sounding like a lovesick schoolgirl. He'd never tell anyone these thoughts, but he secreted them away and kept them safe, bringing them out once in a while to carefully treasure.

With that thought, his mind flickered to the time when he and Lane had been in the bomb blast at Randall's Island and he'd learned of how her parents perished. It explained a lot. He knew she was an only child, which accounted for her independence and some of her ability to hold down an extremely stressful job. He could tell Fio was grooming her for a bigger role. But she had this intriguing mix of maturity and sexy sophistication beyond her years, blended with a kid's enjoyment of life. She drank it all in like no one he had ever met before. Maybe when you faced tragedy like that, you either turned bitter . . . or you drank in life.

But every once in a while there was a flicker in her, a glimpse that made him think she hadn't fully dealt with her past. There was something she hadn't faced yet, and he knew it was coming upon her fast and furious. It worried him. Would she be ready? Would it change her? He knew how brutal the past could be. By God, he did know about that.

It made him want to hold her in his arms and protect her, to help heal those wounds. He thought of the last time he held her tightly, swaying gently in the foyer of her home. And he realized something profound. *She felt like home.* A feeling he hadn't known in a long, long time.

There was a knock at the door of the office. A young police officer came in looking for someone. The secretary up front pointed back to Finn. The officer came over and handed him a note. Finn opened it, and his face drained of all color. He told the officer to stay with him for a minute.

He had a tough choice to make. And he hated the choice, but he needed help. For Lane, he would do anything. Even this. He took his suit coat and the note and paused for a moment as he looked down at his ugly green desk. It was highly likely that the next time he came back to this homely desk grinning up at him, his life would be forever changed. If he came back.

Finn walked down a long hall with the officer trailing behind and opened a door, and a large group of officers turned to face him. At first their faces were friendly and open, then they registered who he was and every face became closed and anything but welcoming.

The tall one in the center of the group was especially closed. Finn tilted his head up and over, suggesting a private meeting, and then said, "Pete, please?" His kind and somewhat imploring tone completely surprised Pete, and he found himself walking over to

Finn. Together, they walked out into the hallway. The officer with the message stood off to one side.

Pete's face was a mask of mistrust. It took everything Finn had not to smack it off him. He said, "Look, Pete, I know you don't trust me. But that's the past, and if you care *at all* about Fiorello, about Lane and Valerie, and about our city, for Christ's sake, then just listen. I need your help."

Pete's face looked like he couldn't completely let go of his misgivings, but then Finn saw something in Pete's face twitch and then relent. He took a small breath, happy to have cleared that first major obstacle.

"All right. This is the deal. Something big is going down tomorrow. . . ." And he filled Pete in on everything.

Finn showed him the note from Lane. "Good God!" Pete exclaimed. "By herself? She went off to Uncle Louie? She started the plan *on her own?*"

"*Mm hm,*" said Finn. "Well, she took Mr. Kirkland. . . ." He looked over at Pete's shocked face. "I know. At first I was angry, then I realized it was exactly what I would have done in her shoes. Admit it. You would have, too."

"I know," he said grudgingly. "But I don't have to like it."

"Yeah. Me, neither," grunted Finn.

Pete actually smiled. A little. Pete took a long, calculating look at Finn. It was obvious to Finn that he still didn't like him and he wasn't able to forgive the past. But there was something there in Pete's face that he hadn't seen before.

"All right. Let's do it," decided Pete.

Finn nodded. "Thank you. Let's go."

He was about to tell the officer he could leave now, but just then, the guy came over to Finn smiling, with a raised hand, and said affably, "Oh, I forgot to say . . ." He chuckled, as if Finn and Pete were going to get a big kick out of this. "I got this message yesterday. I almost forgot to get it to you."

"*Yesterday?*" Finn burst out in savage, primal anger. Pete held him back as he strained to throttle the idiot.

"You better get outta here, you dumbass!" uttered Pete, having difficulty restraining Finn.

*   *   *

Valerie grabbed Ralph by the wrist, Ralph wincing in pain. "You're coming with *me*," she said.

"Where are we going?" he asked, obeying her reluctantly.

"Oh, you don't really want to know that. But you're going. You owe me, and I'd rather have you come along than go by myself."

They found a cab with just a little difficulty. On the way, they both were silent, held captive by their thoughts, fears, and concerns that they hadn't acted fast enough.

They pulled up, and Valerie told the cabbie that she'd pay him double if he waited for them and that they wouldn't be long. He looked hesitant until she said, *pay double*. Valerie marched up to the door and rang the bell. It was after the dinner hour, and she hoped with all her might that he'd still be at home, not having gone out for the evening.

The butler came to the door and gave her a cryptic look as she told him who she was and that it was in reference to Lane Sanders. His eyebrows went up, and he ushered them inside. After only a few moments, he collected them and took them to the back of the grand old house to what looked like an enormous personal office.

They went in the door, and Valerie walked right up to the humongous desk and said, "Mr. Venetti, sir, I know who killed your nephew, Danny."

Uncle Louie's thick, bushy eyebrows almost shot off his face, he raised them with such force. "My dear, you're the second person to tell me that."

It was Val's turn to be shocked. Ralph was utterly, hopelessly distraught, and he looked like he might just melt then and there into the lush carpeting.

"Let me guess, Lane was here," Val offered.

"Yes."

Val put her hands on her hips, taking charge. "Well, I can sense that you like her, as do I, sir. You don't owe us anything, but I was wondering if you might be in a position to help find her. She's disappeared."

Ralph looked as if he might wet himself at Val's gumption. Uncle Louie's eyes looked incredulous, and he started muttering to himself, shaking his head. At first it was in Italian and Val couldn't understand the murmurs, but then she thought she caught something like, *These women will be the end of me.*

After clasping his hands on his desk, deep in thought, he finally looked up and took a good long look at Valerie. He looked at odds with himself. After a long moment, he said, "All right. I *do* like Lane. She is quite . . . unique. I think I found the information she was looking for. And I think I might know where she could be." His face looked pleasant at first, like he genuinely did like Lane. Then, as he said the last sentence, his face turned dark and almost worried, a foreign look for that stony-faced countenance. That dark look scared Valerie more than anything up to this point.

"Mr. Venetti, where do you think they have her?"

CHAPTER 32

I am seeking, I am striving, I am in it with all my heart.

—ML

Despite the constraints in the van, I was able to wiggle my way over to Roarke. Any kind, friendly contact was a lifeline in this journey. We pulled up to our mystery destination, and the engine clunked to a stop. I heard the back doors open, and someone helped us out, leading us into a building. From the night sounds, it didn't seem industrial; there was traffic, but it was quieter than in Manhattan.

We went up some stairs, the kind that led to an apartment versus an office building, and then through another door. Inside I was assaulted by women's perfume, my senses in overdrive, compensating for the lack of vision. I was walking on a rug, then a wood floor, then more rugs. At last, we came to our destination. A door clicked open, we went in, and someone roughly took the bindings off our hands, then left the room, shutting the door behind.

I took off my hood as fast as humanly possible while trying hard not to touch my still very painful head, and I yanked off the gag. Roarke and I looked gratefully at one another. We were, for now, in one piece.

"You okay?" he asked.

I tried a smile and said, "Yeah, thanks. Seems like we're in Queens, huh?"

"I think so. We went over a bridge." I nodded.

"And this is a residential area, not industrial," he said.

"I gotta say, I was scared we were heading back to Metropolitan Hospital."

He shivered. "I thought the same thing."

We took a look around, and we had it pretty good. It was a small bedroom, even had a good-sized bed. Clean, dark colors on the walls, a new bedspread, and there were two lamps that gave off a golden light. There was a pitcher of water on a dresser and some bread and cheese. I went over and sniffed the water.

Roarke snickered. "Think it's been drugged?" he asked sarcastically. "You read too much, Lane."

The water didn't smell of anything bitter. Didn't cyanide smell like almonds? Maybe I *did* read too much. I figured if they'd wanted us dead, they could have killed us easily by now. If anything, there could be something in it to make us sleepy and incapacitated. I ate some bread and cheese, and it made me feel considerably better. Roarke had some, too. Then we drank down some water.

The only odd thing about the bedroom was that there were no windows. There was something that *looked* like a window with curtains, but it turned out to be a solid wall. I started to get an idea of what kind of place we were in. There was no escape.

Turned out, the water was drugged after all. Roarke and I became extremely sleepy. And given the fact that we couldn't escape, Roarke went over to the bed to lie down.

"I told you it was drugged," said Roarke.

"Ha!" I said.

"How's your head, Lane?" he asked softly. Earlier he had looked at my pupils to see if they were dilated abnormally, a sign of concussion. They looked all right.

"Well, it's throbbing again. I think rest would be a good idea."

I looked at his handsome form as I sat next to him on the edge of the bed. He was such an interesting guy. A great friend and someone I could count on. Yet there was something remote about those eyes of his. Like he was always just about to take a trip, like he wasn't able to be completely present.

I sighed. Other than seeing Fio leading a rescue party and knocking down our door, there wasn't anyone on earth I wanted to see more than Finn. *Where is he? Did he get my message? Will he be able to find me even after they moved us from the Meatpacking District?*

Roarke looked at me, his serious eyes marked with dark shadows underneath. "Finn will find us, Lane." He smiled slightly at my look of surprise. "You talked while you were sleeping at the other place. You said his name."

I looked over at him. It was the first time my fears had a chance to catch up and tears were threatening to make an appearance.

"Come here," he said as he reached out a long arm. I laid my head gently on his chest and felt his arm come around me. We fell fast asleep.

When we woke up, I was completely disoriented. It felt like we'd been asleep for hours, but without windows to really know how much time had passed, it could have been one hour or ten. I had a crick in my neck from lying on Roarke's chest for so long, and he was massaging his arm like it had fallen asleep.

After a little while, the doorknob wobbled like someone was tentatively coming in. A girl came in with a tray. She laid it down on the dresser and took up the leftover bread and water. She had dirty blond hair, her movements were skittish, and her face held a world of fear. She was probably all of sixteen years old. She turned to us and put a finger to her lips telling us not to make a sound, pointed to the new pitcher of water, nodded, and made the okay sign. Then she quickly left.

I looked at Roarke in amazement, and he laughed right out loud. It wasn't my imagination that they'd drugged us; the girl had just provided us clean water.

We waited for hours and hours; it was just awful. We had nothing to consume our minds but fear for our friends, for ourselves, and for what was coming for the city. I rummaged around the room and luckily found a deck of cards. We played everything we could think of from poker, to gin, to Old Maid. The waiting was tedious. But more than that, there was a menacing presence in the air. I was extremely grateful for Roarke's company; it would have been infinitely worse had I been alone. Also, I had no doubt we were in the hands of criminal minds who would have no qualms about harming us if the need arose. I didn't take for granted for one second the fact that we were still alive.

The young girl came in a couple of more times to replenish our water and give small offerings of food, still giving us the okay sign in silence. Once, I caught her eye and tried to smile. I thought she might be trying to smile back, but then she looked at the door and ran out. Finally, there was a robust knock at the door, and our two large friends from the night before came in. They informed us that we had a meeting.

We walked through the building, which looked like it was the entire floor of a large apartment building. There were doors all over the place that led to who knows where. But at last we came to what had to be the main living quarters. No expense had been spared. The carpeting, the furniture—it was all top of the line, shiny, and luxurious. We went into a parlor with dark wood floors, a black and white rug running the entire length of the room, and chic black and white furniture perfectly placed. Sitting on a couch, bound and gagged . . . was Roxy.

CHAPTER 33

How can I be useful, of what service can I be?
There is something inside me, what can it be?

—ML

The guards wouldn't let us near her and slammed us both down onto a couch and then walked to the back of the room. Even though the gag marred her face, I could read one expression loud and clear in her eyes: Roxy was *ticked off.* I was so relieved to see her alive, and, although incensed, she seemed unharmed.

The two main doors swung open with dramatic flair, and in came . . . Lizzie. She was nervously clasping her hands as she crept over to within a few feet of us. She started to say something in a quivering voice. "Oh, my God, I found you guys. . . . I . . . I don't—"

My eyes narrowed as I coldly cut her off. "Save it. We figured it out already."

With that utterance, a slow, wicked smile crept across her lips. I watched in dismay as her entire demeanor transformed. She stopped that squint of hers, and her hazel eyes opened up wide; they were much larger and rounder than I had thought. She stood up straight, and suddenly she was just about as tall as me. Her shoulders dropped back, and she had a regal air about her. It was a total metamorphosis. She even shrugged off the little black cardigan she'd been wearing so she could show off her gorgeous figure highlighted by a little black evening dress. The only thing that remained the same was her glorious mane of red hair cascading down her back.

She licked her lips, relishing our shock. I think Roarke was drooling.

"Reel it in, Roarke, sheesh," I said. Lizzie let out a light peal of laughter, enjoying this moment with every ounce of her being. I stole a glance at Roxy and caught her rolling her eyes.

"So, Lizzie, looks like you've been a busy girl." I hoped that my slightly condescending tone would aggravate her and make her start talking; I had a lot of questions that needed answering. It worked. A little too well.

She stalked over to me, looking me right in the eyes. She took one long, bloodred fingernail and stroked the side of my face from top to bottom and said in a slow, husky voice, "Don't *ever* call me Lizzie. Again." Then she drew back and slapped my face a stunning blow.

"My name is Eliza!" She said her name with passion, anger, and something like adoration. I could hear Roarke practically growling. My eyes had tears in them from the sting. This was quite a dramatic performance. It made me wonder if she'd rehearsed it.

I said, through my clenched teeth, "Got it. Eliza." I didn't say anything else, hoping she'd want to hear her own voice some more.

She did. In purring tones, she said, "Oh, you think you've got it all figured out, Lane? I've been playing you since I started working at your *worthless* little office. It was grueling being that ridiculous Lizzie every day. I abhor that name, but it fit well enough. *And*, I acquired my target." She was thoroughly enjoying gloating over me.

I asked, with an innocent voice, knowing full well it would get under her skin, "Were you doing all this to help your mother?"

She swung around with flaming eyes, and I thought she was going to smack me again. I connected eyes with Roxy, of all people, and she gave me wide eyes with a slight turn of her head, wordlessly saying, *Be careful*.

I now knew beyond a doubt that the woman in Metropolitan Hospital, the woman who leered over me while I was in the hospital as a little girl, was Lizzie's mom, not Roxy's. It was Lizzie who had lost a father on that same ice that took my parents; Lizzie who had formed a relationship with Danny; Lizzie who had plotted to kill me. *Lizzie was Louise Franco.*

My dream the night before had slipped the final piece of the puzzle into place. I had been blaming Roxy: the one who had the yellow scarf, the one I was jealous of, the one who was so easy to hate. But the bright scarf around her neck in the dream wasn't yellow; it was red. Like Lizzie's hair. It made me look at everything from a new angle. And there was that hat she had on as she walked the beach. It was the *same hat* that hadn't seemed right at Roxy's apartment. I remembered the line of hat hooks on the wall, and all of them were taken. Roxy was so neat and everything had its perfect place; if the hat had been hers, there would have been an empty hook for it. Secondly, seeing an unremarkable hat on a table is hard to identify, but when you see it on the person's head . . . I remembered seeing *Lizzie* wear that hat to work.

Lizzie, now Eliza, regained her control, and with a calculated twirl of her fingers through her hair, she began again, warming to the topic. "Oh, my mother? No. Not for my mother, Lane. She was a mean drunk to begin with, then crazy to boot. I learned real fast, even as a *little girl*"—she said *little girl* through her teeth with raw hatred—"to hide behind a facade. To become whatever I needed to become to survive. After the accident, which obviously was no accident, that killed my father in Michigan, my mother went even further into the bottle.

"You want to know how twisted my reality became? I was *glad* when the mob came into our lives," Eliza said, with bitter derision. "And it's all your fault, Lane."

My eyes snapped open wide, and I blurted out, "I was ten!"

"I was thirteen! Well aware of what was happening, but still a child. And it was your family who came to peaceful Rochester. And ruined it. Just like your parents ruined my life, I felt it my *duty* to ruin yours."

Eliza took a deep breath and walked back to a bar, where she poured herself a large glass of whiskey and swigged it down in one mouthful. She slammed the glittering glass back onto the bar with such force that it cracked in her hands. She didn't notice.

I kept quiet; she was on a roll. "When Danny came to Detroit with his uncle on business, he discovered me, and we fell in love. Well, *he* thought we were in love," she said, with self-congratulatory aplomb.

"He convinced his uncle that they should help us move out to New York. My *dearest* mother still had her beauty at the time, and plenty of deceit to convince the bosses that she'd be an asset. So we moved. No looking back. But it was only a matter of time before they figured out my mom wasn't all there, so to speak.

"So, in order to survive—again—I had to figure out my own way. I found out that I had quite a mind for business and started my own affairs. I had quite a proclivity, shall we say, for"—she licked her red lips again; I couldn't help but think of a vampire—"giving men what they wanted and getting them to give me what I wanted: money. Information. Leverage. And after I got mother locked up at Metropolitan Hospital, I could begin a new life."

She might have hated her mother, but the theatrics made me think the apple didn't fall far from the tree. I decided to risk another question, as it looked like she might get stuck on reveling in her great accomplishments. "And how did you find me?"

Her eyes flashed. She said, "Oh, I remembered your name and your face. So it was easy enough, what with your aunt's notoriety as a philanthropist and artist. Plus, my mother had talked about you enough. She was obsessed with you. She even went to the hospital when you were in a coma. I think she had in mind to finish the job, but she never got the chance." She sneered at the recognition that must have hit my face.

Eliza went on, "So, I got a job to be close to you, to figure you out. I also sold information from the mayor's office to interested buyers. Plus, my mother had told me of artwork and other valuables that your family was supposed to have. Paintings and books and stolen items from the war. I got wind of someone who was thinking up a scheme to take down our silly little mayor, and I saw my chance. I could get rid of that dago mockery of a mayor while warming up to the new guys in charge, perhaps do some treasure hunting, *and* make your life miserable. All in one fell swoop."

"So, who's behind this big scheme?" I asked. I glanced at Roarke, and I could tell he was barely breathing, trying hard not to break the spell that kept Eliza talking.

"Oh, someone I'm dying for you to meet. But Danny was my

original partner; he wanted to do something to impress his uncle. *The* Uncle Louie. He started working with a couple of guys who wanted to help oust Fiorello. So we started working on some plans. It was a perfect opportunity to form a new and stronger alliance with some movers and shakers. But then Danny had to start getting impatient, taking things into his own hands. Such a shame, too, he was pretty cute." She spoke of him like he was a little pocket dog, a chihuahua she carried around.

"But whatta you do? He got in the way." She made a shooting gun gesture, clicking her tongue when she pulled the trigger. "But by then I'd gone into business on my own. I didn't need him anymore."

"Gone into business?" I asked.

"Oh, yes, my own endeavors were much more reliable and quite lucrative. Danny had already loused up the burglary at your home and the mugging in the subway, and he almost ruined the setup of the biggest event in New York history by setting the bomb at Randall's Island." She shook her head, making a *tsk tsk* sound. "He couldn't be trusted any longer. And my new partners were all about waiting for the perfect time. It's true, Lane, I admit I failed in finding any supposed treasure from your family, if there really was any to begin with. However, I think the next part of our plan will leave you shocked and amazed." Like I was about to attend a marvelous and entertaining circus show. She just needed an evil laugh to make the picture complete.

Eliza was tiring of waiting. *Think think think. How can I keep her talking?* She had been pacing like a caged animal, waiting for something or someone. "And Roxy? How does she fit in with your plan?" I wanted so badly to be sarcastic and rude, but knew that could be quite deadly at the moment. I carefully restrained my roaring emotions.

"Oh, don't you see?" She took a good, sarcastically pitying look at me. She bent a little, putting her hands on her knees like someone explaining something to a little child. "Oh, of course you don't see. But she was so utterly perfect! You were clearly jealous of her and perfectly willing to make her the villain. It hardly took any maneuvering on my part at all." I stole a glance at Roxy as I felt a blush rush up my cheeks, and she gave me an incredulous look. Eliza was gaining steam again, warming to her revelations.

"And to top it all off, my mother has that horrid platinum blond hair just like that bimbo," she said as she thumbed a point in Roxy's direction, which gained a glare from that party. "Oh, my God, I can't tell you how painful it's been trying to pretend to be *her* best friend." I was just as appalled as Roxy at these harsh words. Again I looked at Roxy, and she looked like I felt after I got slapped. Then a look of raw hatred and vengeance came through those baby blue eyes. Maybe she wasn't so bad after all.

"I had you wrapped around my little finger, Lane. Yeah, talented Lane, Fiorello's pet. Outwitted by *me*," she said as she mock-kissed the air. "I planted Roxy's scarf back at that Midtown fire that Danny started in order to introduce himself to you. I planned a whole night with Roxy and a couple of guys in that area. Got her to come to the fire just after you arrived so you could see her in the distance, then goaded her into calling Fio and telling on you," she said, with a smirk.

I recalled that night, running to the scene, seeing the competent and caring Fio watching over his firemen, seeing Roarke furiously writing down his notes . . . feeling Danny pull me into those dangerous shadows.

Eliza feverishly continued, "I had a field day watching your reaction to Roxy as she took over your job when you had a leave of absence from your little tumble into the subway. You weren't supposed to make it out alive, by the way, but this was fun, too. And that incriminating letter about Randall's Island. Now, that was a masterpiece of a red herring. Long ago, I learned how to imitate anyone, any emotion, anything. Even Roxy's excruciatingly neat handwriting.

"Y'see, like I said, Danny wasn't cooperating. He wouldn't listen to me when I told him to back off and quit showing off. He wanted to do the Randall's Island bomb. I knew that number one, he'd mess it up somehow." She ticked off her fingers as she counted down his mistakes. "And two, it could make our *big event* today harder to pull off. I figured a letter in Roxy's handwriting would continue to make her look guilty as well as put you on Danny's incompetent trail to stop it before he ruined the setup. And if you got hurt in the process, all the better." She was thoroughly enjoying this. I was hoping it was making her high, undisciplined, reckless.

Then a noise drifted up from downstairs, and when I looked back at Eliza—her sexy black dress, her flowing red hair and man-eating red lipstick—my heart started to nervously beat as the hairs on my neck rose. I had a feeling these next several minutes would make or break this case. And quite possibly make or break me.

Eliza was electric. Her eyes lit up as if she had a delectable surprise for us and she could hardly bear the anticipation. As Eliza was almost jumping up and down in excitement, Roarke, Roxy, and I quickly looked at each other. We took a deep breath . . . and we tried to speak volumes with fearful, scanty glances. This was it.

The doorknob twisted, and in walked my nightmares: Daley Joseph, Donagan Connell, and, last in line, Finn.

CHAPTER 34

Love is eternal—the aspect may
change, but not the essence.

—ML

Eliza was watching my face like a hawk. Finn looked at Eliza and gave her a devious smile. My stomach turned.

Eliza clapped her hands and then sauntered over to Donagan, her red hair shining in the lamplight. He took her tiny waist in his hands and gave her a disgusting, wet, lip-smacking kiss. And then my eyes were pulled over to Daley Joseph. He was Joseph right now, in his tuxedo and crisp white shirt. But those horrid nostril hairs were as bristly as ever, and memories of the most terrifying night of my life came careening back into my mind: his slightly damp hand curled effortlessly around my throat, Finn standing there doing nothing, the feeling of helplessness coursing through my veins. I could feel the blood drain from my face. Then again, the loathing I felt for Eliza boosted my strength, and I forced myself to be angry at the situation. To think clearly.

Donagan, the obvious leader, broke the silence first. "Well, well, well . . . What a gorgeous collection you have for me, Eliza. Well done." He chuckled his approval menacingly.

"Thank you, Donagan," she purred. "I thought you'd like to see my handiwork in person. Before we, ah, dispense with them." She carelessly swept her hand in our direction like we were a pile of newspapers to be thrown into the trash without a thought.

"Yyyyes," he returned, with an answering deep purr of his own. And then, terrifyingly, he walked toward me. "I've been wanting to see this famous Lane up close." He came within an uncomfortable six inches and scrutinized my face like a doctor looking for a skin cancer.

"You, my dear, keep making things difficult for me. *Mm hmm.*" I wanted to spit in his face. His red, nappy hair was like a rusty aura. He had pale white skin and a tall forehead. He would have been a good-looking man, except that he had a scar across his cheek that marred his lips. And I remembered Fio had said something about his face, how it almost looked like he had incongruous makeup on. It was true, and it gave his face a disturbing sense of a masquerade, like a *Phantom of the Opera* essence. He was overpowering, almost suffocating.

Eliza was drunk with the moment of her victory and made her first mistake. She said flippantly, "I was just filling them in on how incompetent they've been. I had them wrapped around my little . . . finger." She stammered to a halt as she caught a disapproving look from Donagan.

"You've been gloating," he said, with a schoolmarm's disapproval.

"Oh, well, I wouldn't call it gloating. . . ." And then that little snipe did one of her great maneuvering tricks as she took on an innocent, coy look. She slunk over to Donagan and stroked his chest with that same long red fingernail that had stroked my cheek.

"Donagan," she whispered, "I was just having a little fun with my catch, darling. I'm sorry if that made you upset. You're the boss. Show me how you want to handle them." She was *incredible.* He ate it up. When he looked away, Eliza caught my eye and winked.

I had been avoiding looking at Finn. I just didn't think I could take it. After everything we said. Those kisses . . . I pushed *hard* against my thoughts that wanted to drift back to our night during the thunderstorm, that steamy kiss in the park, and our last dance in the candlelit foyer. . . . I *could not* go down that road and survive this. It was too painful.

"We need to be heading to our next stop, Donagan, if we want to stay on schedule," drawled Finn as he looked meaningfully at his watch.

"In a hurry, Finn?" gurgled Daley Joseph, with a wicked grin.

Finn returned that with a casual parry. "Oh, no, only keeping time with the plans that have taken two years to complete. But if you'd like to stay and chat a while, that's fine." He walked over to the bar and poured a whiskey for himself. Instead of slamming it like Eliza had done, he casually sipped it. Like he was doing nothing but enjoying an afternoon at his country club. Then he leisurely walked back over to Donagan, still carrying his drink.

"Finn's right, Joseph," said Donagan. "We'd better head out. Get those two bodyguards to come here and finish up." He said this with a smirk that sent chills up my spine, and the two guards came over, one forcing me to my feet and the other taking Roarke to the other side of the room with a gun to his back.

Eliza looked at me and smiled, then whispered something in Donagan's ear. He grinned and nodded.

"Actually," said Donagan, "I think it's time we truly test the mettle of our friend Finn, here."

Oh, God.

Daley Joseph nodded a quick *come here* to Finn, and Finn walked over to him. "I agree. I think that you have feelings for Lane. I think it's time we find out exactly which side you're on."

I looked at Eliza, and she smirked in triumph.

My guard moved away from me, leaving me alone, abandoned. I looked at Roarke, but the bodyguard had him around the chest, holding him back. He shouted savagely, "No!" I looked at Roxy, her eyes wide with horror.

I slowly, slowly turned my eyes to Finn's. Those deep, dark eyes that I loved. He said with a smirk, "Sorry, love. I have to keep with the plan." He slowly raised his gun. And pulled the trigger.

CHAPTER 35

Someday death will take us to another star.

—ML

In one shocking instant, I was hurtled backward as I violently grabbed my chest. I saw the red stain oozing out through my white blouse, I felt the wetness. I heard a muffled scream from Roxy, a raging, "You bastard!" from Roarke, and a delighted cackle from Eliza. I crumpled to the floor, my eyes slowly closing.

Daley Joseph gurgled a disgusting grunt of approval. I thought I heard Donagan clap Finn on the back like he had just accomplished a noble feat. Someone said they'd let the guards finish up, and then Daley, Donagan, Eliza, and Finn left.

Luckily for me, the bodyguards didn't move too fast. Their bodies lumbered just as slowly as their brains did, so Eliza and her crew had plenty of time to get to their car and depart before they got around to me. I could hear Roxy crying and Roarke swearing. The guards had been debating about how to go about finishing us off, arguing the points of what would take the least amount of effort and cleanup. They hadn't decided on anything, but the one guy came over to check on me while the other topped off his drink at the bar. I could hear the glasses tinkling.

The hardest part was trying not to look like I was breathing. I needed the element of surprise if this was going to work. At one moment, I think I moved my hand a hundredth of an inch too fast and I thought I heard Roarke gasp, but then . . . nothing.

My hand finally made it around my dad's dagger, which I'd been wearing in a hidden slit I made in the inside of my wide belt, the sheath going down into the top of my skirt. The dagger was small, but deadly enough. I'd had to practice this about a hundred times with Kirkland to make sure that I fell to the ground exactly right. Finn knew they couldn't let me live. He would manufacture a way to be the one to do it, but Lizzie ended up making it easy. He would use a rubber bullet, smashing the blood pellet taped to my chest with a metal backing. The bullet hit with such force that I didn't have to fake reeling backward. I had to keep one hand over the blood stain and the other where I could then reach the dagger hilt. All while trying to look natural.

The guard came over to me and bent down, putting his big head within inches of my own. I abruptly rolled over, moving directly under the big guy, and with my right hand I poked my dagger painfully into his throat. His heavy weight was against him; if he made any false move, my knife would do significant damage. Also, happily for me, this guy was a bit smaller than the other one, who hadn't noticed anything as of yet; he was too busy getting another drink. I carefully moved to a crouching position and took Meat Loaf's gun without moving my dagger from his tender throat.

That gasp from Roarke turned out to be exactly what I had thought: He *had* seen me move and must have been ready for anything. Because by the time I got the gun securely in my hand, he had the other guard around the neck in a headlock, slowly knocking him out from oxygen deprivation. He must have been really angry to get the force needed to squeeze that giant neck into submission. But he did. After the meatloaf was out cold, he used the guy's tie and belt to bind his hands and feet. Then he came over to me, and together we did the same to my stunned and ashamed opponent.

Then Roarke swung around and shook me by the shoulders, shouting, "I could . . . I could . . . *throttle you!*" Then he hugged me so tightly I thought I might join the guy on the floor. "You're bleeding; it's fake, I take it? A blank in Finn's gun?"

"Rubber bullet. Yeah, yeah, it's fake," I said, still out of breath. "A big blood pellet I had taped to my chest. Mr. Kirkland helped me with it. And gave me my dad's dagger to use."

Roarke coughed and said, "Unbelievable." We both went over to Roxy and took off her gag and the ties on her hands. She just sat there looking numb. Maybe shock was setting in.

I was feeling good that this part of the plan was going all right and that we were still alive. But when things like this happen in the movies, what they don't show is the massive amount of mental strain and drain that completely taxes your body. My limbs were heavy with exhaustion. My head was throbbing. It was like every nerve in my body was on fire. I was worried about Finn. And I was worried about the next phase of their plan. Where did we go from here?

Then I heard a sound that I will never forget as long as I live: a door being broken down with a great and mighty crash, yelling, *barking*, and then . . . Was that a trumpet? Before we thought it was humanly possible, the door to the parlor was rammed down. And in poured . . . everyone. Evelyn, Fio, Kirkland, Valerie, Ralph, Pete, and even Ripley. *Ralph?*

I was so stunned that I couldn't utter a single word as they all piled in the doorway. But they stopped dead in their tracks when they saw the gruesome blood on my white blouse.

I yelled out, "It's okay! It's fake! I'm all right!" Relief flooded every single one of their faces as they came in and took a good look at the situation. Kirkland knew the bullet was a fake, but a chest full of blood looks pretty terrifying even if you're in on the plan.

My eyes devoured these amazing, wonderful, glorious friends. All of them looked like they were about to start talking at once. It took the short one with the trumpet to bring us all to order.

"Fio," I said. "You brought your trumpet?"

"It just seemed necessary, Lane, my girl. And you know how it worked with the Artichoke King." He waggled his eyebrows in pure enjoyment and then started leading like only he could. With screechy bellowing.

He got us all into order, first having Aunt Evelyn and Mr. Kirkland look at and pat me over thoroughly. I gave Mr. Kirkland a quick rundown of how this part of the plan played out, and he patted my back. Very similarly to how he patted Ripley's head the night he chased out the burglar.

"Nicely done," was all he said in his gravelly voice, but his beaming face spoke volumes. Evelyn had been shooting us both deadly darts with her eyes, and I knew we'd both be in the doghouse for not giving her more of the details. But we could never have been sure who might be on the scene when the plan went down. And for it to work, every single emotion had to be utterly authentic. She'd forgive us . . . at some point. My crazy family had even brought the dog. I got right down to Ripley's level and gave him a big, strapping hug, his huge shepherd head over my shoulder.

Once Aunt Evelyn and Mr. Kirkland were finished with me, Valerie came running over and almost knocked me down as she wrapped her arms around me. She wiped a tear from her eye, but all she said was, "I brought you some clothes." Which made me laugh and then almost cry, too.

I said, "Hey, ah . . . could you . . . ?" I motioned to the stunned-looking Roxy still sitting on the couch by herself.

"Yes, absolutely," said Val. She walked carefully over to Roxy and sat down. She said a few soft words, and Roxy remained silent. But then she slowly, slowly laid her head on Val's capable shoulder.

I ran into the other room to quickly change into the blissfully clean clothes that Val had brought: my best navy blue suit with trousers. Thank God. Something practical. Somehow, I knew this night was not over, and who knew what would be in store?

When I went back in, things were calming down and Evelyn had passed around some medicinal whiskey to everyone. I looked around and couldn't believe they had *all* found us. Pete and Roarke were talking intensely to each other.

"Ralph? What the . . ." I blurted out. I could *not* figure out his presence for the life of me.

Val spoke up. "I'll explain later." Ralph remained quiet, sitting by himself in a corner. His usually wide smile was nowhere to be seen, and he didn't look anything like his happy-go-lucky self.

"All right," began Fio, calling us to order again. "We have a lot to put together here if we're going to figure out where this substantial threat is for tomorrow—well, actually today. And we need to work fast. Listen up people, we can do this. We *have* to do this!"

Roarke and I were completely unaware of exactly how much

time had passed since our capture. It was shockingly well after midnight, practically the early hours of the morning. It was officially August tenth. We didn't have a lot of time. Roarke and I quickly filled everyone in on what had happened over the last couple of days. When I talked about Finn and the rubber bullet in the gun, I couldn't help but flash a look at Pete. He kept his face tight and controlled.

Pete then took the ball. "Finn got your message, Lane, but a day later than you had sent it. The idiot messenger had forgotten about it. I thought Finn was going to . . . well." He passed a hand behind his head, rubbing his neck. Was that a small smile? "From your note, we knew you had been to see Venetti and that you were going to the Meatpacking District, as it was the only place you could think of to try to find a clue. Plus, you'd mentioned Roxy, and maybe you'd be able to locate her since you were worried." When he said Roxy's name, she darted a surprised look at me, and I gave her a small, self-deprecating smile back. Pete kept going. "Finn knew he needed help and came to find me. Finn had to get back to his undercover operation, so he told me the location of the place in the Meatpacking District. I took a few of my best officers to the abandoned warehouse, but we didn't find anything.

"Finn hadn't known the exact address of this place. I guess it's Eliza's place of business?" I nodded. "He had just heard Daley speak about it vaguely, so he gave me what information he could, and then I did some digging and discovered a new high-end escort service had sprung up, and I started putting two and two together. My crew and I arrived right when everyone else did."

Fio had been bouncing up and down from his seat on the couch, enthusiastic about telling us his part in everything. His constant motion garnered a scowl from Aunt Evelyn as she gracefully vacated the seat next to him for a more sedate place to sit. "Okay, I'm next!" Fio yelled happily. "I started thinking more about Roxy's disappearance, and then when Lizzie ended up calling in sick, I began looking at the case from different angles and asking myself questions about who might be behind everything. When I went to the press guys and asked about Roarke, I found out he hadn't shown up for work. I knew then and there that you two were together. Just like Pete, I had also found out about a new madam in town; her standout characteristic was a mane of red hair—Lady Red.

"I knew right where to go to get more information. I found the whereabouts of this . . . *establishment* by pressing one of the government officials whom I figured would be first in line for Lady Red's place. And I was right; he had *absolutely* been first in line, and he divulged the address. I will be attending to him later," he said darkly. "Then, Evelyn and Kirkland and I rejoined, piled into a car, and here we are."

By cosmic design or the hilarity of fate, everyone had arrived at the same time. It took a tense moment or two to figure out if they were all good guys or not, and then they all came bounding up here.

Lastly, Fio turned to Val. "Ah, Valerie. Was that car you came in . . . er . . . Was that who I think it was?"

All heads whipped to Valerie as she blushed a deep crimson, right to the roots of her golden brown hair. "Ah, yes. It was."

She filled us in on what she'd learned from Ralph. She shuffled in her seat a little, like she was avoiding something. "Well, I was at my wit's end. I didn't know where anyone was, and gosh, Lane, I was certain you were in danger. So . . . I knew only one person who might be able to find the target for tomorrow as well as where Lane might be: Louie Venetti."

Pete uttered, "Oh, dear God," and put his head down on his clasped hands. Roarke chuckled silently.

Val told us, her stunned audience, "I was so mad! I traipsed right in and announced to Venetti that I knew who had killed his nephew, Danny Fazzalari." I barked out a loud laugh, which no one understood, and they looked at me in confusion. Val smirked and said, "Louie told me that Lane said the exact same thing to him the day before."

Aunt Evelyn slowly closed her eyes, shook her head, and rubbed her temple with her index finger. Valerie told us that Venetti did, indeed, have an idea of where they had Lane and agreed to bring her and Ralph over here. When they saw the rest of the posse on their way in, his driver dropped them off.

Then she paused, her face taking on a very serious expression, and said, "Most importantly, Venetti did do as you asked, Lane. He discovered exactly what is planned for today."

Suddenly the room, which had held an air of jubilant victory, was once again a room of war strategy. We all took a deep breath.

"The target for the bombing is the Triborough Bridge."

CHAPTER 36

I am doing my very best to make every effort
because I am longing so much to make
beautiful things. But beautiful things mean
painstaking work, disappointment and perseverance.

—ML

This was now certainly official police business, and Pete joined
Fiorello in an intense discussion on what was to be done. Pete had
brought four of his best officers, and they formed a formidable rank
around Fio. One of them was the officer who'd been with Peter
when I had tackled the purse-snatcher in the subway. He kept darting incredulous looks at me, and his grin made it clear that he was
absolutely delighted to be part of this action.

Valerie started a quiet discussion with Roxy. I knew I would have
my own heart to heart with her at some point, but for now my mind
was consumed with trying to help in any way I could. And with
finding Finn.

Mr. Kirkland came over, and whether to keep me distracted or
because he truly wanted to revel in the facts, he had me go over
exactly how we had worked The Plan. When I told Kirkland about
rolling under the assailant and jabbing my knife to his throat and
then carefully taking the gun away from him, his eyes shone with
amusement and pride as he slapped his knee and chuckled his
raspy laugh.

"You know, Lane, you are just like your mother. She gave your
father a lot of grief over the years. They were a team, but after
their feelings for each other became apparent, it was very difficult

for him not to take care of her, to let her do her own work. Yet, he wouldn't have it any other way," he said, reminiscing.

I never felt more a part of my parents' story than I did at that moment. Their story was *my* story. It wasn't some painting that I looked at and admired from afar, as a stranger admiring beauty with an outsider's perspective. I was right in the middle of it.

I must have had a stunned look on my face, because Mr. Kirkland's dreamy look of reminiscence was brought back to the present in an instant. "Uh, Lane? Did I say something that . . ."

"Oh, no, you said one of the best things I could ever hope to hear." I put my hand on his tough, sinewy shoulder. "Thank you."

I got up and made my way over to the police team and Fio. "So, do you have any idea of where to start looking for an explosive device? And can we shut down the bridge?"

They had already sent out one of the officers to shut down the bridge on the pretense of maintenance. (On the newly constructed bridge, just opened this very summer . . . Well, we'd just have to figure out the press on that later.) Then they were going to put teams in place looking for the bombs. Roarke went off with them, performing his journalistic duties. The officers also sent out descriptions of the Schmidt brothers—they'd have to be showing their faces soon—and Lyle, the guy I talked up at that God-awful country bar. They also gave descriptions of Daley Joseph and the elusive Donagan Connell as well as Eliza.

So, what to do now? The police, Fio, and Roarke all had to run off to complete their various tasks. I wanted to help in the worst way, but in most novels I've read, the pushy woman who feels that the police can't possibly do their work without her just ends up getting in the way, and they end up needing to rescue *her*. So I was fine with them doing their job. But it was achingly frustrating and anticlimactic.

Valerie ended up taking Roxy home. I had a few minutes aside with Roxy before she went, neither of us knowing what to say. We just looked at each other like we were both complete strangers. Which we were. I thought I'd been so clever and intuitive. But I had made many assumptions, and the truth had eluded me. Well, at least for a while.

I just looked at Roxy, tried a tentative smile, and then settled for a big sigh. She looked at me, and I knew we had reached a silent understanding. There was something in her eyes that showed *exactly* how I was feeling. We may never be best friends, but perhaps a truce could be arranged.

That left Evelyn and me, eyeing each other from across the room. I still held my tumbler of medicinal whiskey, and I rolled the cool glass between my two hands like a large, heretical prayer bead.

She said with a resigned, wry look, "So . . . you and Mr. Kirkland have been working on this plan of Finn's together, eh?"

I looked closely at her wise, bright face. Her eyes were alive with fire and yet . . . was it amusement? "You knew all along!" I just about yelled, dumbfounded.

Her laughter peeled through the room. "Not really, honey. But when I was painting, I did see you two working with your dagger and pretend jousting, or whatever you call it. I knew you were up to something."

A timid cough sounded from the doorway. Aunt Evelyn and I looked sharply up at each other. I knew who it was, and I felt awful that I hadn't remembered her earlier. She was a prisoner just as much as I had been, yet had dared to help us. I owed her a lot.

Not wanting to scare her, I called out softly, "Please . . . come in."

Dead silence. The silence of someone scared off, or the silence of a mind being made up, we'd have to wait and see.

"Please? I want to thank you. We wouldn't be alive without you."

The door swung slowly open, and there, revealed, was our young friend. I knew she was the one responsible for giving us clean water to drink, not the drugged water probably intended to keep Roarke and me drowsy and weak. Her hands were clasped, the thumbs nervously at war with each other. Her big gray eyes looked up at me, and I felt that perhaps she was younger than I had thought, maybe fourteen or fifteen.

I slowly stood up, my eyes and face smiling as kindly as possible. I had waved Aunt Evelyn down, as I knew her dear heart would make her leap up and throw her arms around the young thing. But that might just scare her to death.

I walked toward her carefully and said, "Thank you. I know it was a risk to give us the clean water." I could tell it took her some courage, but she smiled a little. I took her hand and held it. Then her bravery melted, and she suddenly grasped me around the waist like a drowning victim grabs the sole life jacket thrown to her. I stroked her straggly head, which came to just under my chin, and held her tight.

Then Evelyn could contain herself no longer and she came over, her loving heart apparent in every ounce of her generous being, and the girl slowly let go of me and looked up at her.

Aunt Evelyn cocked her head and said gently, "What's your name, dear girl?"

The girl's eyes looked indecisive for a moment, but after she carefully considered the genuine spirit of Evelyn, giving her a brazenly thorough look up and down, she said in small voice, "Morgan."

Aunt Evelyn smiled with a closed mouth and nodded. She said, "I had a best friend named Morgan when I was fourteen. She had a wonderful gift for making me laugh. And you know? I bet you're about her age when we were best friends."

Morgan nodded slightly, and Aunt Evelyn held out her hand. She took it tentatively, and they walked over to the couch to have a good chat. Evelyn asked if there were any other girls here.

She said, "No, I was the only one for now. Just about a week ago, I was caught by those two big guys and brought here to be a sort of housekeeper."

"I'm surprised the meat loaves were quick enough to grab you," I said, with a grin.

"Meat loaves?"

"Yeah, you know, the beefy guards, the Meat Loaf Twins." They really were the exact shape of a good meat loaf, and just as sharp. She smiled and murmured, *meat loaves.* Then a real, live giggle came out of her. I didn't think it was possible; she looked much more mature and seasoned than her years. Her solemn face turned into a fourteen-year-old's for a split second. I sighed in relief, knowing what we had rescued her from; her duties in this horrid house would certainly have escalated in the near future.

I went back to the bar and poured a large water, still thirsty from the whole adventure of the past couple of days. My mind was racing over all the details, thinking hard about anything I might have missed.

I heard a car pull up, and I went to look out the window. I was ready to vacate the place now that we knew there weren't any other girls around. I didn't want to linger any longer than necessary. Outside, Roarke jumped out of the car and pelted up to the house. His footsteps slapped against the stairs and then he burst in the door.

"Roarke! Is everything okay? What's wrong?"

"Everything's fine, Lane. Sorry to scare you," he said, with his hands out like he was trying to calm a rampaging bull. "There doesn't seem to be any action at the Triborough Bridge. We've had it shut down. The police and police dogs are scouring it, looking for anyone or anything suspicious. But . . . there's something nagging my mind that won't stop, and I *have* to figure it out. There's something wrong. Very wrong."

"All right," I said, my adrenaline kicking in yet one more time. "Any specific part of this that's bothering you that we could go over? Maybe we should sift through the details again, but this time without a gun to our heads."

"Yeah, good idea." He sat down on the edge of a large chair, away from Aunt Evelyn and Morgan, who were having a good chat.

"Okay. So let's go over the day."

We talked through all the details of arriving here, seeing Roxy, getting Eliza to talk, my slap from Eliza. Finally, we got to the part where Finn had come in, and both of us knew we were drawing closer to some black crumb of a detail that we'd missed. My heart was frantic, but to get to the truth, we had to walk through each bit, studiously scrutinizing one piece at a time or we might miss it.

I was saying, "Then Eliza whispered to Donagan. Then Donagan said he thought they should test the mettle of Finn. Then Finn said, 'Sorry, love, I have to stick with the plan.' Then he pulled the trigger—"

"Wait!" exclaimed Roarke, with wide eyes and all the urgency of telling someone to slowly back up from a cliff that dropped a mile to a rocky oblivion. "Wait," he said, with a more tempered tone. "What did Finn say *exactly?*"

"He said, 'Sorry, love. I have to stick with the plan.'"

"No, Lane. He didn't say that. He said, 'I have to stick with Plan B.'"

"He said 'Plan B'? I thought I heard, 'the plan.'"

"Yeah! That's it! I know it! When you were reciting to the group what had gone down, I heard you say, 'The Plan.' But I know beyond a doubt he said 'Plan B.' What do you think that means?"

My mind was reeling and pawing through the possibilities, frantically searching. I knew he had said 'plan' and that word meant he wasn't really going to kill me, it was part of The Plan . . . *Plan B, Plan B.* What could he be trying to tell us?

"Roarke," I said urgently, smacking my hand down hard on his knee. "They must've changed the plan and Finn was trying to tell us."

I gulped, realizing what this would mean.

"It's not the Triborough Bridge."

CHAPTER 37

If I am worth anything later, I am worth something now.

—ML

Roarke stood stock still. His face went ashen as he whispered, "What do you mean?"

"I mean Finn was trying to tell us they switched the plan. It's not the original plan. It's not the Triborough Bridge."

"Well, does that mean we're back to the beginning?" he asked, sounding as desperate as I felt.

"No. No, it *can't*," I said. It was not bearable to think that.

"Okay, okay, let's think," he said, harshly running his hand through his hair as he started pacing.

"Well, they have all the tools, the know-how, and the personnel to handle a bridge. To go and do something completely different would take too long. It has to be another bridge," I reasoned.

"Well, any bridge, frankly, would be a disaster for the city. But what's another bridge that would do just as much collateral and political damage? Are there any other events coming up that would make one bridge over another a better target?"

"Well, the Brooklyn Bridge is an enormous monument to the city, but it's so solid, so huge, it would take a vast amount of dynamite to do the kind of damage that they'd want to do, but I guess it's not impossible," said Roarke, processing out loud.

"Let's see, the biggest event coming up that comes to mind is the World's Fair," I thought out loud. Then it hit us both at the same time.

"The Queensboro," we said, in unison.

"That has to be it. It leads to the World's Fair arena, and an attack on that bridge would have a double impact. That bridge leads to the main causeway to the fair, so it would damage the main route, and there is no way we could repair that kind of damage to the bridge in time. But more importantly, politically, it would make Fio look weak, and the committee would probably take the World's Fair from New York," I said in a rush. "The loss of jobs and finances, not to mention the psychological blow, could cripple the city." I remembered the long line of hundreds of men looking for work the day we broke ground at the site of the World's Fair.

What do we do?

I turned a determined face to Roarke. "Let's send Evelyn to the police; she'll hunt them down and get word to Pete and Fio. Then, I think you and I have to get to the Queensboro Bridge."

"Feels like the Randall's Island deal, huh?" he said knowingly.

I let out a rush of air. "Sure does."

We quickly filled in Aunt Evelyn, and she was ready for action immediately. She, of course, would be taking Morgan with her, Morgan being too shocked about everything to do anything but acquiesce. However, I could see a flame of stubbornness and resilience beneath her sharp gray eyes and stringy blond hair that made me wonder just how long she would stick around.

Roarke and I left. A dead sort of muffled feeling in the air greeted us outside. It was that frustrating predawn time that can't agree with itself if it is truly night or truly morning. There were no cabs to be found, and my eyes went to the van that was parked closest to us, probably the same one they used to bring us here.

"I've always wanted to know how to hot-wire a car," I said.

"I'll show you," said Roarke, with fierce determination.

"You actually know how to hot-wire a car, Roarke?" I squeaked.

"I do. Come on!"

"Huh."

"What? You sound like you don't believe me," he said, with a sardonic look.

"Oh, I believe you, just trying to figure out *how* and *why* you know how to hot-wire a car. . . ." I said, with a critical cocked eyebrow and a tiny bit of concern.

"*Heh, heh, heh,*" he chuckled as he proved his claim.

As we drove toward the bridge, we thought about possible places to begin a search, and the damn bridge was enormous, of course. I tried to pick at this knot, pulling it apart and figuring it out. The best way to handle this would be to find the bombers and persuade them to tell us how to dismantle the bombs. I wanted more than anything to catch Donagan and Eliza, the roots of the mess, but our first objective had to be saving the bridge. The bridge *full* of people going in and out of Manhattan, the bridge that, if collapsed, would also halt the East River barge and boat traffic. Thousands could be killed, and the city would be reeling from not only a physical attack, but a psychological one as well.

As we drove, getting closer and closer to the bridge, we sorted out our thoughts.

"We have to get on the bridge on foot, Roarke. They have to do something to make any work they're doing look inconspicuous, right? And I bet they'll be expecting any trouble to come from the Manhattan side, not the Queens side, so if we enter from Queens, they might not spot us as quickly. Plus, there's that outer lane on the lower level. That lane is always shut down for one reason or another, so it could be a great way to disguise planting the bombs."

"Yeah, that lane is awful," said Roarke, making a valiant attempt at regular conversation. I hated that narrow lane, too. I wasn't exactly afraid of heights, but there was something truly frightening about being on the outside of a monumental structure like a bridge.

"What exactly are we going to do if we find the culprits or the bombs?" Roarke asked.

I flashed my dagger. "I still have this," I said. "*And this.*" I triumphantly pulled out the gun I had taken from the guard.

"I've got mine, too," said Roarke, with a sly grin.

We had accomplished a lot this evening, but I still had a pretty decent grip on reality. Looking for some affirmation, I said, "Roarke, I know this is crazy. I know we can't take down these professionals by ourselves, but maybe we can at least stall them until the cavalry arrives. Right?"

His smile straightened a little, and he focused, locking onto my eyes just for an instant. "Right. We'll do everything we can, Lane," he said. With a resolute look, we kept going, driving closer and closer to our goal.

We took the ramp from Vernon, the road adjacent to the river. We were right by one of the pylons that held up the massive bridge. It was enormous, staggering. It was hard to imagine men building this behemoth. Our van curved up the ramp, and at the point where the bridge began and the ramp ended, we pulled over to the side, with just a couple of horns honking at us. We got out and crouched down beside the metal railing and started to slink along.

A wide light blue sky awaiting the dawn arched over our heads. The east was looking lighter than I expected; I worried that it was later than I had thought. We might run out of time. And we would be caught right in the middle.

"Roarke," I whispered as I beheld the soaring bridge, "this is even more monumental up close. . . . Are we sure this could be the target? How on earth could they take this thing down?"

"I know," said Roarke. "But the Schmidt brothers have taken down entire buildings before. Enough dynamite in the right places can take down anything. And they've had time to work on this. The thing going for us is that Daley Joseph will not be far away. From what everyone has said, he will want a front row seat. They will have set up the wiring ahead of time, but they'll have to set the explosives today; dynamite can be very unpredictable. They wouldn't be able to set it weeks in advance and then come sailing in here to ignite it. No, they'll be here."

All our exhilaration in taking down those thugs back at Eliza's house dissipated just as the night was dissipating into day. Our small victory looked especially insignificant in the shadows of this bridge and the horrific plan to tear it down. Already it was teeming with people. Hundreds of cars, thousands of people. And this bridge spanned not only the East River, but Blackwell's Island. And the end ramps went quite far into Queens and Manhattan. There was no telling the kind of damage it could do if any part of it went down.

We started to skulk across the bridge. We went along the outside lane, thinking it was a good place to spot anything suspicious. That lane was on the lower level, so there were plenty of hiding places and shadows. We had to start somewhere and hope that Aunt Evelyn would be getting through to the rest of our crew.

We jogged a long way, finally making it to the point where we were over water, where it would be logical to place explosives. I felt ready, somehow. I got to the point where I'd had enough of fearing this big threat; I wanted to face it and get it over with. Then I stupidly looked down—way, way, way down—at the water. Roarke must've felt the same waves of fear, because he looked back at me with wary eyes and took my hand. We kept going.

Suddenly, he pulled me to a wall and we pressed up flat against it, trying to blend in. With one finger, Roarke pointed carefully up ahead. I saw them: the unmistakable outlines of the three Schmidt brothers. Two big guys flanking Weasel-Face.

They were in heated debate about something. It looked like Weasel was arguing with the other two. They didn't have anything in their hands, I noticed, like guns or detonators. I liked that. We slowly started to make our way over to them. Roarke motioned for me to go behind the wall and get at them from behind.

I eased each foot out in front of me before I stepped, unsure of my footing in the relative darkness. I moved as fast as I dared and got to the other side just as I heard Roarke say with a cool and level voice, "Gentleman, show me your hands."

"Hey, what are you doing here?" said a thin, oily voice. Roarke could see me now, but the others hadn't heard me with all the traffic behind us.

"No, no," said Roarke. "There won't be any reaching for guns, now. Put your hands on your heads, thank you."

I stepped out of the shadows, my gun leveled at Weasel. "I'd do as he says," I declared firmly.

The big guy closer to me said in a surprisingly high and juvenile voice for such a big fellow, "See, Rufus? I told you! I knew we'd get caught. You always ruin everything!"

"I do not!" snapped Rufus, aka Weasel. This was like a weird family drama on the radio.

"Rufus, it's true," said the muffled, dopey voice from the other big fellow, who had recognized me back at Chesty LaRue's. "He did tell ya, and you do louse up all this stuff."

"*Arrrrrrgh,*" choked out Rufus.

"All right, all right, fellas. I've had enough of this little show here. Tell me what's going down today and you might be able to make some kind of deal with the courts. But we don't have a lot of time. I want to hear you talking about your target, and I want to hear it *now.*" Roarke's firm, stern voice of a mature adult helped snap the big guys to attention. He had more leadership skills in his little finger than their brother could ever hope to acquire.

Weasel made an attempt. "Don't even think about—" But before he could finish his sentence, the other two started ratting him out.

"We didn't know what it all meant!"

"Honest! We just like blowing things up, we didn't know it was gonna be this big bridge!"

"But then Rufus says that we have to . . ."

"Enough!" yelled Roarke, as loud as he dared. "Sheesh! I get it, I get it! Where are the explosives, how do we stop the detonation, and where are the men who hired you?"

They quickly told us: *everywhere, you can't,* and *we don't know.* A helpful bunch. After a little more persuading on Roarke's part, and as we tied them to the bridge with the ropes from their own equipment, they felt inclined to explain a little more fully.

Apparently, the bombs were strung along key places around most pylons and then underneath the upper level of the bridge, so as it blew, it would crash down and tear out both levels with it. There were three main charges that would start a chain reaction. The Schmidt brothers had used all the dynamite they could get their hands on, and it seemed as though it was a substantial amount. As far as their employers, they weren't really sure where they were, but what they were certain of was that they weren't too far away, as they had made it known that they wanted to see the action up close and personal. Oh, and the guy taking the lead on this demolition, they confirmed, was not Rufus the Weasel but Lyle, my slick friend from the country music bar. Weasel (I'm not sure I could really call him anything else) was middle management.

I turned to Roarke. "So, they weren't lying, the explosives really are everywhere."

"So it seems. All right, these guys are out of the way, and since we are leaving them here, I believe they are motivated to be telling us the truth. So, the crucial wire to cut on each of the three main charges is the one with the orange tag. The first detonator is near us, on that second pylon. They said there's a ledge that we can climb to. Let's go have a look. The timers are set for eight this morning, when rush hour is in full swing. We have a little time."

"Okay, let's go," I said. It felt good to have some tracks to run on, albeit terrifying tracks. We both pocketed a couple of tools; I made sure to grab a wire cutter.

The guys had been yelling at us to take them to safety. That was laughable. Roarke rounded on them. "*You* made your beds, now you can lie in them. And you better be telling us the whole truth, because if the bridge goes down, so do you." His golden brown eyes flashed even in this dim early morning light, and his jawline had an angry twitch. For a guy with dimples, when he was angry, every ounce of him showed it in spades. Even the two big guys flinched back and shut up.

We carefully made our way to the nearest pylon. The bridge was over twenty-five years old and repair crews and painting crews frequently worked on it, so I doubted anyone would have noticed the Schmidts' handiwork, especially if they did it at off times or at twilight. Plus, nothing of this magnitude had ever been attempted; no one would think to look. It reminded me of H.H. Holmes, one of the first documented American serial killers, forty years ago in Chicago. No one had even conceived of that happening. Now we knew better.

We got to the first pylon they had directed us to, and sure enough, when we looked down, there was a ledge sticking out just wide enough for a man to walk around with a small fence to prevent someone from falling off. I spotted what looked like a black bag that had to be the charge. The only problem was, we needed a ladder to get down to it.

"*Uhhhhh . . .*" I started to say.

"Here, we can do this. I'd do it, but it's a blind drop. If I lower you, I can direct you precisely. I'll lower you down by your wrists; it's not that far—only about ten or twelve feet. You'll only have to drop a few feet," said Roarke enthusiastically.

I was agitated and scared, but what could I do? There was no alternative. We'd have to try it. The reinforcements weren't here yet; we had no idea when they'd show up.

I stepped over to the edge of the bridge . . . and that ten feet looked more like forty. It was a straight drop. But it looked iffy to me. If a stiff wind came along and swayed us just the tiniest bit too far, I'd be in the East River after a very long free fall.

"Oh, my God, Roarke."

"Lane, it's okay. I've got you—you weigh hardly anything. I will *not* let you go." His eyes were intense, his brow furrowed. I trusted him. I let him take my arms, forcing myself to let go of the precious railing so he could lower me.

For saying I *hardly weighed anything*, he sure did a lot of grunting. But despite this, he lowered me with great strength, very carefully. He said he'd count to three and on three, he'd let go. "Get ready, Lane. One, two, three!"

I knew it wasn't far, but my knees buckled when I landed, nonetheless. But I *did* land. I took a deep breath, gave a thumbs-up to Roarke, and went to the black bag. There were wires coming out of it like black snakes or spider legs. I looked around, and the wires streamed out of the bag, both up and down around the pylon. I looked up, and I could see the faint outlines of oblong lumps that looked like thick candles along the pylon and tucked underneath the second level of the bridge. My heart raced faster.

I gingerly opened the bag. *Orange tag. Orange tag.*

I found it.

I was plagued with *what ifs*: What if this was the wrong wire and we exploded? What if I died right now? What if we couldn't do this in time?

I took a good look at the rest of the wires and thought through if there was anything I was missing. Since we left Weasel on the bridge with us, I had a fair amount of confidence that he wasn't giving us bad information. But there was the theoretical knowledge, and the *I'm about to cut the goddamn wire* reality.

I cut the wire.

And then my heart started beating again. I looked up at Roarke and nodded, giving him another thumbs-up. One down, two to go.

Roarke bent low over the railing, waving for me to come over. I'd have to get onto a step along the wall of the pylon to get just a little more height and then jump up to clasp Roarke's hands. Then he'd drag me up.

The plan worked perfectly. Until my hands just started to reach the top of the railing and a horrifying voice gurgled, "Look what we have here."

CHAPTER 38

Only when I fall do I get up again.

—ML

I was completely blind as I groped for a hold on the railing. I heard a nauseating *thud* and Roarke's arms were wrenched from me. I desperately grabbed the railing and held on with everything I had. I couldn't make purchase with my feet; I would have to use all my shoulder strength to pull myself up. I was doing just that when two beefy hands grasped my forearms like meat hooks. My gut clenched as I struggled and turned my eyes up into the face of Daley Joseph.

My mind roiled with being touched again by Daley Joseph. My skin crawled from his fingers on my arms, even as I struggled to survive, making me debate the choice of letting go. His leering countenance was only inches from mine, his stale breath reeking of old cigars and booze.

"Lane, don't you look extremely hale and hearty for having been shot dead recently," he gurgled with contempt. His strength was astounding; his talon-like fingers were painfully digging into my arms as he kept me aloft without seeming to strain in the least.

"*Hmm,*" he thought out loud in a carefree voice. "What shall I do? It seems a tragedy to drop you from here, after all you've been through. I mean, you deserve a much more glorious death. Seems lazy and unworthy somehow."

A crazy idea ran through my mind: His vocabulary was sounding much more like that of the sophisticated and slightly less cruel Joseph than the bloodthirsty Daley. Could I use that?

"Ah, Mr. Joseph? If you pull me up, there could be a thousand more interesting ways for me to die . . . and you could think about it and make it more . . . worthy of you." Where was I getting this? It wasn't the cleverest thing I'd ever come up with, but hell, I was dangling from a bridge.

He laughed in a mirthless way that said he knew exactly what I was doing but was slightly amused by it. He pulled with a mighty heave, and I was up and over the railing, sprawling onto the cement. Roarke was not far away, crumpled on the ground with a sickening amount of blood over his forehead from his head wound. I could feel the bile rising in my throat. The bravado of a second ago faltering, I looked up at Mr. Joseph.

I was right, he was clearly not his alter ego; his shirt was tucked in and his tie perfect. However, it must have been a quick transformation, because his shirt was the stained, unkempt kind that Daley wore. Of course. Daley had to be there to oversee the carnage, but perhaps the orderly Joseph was unsure of his abilities to pull everything off without a hitch.

My mind raced, trying to account for everything, grasping at straws: Roarke's injury, the bombs, their whereabouts, how to get help, how to save my own skin. But before I could do anything about my thoughts, Joseph turned to me abruptly, saying, "Oh, no, how disappointing. Our delightful little encounter has just been cut short, I'm afraid."

"What are you—"

He cut off my outburst by forcefully turning me around and putting a sharp knife to my throat. Then I saw him.

Finn.

"Look what I found, Finn," said Joseph slowly, like he was enjoying every succulent morsel of each syllable.

Finn came to a tight stop, every muscle taut. This time, his cover was blown, and when I looked at his eyes, that flash of the real him was there. And the fury.

I didn't breathe; I didn't move a muscle. That knife was already making a small cut into my flesh with a painful pinch, and I felt a trickle of blood drip down my neck. I thought of all the options that

Mr. Kirkland had shown me in our short time of training, but none of them seemed like they'd do the trick at this moment. Then an idea crystallized from that crazy thought I'd had earlier.

I said, through clenched teeth, "Daley! Don't you see? Joseph doesn't trust you, he *had* to come out and make sure you didn't louse things up."

"Lane! What are you doing?" yelled Finn desperately.

"He thinks you're a bumbler, Daley."

Joseph tightened his hold on me and jabbed my throat, and I yelped as the knife hurt more than I thought possible. But it worked.

"Well, Lane . . ." said the oily voice of Daley. I could even feel his body change as his alter ego came to life—the subtlest shift of posture and even how he handled the knife, changing his grip. "I didn't know you liked me so much. I would have made a few more visits to you had I but known."

That did it. Finn dove at us as I kicked back into Daley's knee, striking him off balance, while I simultaneously pulled at his arm holding the knife to keep it from cutting into my precious neck. I relentlessly kicked and thrashed for everything I was worth until his arm released me.

I stood up, grabbing my gun out of my belt, ready to shoot. But Finn and Daley were in a death grip, wrestling on the ground. Daley had his knife out, and Finn held his gun, trying desperately to point it toward Daley while warding off that knife. If I tried to shoot, I could hit Finn. Just as I was about to jump in and at least start hitting Daley over the head, I caught the look on Finn's face.

It was a primal mass of rage. "I said . . . I would *never* let you touch her *again*." With one final, savage burst of energy, he head-butted Daley, and with arms and legs tangled in the deadly wrestling match, a shot rang out.

I screamed, "No!" My God, they were so closely entwined.

Then Finn said breathlessly, "It's okay, Lane! I got him. He's done."

I had been knocked to my knees. Daley was still holding on to the knife, blood spreading quickly from his chest wound, which was certainly lethal. Blood streamed from his grotesque mouth, his eyes slowly turning over to look at me. And then his head rolled to the ground with a low thud as his life ebbed away.

Finn rushed over to me. We wrapped our arms around each other like we were holding on for dear life. His hand held my head to his chest as he kissed the top of it. I exhaled as if I'd been holding my breath for hours.

We pulled away and ran over to Roarke. Thank God, he was still breathing. The head wound was serious, but his heart was still beating and his lungs were working. Finn took off his suit coat and laid it on top of him to keep him warm. I took Finn's tie and my scarf and tied on a rough bandage to slow the blood loss. To my relief I could see that it was already clotting. I didn't want to move him without a doctor, though.

While we were taking care of Roarke, I quickly brought Finn up to speed.

"Okay," he said, fully alert to the critical nature of our next steps. "We have two more charges to take care of. Let's go."

We started running toward the next pylon, which had the detonator for the midsection of the bridge.

"But, Finn, where are Donagan and Eliza? How did you give them the slip?"

We were running side by side, the next pylon seeming impossibly far away. "Said I was going to go check on things, make sure Daley was handling everything all right. That was a stroke of genius back there. I'd never seen Daley drawn out before."

"Thanks!" I was panting now as we ran. "At first I was glad to see it was the slightly less terrible Joseph, but then again, he was much more calculating. I was gambling that if Daley were there, he might make a rash mistake or misjudge something—anything! I had to try *something*."

"Nice." I caught that he was smiling broadly, but then we cut the niceties short as we were both spent. We sprinted in silence, the rhythm of our feet pounding the pavement and the panting of our breath blending with the noise of the traffic.

When we got to the next pylon, I told Finn how Roarke and I handled the first one. He lowered me down without hesitation. We were running out of time now. I found the pouch, cut the wire, and shuddered as I saw many, many bundles of dynamite underneath the bridge now that I knew what to look for. I jumped up to Finn's waiting hands, and he lifted me up and over.

We started off to the final pylon, the one closest to Manhattan. Rush hour was in full swing now. I noticed a couple of curious on-lookers as they passed by on their way to work, but the busy New Yorkers were used to seeing everything, so we really didn't stand out too much.

The final pylon was within reach, when out from behind it strode Donagan Connell and Eliza. Donagan's gun was at the ready, point-ing right at us. We lurched to a stop and put up our hands.

From a half-amused, half-irritated Donagan, I heard for the sec-ond time that morning, "Well, what do we have here? Set your gun down, Finn." He did.

Eliza murmured sulkily, "I knew it was too good to be true. Should've stabbed her myself."

"Quiet!" snapped a now fully agitated Donagan, but then his voice became silkier, as he had second thoughts about his rebuke. "Well, actually, Eliza, my dear, maybe we'll just give you your chance." The pouting Eliza brightened up at that. Finn put out his arm and barred me behind him.

Donagan's eyebrows went up, and he said interestedly, "Really? You mean Daley was right after all? Very intriguing."

I hated that man. It felt like my blood was boiling.

Finn chose not to take the bait. He mastered his face and re-mained motionless.

But then Donagan looked past us, where I knew he could see the form of Daley lying flat on the cement. I closely watched Dona-gan's face as he took in that fact. Eliza was still consumed with her-self, as usual, and probably dreaming up torture scenarios for me. Donagan's face registered disbelief, then shock, then anger . . . and finally indifference. The worst of insults.

"Oh, well," he said, as if someone had just knocked over an in-consequential glass of milk that would quickly and easily be re-placed. "And I assume you've taken out the first two charges?" He looked at our faces and got his answer.

He took a good look at the final chain, around and above us on the underside of the upper level of the bridge. Everything was still in place. "Well, it won't be as spectacular as I had hoped, but it will still do the trick. Pain, plenty of mayhem and destruction, and your precious mayor will be out on his ass. And of course, I'll be there to pick up the city's pieces!" he said, with a satisfied smirk.

So, that was it. Donagan not only wanted to create chaos, he planned to swoop in and be the savior to the city. With his ties to Tammany, that was a pretty likely scenario. If we didn't stop him.

From what the Schmidt brothers told us, we probably only had about fifteen minutes left to stop this charge. Donagan was too cool and collected to manipulate like Daley. They had walked right up to us, both within a few feet. How could we distract them?

Suddenly, there were loud yells, running feet . . . then that ridiculous, wonderful trumpet. And there he was, my knight in shining armor. Well, my short, round knight in rumpled suit and off-kilter fedora. Fiorello was leading the charge. Eliza and Donagan looked to see what the commotion was about. Finn saw his opportunity and grabbed Donagan's gun, pointing it away from us. He was just about to wrench it out of his hand as Eliza reached to her thigh and, quick as lightning, brought out a gun.

The silver gun.

The flash of silver caught Donagan's eye. He looked thunderstruck and uttered, "You?" That split second allowed Finn to wrestle him to the ground.

I grabbed the muzzle of the silver gun and pointed it away from me as I grappled with the seething, writhing Eliza. All the past months and years of internalizing her acute hatred started to boil up and over. Her sheer strength was almost too much for me. Her face was a ragged, hateful mask with bared teeth. Her knife-sharp nails were biting into my hands, blood starting to drip, mingling with the red scroll on the handle of the gun. My wrists were shaking with the force needed to keep that gun from pointing at me.

Finn was having the same problems with Donagan; they were matched physically. The rescue group was almost upon us, and I glimpsed a pistol waving in Fio's hand. They were gaining on us, but I had no idea how long I could hold out against Eliza's fierce wrath.

I heard a thud as Finn brought Donagan down hard to the pavement, having kicked his knees out from under him, and punched him over and over again. Donagan's gun skittered across the ground. I finally kneed Eliza hard in the gut, but as she doubled over, she knocked my feet out from under me. She stood over me, the silver gun not wavering one iota as it pointed at my heart.

Before I could even blink, a gun went off. I winced, shutting my eyes, certain I'd feel my flesh tearing. Instead, Eliza was struck. Her hand came up to her chest. Her eyes were wide with shock, and her knees began to wobble. She staggered backward. A sharp spasm of pain hit, her face wincing with agony. Her feet faltered, making her lose her balance. She fell hard to the ground, her head hitting the pavement and her hand, with the silver gun, coming down last with a crack.

The gun slid from her grasp. The silver gun of my nightmares skidded inexorably toward the edge of the bridge.

Donagan uttered an agonized, "No!"

The gun went right to the edge, slipping beneath the railing. Its heavy handle went over the side, slowing nearly to a stop. Then it gently tipped, the weight of the handle dipping downward, and it fell.

CHAPTER 39

Art is to console those who are broken by life.

—ML

I scrambled to my feet. There, standing behind Eliza, was Fiorello, looking shattered. His gun was smoking.

I walked slowly over to Fio, took his gun gently from his hand, and handed it to Mr. Kirkland. Then I bear-hugged my hero.

"Fio! I knew you'd get here in time." That broke the spell that had kept him stunned. Then I went to Mr. Kirkland. I looked up into his bright blue eyes, his gray hair forming an incredible halo around his rugged face. I threw my arms around him, too. "Thank you." He didn't say anything, but for our first real hug, he did a bang-up job.

The last charge.

I ran to Finn, who was just getting up from a mangled, but breathing, Donagan. "Finn!"

"Yeah. Let's go."

He lowered me down, to much yelling and disagreement from the ones who had been running up to us, including most of the police force, who had shown up from Pete's crew. But we had already done this, and we could do it faster than anyone.

We were cutting the timing terrifyingly close. I located the bundle, found the wire with the orange tag, and cut it without an ounce of hesitation.

I slowly, carefully stood up on my narrow platform, holding tightly to the railing. As I paused, I was given a moment of total clarity, an intense moment of deep thanks and peace. The cheery yellow and orange from the rising sun splashed onto the shining buildings in a beautiful scene that took me completely by surprise. My town. My city. Above the traffic, I heard the lonely cry of a gull in the quiet of the morning.

A new day. A slow smile spread across my lips.

I looked up at the men lining the edge of the bridge. I raised my arms above my head in victory, like a runner crossing the finish line. "Got it!" I yelled, full of ridiculous happiness. Suddenly a dozen faces broke into enormous smiles. Cheers, hand-shaking, and manly hugging spread everywhere at once. A particularly burly fellow reached his arms down and said, "Okay, doll, let's get you back up here."

Finn interrupted and patted the guy on the back. "Thanks, pal, I got her." And he reached his arms down to me. He grinned, his eyes glinting with enjoyment. "Come on, Lane!"

I jumped with more energy than I thought possible, and he gripped my arms. He pulled me up, and as I got closer to the top, several kind hands helped me up and over the railing. Many hands slapped me on the back. I hugged the burly guy.

Finn put his arms around me in a quick embrace, whispering into my ear, "Nice job, love." We had so much more to say, but we'd have to wait a little longer.

Our friends, firefighters, and policemen all gathered around. Finn and I quickly told the other officers everything we learned concerning the rest of the explosives. The police were already clearing the bridge, and they had the professional bomb crews out checking the charges and safely retrieving the dynamite bundles. We also filled in the police about Daley's body, the Schmidt brothers at the other end—still tied up, hopefully—and then Donagan and Eliza. A medic was already covering up Eliza's body with a white sheet.

Another medic quickly bandaged my throat. The bleeding had stopped, but I was going to need some stitches. Finn looked like his shoulder was bothering him, and he had a couple of good bruises appearing on his face, but I didn't see too much blood or broken bones.

They wanted to take us to the hospital, but we both thought that was overkill. However, my need for stitches ended our arguments about the matter. At least they didn't strap us down to stretchers. I was swept away toward one ambulance, Finn another.

I suddenly caught sight of Roarke being wheeled into an ambulance nearby, and I went over to him to talk for a minute, even though the traveling nurse wanted to force me right into the ambulance. I swatted her away.

His head bandage was showing some blood through it, and his face was pasty. His eyes were shut, but when I went to him, the golden lashes fluttered open.

I gently rubbed his arm, afraid to touch anything else, and whispered, "Roarke, are you okay?"

He smiled dimly. "Lane . . . did we make it? I didn't hear any explosions."

"Nah . . . no explosions. Our plan worked, Roarke. And you wouldn't believe the cavalry that rode in to save us. Fio even had his trumpet."

"Oh, God, that's good to hear. I thought I heard a trumpet. I thought I was hallucinating."

"No, no hallucinations. Just our mayor. He only lacked a white steed and Excalibur."

"God. What he would do with that . . ."

I snickered, then I paused. "Roarke, they say you have a concussion, but you're stable. You lost a *lot* of blood. I . . ." I shook my head. I couldn't finish my thought.

"Oh, Lane, it would take a lot more than a pistol whip from that greasy, pitiful excuse for a man to take me out." He paused for a minute. "I thought I saw Finn over there. Is he all right?"

"Yeah, he's fine." I quickly filled him in on all that had happened.

"So Eliza had the silver gun?"

I nodded.

"Well, that's interesting."

"*Mmm.* Sure is. And she lost it. The gun fell over the edge of the bridge when she was killed."

"*Hmm.* I guess that's the end of the silver gun, huh?" he contemplated. For some reason, I wasn't so sure about that. "Who shot her?" he asked.

"Fio."

"Oh, my God, what I would give to write up *that* scene. It's painful I can't do it."

"Who says you can't? Here, I have my notepad and my pen. I'll describe it all and you put it to your own, heroic words. Make sure you put in your part. We wouldn't have been able to do this without you, you know."

He smiled a full-dimple grin at that. I reciprocated. Minus the dimples.

I searched his golden brown eyes and said intently, softly, "Roarke. Thank you for going through all this with me. It wouldn't have been survivable without you."

He gazed at me, then slowly raised his left hand and put it over mine, which was still on his right arm.

"Come visit me in the hospital, Lane. I want that story." I smiled. He'd be just fine.

The medics wheeled him over to the ambulance, lifted him in, then closed the doors with a bang.

CHAPTER 40

For my part I know nothing with any certainty,
but the sight of the stars makes me dream.

—ML

I arrived at the hospital and, sure enough, ended up with six stitches. They were quite painful, but Fio got the best surgeon he could find who specialized in a new surgical method that left minimal scarring. Fio would have nothing but the best.

I didn't have to stay under observation, so they allowed me to go and find Roarke. I gave him the entire scoop with as much description as possible. He wrote furiously, and I could see the gears of his mind turning; it was like he'd never been wounded. He was captivated, fully enthralled with getting this good story. *This* was his life blood, *this* was his mistress. She was a keen, bright flame.

Aunt Evelyn told me they'd released Finn and that he said he'd come by tonight for the debriefing she'd scheduled. She took me home. Mr. Kirkland was waiting for us there, and I have to say, home never looked so good.

It was early evening, and a golden glow of lamps and candles shined from the front windows, and my Ripley was at the side window of the front door. I looked up at the face of our home: the red bricks, the bumped-out bay window in the front with the green copper roof, the little curved dormer windows way at the top in Aunt Evelyn's studio . . . taking it all in as if I'd been on a long, long voyage and was returning home at last.

Inside, the heavenly aroma of Mr. Kirkland's cream of potato chowder, fresh bread, and brownies just about overwhelmed me, as I was *starving*. Luckily, Aunt Evelyn and Mr. Kirkland knew me well, and we had dinner right away at the scrubbed pine table, with Ripley lying directly on my feet, letting me know in no uncertain terms that I would not be going out tonight, possibly ever again.

As if the three of us had made a silent agreement, we didn't discuss anything of the case or even of the remarkable events of the past few days. We were just happy to be in one piece, and together. We talked of trivial things and delighted ourselves in the normalcy of life.

I did ask what had happened to Morgan, wondering why she wasn't here for dinner. After she and Aunt Evelyn talked, she had decided she felt most comfortable going to live, at least temporarily, at a new home for women that Ellie and Evelyn were helping to organize. Morgan was younger than most of the guests who had been on the streets, but could relate to them in ways we never could. But we'd be checking up on her in the days to come, figuring out some schooling and a plan for her future. She was so young. But I could also see a bright streak of defiance, strength, and independence in her. I liked her, and I wondered if she would let us help her, or if she'd decide to go her own way.

Just as we were finishing up our simple dinner, the invitees to Aunt Evelyn's debriefing started to arrive. No room but the parlor was big enough for us all to congregate comfortably. Aunt Evelyn, Fio, and Mr. Kirkland took the Command Central seats at the front windows. Val sat next to me on the large sofa; Peter sat on the other side of her in a high-backed chair. Roarke had to stay in the hospital and left a noticeable void.

Lastly, the bell rang. I walked over to the door. "Hi, Finn," I said as I opened the door.

"Hi, Lane," he said quietly, with a smile. Then his brow furrowed and he looked closely at my neck as he stepped in. The chattering from the other room was nice and loud, letting us have a minute of solitude. I smiled at him. He drew close and took a good look at me. I had changed into a soft pink pencil skirt and white blouse, which was open a couple of buttons at the collar to give my poor neck some room. He winced as he took in the stitches.

"Is your neck all right?" he asked as his hand softly came around my jaw.

"Yeah, I took some aspirin, and the six stitches hardly seem noticeable."

"*Six?*"

"Finn, it's okay. I'm good." His face looked tired, but his dark eyes were mesmerizing, and it just felt *good* to have him here. His brow cleared as he looked into my eyes and found that I meant it: I really was all right.

Finn greeted Aunt Evelyn and took the offered cup of coffee from Mr. Kirkland, then came to sit down on my other side on the sofa.

"Were there brownies?" he asked abruptly and a tad forlornly.

"Smells good, huh?"

"I'll bring out some more brownies for everyone," said a grinning Mr. Kirkland.

Finn ate his brownie with complete devotion, no crumb going to waste. If it had been proper enough, I was certain he would have licked his fingers.

Aunt Evelyn brought the meeting to order with an *ahem*, and all the little conversations happening around the room came to a halt as we turned our attention to her. In her usual, methodical manner, she'd given the order of events some thoughtful consideration.

"Lane, I believe we are all up to speed from the part where we left Eliza's um . . . house of . . . ah, yes. We'll just leave it at Eliza's. The police were informed of the attempt happening at the new Triborough Bridge. Could you enlighten everyone as to how you all ended up at the Queensboro Bridge?"

"Certainly," I said.

I filled them in on all the events that happened, from leaving Eliza's place up until now. Much of it sounded unreal even to my own ears, proving the point once again that reality is stranger than fiction. Well, at least my reality.

"Thank you, Lane," said Aunt Evelyn. Her eyes took on a beady look of determination and deep thought. "Peter, the police took in Donagan and the Schmidt brothers?"

"Yes, ma'am. We also picked up Lyle."

"And the bodies of Daley Joseph and Eliza?" asked Mr. Kirkland.

"Yes, sir," replied Peter. "They've been taken to the city morgue. We'll have to send someone to officially identify them tomorrow."

Fio and Finn said that they would handle that the next morning.

Peter piped in again. "So, I understand the motive of getting Fio out of the way but, may I ask, how does the art theft here and the subway mugging connect with everything? Were they really connected or just coincidence?"

Finn replied, "The answer to that goes back to Danny Fazzalari and Eliza. There were multiple motives. Overall, Daley and Donagan wanted to discredit Fio and make the city ripe for a new leader. I think Donagan thought he could become the new Jimmy Walker. But those other incidents were Danny going rogue. I'd always felt that the subway incident, the home theft, and even the Randall's Island bomb were too messy, too aimless for Donagan and Daley. I couldn't figure it out until yesterday, when I finally got to see Eliza and Donagan together. Eliza started out just trying to get back at Lane, hating her and her family. But Eliza's plans became much bigger once she got tight with Donagan. Danny was no longer necessary. Not only that, he had become a menace to their carefully laid plans. That's why Eliza eventually took Danny out. He had filled her purposes well enough for a while. I think he did all that to try to impress her and Donagan. Being Uncle Louie's nephew, he had a lot to live up to."

Valerie piped in, "I get why Eliza wanted to get back at Lane. But it seems like Lane became more of a target than just that."

I nodded. "Yeah. Lucky me. Well, if Danny's plans had actually killed me off, it wouldn't have been too bad for them." Evelyn winced. "But I survived. And I started asking questions and basically making a nuisance of myself. What was that, Finn?" He'd snorted.

"Nothing," he said, grinning.

"So, I became a target because they realized I wouldn't let it go. They tried intimidation with Daley visiting me that night." I carefully felt my aching neck, remembering that choke hold. "But that didn't work, it just made things worse. And they had to kidnap Roarke and me when they discovered us at the Meatpacking District, to find out what we knew before they could just get rid of us, in case they had to do any damage control."

Finn said, "And that is actually why they changed their plan from the Triborough to the Queensboro. They originally liked the Triborough Bridge best, being that it just opened this summer. But Donagan and Daley figured one last change of plan would be a good thing, to confuse anyone who might have gotten wind of their intentions."

"How about Roxy, Val?" asked Aunt Evelyn. "Did she suspect anything? And how did she hold up when you took her home?"

"Roxy had started to notice some peculiar behavior from Lizzie, and she's no dummy. However, she had no idea of the magnitude of what was provoking Lizzie's strange behavior or that she herself was Lizzie's scapegoat. Roxy kept her suspicions mostly to herself. But she finally confronted Lizzie with the strange absences, the dark circles under her eyes, and the fact that she knew that Lizzie and Danny had been an item and yet she had no *real* reaction to his death. She let her know enough that Lizzie got nervous, forcing her hand, so she had Roxy kidnapped. But she's a tough cookie, I think she'll be fine."

"Good," said Aunt Evelyn. "Now, have we covered everything?"

Fiorello leaned forward, clasping his hands, elbows on his knees. "I'd like to thank all of you," he said, with an earnest smile. "What you did today and what you've been working on for these past weeks has saved many, many lives. And you've also helped *me* more than I can say," he declared as his voice started to break. "Thank you—all of you."

Aunt Evelyn wiped a tiny tear from the corner of her eye and said just as earnestly, "Fiorello? You are worth it, dear friend. All right, then," declared Aunt Evelyn. "How about some coffee, and I think we can find some more brownies." The meeting was adjourned, and we broke up into small groups, chatting and enjoying the company of friends.

Fio called Finn over in a rather hush-hush way. So, I went to the kitchen, where Mr. Kirkland and Aunt Evelyn were assembling another plate of brownies. There was a little plate and a big plate.

"You made Finn his own plate, didn't you?" I said.

"Well, it was pretty obvious he enjoyed them. I always try to favor the fans of my cooking," said Mr. Kirkland, in a mock snooty fashion.

When I went back to the main group, Fio and Finn were still in deep conversation, but then they waved me over. "What's up, fellas?" I asked. "Mr. Kirkland made you your own plate, Finn," I said, handing it to him.

"*Oooh,*" he exhaled, taking the plate eagerly.

"Well, Laney Lane?" Fio screeched happily.

"*Grrrrr.*"

"*Heh heh heh,*" he cackled. "We were just discussing that Finn's undercover assignment is finished. Valentine and I already came to the conclusion that he's done all he can to uproot the corruption and work with Daley and Donagan in his current role. So? He's back to being a regular detective." I was pretty sure Finn could never be classified as *regular.*

Fio continued on, "Valentine is already set to make the record straight about Finn's *incorruptible* self and his role. In fact, Finn, guess who offered to make the announcement with Valentine tomorrow morning?"

Finn looked relieved, and his shoulders lowered, letting go of the years of tension as he exhaled deeply. Finn shook his head as he smiled. "I don't know. Who?"

"Pete."

Finn shook his head. "Well I'll be . . ."

CHAPTER 41

I wish they would just take me as I am.

—ML

I walked in the honey brown doorway. The kitchen step creaked the same way I'd heard it creak a thousand times. The clock on the wall made its quick tick-tick-tick, the heartbeat of the kitchen. The gold, flat knobs on the cupboards, the short curtains fluttering in the windows, the butter yellow walls. How many times had I eaten vegetable soup, Swedish steak, mashed potatoes, turkey . . . in this very room? So many good meals.

I walked through the door, through the kitchen to the living room with its lovely high beams, and up the stairs. I felt the cool banister beneath my fingertips, every ridge, every curve, every nick . . . I knew exactly where they would be before my fingertips felt them. I turned to the right at the top of the stairs toward my parents' bedroom. I saw their oak bed ahead of me, the dresser on the right, the chest of drawers on my left. I felt the little decorative knob that I touched and admired every day. I was looking for something. But I couldn't find it. There was the nightstand clock, the mirror on the dresser, the scents of my father's cologne and my mother's face powder. It was a lovely feeling of being back, of knowing what to expect and then seeing it. I half-understood that I was dreaming, but then again, there was a real quality to it all. And then it hit me. What I was looking for wasn't here.

There was no music.

I was suddenly outside at the front of the house. There was the little black statue of a young boy riding a serpent, with a fountain of water flowing out of the fishy mouth. I ran my hands along the seashell-shaped base and felt the cold water that was collecting, the sound of the fountain bright and clear and familiar. I turned to my right, and there was my tree, overshadowing the sadness, offering its happiness.

My purple maple tree with the one branch reaching out to the left like a leafy giant, kindly holding out his arm to invite me to play. My hands automatically went to that branch, and the smooth, brown bark felt cool, and it was like an old friend. I eagerly pulled myself up onto the branch, followed it along like a balance beam to the main trunk, and climbed my tree like a natural ladder.

High, high up, I found a good foothold and leaned back against the strong, supportive trunk. I looked down and saw my father on a ladder, fixing something near the roofline of the house. I saw my mother in that corner window above the kitchen sink, and she smiled up at me and waved. I took in the brick planter near the road, full of flamboyant purple and pink petunias. Across from me was the tall pine soaring way up over our house while a fresh wind blew its Christmasy scent to me.

This was a gift, I knew. Simultaneously, I was filled with joy and heartbreaking sorrow. The tears from both overcame me, and my head ached with them. They spilled out over my cheeks and dripped onto my hands, which were still tightly clasping my tree.

I woke up.

Then, slowly, slowly, the heartache ebbed . . . a little. I uncurled my body and rubbed my hair out of my face. I wiped the tears that had run down my face. I drew slow, big breaths and filled my lungs and my heart with the cool air of the night.

I never went back to sleep. I wasn't afraid to go to sleep; The dream hadn't been a bad one. Just heart-wrenching. In fact, part of me wanted to go back to it; I had so much more to look at and to experience again. I mentally walked through that dream again and again, marveling at the crystal clear details that had come back.

Around six, I finally gave it up and got out of bed. I wasn't that tired for having been up the past two hours or so. I took a shower and put on my clothes for work: a deep rose–colored dress that had a wonderful cream-color collar that came up high on my neck to hide some of my bandage, but was wide enough to be comfortable.

I brushed my hair and let it fall loosely to my shoulders, wanting a soft curtain of protection and comfort.

I went downstairs and was surprised to hear Mr. Kirkland in the kitchen. I went in quietly and took a stool at the kitchen counter. There was already a steaming hot cup of tea in place.

"Heard me up, huh?" I asked quietly.

"I heard the floorboards creak a bit. Did you sleep all right? I didn't expect you for a couple more hours."

"I slept all right. Until I had a very vivid dream. It was about our Rochester house. I hadn't recalled some of those memories in a long, long time."

He nodded his head, listening intently, sipping his hot coffee.

Aunt Evelyn walked in, still in her fluffy blue robe. She looked quiet, contemplative. "The Rochester house, Lane?" she asked, with a soft smile. She came and sat down next to me, where the other cup of hot tea lay.

"*Mm hm*. And my maple tree," I remembered, with a smile. "Gosh, I loved that tree. It was like a friend."

"That red maple out front?" asked Mr. Kirkland, with a grin. "I remember you climbing that tree to the very top; made your mom very nervous the first few times you did it. But your dad just taught you how to be sure of your footholds, and after a few dozen safe climbs, your mom grew to love the sight of you way up there."

"You know? I think I need to go back there soon. Through all of the details of this case, I feel like I've learned something about our home in Rochester."

"What's that, dear?" asked Aunt Evelyn interestedly.

"Well, I caught myself talking about my mom and dad as 'them' and 'their life' and 'their home.' Well, I'm realizing that it was *my* home, too. My life and my story. I feel like I need to know more, and I think that house might have some answers, if only to help me make those memories more substantial."

Aunt Evelyn was nodding. "Yes, Lane. I think you're correct. I do think, however, that we should wait a bit. First of all, your twenty-fourth birthday is in just over a week." That completely took me off guard. I was usually very on top of my birthday—I love birthdays—but I had completely forgotten it was coming up. "Your parents left some things with their lawyer that were to be given to you on that day. I think it would be wise to see what those things are before we go to Michigan."

"My twenty-fourth birthday?" I asked incredulously. "I know they were eccentric, but why not twenty or twenty-five? That would make more sense."

"Well, er . . ." started Evelyn, looking awkward. "They really did mean for it to be for your twenty-fifth birthday. However, there was a built-in caveat that said we could give it to you earlier if, and I quote, 'there are strenuously extenuating circumstances deeming that Lane should receive it earlier.' And we think that these past months have indeed been strenuously extenuating circumstances."

"You could say that again," I said, with a laugh.

Aunt Evelyn looked at me closely. "You know, Lane, it's interesting that you said you felt like you were an outsider to your old life. How did you say it? Like you were looking in on something that you wanted to be in the middle of. . . . It reminds me of a friend of mine."

I smiled knowingly. "ML?"

"Yes, dear," she said. "I think on your birthday we shall chat a little more about that, too."

I sank into my little white chair next to the window in my blue room to read a while, but it was almost impossible to focus. I gave up and headed in to work. I had told Fio that I'd make my own way in today; I liked the idea of having the time to be by myself. I had gotten a new pair of cream high heels with bows on the toes. They looked great with my dark rose dress. The high-strung events of yesterday's big adventure mixed with the emotional, gut-wrenching feelings from the night, left me wilted and melancholy. But as I walked down the street, seeing the familiar sights of my neighborhood, breathing in the festive city air, and doing something normal and natural like going to work, I began to feel more like myself.

I was one of the first to arrive at the office. I walked in the door and stopped abruptly. I was face-to-face with Roxy. I almost dropped my purse. She looked surprised as well, and the fleeting emotions on both of our faces would have been worthy of a major motion picture had anyone witnessed them.

There had been a lot of drama: the best friend turned enemy, the enemy turned sympathetic victim, and on and on. . . . What could you say about all that? I looked at her lovely, fair face, her white-blond curls, her perfect figure. I looked at her eyes again. Maybe for the first time. Then my shoulders relaxed, my arms fell to my sides. And I started to laugh appreciably at our *situation*.

"Come on, Lane, let's get a cup of coffee," said Roxy, through a commiserating chuckle. We both surrendered. We put our stuff down and trooped over to the coffee room together.

We were still the only ones in the office, so after we clinked our coffee mugs in a show of solidarity, I filled her in on the whole story. Valerie had gone back last night to tell Roxy about Eliza being shot. But she deserved to hear *all* the details of what had been going on the past couple of months. Again, her emotions were all over the place, from stunned to angry to relieved.

After a long drink of her coffee, she asked with a sly squint to her eyes, "So, did anyone see Lizzie's hat on my dining room table?"

"Aha! I *knew* it!" I yelled.

I made her jump at my jubilant outburst, but she shook her head, laughing. "I should have known you'd be the one to find my clue. When Lizzie came over that night, she had brought a couple of her thugs to help *persuade* me to come along. I didn't know what she was up to, but I couldn't leave a note or anything to let someone know I was being kidnapped. At the last second, I saw her hat that I had borrowed on the small table by the door. I managed to grab it and throw it onto the kitchen table. I thought . . . well, I *hoped* someone would recognize that it wasn't mine and that it was totally out of place."

I was nodding encouragingly. "It took me a while to figure out that I was seeing a clue, but it finally came to me."

We just looked at each other for a moment. We were both stuck: me having trouble saying, *Sorry I thought you were an evil master-mind*, and her unable to say, *Thanks for coming to find me when an evil mastermind kidnapped me*. We were rescued from the awkwardness as we heard someone come into the office.

"Hi, Peter!" I called out to him gratefully. "What are you doing here so early?"

"I'm looking for Mr. LaGuardia. Is he in yet?"

"No, it's just us," I answered. He was agitated, with his legs and arms moving constantly to some unheard rhythm as he paced around the place, searching, in case we were hiding the mayor.

"Can we help you at all?" I asked him sardonically.

"Well . . ." He gave a great pause, weighing something in his mind. "Well, maybe you can. We need to identify the body of Eliza sooner rather than later. I was hoping to get Mr. LaGuardia to the city morgue ASAP." I stiffened, knowing what was coming.

He sighed apologetically. "Do you think you would be able to do it? I know it's asking a lot. But . . ." He left the question hanging.

Roxy stepped up behind me and said in a very firm voice, "Yes. Absolutely, we can do it."

I nodded in agreement.

"All right, ladies. Let's go."

We got to the city morgue, none of us feeling particularly chatty. The building was just like any other government building on the outside. The interior looked like a rather dark hospital with unending tiled walls and bleached floors. When we approached the actual room where we would encounter her body, Peter prepped us. Eliza would be under a sheet. The medical examiner would uncover her face and then cover it back up again. We drew big breaths, subconsciously not wanting to breathe in the air of that room.

The medical examiner was there, standing beside the body. He told us this was Louise Franco, aka Lizzie Frederickson, aka Eliza Franco. I felt Roxy stiffen as he said 'Lizzie.' He lifted the white sheet, and I saw that beautiful mane of red hair. And that was the first time I felt great pity, seeing something human about her that made me think of the girl, not her actions.

Roxy gasped. "That's not her."

I exclaimed, "What?" at the same moment that Peter said, "I knew it!"

I bent closer to her and looked directly at the face. It most certainly was *not* Eliza.

We all went back up to Pete's desk without saying a word. We sat in the ugly old chairs he'd pulled over for us, looking at him in listless, dumb shock.

"All right, this is the deal. The police got to the bridge yesterday just as we all did. I was able to radio ahead to get as many men there as possible. Eliza's body was located just where you told us. The medic pronounced her dead on the scene, and her body was covered in a sheet.

"After debriefing at Evelyn's last night"—he looked at me pointedly—"I came back here to get started on my paperwork; there's a lot of it, the case is so damn complicated." Roxy and I nodded numbly.

"I was putting my notes together when the medical examiner comes up and says that there's a discrepancy with his notes. I went down with him to the morgue, and he showed me the body. I only ever saw her from a distance, but I knew her hair. Eliza is a natural redhead, and this gal had obviously dyed hair; you could just see the small roots of brown coming in. That's when I needed to get someone close to her to confirm our suspicions."

"What on earth could have happened?" I just about yelled in frustration. "I watched her go down, I saw a blood stain on the front of her shirt. It was Fio's bullet, damn it."

Pete looked just as frustrated as I felt. He continued, "Well, someone obviously got to the body before it got to the morgue, and put this one in its place. So, either the body was important to someone, for reasons I can't figure, or"—he paused, looking meaningfully at us—"Eliza is still alive, and someone used this decoy to stall us. In either case, it took someone with cunning and considerable power to pull it off."

CHAPTER 42

I can't change the fact that my paintings don't
sell. But the time will come when people will
recognize that they are worth more than
the value of the paints used in the picture.

—ML

August twentieth rolled around, the eve of my twenty-fourth
birthday. The previous week and a half had flown by as the police performed a dedicated search to find Eliza Franco or her body.
Nothing turned up.

We visited Morgan a couple of times, but despite her obvious
appreciation for me and Aunt Evelyn, I could see that this new life
wasn't taking. And it was with a bit of sadness, but not surprise, that
I heard she ran away. Aunt Evelyn was quite distraught, but I told
her that Morgan knew how to get hold of us, and I truly believed
she would if she got into trouble. She'd been on the streets for so
many years, it was going to be hard to turn away from that.

Mr. Kirkland, Aunt Evelyn, and I were sitting in the parlor. I was
fairly shaking with questions, curiosity, and surmises. They were
laughing as they looked at me sitting perched on the edge of my seat.
We were about to finally have that chat about the mysterious ML.

I started to rapid-fire my questions, Fiorello style. "Okay, who is
ML? Was there anything more than coincidence behind the painting Danny had stolen? What valuable art do we have in the family
that could inspire such an interest in us? Who—"

"Whoa, whoa, Missy!" exclaimed a chuckling Mr. Kirkland.
Aunt Evelyn laughed out loud.

She took the floor, and in her businesslike, efficient manner, she brought the room (meaning me) under control. She stood up, and, clasping her hands with all the formal pomp of a professor lecturing at Cambridge, she began an orderly account.

"Lane, dear, we have many answers to your questions, but I'm afraid we don't have all of them. Don't worry," she said, replying to my crestfallen look. "You will be satisfied with what we have to share with you today. No more secrets. You are old enough, responsible enough, and wise enough to handle the rather remarkable truth."

She piqued my curiosity even further with this statement, and Mr. Kirkland gave a tiny *ahem* that prodded her along. Enough with building suspense already.

"All right, first of all, do you have the journal with you?"

"Yes, here you go." I handed her the lavender journal that had become a companion and champion of sorts. ML's words were somehow soothing to read, as I could identify with so many of his thoughts these past few weeks.

"What were your thoughts as you read this, Lane?"

"Well . . . ML is a man of deep beauty, color, passion, intensity . . . and somewhere in there . . . very tragic, too." I put my chin in my hand as I pondered ML. "Like you alluded to the other day, it feels like he's looking in on something that he wishes he could be a part of, but can't."

"Very insightful, Lane. That is exactly why I wanted you to read this journal. He was someone who was trying to put his life together. He felt separate from the life he wanted at times, like you do with your parents, Lane. And his thoughts are just so beautiful. You see, ML was a man I met when I was a young girl in France. I was about eleven. I was visiting my uncle for the summer, and I met some of his patients who were artists. When I first met ML, he was out in a barn I had wanted to explore. He was studying his painting of lilies, and they immediately captured my imagination. From then on, I called him Monsieur Lily. ML." Her face revealed that she was back in that time, remembering, remembering *him*.

"I visited him frequently. He was painting nonstop; the quantity of his paintings was absolutely staggering. He would pile them up and stack them in the barn. I thought they were all genius. Of course, like I said, he never sold anything back then. He was the one who inspired my interest in art," she marveled. "Let me ask you something else, Lane. Do you remember the painting that was stolen out of my studio?"

"Sure, I remember there were a lot of blues and black, and I think there was a moon at the top and a small town in the distance."

"Right. It was just my attempt at a recreation of the original, with my particular style. Here . . . is the original."

She uncovered a painting on an easel that stood behind her. I stood up, thinking that I felt like I'd seen it before but couldn't quite place it. I looked at it closely after shooting Aunt Evelyn a sharp glance.

"I feel like I've seen it before. . . ." I said.

"You have, in a few magazine articles. ML gave it to me."

Again, I looked very closely at the painting. I carefully sat down on the sofa, thinking. I'd read a few articles about a newly discovered artist who was rapidly gaining fame, but I couldn't remember his name. Although ML was not thoroughly recognized yet, this painting wonderfully exhibited that desperately sought-after *transcendence*.

Aunt Evelyn had taken a seat as well and took up her account. "Yes. You've seen some of his works. Lane, dear, ML was an artist who died having sold just one of his works. But now, the world is just beginning to see his genius. ML was a man named Vincent van Gogh. My eccentric uncle was Dr. Gachet, van Gogh's doctor, who specialized in diseases of the mind. I was there in Auvers-sur-Oise, France, during the last couple of months of Vincent's life.

"*Tragic* is just the word for the poor man. He was capable of such strength and beauty, but also a horrifying distrust of himself and of life. When he talked with me, just for minutes at a time, as he was so consumed with his paintings, he'd often leave me with a tiny note. The ones in that journal.

"My uncle filled in a lot about Vincent's past, once he gave in to my persistent questions. For years, Vincent wanted to work for the church in some capacity. But he was a bit of a loose cannon, to put it mildly. Vincent then forced his attention to flow into his other passion, hoping that through art, he might be able to express what his words and his actions were incapable of doing. And he was no saint, by the way, believe me. His physical self always wrestled with the spiritual; he could never seem to find a place where both could coexist.

"Anyway, in this piece, *The Starry Night*, the heavens are a beautiful but turbulent swirl above, and in the center, the view looks *in* toward the church. And it grounds or completes the painting. If it weren't there, it wouldn't look right, see?" She demonstrated by covering the church with her hands, then removing them.

"I believe he always felt like an outsider—with the church and with life in general, I think. What turned out to be the last week of his life, I begged him to let me have *The Starry Night*; it moved me so much. I wanted to look at it every day.

"I didn't see his demise coming so shortly. He was horribly worried about his little nephew, who had become ill, and he felt that he was a burden to his brother, Theo, despite Theo's best efforts to reassure him. He felt certain his sadness would never end. He shot himself out in the fields only days later."

"Oh, Aunt Evelyn," I said, with my hand to my mouth, shaking my head. "I'm so sorry."

She nodded, with a sad smile. "My uncle allowed me to go to the funeral. Vincent's poor brother was completely shattered, as well as many of his artist friends. I remember his one friend, Émile Bernard, wrote a piece about the funeral. He articulated what we'd all been feeling. That day there had been a glorious blue sky, and his grave was overlooking beautiful fields that Vincent would have loved. We couldn't help but wonder if this particular day was beautiful enough to think he could have still been happy. We wished it were so. There are always so many what-ifs, aren't there?"

She sighed and took a sip of her tea. "I left my uncle's and returned home. But I was changed forever. And *this* is my most prized possession." She clasped the journal to her heart.

"My God, Aunt Evelyn. I don't know what to say," I whispered.

Mr. Kirkland took up the story. "And this little journal is what we thought the thieves were after when they assaulted you in the subway and then broke into our home. The Museum of Modern Art is trying to buy this piece, and we were wondering if word got out about the journal. Trust me, he's going to be a household name one day."

"So . . . You . . . Van Gogh . . ." I was stuttering in my efforts to put it all together, and I caught a mischievous glint in my preposterous aunt's eye.

I couldn't help but smile. I said, "So, Aunt Evelyn, your journal is unquestionably valuable. But, given the fact that it was Danny who burglarized the house hunting for random treasure, it seems that no one does know about it."

"Right. But what is delightfully ironic"—she chuckled like she relished this part—"is that the thief stole something worthless that, unbeknownst to him, actually points to the real treasure. That painting of mine had been my take on *The Starry Night*, with my personal technique." She looked lovingly at the painting.

"What are you going to do with that, Aunt Evelyn?" I asked curiously.

"Oh, I knew for years what I had and that I wanted to keep my connection with Vincent private. I have been working with friends who will eventually sell it permanently to the Museum of Modern Art on my behalf, keeping my part anonymous," she said.

"So, as far as you know, are there other treasures in our family that could have started those rumors? Treasures that my parents might have . . . acquired?"

She and Mr. Kirkland exchanged a glance, and I felt compelled to remind them, "You said no more secrets."

Mr. Kirkland fixed me with his light blue stare. "Lane, *I* didn't promise that, and I can't. But what I can tell you is, I don't really know everything your parents were involved with near the end of the war. We worked together frequently, but we all had our secret missions. One day, I think we may find some answers in Michigan."

The puzzle we had so neatly figured out last week had just led into a more intricate and enigmatic chain of events. What were my parents involved with? How much did Eliza know? Was this all leading down a road that I was meant to traverse? Or was it one that I would wish I had never followed? Well, for better or worse, I knew one thing: There was no way that I wouldn't take this path. I *had* to know.

Underneath it all was that silver gun. It did, in fact, point to our villains. I thought it pointed to a lot more, too, yet it was gone. The police sent a search party underneath the point where it fell off the bridge, and nothing was found on the shore or in the water around the area. They said it must have sunk into the murky bottom of the East River. The other one that my dad must have had, the twin gun that I must have seen or even touched, was nowhere to be found for decades. Maybe that was lost, too.

Something lifted, shifting a ponderous weight off my mind. What if this meant the end? What if that gun had disappeared into the mud forever, where it belonged? Maybe this meant the nightmare would stop.

CHAPTER 43

Be clearly aware of the stars and infinity on
high. Then life seems almost enchanted after all.

—ML

The next night, Valerie, the LaGuardias, Roarke, Aunt Evelyn, Mr. Kirkland, and I all had dinner together in celebration of my twenty-fourth birthday.

We were busy chatting, setting the finishing touches on the table, and drinking festive drinks like prosecco with cranberry juice and lime. Just as I was about to sit down and enjoy an appetizer, the doorbell rang. I ran for the door.

"Finn!" He bounded in, dropped a shiny red box on the table, and grabbed me up with both arms.

My breath whooshed out of me as he squeezed me tight and said into my ear, "Happy birthday, Lane."

We walked into the dining room holding hands, with six people grinning at us.

Fio nonchalantly kissed Marie's hand. That old softy. Roarke and Valerie were talking about *The Great Ziegfeld* and laughing as they chatted about the bigger-than-life dance numbers and how much they loved the music. I looked about the room as we took our chairs: the people I loved, the warm room full of old memories and new ones in the making. The only feeling of sadness was a small sting from a leftover memory of that dream about my parents and our home in Michigan. It was nagging, irritating like a rusty old nail stuck in a board. My parents couldn't be part of this.

That sting grew a dangerous little bit.

But it was a wonderful night of laughter, happy bantering, and delicious food. The LaGuardias' birthday present was a couple of new albums by Benny Goodman and Fred Astaire. Valerie gave me a beautiful new scarf with reds and purples all swirled together and a big ruffle along the edge. It looked like a wonderful painting. Roarke gave me a delicate pearl necklace from one of his travels. Aunt Evelyn and Mr. Kirkland gave me a new journal in deep blue silk and a new Agatha Christie novel that I kept leafing through, dying to dig in.

Lastly, I opened the lovely red package from Finn. It was an oval, black lacquer jewelry box. I opened it, and inside there was a small engraving on the lid that read, "Lane—With all my love, Finn."

"Thank you, Finn. I love it." I reached over to him and kissed him on the cheek.

At the end of the night, all our guests left except Finn. He and I were helping Evelyn and Mr. Kirkland wash the dishes. It was a cheery room with the warm glow of the lamps, a bright red rose at the pine table, and the good scents of dinner and coffee still wafting through.

At the last glass, Aunt Evelyn said, "All right, my dears, to the final event of the evening."

We sat down at the kitchen table, and she brought me a large, white envelope.

"From my parents?" I asked.

They nodded.

It was from the lawyer telling me that my parents left two keys for me, which were contained in the envelope. One would open a safe deposit box located at a bank here in New York City. The second would open a safe located in the Rochester house.

Mr. Kirkland promised to get the contents of the safe deposit box the next day. So Finn and I planned a dinner date, then we'd come back here to find out what was in the box.

The next morning, I stood at my dresser taking a good look at the person in the mirror. It was the same face as always: blue eyes, big smile, framed by brown hair. A girl-next-door look. But those eyes had seen a lot. Experienced a lot for being only twenty-four years old.

I looked down at my hands. My left was making figure eights on the top of the smooth oak dresser. My right was balancing the pearl dagger perfectly on my middle finger, blade side up. Then, with a deft flick of the wrist, I flipped the blade down, its tip now just touching the dresser. It stood nice and steady with that same middle finger gently holding it straight. I had clearly done that a hundred times. It was natural. *I'm pretty sure that's not normal.*

I smiled. When Mr. Kirkland gave me this dagger, the weight of it was as familiar to me as the branch of that maple tree back in Rochester. My hands knew exactly what to do with it. Memories of my father that had been buried deep down came into focus like they had just been patiently waiting around the corner for me to call them.

They were good memories: camping up north in Michigan, rowing around a crystal clear lake (where I first learned to hate rowing), archery, throwing a knife at a target that my dad had made on a dead tree, roasting marshmallows. . . . He loved to teach, and I loved a challenge even then. Some things never took. But archery and the knife? Piece of cake.

I fingered the beautiful curves of the mother-of-pearl inlaid in the ebony on the handle. Wanting the confidence of having it nearby, I put it in my purse. I had an important meeting.

CHAPTER 44

It is a pity that, as one gradually gains
experience, one loses one's youth.

—ML

I was sitting on a bench overlooking the water. The Brooklyn Bridge looked as majestic and steadfast as ever, and I had a whole new appreciation for just how grand bridges were. A warm gust of wind whipped through, making my new scarf from Valerie flutter about as I settled on the bench. It was perfect against my black blouse and cranberry red pencil skirt and shoes. I had brought a newspaper with me, to look like I was taking a leisurely break.

From behind, someone cleared his throat in introduction, and a large man sat down next to me. He had on a black suit with wide pinstripes, and the fedora with the white band and white feather. From my peripheral vision I could see his massive gray and black caterpillar eyebrows.

"Mr. Venetti, thank you for meeting me."

"Hello, Lane. I must say that I was surprised to get your message this morning."

"I would have come to you, but I thought that you might prefer an inconspicuous place."

"I do, that I do." He looked down at my paper in my hands, and a smile tugged at his mouth.

"What?" I said, slightly defensively.

"Oh, nothing."

"Mr. Venetti, I'll get right to the point. I'm assuming you heard about the body of Eliza Franco?" It wasn't in the papers, but I figured he had ears and eyes all over the place.

I kept my head turned to my paper, but I darted my eyes over to his face to see his expression. It went dark, and his brows lowered. I was glad that *my* name didn't provoke that response in him. Despite the fact that this was not our first meeting, the man made me very nervous. His power was something tangible and potent.

"I figured you had. I've been speculating on what could have happened. But I wanted you to know that in our last hours together, she did confess to murdering Danny. And though I don't know what happened, I think she's still alive."

He paused, breathing in and out slowly, deliberately. It felt like a bull trying to contain his rage. I tensed, ready to run. I knew his anger was not focused on me, but like I said, I had an excellent sense of self-preservation.

His voice came out deep and raspy. "I'm certain, too."

Okay, then. I fought the urge to scoot farther away from him on the bench. I had a small idea forming in the back of my mind that I wanted to ask him about. "Sir, have you heard anything about a new person in New York in your line of . . . *work?* Someone who may have assisted Eliza?"

I saw his chest move from a soundless chuckle. "You might not like this, but you and I think a lot alike, Lane. Let me leave you with this. It's not someone *new* to the city, in fact, he's been here quite a while. People have seen him fleetingly, but no one knows his name. There's power and menace to the mystery of a man. Let's just say, if I were a betting man—and I am—I would think he's involved. The only description I've heard about him is that he wears a large ruby ring on his pinky finger."

Uncle Louie stood up from the bench and looked around, his eyes lingering on the bridge. "Lane? It was delightful meeting with you once again. Be careful. You're running in crowds that can be . . ."

I whispered, "Deadly."

"Yes."

He was about to leave, but I blurted out one last thing. "Uh, Mr. Venetti . . . thank you. Thank you for helping me. And Valerie."

He put a cigar in his mouth and looked at me closely, slightly squinting his eyes in calculated thought. He nodded minutely. Then he turned on his heels and walked slowly up the bank toward his muscular bodyguards. I stayed on the bench for a few moments longer, getting my heart rate back down to normal, then hurried back to the office.

CHAPTER 45

In the end we shall have had enough of
cynicism, skepticism and humbug,
and we shall want to live more musically.

—ML

I felt *off* the rest of the day. I couldn't shake the image of a new gangster to worry about. It had to be an extremely powerful man to have executed a plan involving a body-exchange, for crying out loud. It had to be someone who followed us around, who knew our movements, and was waiting. Watching.

Finn picked me up early. As we left city hall, I found that I desperately wanted to unburden myself of all this information. So I bared my soul about Venetti and my own musings, spewing out everything in a rush to get it over with. Finn and I had been walking down the street. In my exuberance to get everything off my chest, including my fears about damn Eliza and the *über* gangster, I found myself winded. I'd been walking faster and faster with the intensity of my words.

Finn pulled me over to the side and said, "Whoa, Lane! You can slow down. We're almost sprinting down the street." His eyes were crinkling with amusement, and yet his brow was furrowed. I was breathing pretty heavily; I hadn't noticed that I was walking at breakneck speed.

"Sorry," I said, laughing at myself.

He smiled reassuringly. "It's okay, Lane." He brushed a strand of hair that had fallen into my eyes and put it behind my ear. "Do you feel better? Got it all off your chest?" His Irish accent was in full voice.

"Yes, I do feel better. No, ah, recriminations? Admonishments?"

"Well, Lane, I learned a while ago that you march to the beat of your own drummer. And, I do worry about you, but I trust your instincts." His brow darkened for a second. He looked to the side and said, as if in deep contemplation, "Your intuition and instincts about the case were *terrifyingly* like my own." Ho boy, if he only knew Uncle Louie said the exact same thing. . . .

We made our way to Copioli's, and we had a delectable meal of fettuccine Alfredo, salad, and fresh bread. And those amazing crusted olives, of course. We talked about current movies and old books, and delightfully normal things.

"You gonna let me have one of those olives?" asked Finn as I dipped my hand into the bowl yet again.

My eyes narrowed. "You can have one. Or two." He chuckled.

The little band walked out just then, and people started moving tables like last time. As we were just about to get up ourselves, the first few beats of "Mambo Italiano" started to play.

Finn fixed his eyes on me, and I replied to his look, "Oh, definitely."

We moved our table without taking our eyes off each other. He reached out his right arm and pulled me to him. My right hand clasped his left, and we moved and swayed to the rhythmic, swinging song.

Hey mambo, mambo Italiano . . .

The candles glowed, the music swelled around us, and once again we were in a room crowded with others, yet completely alone.

We both smiled, content and just plain happy. He held me closer, and I laid my head on his shoulder.

I said, "I finally figured it out, Finn."

"Figured it out?"

"Yes. Something about you that I've been trying to place. A certain feeling."

"What is it?"

"You feel like *home*."

I felt him take a big breath, and his hand came up and pressed my head to his chest.

"Let's keep dancing," he whispered. I looked up at him. His eyes dark, he bent farther down and kissed me gently. He pulled me even closer, then we danced . . . and danced . . . and danced.

Then we had a cannoli.

CHAPTER 46

I often think that the night is more
alive and more richly colored than the day.

—ML

Much, much later, Finn took me home. We went up the front steps of my townhouse and slowly, reality started to come back to both of us. I had a box to open.

After greeting Ripley, we walked into the quiet house; Mr. Kirkland and Aunt Evelyn were already asleep. We found the contents of the safe deposit box from Mr. Kirkland waiting for us. We both sobered. There was only one item. It was a shiny, heavy black box. Black lacquer, not unlike the shiny jewelry box Finn had given me. But this was much bigger, a good two inches thick and about ten inches square. I handed it to Finn. His strong yet gentle hands turned the slick box over, feeling the smooth, glossy finish, the satisfying heaviness.

There was a note attached. It was in my father's handwriting. It said:

> There's a key for this box in the piece of furniture we
> gave you for your tenth birthday. Underneath, front
> right corner. The combination is the numbers that
> correspond to your real name.

"Huh," I said. "It's like a treasure hunt. Let's go!" I grabbed his hand and walked upstairs to my room. We walked into the blue and white room, which was softly lit by the lamp next to my bed. I nodded at the dresser.

"Is that the piece of furniture from your parents?"

"*Mmm hmm.*" I nodded. "They got it for me for my birthday. I wanted a unicycle. But I got a dresser. Let's see. . . ." I said as I lay down on the floor in front of it, looking underneath. "Front right corner. Wow, there really is a wooden combination lock of sorts. Looks old."

I looked up at Finn and motioned for him to come down and see what he thought. He helped me up, then took my place on the floor, looking underneath. "So, the note said the numeric code to your real name," he said, smirking. "But there are six spaces here."

"Uh-huh, smart guy. I recall you saying you knew what my real name was—my full name. Are you having second thoughts?"

He stood up suddenly, with the smooth, powerful grace of a panther, and took me in his arms. I was so shocked at his sudden movement that I gasped.

"Lane, I *do* know your name," he said huskily.

"How do you know?" I asked, just barely above a whisper.

"It's just Lane. *I know you*, Lane." I believed him. His lips came down on mine heavily, urgently. A wave of pure, intense desire came up and over me. . . . He pulled away, bracing himself.

"You better get that key," I whispered.

"Yeah . . . that's a good idea," he said, rather breathlessly, as his eyes lingered over my deep neckline. Then he nervously looked at my open doorway. A flicker of fear raced over his face as if he were imagining Mr. Kirkland's form materializing before him. Or worse: Aunt Evelyn's. I bit back a smile.

He quickly lay back down in front of the dresser and started to work the combination. I bent down on the other side of him and watched him turn the wooden rollers underneath the dresser. I heard the old gears shifting and clicking as he turned, and I thought about those six spaces. If you used numbers for each letter in the alphabet, Lane was twelve, one, fourteen, five. Exactly six numerals, if you entered one, two, one, one, four, five. *Honestly, whose parents do this sort of thing?* Then I heard a little *plink* as something metallic dropped to the wood floor. It was the key. Goddamn, he did it.

We grabbed the key and the box and practically ran down the stairs. We stopped in the parlor, and I turned on a couple of more lights. I went and sat down next to Finn on the sofa. I looked at him: his tousled hair, his dark eyes, his shirt that was loosened at the collar. He looked delicious.

"Right. Okay, we've put this off long enough. You have the key?" I asked. He nodded. I gave him the box; he put the small key in the keyhole and clicked it to the right. It was smooth, like it had just been oiled.

The top clicked as it unlocked.

"Are you ready, love?"

"As ready as I'll ever be," I replied.

Had I known what was coming, I would never have been ready. I should have taken more time to consider my options, and think about what this package that my parents so mysteriously gave me on my birthday might mean. I should have stayed Finn's hand as he started to lift the lid. It was like it was in slow motion, and a prickly fear began to creep up my body.

"Um, Finn, maybe we shouldn't . . ."

But it was too late.

"Oh, my God," whispered Finn.

There, on black velvet, were two identical compartments that fit into each other like a malevolent yin and yang. One compartment was empty, and one was full. There, right in front of me, was the shiny silver gun with a bloodred scroll on the handle. The one my dad had retrieved when they killed Rex Ruby. The one that I must have seen and touched when I was young. My dad wanted me to have it for some reason.

At that moment, I knew beyond a doubt the other one was still out there. Like the yin and yang that weren't complete without their partners, that gun had a life of its own. Its destiny hadn't come full circle. It was still pointing to more.

The nightmare was coming back.

I took a deep breath and looked at our parlor, which had been both a war room and also a peaceful place for my birthday celebration. I looked at Ripley, whose tail beat a rhythm on the wood floor expectantly. And then I locked eyes with Finn, who had a spark of adventure glinting from within and a small smile pulling at one side of his mouth.

The power of the nightmare is the unknown and the inability to control it. But things had changed over the past few weeks. *I* had changed over the past few weeks.

I thought about my city, which had been plagued with the effects of the Depression for years now. But we were still forging ahead. Still creating. Still loving. And still celebrating with cocktails. Who was to say we would've had the same intensity of innovation and brilliance that New York had at its heart without the wrenching demands of those years?

Well, now. The silver gun had a destiny of its own.

So did I.

> Love many things, for therein lies the true strength,
> and whosoever loves much, performs much, and can
> accomplish much, and what is done in love is done well.
>
> —Vincent van Gogh

EPILOGUE

Her red hair shone in the light of the lamp. She'd been out cold for an hour or so after the doctor came in and stitched her up. Her eyes were starting to flutter; she'd be awake soon. Goddamn good thing he hadn't let her out of his sight.

It would have been workable if she'd been killed outright, he considered, but he couldn't be one hundred percent sure it had been a lethal shot. And to have her in custody? No way. Not a chance in hell he'd let that happen. There was a delicate balance to his meticulous plans. It would be best if she were still around; it was optimal to still use her.

As always, he was thorough, and he'd had the foresight to take some precautions. He'd gone to great lengths to protect what he'd been building. He had personally tailed Eliza for days, and had several of his people ready in the wings in case there was a hiccup in Donagan's plans.

He'd worked too hard to keep his anonymity and the power that came from that mystery, starting back in the Detroit days. But goddamn, after he saw that gun fly from her hand and topple over the side of the bridge . . .

The silver gun. The gun he'd been certain was lost once Rex had been killed.

Once he'd gotten Eliza into the ambulance he'd arranged, he had almost strangled her himself over that loss. Where on earth did she get it? She must have had it for years. . . . He put a hand to her throat, his loathing almost getting the better of him. Almost. He withdrew his hand.

Later, he'd scrambled to the point where he saw the gun fall as soon as humanly possible; it could've hit the side of the shoreline instead of sinking into the murky East River. Maybe. He scoured the area for hours but found nothing. It was lost. Once and for all.

She moaned and started to sit up. "Oh, my God, I feel like I got run over by a truck."

"Worse," he said as he threw back a shot of bourbon.

"All I remember is that bitch and me fighting. I was just about to shoot her and then . . ."

"Yeah," he said coldly. "You were shot. Clean shot, hit closer to your shoulder than your heart. You're lucky."

She turned her head sharply to him, then cringed as the sudden movement made her shoulder and chest spasm with violent pain, the nausea almost overwhelming her.

"*Unh*," she moaned again. "Yeah, real lucky. Do you have any more of that bourbon?"

"Here," he said as he handed her a cold glass. He was watching her closely, carefully weighing the pros and cons of her worth. She'd really fucked up.

She looked up at him, trying to read his unfathomable face, his dangerous thoughts. "You think this is *my* fault, you son of a bitch?"

"Careful, Sis. Don't forget, we *are* related," he said, in a mocking voice.

She took in his countenance. His wonderful hair, beautiful eyes. His collar was opened a couple of buttons, as he'd taken off his tie. She thought that she had never seen a more diabolical face in her life. She'd been raised with that face and had learned from that face all her deceptive mannerisms and tricks of the trade. But, by God, he was flawless. He could look so innocent, so wholesome. And then turn around and have a smile that would say he was about to strangle the life out of you with his bare hands, and he was going to enjoy doing it. She marveled at his talent just as much as she was horrified by it.

With that sobering thought, an even more horrific thought crept into her foggy mind.

The gun. She'd lost the silver gun.

The blood drained from her face. But then again, he hadn't known she'd had it. No one did. Did Donagan? She tried hard to remember if he'd seen it back on the bridge. She just couldn't recall. She wrestled her temper and fear into submission. She'd better do her best not to provoke him. Or let him see her anxiety. She turned her face to him, but kept her eyes on the floor, unable to look straight at him.

"All right, I'm sorry. Thank you for getting me out of there. I admit it, the plan was fouled up. I thought I had her, too. She is such a goody-goody, goddamn pain in the neck." Her anger was coming back, obviously. She took a steadying breath. "I suppose you haven't made any more inroads with her?" she asked him.

He'd been watching her mental gymnastics and was fairly certain she'd remembered the gun and was debating whether she could keep that loss a secret. At her last remark, his face clouded over, and she flinched a little. "No, *Sis*," he said condescendingly. "I told you, there was something holding her back, something keeping her from giving in to me. Like they all do sooner or later," he said, with a one-sided smirk. He was smug and arrogant, and he was right. She'd never seen more women go head over heels for any other guy.

"I have to admit, she was maddening; hot one moment, cool the next."

"Oh, I can tell you what was in the way. His name is Finn Brodie. He played us all, even Donagan. He's in love with her."

He looked carefully at her, with an intense scrutiny that made her uncomfortable and agitated. She shifted around, anxious in his piercing gaze as he fingered the large ruby on his pinky finger. "Hmm. I'll have to give that some thought. Finn Brodie. I take it he's an undercover cop?"

"Yes," she said derisively.

"Well, well, well, little Lane likes a little danger in her men, huh? Not the innocent, reliable farm boy for her. . . . Maybe I'll take a different tack." He poured himself another glass as he ruminated over this new approach. Then he murmured to himself as he shook his head with a small, self-deprecating smile, "God she was funny. . . . Fantastic kisser . . ."

"*What* did you say?" she asked, with a demonic look in her eyes.

"Ah, yes, Eliza, dear. I'll work on a new tack with Lane. I have big plans for the future, and I feel certain I can pull her in. I've never failed yet," he said, with a sneer.

She nodded. Eliza had no doubt he'd be able to do it. She drank a big swig of her bourbon, then inhaled deeply, preparing for what lay ahead. She exhaled and looked directly into his blue, piercing eyes.

"All right, Tucker. Give it your best shot."

A Word from the Author

Most of Fiorello's antics were taken right out of reality. I've often told friends that he was so outrageous, people won't know which events in my books are fiction and which ones are truth. The Artichoke King event (with the trumpets), hammering slot machines with a sledgehammer, scurrying all over the city (especially the fires), having an office and two gun compartments in his car, listening to a line of people with problems every day at city hall, the Boner Day awards, and the funny escapade of jumping onto a motorcycle, complete with sidecar, yelling, "I am not a sissy!" actually happened in real life. And much more . . . He has many more antics to come.

Many of the specific places in New York City that are mentioned are around today. I tried to bring in as many real places as possible. The neighborhood where Lane lives still has many of those stores and restaurants. The original city hall is alive and active; you can even get tours on Wednesdays. The scroll really is on the Glade Arch bridge near Cedar Hill in Central Park, and you can still admire Jagiello's statue.

Blackwell's Island is now Roosevelt Island and is a lovely place to live. You can still see the octagonal tower of Metropolitan Hospital (now an apartment complex with a pool in the back), the ruins of the smallpox hospital, and those red and white factory smokestacks are still there, too.

Hulbert Footner, in his book *New York: City of Cities*, said, "Every night [New York City] is the same yet not the same." After living here for almost two decades, I understand what he meant. The city is always changing. Restaurants and buildings come and go. Fashion and music and car designs progress. But there is this element of the city that the more it changes, the more it stays the same. Maybe it's the long history it holds, with those wonderful ghosts and memories sticking around. Because of that, I mentioned a couple of places that are accurate to the feel of the time and scene, but are modern (such as Firenze restaurant) to add just another touch of the city's peculiar way of straddling time and space. And once in a while, I created a completely fictional place because I needed a certain element for the story.

I have loved the work and the thoughtful words of Vincent van Gogh for a long time. He wasn't always a household name, and I thought that taking a look at his words might be interesting. Of course Aunt Evelyn is fictional, but I do believe that she and Vincent truly would have liked each other. All of ML's quotes are Vincent van Gogh's actual sayings, taken from the many letters that he wrote. However, the one quote from Chapter 12, "I would rather die of passion than of boredom," is actually credited to both him and the artist Émile Zola. Vincent quotes Émile in a letter to his brother, but Émile is the originator.

What I love most about taking a fresh look at the Thirties, a time period that is usually pigeonholed in the era of the Dust Bowl and *The Grapes of Wrath*, is that it has something profound for us today. Despite the afflictions of the day, the people of the Thirties kept striving and accomplished truly great things. We live in a similar era as Fiorello and Lane. Economic depression, crazy steps forward in technology that are hard to keep up with as much as we love it, great strides toward human rights and the environment, yet deep-seated corruption, too. However, despite the odds being stacked against real change happening, it did. And it can today. With all the humor, love, zest for life, and, of course, cocktails to boot.

If you're interested in seeing some of these places as they are now, you can check out @LAChandlar on YouTube for behind-the-scenes stories.

ACKNOWLEDGMENTS

It really does take a team of wonderful people to take a book from an idea, to the first draft, to a better draft, and on and on until it's read in its final version.

My profound thanks to my husband, Bryan, who witnessed my satisfied tears the first time I wrote those magical words The End. You've been my best friend and the one who knows just how much my writing and my stories mean to me. You have my heart and my eternal gratitude. To my amazing sons, Jack and Logan, you have been so supportive and compassionate during the hard parts of "putting yourself out there" and have celebrated joyously with the victories. You're just the best.

My thanks to my first readers of what my friend Suzy calls the SFD. The Shitty First Draft. You were my cheerleaders and careful critics. I love you dearly: Judy and Fred Freeland, Bob and Lin Cracknell, Alicia Horvath, Arlee Leo, Michelle Beaker, Mindy Kaspari, Angela Koch, Colleen Fleshood, Patty Oeffinger, Beth Ann Harper, Melissa Moskowitz, Amy Liblong, and Christy Krispin. I would also like to thank Amy Elizabeth Bennett for your splendid early round of editing. To Suzy Welch, I so appreciate your guidance and encouragement in this whole process. And thanks to Heather Greenberg for loving history with me, and for your excellent counsel with regard to dear Vincent van Gogh.

Thank you so much to my crew of friends who have been super supportive and encouraging through talking things over a coffee (or a wine . . . or a martini), asking great questions, and just being interested. It has meant so much! Thank you, Pam Mittman, Heather Greenberg, Meredith Berkowitz, Karen Reeves, Troy and Allison Patterson, Don and Darla Wilson, and Jeff and Mindy Kaspari.

Thank you to James Romaine, for the fantastic lecture on Vincent van Gogh. I obviously never forgot the way you pointed out how the church in the middle of *The Starry Night* visually grounds the work. Ever since that lecture (years ago!) I have had a special place in my heart for Vincent.

Thank you to Kevin Fitzpatrick, whose NYC tours and books have helped me immensely, not to mention introducing me to Club Wits End, a place that is almost as good as going back in time.

Thank you to my agent, Jill Grosjean, who was the first literary professional to believe in me and Lane. I've so appreciated your insight, your editing, your fortitude, and of course, our shared love of animals and Amelia Peabody.

Thank you so much to Esi Sogah at Kensington. Your spirit and energy are contagious, and your professional guidance has been invaluable. Many thanks to Morgan, whose ideas are fabulous, and the art team who have incredible talent in helping Lane and her stories come to life visually. Thanks to the production editor, Paula Reedy, for making decisions that made the story its best. And to my copy editor, who fact-checks like a rock star and undangles my participles, Linda Seed.

Lastly, my heartfelt thanks to you, wonderful Reader. Your imagination and love of reading is the most important part of a good book. It is my dearest hope that my books will somehow increase your delight in life.

SELECTED BIBLIOGRAPHY

Abbott, Berenice, and Elizabeth McCausland. *New York in the Thirties*. New York: Dover Publications, 1939.

Brodsky, Alyn. *The Great Mayor.* New York: St. Martin's Press, 2003.

Ferloni, Julia, Sophie and Mikael. *Vincent van Gogh.* New York: Konecky & Konecky, 1994.

Footner, Hulbert. *New York: City of Cities.* Philadelphia: J. B. Lippincott, 1937.

Jackson, Kenneth T. *The Encyclopedia of New York City.* New Haven & London: Yale University Press, 1995.

Jeffers, H. Paul. *The Napoleon of New York: Mayor Fiorello LaGuardia.* New York: John Wiley & Sons, Inc., 2002.

Jennings, Peter, and Todd Brewster. *The Century.* New York: Doubleday, 1998.

Lowe, David Garrard. *Art Deco New York.* New York: Watson-Guptill Publications, a Division of VNU Business Media, Inc., 2004

Powell, Elfreda. *The Letters of Vincent van Gogh.* London: Constable & Robinson Ltd., 2003.

Stolley, Richard B. *LIFE: Our Century in Pictures.* Boston, New York, London: Bulfinch Press, 1999.

Tauranac, John. *The Empire State Building: The Making of a Landmark.* New York: Scribner, 1995.

Wallace, Robert. *The World of Van Gogh.* New York: Time-Life Books, 1969.

THE SILVER GUN

L. A. Chandlar

ABOUT THIS GUIDE

The suggested questions are included
to enhance your group's reading of
L. A. Chandlar's *The Silver Gun*.

DISCUSSION QUESTIONS

1. When you think of the 1930s in America, what comes to mind? Did the representations of the '30s surprise you? Why or why not?

2. Just like art, stories speak differently to different people. Discuss the overarching themes of the book. For you, what was the main theme?

3. When you think back to the book, what scenes keep coming to mind? What has been the most memorable thing about the book?

4. Who do you think the hooded figure is in the Intro? (Hint: We will find out who it is in the next book, but it is someone who has already been introduced in *The Silver Gun*.)

5. Did you read the quotes at the beginning of the chapters? Why or why not? Why do you think art is a theme in this series?

   (My answer: I confess I sometimes don't read the epigraphs at the beginning of the chapters. It's like I can't wait to get to the story. For this series, though, I wanted those quotes because I wanted to underscore the idea that art was a serious theme in society at the time. And even today, art has a capacity to "open the shutters of our heart," as a friend of mine likes to say. I think we can see things through art that we cannot see otherwise.)

6. If you did read the ML quotes at the beginning of chapters, did you see how they connected to the chapter theme? Were there any that stood out to you? If so, why?

7. How do you think van Gogh's search for acceptance mirrors Lane's (and Finn's) desire for home? What might Lane find

when she ventures to her childhood home in Rochester, Michigan?

8. Just like the art and vitality of the 1930s being overshadowed by gangster stories and the Great Depression, van Gogh's reputation is a mixed bag. His genius is loved and understood these days, but sometimes the fact that he cut off his ear overrides everything else. Did you know some of this history of van Gogh? What was new to you? Did you recognize any of his sayings before it was revealed just who ML was?

9. In Stephen King's book, *On Writing: A Memoir of the Craft*, he has a quote that says, "Life isn't a support system for art. It's the other way around." Do you agree that art is a support system to life? Why or why not?

10. The epilogue gives a clue to Tucker's role in the next book. What do you think he'll do and what is his main objective?

Connect with Us

Visit us online at
KensingtonBooks.com
to read more from your favorite authors, see books
by series, view reading group guides, and more.

for sneak peeks, chances to win books and prize packs,
and to share your thoughts with other readers.

facebook.com/kensingtonpublishing
twitter.com/kensingtonbooks

Tell us what you think!

To share your thoughts, submit a review,
or sign up for our eNewsletters, please visit:
KensingtonBooks.com/TellUs.